The Last King of
Scotland

The Last King of Scotland

GILES FODEN

 Alfred A. Knopf   New York   1998

THIS IS A BORZOI BOOK
PUBLISHED BY ALFRED A. KNOPF, INC.

Copyright © 1998 by Giles Foden

All rights reserved under International and Pan-American
Copyright Conventions. Published in the United States by
Alfred A. Knopf, Inc., New York.
Distributed by Random House, Inc., New York.
Originally published in Great Britain by
Faber and Faber Ltd., London.

www.randomhouse.com

Library of Congress Cataloging-in-Publication Data
Foden, Giles, [date]
The last king of Scotland / Giles Foden. — 1st American ed.
p.   cm.
ISBN 0-375-40360-4 (alk. paper)
1. Uganda—History—1971–1979—Fiction.   2. Amin, Idi, 1925–
—Fiction.   I. Title.
PR6056.O27L37   1998
823'.914—dc21   98-36722
CIP

Manufactured in the United States of America
First American Edition

Loose ends, things unrelated, shifts, nightmare journeys, cities arrived at and left, meetings, desertions, betrayals, all manner of unions, adulteries, triumphs, defeats . . . these are the facts.

—Alexander Trocchi, *Cain's Book* (1960)

Acknowledgments

Insofar as this is a historical record (and, indeed, otherwise), I am greatly indebted to the following for source material in books, newspaper reports, films and photographs; also, in certain cases, for eyewitness statements dictated to the author: Mohamed Amin (deceased); Tony Avirgan; Adioma Ayubare; Philip Briggs; Wilson Carswell FRCS; John Craven FRCS; Anthony Daniels; Richard Dowden; Richard Ellis; S.S. Farsi; Mary Anne Fitzgerald; Sandy Gall; Iain Grahame; Max Hastings; Denis Hills; Martha Honey; John Isoba; Judith, Countess of Listowel; Bishop Festo Kivengere (deceased); Henry Kyemba; David Lubogo; Ali Mazrui; David Martin; Yoweri Museveni, President of Uganda; Edward Mutesa, Kabaka of Buganda (deceased); Phares Mutibwa; A.F. Robertson; Barbet Schroeder; George Ivan Smith; Rolf Steiner; Dr. Harriet Stewart; John Stonehouse (deceased); Brian Tetley (deceased); Philip Warnock.

I would further like to express my thanks to those personal informants currently living in Uganda who gave interviews but asked for their names to be withheld— and to the many friends and colleagues who kindly read the manuscript.

Part One

1

I did almost nothing on my first day as Idi Amin's doctor. I had just come in from one of the western provinces, where I'd worked in a bush surgery. Kampala, the city, seemed like paradise after all that.

Back in my old neighborhood, I'd seen to Idi once. On his bullying visits to the gum-booted old chiefs out there, he would drive a red Maserati manically down the dirt tracks. Walking in the evenings, under the telegraph poles where the kestrels perched, you could tell where he'd been—the green fringe of grass down the middle of the track would be singed brown by the burning sump of the low-slung car.

On this occasion, he'd hit a cow—some poor smallholder had probably been fattening it up for slaughter—spun the vehicle and been thrown clear, spraining his wrist in the process. The soldiers, following him in their slow, camouflaged jeeps, had come to call for me. I had to go and attend to him by the roadside. Groaning in the grass, Idi was convinced the wrist was broken, and he cursed me in Swahili as I bound it up.

But I must have done something right because, a few months later, I received a letter from the Minister of Health, Jonah Wasswa, appointing me to the post of President Amin's personal physician—Medical Doctor to His Excellency—at State House, one of his residences. That was Idi's way, you see. Punish or reward. You couldn't say no. Or I didn't think, back then, that you could. Or I didn't really think about it at all.

I explored the planes and corners of my gleaming office, which stood in the grounds of State House and came with a next-door bungalow thrown in. I felt rather pleased with its black couch and swivel chair, its green filing cabinets, its bookshelves stacked with medical reports and back issues of the *Lancet*, its chrome fittings and spring-loaded Anglepoise lamps. My immediate tools—stethoscope, a little canvas roll of surgical instruments, casebook and so on—were laid out tidily on the desk. The neatness and the general spotlessness of the place were the work of Cecilia, my nurse. She was a remnant from my predecessor, Taylor. After suffering my attentions at the roadside, Amin had summarily dismissed him. I knew I ought to feel guilty about this, but I didn't, not really. Cecilia made it quite plain that she didn't like or approve of me—I reckon that she must have been half in love with old Taylor—and that she soon would be going back herself, back to Ashford, Kent.

Let her go, I thought, pushing aside a paper on disorders of the inner ear: my private study, my little problem. I was just glad to be out of the bush and to be earning a bit more money. The sun was shining and I was happy, happier than I'd been for a good many months. I stared out of the window at a cultivated lawn which swept down a hill towards the lake, glittering in the distance. A breeze moved the leaves of the shrubbery: bougainvillea, flame tree, poinsettia. Through the slatted blinds I could see a group of prisoners in white cotton uniforms, mowing the grass with sickles. They were guarded by a sleepy soldier, leaning on his gun in the dusty haze. Swish, swish, the noise came quietly through to me. I watched the prisoner nearest, slightly hypnotized by the movement of his cutter and the articulation of his bony arm. I shouldn't think they were fed too well: a bit of steamed green banana or maize meal, some boiled-up neck of chicken if they were lucky.

Turning away from the window, I resolved, since there didn't seem any likelihood of a presidential consultation that afternoon, to get a bus into town. I used to wear just shorts and shirt in the bush and needed to get a linen suit run up for tonight. The street-side tailors—there were whole rows of them—with their push-pedal, cast-iron Singers, their bad teeth and worse English, were just the fellows for the job. They could sort you out a suit in a cou-

ple of hours, while you looked round the market or went to one of
the astoundingly understocked grocers. Not quite Savile Row, but
good enough for here, good enough for Idi, anyway. Though he
himself did wear Savile Row tailoring, with its luscious, thick
lapels and heavy hem drop. Zipped up in their polypropylene
bags, the suits came in on the weekly flight from Stansted, hung
on racks among crates of Scotch, golf clubs, radio-cassettes, car-
tons of cigarettes, bicycles tubed in cardboard, slim-line kettles,
sleek toasted-sandwich makers with winking lights. And plain
things, too: sugar and tea—products that might well have come
from here in the first place, swapping their gunny sacks for cellophane packaging on the return trip.

I needed a suit quickly because this evening Idi was to host
the Ambassadors' Dinner, the annual bean feast at which he
entertained Kampala's diplomatic corps, assembled local dignitaries, senior civil servants, the wealthier concessionaires (Lon-
rho, Cooper Motors, Siemens), the top figures from the banks
(Standard, Commercial, Grindlays) and tribal chiefs from all over
the country. Wasswa, the Minister, had told me that His Excellency had given specific orders that I should attend. "As you
know," he had said (I had read Amin's medical records, such as
they were—chaos really, since His Excellency insisted on editing
them himself), "President Amin occasionally suffers from a slight
gastric difficulty."

As I shut the door of the office behind me, the draught from
the corridor set the blinds tinkling, like little cymbals. The noise
reminded me of something I once saw on holiday in Malta—a set
of tiny, shiny knives hung up like wind chimes outside a knife-
grinder's shop. "Aeolian sharps," as a friend remarked at the time.

On my return from town, I took a shower in the concrete-lined
cubicle in the bungalow. The big steel rose spurted out only a single stream of tepid liquid, under which I held up my hands, sending it spattering, planing down my back. Afterwards, as I went
through the rough archway that separated the steamy bathroom
from the sweltering bedroom, it was like going from one dimen-
sion to another. Fresh sweat mixed with the runnels of shower
water.

I then found myself, irritatingly, needing to defecate, which I always hate doing just after a shower—it seems like a form of sacrilege. As usual, I contemplated what I had produced: it was the easiest way of determining at an early stage the presence of a parasite, which could take hold in that fetid climate in a matter of hours. This evening's offering, I was worried to notice, was paler than usual, suggesting that bacteria had been absorbed into the bowel. I made a mental note to run some tests on myself in the morning.

The effort of expulsion had caused me to perspire even more, so when I put on my new suit I was already wearing what I used to call my African undertaker's outfit: the envelope of moisture which covers the body day and night. This tropical monster, ghostly presage of a thousand sallow malarial deaths, squats on one's shoulders and then, trickling down, concentrates its peculiar force in the hollows of the knees and ankles.

It was in this morbid state that I strolled across the lawn to State House itself—hair brushed and shining nonetheless, a blue, short-sleeved shirt and natty green tie under the cream suit. On my way, I saw that the sicklemen were being herded into the lorry that would take them back to the gaol on the outskirts of town. One by one, the mowers disappeared through the canvas flaps, throwing their cutters into a wooden box below the tow bar as they did so. Their guard lifted a short stick, acknowledging me as I passed.

A marabou stork was poking about nearby in a pile of rubbish, and I gave it a wide berth. These birds, the height of a small child, stood on spindly legs, their large beaks and heavy pinkish wattles making them look as if they might topple over. They were urban scavengers, gathering wherever there was pollution or decay. I hated them, yet I found them intriguing; they were almost professorial in the way they sorted through the heaps of rotting produce scattered all over the city, the organic mass mixed in with mud and ordure, scraps of plastic, bits of metal.

Going through a gate in the wall, I walked to where the big black cars of the ambassadors, the Mercedes of the richer merchants, and various white Toyotas and Peugeots with a smattering of dirt about the wings were beginning to pull up outside the main portico. An official in a red coat with brass buttons (it was too tight for him, the buttons strained to close the gap) ushered them into parking spaces, smiling and inclining his head.

Once inside, Wasswa, the Minister, beckoned me impatiently from the top of a wide staircase. He and various other ministers and senior army officers were waiting there to greet the guests and progress them through the great ebony-paneled door into the main hall, where the banquet was to take place.

He was definitely one of the solemn ones, Wasswa, his sharp young face (he couldn't have been much older than me—under thirty, anyway) frowning with the burden of office.

"Ah, Garrigan, you have arrived. I was hoping that you would be here in good time. You must be on hand if any of the guests are becoming unwell."

"Of course," I said, obligingly.

He looked ridiculous, my boss—somehow he'd got hold of a dress suit, but the sleeves were too short, and his cuffs, fastened with twisted bits of fuse wire, stuck out like the broken wings of small birds.

Already a long queue had formed down the stairs as the dignitaries waited for a handshake from Idi. He was wearing a blue uniform today—air force, I supposed—with gold trim and lacy epaulettes. He looked splendid.

Wasswa propelled me into a knot of three in the straggly queue. One of them was Stone, the fair-haired official at the British Embassy who had logged me in his book when I first arrived in the country, before I went into the bush. The other couple, I guessed, were the Ambassador and his wife. She was small but sinewy, in a dress printed with flowers. Coming closer I studied her covertly from over Wasswa's shoulder; then her eyes, long-lashed in a composed but unsmiling face, surrounded by a dark bob, were suddenly meeting mine, and I had to look away. Her mouth was pursed like a little fig, and her face had momentarily registered some expression as she looked at me. Not a totally unpleasant one, I thought.

She was a bit younger than her husband, who was standard Foreign Office issue: plastered-down hair, a large body shifting in its bristly suit, round glasses in a round face—a sponge of official easing-along, ready to soak up whatever discord the world threw at him.

Wasswa introduced us. "Ambassador Perkins, you have met our new doctor at State House, Nicholas Garrigan?"

"I haven't, in fact, but Stone here has told me all about his good work out west. So you've come to keep things in order back up here? We've been a bit lost since Doctor Taylor went, I can tell you."

He looked meaningfully at Wasswa.

"This is my wife, Marina. And Stone you already know."

Stone lifted his nose up in the air. Even then, there was something in his manner that irked me.

"Hello, Mrs. Perkins," I said.

She held out a hand to me, leaning her head to one side, her teeth showing slightly through her lips as she spoke.

"It's good to have a doctor nearby again. One gets so terribly worried."

When it was the turn of our little group to take its salutations from Idi, he clapped me on the shoulder with one great hand and waved the other in front of my face.

"So you see, Doctor Nicholas, I am fully recovered from my tumble. But although I am as strong as lion, I have some small wounds in my belly which you must fix for me."

Greeting each of us in turn, relaxed and charming, he chuckled as we moved past, beneath the twinkling chandeliers. There were some loathsome tribal masks on the walls, and also a line of stiff, heavy portraits of governor-generals from the colonial era: several had mutton-chop whiskers, and one looked slightly like my father. We searched out our seats at the long mahogany table, which was already filling up with grim-faced army officers and assorted civilians. There were a couple of journalists dashing around with notebooks, and also a photographer, his camera hung round his neck on a broad canvas strap. Some of the guests were in dinner jackets and evening gowns, some were in linen suits, cotton dresses, safari suits, saris; some (though by no means all) of the chiefs were in traditional clothes, and several matrons wore wraparound frocks of colorful cloth. One young Ugandan woman—a princess, it was later pointed out to me—was wearing a trouser suit that seemed to be fabricated entirely from pink cashmere. But she didn't, under those whirring hardwood fans, appear to be any hotter than the rest of us.

The company hovered, ill at ease, behind the tall chairs, waiting for the greetings to come to an end and the meal proper to begin. I discovered my own label. Name spelt wrong, in uneven type: Doctor GARGAN. Mrs. Perkins was next to me on one side, Wasswa on the other. Perkins and his American counterpart, Todd ("Nathan Theseus Todd," if you please), faced us. Beyond—the Italian, Bosola, the East German, Lessing, the Portuguese, Dias. All were fat, or fattish, and full of savoir-faire; they must make them in the same place, these ambassadors.

I looked down the table, over the rows of silver and crystal, towards the opening of the kitchen, where processions of waiters were bustling in and out. A slight aroma of woodsmoke, a whiff of reality, drifted up the table, fanned by the doors. All this—the china, the doilies, the display of tropical flowers, the perfumed fingerbowls, most of all her, Marina Perkins, next to me—was a bit overwhelming after those long months in the west; it all promised, it all suggested too much.

Wine was poured. Conversation bubbled quietly as we waited for Idi to finish greeting the guests. Eventually he bowled in, smiling genially as he made his way to the top of the table, to the carver chair. Behind him on the wall was a large disc of golden metal, emblazoned with the country's emblem, a Ugandan crested crane.

Our party was two or three down from Idi's place at the head of the table. Perkins and Todd were the most significant emissaries, politically speaking, but as they had presented their credentials only relatively recently, ancient diplomatic practice decreed that they were not placed hard by the seat of local power. About which, I suspect, they were secretly ecstatic. It's a lesson worth noting that apparently burdensome convention can sometimes work to individual advantage.

So there he stood, Idi, solid as a bronze bull, almost as if he, too, was waiting for something to happen. What did happen was that a greying official in tails, some sort of major-domo who had been scuttling up and down ever since we entered the hall, sounded a gong and then, straightening up, read from a paper:

"His Excellency President for Life Field Marshal Al Hadj Doctor Idi Amin Dada, VC, DSO, MC, Lord of All the Beasts of the Earth and Fishes of the Sea and Conqueror of the British

Empire in Africa in General and Uganda in Particular welcomes the Court of Kampala and assembled worthies of the city to this his annual banquet."

I looked down at Marina Perkins's hands resting in her lap. "I wonder how long this business is going to last," I muttered.

"Mmm," she said, turning towards me. "Longer than you think, probably . . ."

She raised her eyebrows mischievously. But at that moment, the toastmaster's voice rose in a crescendo.

"Ladies and gentlemen, welcome. Field Marshal Amin has requested that you should begin eating only after he has made a few introductory remarks concerning domestic and international affairs."

Amin drew himself up to his full, impressive height, the light of the chandeliers dancing on his shiny dome, his sharply angled cheeks. The girl in pink was seated next to him.

"My friends, I have to do this because if I do not speak now, you will become too drunk to hear my words. I have noticed there can be bad drunkenness in Uganda and indeed across the whole world, from beer and from spirits. This is true of the armed forces especially. For example, looking at the faces of the Entebbe Air Force Jazz Band, I know straightaway they are drunkards."

The diners tittered, turning to look at the jazz band, seated on a podium in a shadowy corner, waiting for their turn. Having looked doleful at the outset, and then worried at Idi's remark, the musicians were now laughing energetically.

"Yes, some people look as though they are painted with cosmetics just because of too much drinking of alcohol. And cosmetics too can be bad themselves, and wigs: I do not want Ugandans to wear the hair of dead imperialists or of Africans killed by imperialists."

He patted the pink princess on the head. For a moment he paused, blinking as if confused, or unsure of what he was seeing— his eyesight, I knew from the files, was bad. Then he sniffed the air and continued.

"No member of my own family is to wear a wig, or she will cease to be my family member. Because we are all one happy family in Uganda, like it is we are gathered around this table in our single house. Myself, I started cleaning the house until I succeeded in placing indigenous Ugandans in all important posts. Can you remember that even cooks in hotels were whites? Except for me. I myself sold sweet biscuits on the roadside as a young boy and was a cookpot stirrer in my first army position, before I became General. Otherwise, insecurity prevailed before. Now, if you go into the countryside, you will see we have enough food. We are growing crops for export and we are getting foreign exchange. Also I have here a report from the Parastatal Food and Beverages Ltd: it says we are selling Blue Band, Cowboy, Kimbo Sugar, salt, rice, Colgate, Omo and shoe polish. So you see, you do not hear anywhere Uganda has debts, only from the British press campaign to tell lies."

Perkins wiped his fork on his napkin, then lifted it up close to his face, examining the prongs. He looked slightly liverish.

"Because the World Bank is very happy with Uganda. In fact, I have decided to help the World Bank. I have decided to offer food relief to countries with food problems: millet, maize and beans shall be sent in sacks to all thin countries. And cassava also."

I thought of the terraced plots back in the west. I used to watch the women set out to work as I ate my breakfast on the wooden veranda. They carried strange, broad-bladed hoes on their shoulders and had children strapped to their backs and bundles balanced on their heads, their chatter floating up to me as they walked by.

"Ambassadors who are here, please ensure that the food delivered in your countries is equitably distributed. Even you who are from superpowers. Remember this: I do not want to be controlled by any superpower. I myself consider myself the most powerful figure in the world and that is why I do not let any superpower control me. Remember this also: superpower leaders can fall. I once went for dinner with the Prime Minister of Britain, Mr. Edward Heath, at his official residence Number Ten Downing Street. But even he could fall from a great height, even though he is my good friend."

"I don't think we need give too much credence to that," muttered Perkins. His wife fiddled with her spoons, putting the dessert spoon into the curve of the soup spoon. And then she changed the arrangement around.

"But the truth is, I would like to be friends with all of you. As I have repeatedly emphasized, there is no room in Uganda for hatred and enmity. I have stated I will not victimize or favor anybody. Our aim must be unity and love. And good manners. So guerrillas against the country will be met with countermeasures. You will forgive me for ending my speech here. I have said it before: I am not a politician but a professional soldier. I am therefore a man of few words and I have been very brief throughout my professional career. It only remains for me to draw your attention to one thing more: the good foods coming to the table before you. A human being is a human being, and like a car he needs refueling and fresh air after working for a long time. So: eat!"

With this last declamation, he threw up his arms and stood there motionless for a second, like a preacher or a celebrant at the Mass. Behind him, his raised arms were reflected dully in the great gold dish on the wall, altering the pattern of light as it fell on the tablecloth.

And then he sat down. The diners hardly stirred, staring at him still. Idi savored the sight of it, his own lips moving silently, as if he had carried on speaking. Only the rattle of the trolleys, bringing in the starters, broke the spell, and everyone began to applaud.

The hors d'œuvre were placed in front of us, a triple choice: fillets of Nile perch, thick gumbo soup made from okra and crayfish, or, most disturbingly for the Europeans (it was the kind of thing Idi would do on purpose), a variety platter of dudu—bee larvae, large green bush crickets, cicadas and flying ants, fried with a little oil and salt. They were actually quite delicious—crisp and brown, they tasted a bit like whitebait.

"I think I'll stick to the gumbo," said Todd, horrified, as Wasswa and I crunched up a few.

Wasswa pushed the dudu platter towards him. "But these are a local delicacy. You may not know, sir, that gumbo is an imported dish even in our own Uganda. It is from just over the fringe of our southwestern province, into Zaïre, where, as you may know also, many of the border peoples speak Swahili like our Ugandan soldiers here, and come to trade fish or to be treated medically by such fellows as Doctor Garrigan, who was in those parts before."

"That's right," I added, lamely. "I was in the west before I came to Kampala."

"I guess it must have been quite rough to live out there. I went down there on tour last year," said Todd.

"But in Zaïre it is too bad more," interjected Wasswa. "They are real washenzi, savages, in that place. In that country, sir, this gumbo, it is called nkombo, which means 'runaway slave' in the Nkongo language—it is how he, this dish here, came to your country America. I am sure you were not knowing this."

"No, I can't say I was aware of that, Minister Wasswa. Of course, American cuisine is nourished by all manner of national traditions: Dutch, German, English, but also Korean and, as you say, there's the whole African-American thing. The melting pot, you know. It is fascinating, isn't it, this gourmandizing business? Every plate tells a story."

"I thought you chaps just ate hamburgers," said Stone. It was hot in the banqueting room, and two damp strands of flaxen hair fell over his forehead like tendrils of seaweed.

"Now don't you mock me," the American replied, chuckling. "I had a Paris posting when I was young. They'd call you Monsieur Rosbif there, or John Bull."

"But in Zaïre, too, those people eat monkey meat," Wasswa said loudly, laying it on thick, piqued at no longer being the center of attention.

Suddenly Amin himself, overhearing, called down from the top of the table.

"And what is your fault with monkey meat, Minister of Health? I, your President, has eaten monkey meat."

Wasswa, craven, toyed with his cutlery.

"And I have also eaten human meat."

This His Excellency almost shouted. A shocked silence fell over the table—almost visible, as if some diaphanous fabric had come down from the ceiling and settled over the steaming tureens and salvers. We looked up at him, not sure how to react.

Amin finally rose to his feet. "It is very salty," he said, "even more salty than leopard meat."

We shifted in our chairs.

"In warfare, if you do not have food, and your fellow soldier is wounded, you may as well kill him and eat him to survive. It can give you his strength inside. His flesh can make you better, it can make you full in the battlefield."

And then he sat down once again. The candles fluttered light onto the silver, which threw off distorted images of the faces round the table. Oddly, I found myself thinking of ants, clay mounds, the distribution of formic acid—I suppose it was having eaten the insects.

No one said a word until the waiters wheeled in the center-piece of the main course. It was a whole roast kudu hind. Her lit-tle stumped-off, cauterized legs stuck up in the air like cathedral spires, and she was stuffed, so the menu told us, with avocado and sausage meat. The latter spilt out, crusty and crennellated, at one end, the Limpopo-colored fruit-vegetable at the other.

The display rolled up to Idi. We watched him rub knife against steel, rhythmically, the noise marking out still further the silence over the table. Then he slit the torso and, with a rough majesty, hacked off a ceremonial slice of meat for himself, flipping it onto the gold-rimmed plate. A drop of grease flew onto the princess's cashmere, causing her to jump back in her seat and then, when Amin looked down, to smile at him obsequiously. Finally, he handed the knife to one of the waiters, who proceeded dextrously to layer slice after effortless slice—the meat falling away like waves on a beach—on the edge of the platter, while others shuffled them onto plates. Yet more waiters, moving swiftly behind the chairs in a complicated shuttle system, sliding along the parquet, brought them to each guest.

I prodded the kudu steak in front of me. A thin trickle of juice came out. I thought about how the beast must have been stalked and shot, dragged or perhaps carried home slung on a pole, flayed and gutted, the crouching hunters palming prize portions (heart, kidney, liver) into bloodied banana leaves to take home to their wives. And the carcass itself, too, might well have been wrapped for transport by lorry back to Kampala: as well as keeping off flies, the banana leaf is said to contain a tenderizing enzyme. Out in the bush, I'd often mused about analyzing and isolating it, selling the formula to make my fortune back home.

Nathan Theseus Todd attacked his steak with gusto. He cut off such a large piece that the dark meat, darker than beef, covered his mouth as he forked it in, making it seem—ever so briefly—like a gag. Or another mouth altogether. A second mouth.

Nauseated, I turned to Marina Perkins. "What's really interesting about all this, is that none of the meat is chilled at any point; refrigeration breaks down the cell structure of the meat, you know. That's why it tastes different from English meat."

She looked at me slightly quizzically. "You're lucky, being a man of science. I sometimes wish that I had a better idea of how things fit together."

The accompanying dishes for the kudu began piling up: a little ramekin of chili relish; mounds of vegetables—sweet potato rissoles, yam chips, fried groundnuts, pigeon peas; and a chopped mess of green I called jungle salad: spinach, shu-shu and black-eyed-bean leaves.

"Watch out for this foods," called out Idi, tapping a dish. "There is an old Swahili proverb: if you give pigeon peas to a donkey, he will fart. That is why I never eat this foods."

I thought of the donkey I had as a child in Fossiemuir. It died from bloat, having eaten grass cuttings I'd left in a bin outside the paddock. They'd fermented in its stomach, blowing it up like a balloon. The only way to cure it was to stick the point of a knife between the beast's ribs, cutting into the stomach wall where it pressed against them. I remember how the green liquor came out, when the vet did it, but the animal was too far gone—we couldn't save it.

Nathan Theseus, excited by mouthfuls of meat, waved his fork in the air.

"We saw these wonderful cows when we went down to the Rwanda border. You know, the ones with the long horns and humped backs. Herds and herds of them, with white birds sitting on their backs."

"They are called zebu," said Wasswa. "The birds eat their ticks, and the hump is for storing fluid during drought."

"Like a camel, I suppose," said Perkins. "Don't cows have two stomachs, Doctor Garrigan?"

"Three. Grass is very difficult to digest. Though I believe the digestive structure of zebu is even more complicated than that of the European cow—more like buffalo or wildebeest."

"You have buffalo cheese in Italy, don't you, Bosola?" asked Todd, leaning forward.

"Yes, mozzarella. But it is mostly made from ordinary cow's milk these days."

Amin cut him off, booming. "Only in Africa are there real buffalo, strong like me."

"A nice display," Marina Perkins whispered to me, touching the flowers in front of us. It was the first time I saw her smile. I lifted up my glass of wine and looked straight into her eyes over the rim.

The sweet, like the starter, was a choice of three: guava fool, pumpkin pie with cream, and, as the menu put it, "Delicious Pudding"—some kind of blancmange, each portion molded into a quaint little castle shape.

This last Idi himself had, scooping it up swiftly, closing the distance between mouth and plate with every spoonful. By the end, he was almost bent double.

"All gone," he said then, pushing it aside like a little child.

As I finished my own Delicious Pudding, the waiters began to bring in the coffee and liqueurs, and the jazz band struck up for the dancing. I watched transfixed as, in one fluid, seamless movement, Nathan Theseus brushed a bead of sweat off his brow, reached into his jacket, pulled out a cigar from one pocket, a clipper lighter from the other, cut and lit the cigar and put the silver contraption away again. All in a matter of seconds. It was a quite astonishing piece of prestidigitation. I almost felt like asking him to do it again, to prove that it had happened at all. But it was final, this perfect execution: the tip of the cigar was already glowing fiercely.

Much later that evening, I took a walk down by the lake. The moon was high and the first birds had begun calling from the shrubs and marsh grass by the edge. As I looked out over the water, I supposed the crocs were moving in the dark shallows that stretched out towards the fires and lamps of Kenya on the other side. And I fancied, standing there, that I could see the circles of tilapia rising to the surface for crane flies, rising as if coming up for air; denizens of the lake, our scaly forebears: white eyes, blind mouths.

2

All that, it feels so long ago. Strange times in a strange place. But things here seem strange enough, in their way. For instance, a bomb went off last week. A "device," as they put it, was remotely detonated on the mainland. An electricity pylon was knocked over and one person was killed. They showed the funeral on the television. There was a shot of the steeple and you could hear the knell—you could hear the clank of it—and that reminded me of something.

What it put me in mind of was a very bad joke that once ran in my family. Ask not for whom the Bell's tolls, it tolls for you. That's what my father used to say whenever he took a glass of the hard stuff. This wasn't often, but the repetition of the joke made it seem so.

Perhaps, to begin with, I really ought to explain how I've come to be writing this, my tyrannical history, my rainy-day rhapsody. Rather than stumbling around like a drunken man. Which, I must concede, I am. Though only a little.

The dwelling I presently inhabit is little, too. It seems an inappropriately northern place to embark upon this tropical tale. For as I take up my pen, the snow has been falling for several hours, and it seems likely that the road will be blocked by morning. I know the portents of my new habitat, I have been learning my local lore. I know that "track to the village impassable, NG runs out of milk" will be tomorrow's story.

The real story, of course, lies somewhere quite other: "I am going to write it all down in my book. I am going to write what I did bad and what I did good." These are, truly, the words of the man—H.E., His Excellency, Idi, the number one id—whose deeds I am about to describe. He has never written it, so here I am. It is a story of various strange happenings in Central Africa, happenings which involved the author, Nicholas Garrigan, in a professional and private capacity. I have resolved to publish not for the purpose of exonerating myself, as some will no doubt believe, but to provide a genuine eyewitness account. For while the newspapers continue to execrate me, I'm committed to preserving for posterity a fair judgment on a history of blood, misery and foolishness.

I want to do this right. My father was a Presbyterian minister, and I was brought up according to the strictest precepts. "Sometimes I do think," he would say over his steel spectacles at the breakfast table, after some misdemeanor of mine had been reported to him, "that you are as set for damnation as a rat in a trap."

My sister, Moira, would giggle into her bowl, and my mother would sigh, readying herself for the concentration—upon me, over the toast and marmalade—of the full force of my father's oratory. This was considerable. His sermons at Fossiemuir were well attended. Yet for all his proverbial fire and brimstone, my father was not a violent man. He had a sort of dry, if unadventurous, humor in him, as suggested by that dreadful Bell's adage.

I should point out that he died himself while I was abroad. It's a matter of eternal regret to me that I didn't have the chance to make some kind of reconciliation with him (though we hadn't exactly fallen out), not least because my mother's death followed hard on the heels of his own. Pure grief, she died of: the learned doctors may not have rehearsed it to me on the hard wooden benches of the lecture halls of the university, but I know it can happen.

Apart from its ecclesiastical atmosphere—religion covered our family like the fine soot that would sometimes come down from the clouds, spewed out by the automotive products factory on the edge of Fossiemuir—my early life was unremarkable. I attended the local school, went to the swimming baths on Wednesdays and the cinema on Saturdays. I chased about with my friends in the pine-wooded hills above the town—the hills that began at the end of the paddock where my donkey grazed, and might have stretched, so far as I was concerned, up to high heaven. Emotionally speaking, the death of "Fred" was the most significant thing that happened to me as a child; I cannot see crème de menthe but think of that green stuff coming out of his stomach.

But even then, I didn't let it show very much: while I had inherited from my mother a capacity for hard work and for worry, from my father I had learned that feelings, if one is to be successful in life, must be strictly controlled. There was none, in our household, of that "express yourself" mentality that is today's common wisdom. So if I was ever wild as a young boy, I was wild in my head, which was full of wandering yearnings: I was mad for maps and stamps and adventure stories. Firths and fishing villages, hills and golf courses—Fife's rich, venerable landscape bored me, and in my overheated imagination I played out stories of Hickok's Wild West, Tarzan's Africa, the Arctic of Peary and Nansen. And I, oddly, was always the Red Indian, the Zulu, the Eskimo . . .

Come puberty, these evagaristic longings were transmuted in the customary fashion, though I didn't lose my virginity until my post-Highers year, with the daughter of a neighbor. At that stage I took some specialist scientific subjects, my natural sense of orderliness standing me in good stead in this respect. Oh, the files I had. Then came Edinburgh and the long hard slog of a medical degree and the various hospital training jobs that followed.

My student life was eccentric, rather than revolutionary or louche. My college friends and I did have a dog-eared old exercise book, called the Sweaty Betty, in which we recorded the results of our weekly poker game and odds for proposed (and most unlikely) sexual conquests—but it wasn't like it seems now. As for those 1968, paving-slab ructions, we didn't see any of that, not in the medical faculty at Edinburgh at any rate.

We did like a drink, though. This image sticks in my head: several of us stumbling out into the stony light of the High Street at dawn after a fancy-dress party, one a clown, one a pirate, one holding a plastic skeleton kidnapped from the faculty. I myself was Dracula, my lips (I saw, as I caught my reflection in a shop window) conveniently stained red from the night of wine: a happy vampire!

Such antics aside, I lived in digs while I was at Edinburgh, along with another doctor and two humanities students, under the watchful eye of Mrs. Berkeley. She was a nice old bat really, but I think it was partly the combination of her refusal to let us bring girls back to the rooms and my slightly oppressive home life that made me want to spread my wings when I qualified. I had a brief, raucous holiday in Malta—it was cheap—with a couple of my friends, and then pondered what I would do.

In the end, rather than going for consultancy or into general practice, in October 1970 I took the Civil Service (Medical Division) exam, having specified in the application that I was looking to go abroad. Most of the others were Foreign Office hopefuls, taking the main examination. As we waited in the cold on the steps outside the hall, they were all talking about the PLO bombs in Israel and the fate of a British diplomat some Québecois separatists had taken hostage in Canada. I kept myself to myself.

Naturally, it was an uncertain period of my life, waiting for the results—everything pent up as I thumped down the stairs for the post each morning and disconsolately picked up the *Scotsman* instead. The envelope finally came on the day the electricians went on strike. I remember, that evening, obsessively rereading the letter by candlelight. I was in. I was one of the elect. Not according to my father, however, who wanted me to practice as a GP in Fossiemuir. We argued about it, and when I left, I left under a cloud.

It was against this background that I arrived in Uganda—on Sunday, 24 January 1971—to take up a post as a medical doctor attached to the Ministry of Health. Though I was on secondment from the British government's Overseas Development Agency, I was to report directly to officials at the ministry. My specific brief was to join a clinical practice in a remote rural area, and to pursue whatever more generalized researches in the name of public health my superiors desired. Had I known, on arrival, the breadth of activity that this later would involve, I should have gotten straight back on the airplane.

As for the narrative I am presenting in these pages, it is nothing but the working-up of a journal I made at the time. I also had the opportunity of conducting a number of interviews with Idi Amin, at his own behest. Some of this material will already be familiar to readers of newspapers and to broadcast audiences around the world. But until now, only a fraction of the "dictator-phone" tapes, as the caption writers have insisted on calling them, have been revealed to the outside world. It is eerie, now, to press the button on the machine and hear his voice: I should not, I know, listen so long, so eagerly.

These thoughts bear down on me as I sit here on this third night of writing. Gazing down over the outline of woody sand-hills and rocky outcrops that stretches down to the quay and out into the never silent Inner Sound, I'm overwhelmed with an awful sense of regret. Because good things seem bad to me now—even the light is cross. In the lamps hung in the windows of my neighbors, in the dark-beleaguered cluster of gold that signifies the port village and in the gleaming traverse of the occasional ship, I see a picture not of others but of my own isolation.

Though I know that those village lights promise companionship, just as the magnificent white horses of the bay promise another sort of consolation, I am steeped in my churning memories. Like the roar of the Sound, the question comes incessantly. Can you tell the truth when you are talking to yourself? What is the truth about a man on an island?

3

During the flight to Kampala—twelve hours' worth of stale air from London, with stop-offs in Larnaca and Nairobi—I read one book, *Uganda for Travellers* (thin) by Charles Sabon-Frazer, and flicked through another, Bailey and Love's *Short Practice of Surgery* (fat). My nose and ears kept blocking and unblocking as I read, as the pressure in the cabin changed—almost, it seemed, with every turn of the page.

> From the snowcapped Ruwenzoris, the "Mountains of the Moon" described by Ptolemy, to lush rainforest and arid desert, the Ugandan landscape offers a rich variety for the adventurous traveller. Abundant with flora and fauna, it boasts the source of the River Nile, waterfalls like the impressive Murchison Falls and two of Africa's greatest lakes, Lake Victoria and Lake Albert . . .

When the pilot said we had crossed the Uganda border, I looked out of the window. I looked down and I imagined myself being regarded as I passed above—as with every wing dip and aileron flutter, the plane changed its relation to what was below: the animals on the plain, the tin roofs of isolated buildings, the gullies of the eroded land, the fertile green squares where farmers tended coffee and bananas. Even, so I wondered, the tawny, cross-eyed tigerfish moving beneath the glittering surface of the lake.

For that was the approach: Lake Victoria Nyanza. Then we banked and, coming steeply down, went through a breach in the seven hills that surround the city of Kampala. We hit, with the habitual moment of fear, the tarmac. Then, as the rumble of the reverse thrust kicked in, the bumpy scrub of the strip—trees in the distance, sun-scorched grass at the margin—was whipping by like it wouldn't stop.

The heat was the most of it, I should have expected that. *Uganda for Travellers* had told me that: "though more temperate than other East African countries due to its height above sea level, Uganda is on the equator and . . ." etc., etc. But nothing could have prepared me for the hydraulic blast of hot air that came as I stepped out. It was about four o'clock, local time, and although the main of the sun was over, the ground was still giving out all that it had stored up during the day, heat and dust mixing with the smell of aviation fuel in the upward currents.

I had watched the runway attendants wheel the mobile stairway past the cabin window as we taxied, peering out through its smeary plastic lozenge. Now, as I climbed down the rickety steps, I looked at the men in the hot air—the jet heat making unnatural patterns in natural light, they in their blue overalls unwinding fat tubes, opening hatches or just plain standing around. And they stared back, but without interest. Or so I supposed. Who's to tell from a face?

I walked with the other passengers across the apron to the glass-fronted terminal: so much smaller than in Britain, and self-contained. This was the airport *tout court*, you could see it all—including, which was a shock, a squadron of military jets neatly parked in formation. I turned at the terminal door for one last look at them, their wings sloped like the back of an envelope.

Inside, I proceeded towards immigration and customs, as the sign directed. After immigration I collected my bag from the carousel. Craning my neck, I eyed the rubber flaps anxiously as they parted to reveal a glimpse of daylight. I saw the hand of an attendant reaching into the wire-sided cart outside. After a while, I recognized my own case rotating, by virtue of some weird physics, on its own axis as it came round towards me.

We stood in the customs queue, grasping passports in sweaty palms. At least, mine were sweaty. Soldiers were leaning against the walls, their guns slung at awkward angles as they smoked and chatted. Up ahead, an Indian man with a large family and cardboard stereo boxes bound up with string (AIWA in red letters: bisected by two lines of yellow twine), was gesticulating violently. But no problems for me, when it came to my turn. Slumped in their booths, the officials stamped my papers slack-handedly and nodded me on: case opened, case closed, the blink of an eye.

In the arrivals hall, I changed some sterling into Uganda shillings at a little Barclays Bank booth. I looked about. Someone from the ministry was meant to meet me. There was no one. I strode out of the hall into the sunlit car-park. Outside the door was a tall, bushy tree. In it were perched twenty or thirty bright green, parrotlike birds, squawking very loudly. It was an odd sight. I watched them for a short while, and then looked around again. No one. I went back into the terminal.

All in all, I waited about an hour, walking in and out of the terminal with my hard blue suitcase and the little BOAC shoulder bag. I soon found myself beset on all sides by a ragged band of boys. "Taxi, bwana," they cried. "Taxi! We find you fine good taxi, fine good hotel." They tugged at the handle of the big case and gestured to the rank—to where the drivers sprawled on their bonnets in the sun, confident of eventual capitulation.

They were right. Jealously clutching my bags to myself, I finally clambered into one of the old Peugeots. "A hotel in Kampala, please. Somewhere clean."

Flies buzzed about in the cab. Distracted, I heard the voice of the cabdriver, repeating himself. "I will take you to the Speke Hotel, bwana. It is a good place. Very clean indeed. You have come from London?"

I told him, yes, I had, then, suddenly tired from the journey, tried to avoid further conversation. We drove along an initially well-tarmaced road, past the docks and some ranks of sheds with rusty tin roofs, and then out into a rural area. I could see the blue of Lake Victoria on my left. On the other side were straw shacks with piles of produce outside—stippled ovals of jackfruit and avocado, painted wicker stools, stacks of firewood, charcoal and irregular bricks made of dried mud. Behind the shacks stretched miles of rough grassland, punctuated now and then by yellow-flowered acacia trees and the mysterious brown shapes of termite mounds.

After about twenty minutes and the final dilapidation of the tarmac into a sort of beaten clay, we came to a roundabout. In the middle was a spiky multiple wooden signpost, black letters on peeling white paint: NORTH (Kampala, Gulu, Sudan); EAST (Jinja, Tororo, Kenya); SOUTH (Entebbe, Lake Victoria)—the direction from which we had come; and WEST (Mbarara, Rwanda, Tanzania, Zaïre). I had never seen countries on a signpost before, it made me feel like anything was possible—like I was the king of infinite space.

I dumbly watched the bush landscape reel by as we headed towards Kampala. The engine groaned with the effort as the driver shifted the gearstick to cope with the inclines, tutting with frustration each time he did so. Through the gap between the front seats I could see the stick's dusty canopy of weary black rubber. Above that was a dark hole where the heater or radio should have been. Some kind of charm made of bark, animal skin and beads dangled from the mirror, swiping the road ahead as it dipped up and down into the distance, bush on each side. I watched it all, until trees developed into shacks, shacks into concrete buildings and we were suddenly on a major highway in the middle of the city.

Installed in the Speke, I took a shower and came down from my room. Already prickling with sweat, I went in search of the bar. The room was enormous, a high ceiling with rose reliefs, and on the walls dark wooden boards with the names of cricket and rugby players—Rider, D.G., Inglis, R., and many a long-dead Brown, Smith and Jones—picked out in white and gold. In between these, at intervals, were the horns of antelopes mounted on plinths and one lonely, gigantically long, grotesquely distorted rhinoceros horn. Underneath, out of place amid the colonial bric-a-brac, were three or four gaming machines—pinball, and several of the old-fashioned, one-armed-bandit type with whirring dials.

Idly, irrationally wondering whether anyone from the ministry was about, I looked around. Above the optics was a large sign:

YOUR COUNTRY IS YOUR FAMILY. There was also a cloth picture of a man I took, from the grainy photograph in *Uganda for Travellers*, to be President Obote, the incumbent. A group of women in nylon dresses and plastic jewelry sat together at one end of the bar, watching me and muttering amongst themselves. A fleshy barman in a smudged white jacket looked at me expectantly as I approached.

"Prisoner?" he said.

"Sorry?" I did a double take.

He looked pained. One of the women, as if they had made a decision between them, stood up and began moving along the dais towards me. A tooth-filled smile traveled before her, as if it was separate from her tiny face and some kind of mechanism was training it down the bar. I edged nervously away, crab-walking my elbows.

"You drink Prisoner?" The barman repeated himself, gesturing irritably with his thumb at the rack of bottles behind him.

Then I understood: Pilsner.

"Yes," I said, and handed over some of the shillings I'd converted at the airport.

"There's been trouble in the north, you know that?" a white man said abruptly, jerking his head round in front of me as I clasped the bottle. He had a big black beard, an open-necked khaki shirt, and a strong South African accent.

"Oh," I said, surprised.

His body, his manner, everything about him was chunky and muscular, even his face: it was as if, above the sprouting black hair, he had biceps for cheeks.

"Off you go," he said.

For a second, I thought he meant me, but then he waved the girl away, brushing at her shoulder imperiously. She was right next to us by now, my crablike escape having been thwarted by a thick post of rough-carved wood going down through a hole in the dais. Pulling a face, she turned on her heel.

"You want to watch out for that lot," the South African remarked, "they'll have every last shilling out of your pocket before you can say jack rabbit. And then there's, you know . . . the disease and all that." He finished his sentence with a hearty laugh.

I smiled, embarrassed, and turned to walk across the room to a table. But he came with me, walking alongside.

"Don't mind if I join you, do you?" he said. He had a dog with him, too, I realized: an Alsatian was trailing along behind us, its claws ticking on the parquet floor.

"No," I said. "Please do."

We sat down at a table. "Name's Freddy Swanepoel." Taking a cigarette himself, he tossed the packet across the wood.

"No, thanks . . . Nicholas Garrigan." I held out my hand.

"Pleased to meet you, Nicholas. What you doing in Kampala?"

I bristled slightly, half-annoyed, half-flattered at his interest. "I'm a doctor, I've got a government contract."

"Contract with the devil, more like. Anyway, plenty of work here for you, then."

He sipped his beer. As we exchanged information, the Alsatian sat at our feet, licking the salt out of an empty crisp packet. It occasionally looked up at its master with soulful eyes.

"Boetie, he's called," said Swanepoel, seeing me study the delicate salt-licking operation. "Take him in the plane with me sometimes." He patted the dog's head proudly.

"And what do you do?" I asked.

He explained that he was an émigré South African, based in Nairobi. "I'm a pilot. I work for an outfit called Rafiki Aviation. We run things about for the Kenyan and Ugandan governments. And other bits and pieces."

"Don't they mind you being a South African? I didn't think you were allowed up this far."

He raised his eyebrows. I realized I might have sounded rude. There was an awkward pause before he answered my question.

"My mother was English, so I managed to wangle myself a Brit passport. That's how I get to work in black Africa. The British Coat of Arms. Otherwise they wouldn't let me in here, you're right."

I began to quiz him about the situation in the country.

"A coup in the offing, I had it from one of the air force boys. No worries—I've seen it before in these places, they usually leave the whites alone."

We talked a bit more, and then I levered myself out of my

chair to get us another round of drinks. Feeling as if I'd left part of my body back in the chair, I walked over to the bar and bought the beers.

As I turned round, there was a sudden commotion at the door. A group of five or six men, all in flared trousers and dark glasses, burst into the room. One had on a flowery toweling sun hat, and there was something heavy weighing down the top pocket of his safari-suit jacket. They marched straight up to Swanepoel, beckoning and shouting. I stopped in my tracks, a beer bottle in each hand.

The one in the sun hat whispered excitedly to the South African, pulling at his sleeve. Swanepoel, however, put his feet up on the table—deliberately, as if to annoy him. The man cuffed his feet. Swanepoel got up, leaning over him threateningly. The dog scrambled up, too, and growled. The man took a step back, delving into his heavy pocket. I saw the black of a gun.

Then Swanepoel laughed out loud and patted the man in the toweling hat on the shoulder. The man in the toweling hat laughed, too, and put the gun away, and then everybody laughed. Swanepoel gathered up his cigarette packet and lighter, put them in his shirt pocket and took a last swig of beer. He paused to make an apologetic, can't-be-helped gesture across the room to me, and followed the group of men out the door. The dog padded out behind them.

Bewildered, I went over to the table and spent the next half-hour stalwartly drinking the two bottles. Then I went up to my room. As I opened the door, I caught a glimpse of three cockroaches scuttling across the linoleum. Each one was fat as a hand-rolled cigar.

I got undressed and lay on the bed. A dirty mosquito net hung above me. My opened suitcase was on the floor, its contents in disarray from when I'd got a fresh change of clothes out after my shower. Now I felt unclean again. The room was stale and airless (the window was stuck) and the beer was making my head swim. I took out the guidebook from the suitcase and tried to read.

Following the appearance of Arab slave-traders earlier in the century, the colonial period in Uganda effectively began with the arrival of John Hanning Speke in the country on 24 January 1862. Thereafter followed a large number of European explorers, merchants (the Imperial British East Africa Company) and evangelical missionaries. The period of 1885–87 was a trying one for the newly converted Christians in Uganda, many being killed by burning, castration and dismemberment, as antagonism flared between them and supporters of the Kabaka, the King of Buganda. In 1892, war broke out between the converts themselves, the Anglicans favouring British, the Catholics French or German colonialism . . .

While British rule would continue, in Protectorate form, until Independence in 1962, an odd turn in Ugandan history took place in 1903, when the country was offered by the British Secretary for the Colonies, Joseph Chamberlain, to Theodor Herzl and the World Zionist Organization as a possible Jewish state. The offer was refused, as the Zionists were alarmed at the diversion of energies from Palestine . . .

Finding myself unable to concentrate, I set my alarm clock to Uganda time from my wristwatch and turned off the lamp. I kept thinking about the cockroaches, every now and then flicking on the switch to see if they were there. They were too quick for me. This, and the sound of heavy machinery passing underneath the window, kept me tossing and turning.

And thinking. I was a terrible insomniac when I was a teenager, but never on account of cockroaches. I used to lie awake worrying about myself. And when I did sleep, I fell victim to dreadful dreams: that I had been tossed into the flames, or into the icy floes of some Stygian river. I labored under the misapprehension that I had committed some inexpiable crime—some nights I even thought I was the devil himself, that his malleable form had insinuated itself into mine, that his scaly horns had become my own dark locks. But it wasn't all one way. Other nights I went so far as to imagine myself the new Christ—that I had a mission on earth and all these demonic identifications were mere temptations.

All of these dreams visited me within a sensuous geography of temples and jungles and so on. It was all very exotic—and it all disappeared abruptly the moment I had my first assisted seminal experience. This took place in the copse above our house, in the hands of Lizzie Walters—that same neighbor's daughter. She married young and, so far as I know, still lives in Fossiemuir. Whenever, on trips home from university, I used to see her walking down the street, with her pram and her shopping bags, all I could think about was that exquisite moment: the branches in my back, a celestial light in my head, her sly giggle—and then the wetness on my stomach.

I smiled to myself as I remembered all this, and eventually dozed off into a reasonably peaceful sleep. Or so I thought. Later, in the early hours, waking with a full bladder of Pilsner, I turned on the light once more. On top of my big white alarm clock sat a cockroach bigger than any I'd seen, waving its antennae and eyeing me speculatively. I knocked it to the floor and whacked it with the guidebook.

The cracking of its carcass gave out a loud report. Pulling on a shoe, I toed the yellow mess towards a corner. I pushed the shoe off with the other foot, and then sat naked on the edge of the bed for a while. Disgusted but triumphant, I finally lay back down, confident that the revolting trophy in the corner—like the jackdaws, jays and stoats that Scottish gamekeepers hang on barbedwire fences—would ward off the others.

I turned off the light and had almost gone back to sleep when I heard the rumbling of machinery again. Much louder this time. It was now about three in the morning, and I was feeling pretty sick at heart about my first night in Uganda. It was hot, and the sheets were clinging to me like a shroud. I got up and went over to the window. The warm, dirty lino stuck to the soles of my bare feet, and yet softened with each step through the unlit room. I felt like I was leaving impressions—Man Friday tracks for some hunter as yet unknown.

But it was me that was the stalker as I pulled aside the curtain and stood there amid the blankness, an observer hidden from the world outside. Below me on the street, a column of tanks was moving past, their black shapes outlined, in the way of things in darkness, by the obscurity of the night. As they passed by, I could also see the silhouettes of men in helmets in the turrets, and now and then thought that I could hear shouting through the jammed, smeary glass.

Though I knew that they couldn't see me, I was conscious of my nakedness, of my pale, presbyter's face with its straight, jet-black hair, my narrow chest with its own damp, hardly there tuft in the depression, the sharp curve of my iliac crests—those pelvic bones above the thigh—and of my long, thin legs. Like a pair of pokers, my mother used to say, and I'd look at the companion set by the hearth, that small coal fire that glowed like a red eye but never heated the place up, and think, no they are not.

4

I took breakfast by the veranda doors, down in the Speke's dilapidated dining room—a pulpy, orange-colored fruit I didn't recognize, a boiled egg with a grey yolk, and coffee in a battered silver pot engraved "E.A.R." Below, in smaller letters, "Property of East African Railways." I remembered what my guidebook had called it, "the Lunatic Line," and how Winston Churchill had entered Uganda by it, strapped to the cowcatcher of the train to get a better view.

I noticed that the waiters were all crowding round the copper radio grille in the wall near the lift-hatch to the kitchen. At the time I was not aware of the significance of what was being emitted. This was about the sum of it, in the rather shaky "Voice of Uganda." I strained to hear it from the table:

> The Uganda Armed Forces have this day decided to take over power from Obote and hand it to our fellow soldier Major-General Idi Amin Dada . . . and we hereby entrust him to lead this our beloved country of Uganda to peace and goodwill among all . . . We call upon everybody . . . to continue their work in the normal way. We warn all foreign governments not to interfere in Uganda's internal affairs. Any such interference will be crushed with great force . . . because we are ready . . . Power is now handed over to Major-General Idi Amin and you must await his

statement which will come in due course. We have done
this for God and our country.

My belly danced with fear, in spite of the food I had just
eaten. The muscles in my shoulders knotted as I got up from
the table. Coffee cup in hand, slopping the liquid in its saucer,
I went out onto the terrace. The balcony gave out onto the
hotel forecourt, with Nile Avenue and the corner of Pilkington
Road beyond. There were drowsy clusters of bats hanging upside
down in the trees in the forecourt—dark and wrinkled, like big
sultanas—and a smell of woodsmoke in the air. I sipped the coffee
and looked anxiously around for signs of disturbance.

People were gathered in the avenue, talking in little groups
round parked cars. They didn't seem unduly perturbed. Many
were apparently going about the routines of their daily business:
produce sellers balanced piles of green bananas and laid out rusty
iron pails of peas and beans; carvers arranged ebony figures on
hessian mats; foreign-exchange dealers looked on, leaning against
the walls in their shiny suits; women in colored dresses printed
with President Obote's face took charge of children and shopping.
Others were passing by on bulky black bicycles, some with bales
of cotton or churns of milk strapped to the back, or in old cars
with rounded roofs and wooden boards on their wings.

This was what I saw. None of it seemed that strange, really,
considering the news on the radio. Yet I realized, standing there,
sipping my coffee, that I had tipped up in Uganda in momentous
times. And I wasn't quite sure how I felt about that. I remembered something Swanepoel—the man in the bar—had said:
"Coups in Africa are normal, they just come round, like the rainy
season and the dry season."

Looking back, I'm aware that he was, in fact, quite wrong
about that—I mean, there are plenty of peaceful places in that big
continent, aren't there? Though it has often struck me that it
looks, cartographically, like a gun in a holster.

I scanned the Speke's crumbling façade to my right and left.
Then I put down my cup and saucer and walked to the end of
the balcony, where my eye followed the dingy stucco colonnades
of the shops along Pilkington Road. My gaze was caught by a

group of women washing clothes at a stirrup pump, singing as they scrubbed and pummeled. They took a sheet at either end and began to shake the water out of it. As they shook, the sheet clapped against itself and an unnatural sound, half like a drumbeat, half like a slap on human flesh, echoed between the trees outside the hotel.

At this one of the bats suddenly took flight; or *dropped* into flight—fell straight down from its branch, then twisted about and, becoming a black spot at the edge of the retina, disappeared into the sky.

Mixed in with the sound of the washerwomen, there gradually came another, more uncertain one. Nile Avenue began to fill up with a crowd, so much so that people soon had to stand to one side. What started as a trickle, a noise in the distance, in minutes turned into a walking, running mass of bodies, shouting slogans and ululating. Army jeeps with long radio aerials and mounted machine guns appeared round the bend of the road, threading their way through.

Teenage girls leaped onto the running boards of the jeeps, handing garlands to the soldiers. Shouts rang out, rising to my balcony: "Welcome, Idi Amin Dada! Eh, eh, eh, eh, eh, we support you! Major-General Amin is the one for Uganda! Amin is the savior of Uganda! Eh, eh, eh, eh!"

I was amazed at this sudden endorsement of an enforced government, and shocked at the speed with which the character of the street had changed. Cars and vans rolled through the crowd, in the wake of the jeeps. Their occupants waved out of the windows. Buses and bicycles, too, joined the parade, and also a solitary tank—ungainly, the barrel of its gun quizzical as the antenna of an insect. I wondered what had happened to the tanks I had seen passing in the night, around which vital locations they had been positioned.

Vehicles and people both were festooned with banana leaves—symbol of rejoicing and fertility, I later learned. I found myself recalling one of those Green Man pubs I saw on a trip to England, the face itself a wreath of vegetation, swinging on the sign in the wind. Then my attention was suddenly drawn by a group of young men ripping down an Obote poster from one of the colonnades.

"Obote afude!" they cried, stamping on the shreds of paper.

Obote is dead. (Not true, I discovered later. In fact, returning from the Commonwealth Conference in Singapore, Obote had diverted to Kenya, where he had received short shrift from Vice-President Moi, and from there fallen into the consoling arms of President Nyerere of Tanzania.)

And then I saw another group of young men, carrying burning images of Obote on spikes, and smashing to the ground melons painted with his face. It was more comical than sinister—though I suppose there are ways in which those two things can be one and the same.

I decided, after some thought, to go down into it all. After all, whatever was going on in this godforsaken place, I still had to present my credentials at the ministry. I wondered whether I ought to report to the British Embassy, too, just to be on the safe side.

So down I went, pleased with my rare flash of courage. Outside, the mob surged around me, retiring and returning like a spring tide. There were soldiers everywhere by now, shabby-looking in peak caps set askew and ill-fitting camouflage. Ahead of me, I saw, the tarmac had been churned up by the passage of the tank. I walked on, stepping from side to side to avoid the crowd. I passed the window of a clothing store with a brightly painted sign: "Khan Fashions." Across the street, one of the women in a dress with multiple images of Obote's face on it was suddenly surrounded by the same young men who had earlier pulled down the poster. Jeering and chanting, they thrust her down on to the curb. Her head hit the concrete with a sharp crack.

I turned away, scared and not wanting to get involved. The proprietor of the clothing shop, an Asian, was rolling down the steel blinds in front of his display of bolts of cloth and mannequins draped with saris. He turned briefly towards me as he ducked under the blinds, shaking his head at once despairingly and apologetically—as if explaining both that he couldn't let me in and that he, too, was nothing to do with all this—and then slammed the door.

I carried on walking through the crowd. A little way along was a small shack with a stripy canvas roof, where an old woman was selling fizzy drinks out of a cool-box. The awning bore the legend "Shongololo Bar and Eating House" and then below: "Coca-Cola: the Real Thing." I ordered a Coke and sat down at a rickety table, glad to be out of the crush. There was a brazier in a corner, where bits of chicken on wooden skewers were hissing over the coals.

Nearby, at another table, two men, two citizens of Kampala, were talking animatedly. One was a big, greying elephant of a man, wearing a safari shirt, the other long-legged and bespectacled. Very tall, he looked donnish, or like one of those marabou storks. I listened to their conversation, pretending to be distracted by the cavalcade passing by outside.

"Ever since the UPC conference, I knew this would happen. They are saying now it was Amin Dada's bullet which smashed the cheek of Obote that other time. But I have also heard that Amin took flight over a barbed-wire fence when the shot rang out, and was telling Obote that he was fearing an attempt on his own life."

"Well, from then all the time Obote has been chasing him. But he could not catch him because Dada runs too fast. You know he was, in the white man's army, the champion of sprinters. He is fast as a cheetah."

"He boxed with the whites also, and played in their front line for rugby, and the white soldiers who were playing, they hit him on the head with a hammer before the outing, many many times, to make him go faster still. They must have been nothing more than animals, those people."

"Maybe things will work out now. I hope so. You know that when Dada went on the Hadj to Mecca, people were saying that he would be put in gaol when he came back."

"Mecca is a great thing in this affair. It is because Dada is a Moslem man that the favor of Obote fell no longer upon him, and because he is a Kakwa man, and not of the Acholi or Langi tribe like Obote's fellows."

"And because Obote is a left-wing man and Dada is a right-wing man. The wazungu in Europe and the United States—of this fact I am sure—they must have blessed this movement today, for fear that we should become like the Chinese bandits of Dar es Salaam and Maputo."

"And for us Baganda people this can only be good, for Dada will surely bring back our king. It was Obote's orders, for certain, that sent Dada bombing to the palace and sent the Kabaka to England. Kabaka Yekka!"

"Kabaka Yekka!"

They got up to leave, exchanging some words with the old woman and then going out into the street. Swiftly finishing my Coke, I stood up and went after them, to ask for directions.

"Sir, it is not wise for you to be in this place," the man in the safari shirt said, with concern. "It is wiser for you to return to your lodgings, there are many things happening here in Kampala today."

"I'm on government business, I have to get to the Ministry of Health." The crowd jostled me as I spoke.

"But, sir, the government has changed," protested the other. "The soldiers, they are saying that wazungu must return to their homes. I have heard some missionaries, several of the White Fathers order, got shot at the airport. I am afraid that some of these army men can be very cruel."

"I really do have to get to the ministry," I said, anxiously. "And I need to go to the British Embassy as well."

"The ministry is on Kimathi, near the Neeta cinema just down there, the embassy on Parliament Avenue, which is farther, first you must . . ."

I repeated their directions to myself as I pushed through the mob. Having passed the cinema, outside which gaudy posters were advertising a Hindi film, I eventually reached my destination—a grim block with an empty car park. The askari at the gate, towering over me in his brown uniform, asked me what I was about. I said I had to see Mr. Wasswa, the Minister. He looked at me suspiciously through bloodshot eyes, then shrugged and let me pass.

Inside the ministry, I climbed several flights of stairs and went from desk to desk until I could find someone to help me. In the end I had to wait for half an hour outside an office on the top floor, while one of the secretaries, a tall girl with shiny ringlets and bright lipstick, made my representations. As I waited, most of the staff were hanging out of the windows, looking down at the crowds and talking excitedly. I watched them watching, my thighs getting sweaty on the plastic chair to which the secretary had consigned me.

Finally she came out, clutching a clipboard. I stood up.

"I am sorry," she said, "Mr. Wasswa is away."

I noticed that her lips were chapped.

"Well, what should I do? I'm due in Mbarara tomorrow. How am I meant to get there?"

"It will be possible to make the journey. By bus is the best way. You must find Doctor Merrit. He is the man you will be working with in Mbarara. This is his phone number. I also have a file here of papers for you to take away, papers to show you are the real thing. And here is one also that you will sign for me."

It was a disclaimer, stating that if any patient made allegations against me that were upheld in the courts, the Ministry of Health could not be held responsible. I took it from her and signed, balancing awkwardly as I leant the clipboard on one knee.

"Is it possible to have an advance on my salary?" I said, handing it back to her. "I've only brought about 300 English pounds with me."

"In Uganda 300 English is much money. I only get what is 10 pounds a month, and that is not enough; sometimes I have to go without breakfast and lunch to survive." She looked at me accusingly.

I didn't know what to say.

"It would need the Minister's signature," she continued, "and is not possible anyway. Unfortunately, Minister Wasswa was on the plane with—former Prime Minister Obote. We do not know if he will be coming back."

I left the minister-less ministry in slightly sour temper. Carrying my accreditation papers under my arm, I tramped off through the now thinning crowds to the Embassy. I discovered it to be a grand, white building with tall radio aerials on the roof. A pair of sunburned British soldiers were in the gatehouse.

I peered through the wire-net partition. "I've just arrived here. I have to see someone about my job."

"What job would that be, sir?" said one of the soldiers. He had a ginger moustache, and a Geordie accent to boot. The sound of it was a comfort.

"I'm going to be a doctor, somewhere called Mbarara."

"You'll be wanting to see Nigel Stone, sir. If you just wait a minute, I'll ring up for you. Can I please see your passport, sir? I know you sound British, and you look British, but we get some funny types trying it on here."

Stone was looking out of his window when I entered the room, his back to me. A teleprinter was chattering away in the corner. I coughed.

"Ah, Doctor Garrigan," he said, turning and coming across to shake my hand over his desk. He had wispy fair hair and a forehead so shiny it looked like he polished it each morning.

"I'm glad you've come. Take a seat. We usually keep tabs on British nationals coming into the country, and I'd wondered what had become of you. As you've probably gathered, things are a bit hectic round here. There have been a few changes. We're actually advising people to stay in their houses, but it's safe as . . . well, safe as the bush"—he gave a little laugh—"where you're bound, so you might as well head off. All the trouble's been in the city really, you see."

"You think I ought to just go, then?" I said.

"Absolutely. I think things will calm down very quickly. We're actually quite glad Amin has stepped in. Obote had some pretty odd ideas about how to run a country and Amin, well, he's one of our own. If not too bright. We think we'll be able to help him out. And vice versa."

There was a knock at the door. A thin man in army uniform came in, walking with a limp. The aging skin around his throat and cheeks drooped lugubriously, like a turkey's wattles.

"Stone," he said, ignoring me, "my boys haven't turned up. A little coup and they're cowering under their beds."

The man had a distinct Edinburgh accent. He sat down in the armchair in the corner of Stone's room, dangling his good leg over the arm. "I mean, how can I be expected to train such a bunch?"

"Doctor Garrigan," said Stone, "this is Major Weir, he's our Intelligence Officer, he's training the new Ugandan Army Intelligence Corps. The doctor's heading out to Mbarara, Major, where he's joining Doctor Merrit's clinic. He's a fellow Scot."

"Is that a fact?" said Weir. There was, I thought, something slightly frightening about him. He disturbed me, and I couldn't tell why.

"That's right," I said. "Fossiemuir." His name, that's what it was, it struck a chord with me—I think it was an old folk tale that my father liked to tell, something to do with a bonfire, a monkey and a walking stick. I couldn't remember what it was.

"Know it well. Good luck, anyhow. You're just the sort of fellow we want out here. You'll be aware that all the great things in this country have been achieved by Scots—Speke, Grant and the rest of them. Yes, Uganda was built out of the mills and girders of Scotland."

"Well," I said, with a half-embarrassed laugh, "I suppose we had to get out from under the feet of the English."

Weir stood up and gave me a strange look, ash-grey hair melting into ash-grey eyes. "Indeed," he said slowly, as if he was thinking of something else, and then, declamatory, and to my amazement: " 'What rhubarb, cyme or what purgative drug, would scour these English hence!' . . . *Macbeth*," he explained, and turned to go abruptly. "Let me know if any of my mugs show up," he said to Stone. "I'm going to fly my kite on the lawn."

Stone grinned at me apologetically as Weir closed the door. "Interesting chap, Weir. Decorated in the war. Very talented pilot. He transferred from the RAF to Intelligence after he was shot down—you saw the limp?"

"What did he mean—about flying his kite?"

Stone looked at the window, and then said, cryptically, "Oh, you'll see. Now," he continued briskly, sitting down at his desk, "let's get you signed up. We don't want you being left behind in Mbarara if the balloon goes up. Let's start with the basics."

He opened a leather-bound book and picked up a fountain pen. "Next of kin?"

"George and Jeanie Garrigan, Tarr House, Fossiemuir, West Fife."

"Fossiemuir? Is that with a *y* or an *i*? I'm not up on Scottish names, I'm afraid."

I spelled it out, and he wrote it down. I noticed a small bald crown on the top of his head as he bent over the ledger. The pinkness of the skin and the yellowy hair around it—eggs and bacon, I thought.

He looked up as I was studying him, raising his blond eyebrows as if he had divined my thoughts. "How much money have you brought with you? We've had terrible problems recently, repatriating folks—hippies, mean-wells, so on—who've thought that just because it's Africa they can wander about without a bean in their pockets. I know it won't apply to you, but it's a question we usually ask."

I told him about my £300.

"And how are you planning on getting to Mbarara?"

"Well," I said, "I thought I'd get a bus. I've heard about these—well, I've read in a guidebook about these—matatus, the vans that go all over the country."

"Death traps," he said with a sigh. "It's a shame we don't have an Embassy car going down, else we could give you a lift. Ah, well, I suppose you'll get there in one piece."

I must have looked a bit shocked when Stone said this.

"Oh, I'm sorry," he added quickly. "I've put the wind up you now. It's just that the accident rate on East African roads is phenomenal. I remember once—on the Mbarara road, as it happens—a tanker coming towards us skidded and came down the hill totally at right angles. We had to pull off into the scrub. We nearly hit a tree stump. The tanker turned over and blew up. The driver was killed—we went up to look when the flames died down. Everything was charred."

He closed his book, as if signaling that the conversation was over. I got up to go, gathering the papers I had brought with me from the ministry.

"Doctor Garrigan," said Stone, "just one more thing."

"Yes," I said, halting my upwards, paper-gathering motion to settle down on the seat again.

"Do you mind if I tell you a bit about my work here?"

"Go ahead," I said, surprised.

"You'll appreciate the exigencies of our role at the Embassy: keeping an eye on the interests of Her Majesty's Government in such a place as this is, how shall I put it? . . . delicate. Sometimes those who you thought were your friends turn out not to be."

He paused.

"Obote, for example. I was here for the Colonial Office, you know—before this, my very first job—and I saw the Independence, the Uhuru, ceremony. The flag raising, the teas on the lawn, the band playing the new national anthem, the freshly promoted African soldiers marching past. You know the sort of thing. Amin was one of the soldiers, by the way, he escorted the passing of the Royal Colour. It was the Duke and Duchess of Kent who were there. I stood behind them in the box, listening to the legal rigmarole and the prayers from the Archbishop and the Moslem cleric."

The teleprinter gave a sudden chirrup and spewed out reams of paper. The connecting sheets, folding awkwardly along their perforations, settled in a rough white nest on the carpet and the machine returned to its poised silence.

"Anyway, Obote let us down. He started consorting with the Chinese—Mao's very influential in Southern Africa, you know—and all sorts, and he made a pig's ear of things on the tribal front. And I have to say, we didn't see it coming. So now we want to be extra vigilant: you never know what Africa's going to throw at you."

I wondered where this little lecture was going. Stone was becoming quite demonstrative, moving his arms and hands as he spoke.

"What I'm driving at," he continued, as if in answer to my thought, "is that we need reliable Brits to keep their eyes and ears open down in the country."

"You mean, be a spy?" I said, incredulously.

"No, no, not at all. Let me put it like this: I have to file reports to London, and I have to put something in them. Up here in Kampala, we sometimes don't see the wood for the trees. That's what happened with Obote. Now out where you are, almost up in the trees—I'm joking—a body might get a feel for what's afoot earlier than we would. That's all it comes down to."

He leaned forward, his hair flopping down as he did so. "Grass roots, that what African politics is, you see. As you're down there, it wouldn't be any bother to keep a weather eye out for anything untoward now, would it? Just on a casual basis."

"Well," I said, "I suppose not, but I don't really know what you mean. What sort of things am I meant to be watching out for?"

"Nothing in particular, just drop in to see me when you're next up here. Let me know the lie of the land. I'll buy you lunch."

As he stood up—the interview really was concluded this time—I heard a strange whirring noise. At first I thought it was the teleprinter again. But it came from outside.

"Ah," said Stone, turning his head towards the window,

"that'll be Major Weir's magnificent flying machine. Come and have a look."

I followed him over to the glass. The whirring noise got louder. Through the louvers, and the steel mesh of the mosquito net, I could see suspended—almost directly in front of us—something I'd never seen before but had often wished, as a boy, to possess: a radio-controlled model helicopter.

It hovered there for a moment—bulbous and tubular, its rotor a blur—before dipping off to one side, out of view, in a florid movement that reminded me of a servant giving a bow.

"There's Weir," said Stone, pointing.

Down on the lawn, with a semicircle of uniformed British soldiers and African servants in white tunics behind him, stood the Major. A squat box was in his hands, with a tall aerial shooting up out of it, and there was a jumble of equipment at his feet on the grass.

We stood and watched in silence for a few minutes, until the machine swooped back into view below us and Weir, fiddling with his control levers, brought it gently down on the grass. The audience clapped and cheered. Weir handed his transmitter to one of the soldiers and limped a few paces towards the model. Once the rotor had stopped spinning, he went down on one knee to check it, and then stood up with the helicopter held out gingerly in front of him.

"It's his little joke," said Stone, as we walked to the door. "Every time he flies it, he sends it up here to buzz my window. It's just a toy, but it's astonishing all the same. He built the thing himself."

5

Filled with silky-haired goats, chickens and what must have been nearly thirty human bodies—in a space meant for about ten—the matatu didn't feel like a vehicle at all. With its windscreen cracked and browned, several of the door handles sheared off, one of the wheel arches missing and a general weariness distributed throughout the whole structure, onto which various bits of wood and steel plate had been tacked, it seemed less like a machine than an ancient artifact, something to worship or view at an exhibition.

I was tired even before the journey began. After walking from the Speke the next morning, and struggling with my bags through the crush of the matatu park, trying to seal off from my hearing the relentless beeping of horns and blowing of whistles while deciphering the destination calls of the touts—who tended to hang, at the acute angle of slalom skiers, by one arm out of the sliding doorways of their vans—I had finally taken a seat at the back of (to be specific) Matatu Number 8.

This number wasn't displayed prominently, however, either at the front or at the back of the vehicle. It was on a little square of torn cardboard propped against the windscreen—and I only noticed that once I was installed, having made laborious enquiries. Walking round each minibus, wherever you might have expected a number to have been, there were brightly lettered messages instead: "Travel Hopefully," I remember, and "Go with God." Elsewhere, "Africa Superstar Express." Inside the van, stenciled above the driver's head, was yet another sign: "No Condition is Permanent," it said, whether warning or comfort I could not tell.

My seat, under which I had stowed my luggage, was only partly covered. The springs came through, poking up between fibrous stuffing and remnants of plastic. I moved about uncomfortably, listening to the thumps on the roof as they loaded up the cargo. I saw crates of Fanta and Coca-Cola, bundles of newly planed wood, heavy sacks of rice or grain stamped with an inky logo, a long tower (almost as long as the bus itself) of red plastic washing bowls, one inside the other, the inevitable stalks of matooke, or green banana—and so much more being passed up, that I wondered how we would ever manage to travel.

While we were waiting, I looked out of the window. On the ground nearby, ignoring the human bustle around it, a crow was picking at something, tearing at something, holding it down with its foot. I looked more closely. It was the carcass of a brown animal. I realized that it was one of the species of big rats I had seen gamboling by a wall on my way back to the Speke the evening before. Or, as I'd fancied, dancing strathspeys and reels—on account of it being Burns Night, as I'd suddenly realized: Amin's first night of power. I say rats, but they were more like rabbits, one sitting up on its hind legs to give me a curious look as I passed by.

Watching the beak of the crow as it tugged at the fur and the pink flesh beneath, I began to feel sick. This surprised me, since I had always had quite a strong stomach when faced with dissections. I supposed it was the difference of the dissections being scientific, the smell of formaldehyde on my hands disguising, back then, during my practicals, the fact of the matter.

By the time the last of the freight had been humped up and the tout, who also doubled as conductor, had given his final catcall and grabbed his last fistful of grubby notes, my thighs were beginning to hurt a great deal from the metal coils in the seat. As we roared off with crashing gears and a cloud of dust and exhaust, I folded my jacket and put it underneath me. This action disturbed one of the goats, which was doubled up next to my suitcase under the seat, its shanks horribly tied with wire flex. It also caused a certain amount of merriment among my neighbors. The old woman next to me said something loudly. I caught the word "muzungu"—

meaning white man, I'd already worked out. A titter went around the van, everyone looking at me as if I were some kind of zoo animal.

I just grinned back awkwardly, as we bumped along the pot-holed road out of the city—grinned at the mixed bunch of merchants, mainly women, with their goods and animals (one had a live chicken squashed into a basket on her knee), farmers and crying babies. All were very poor, although I noticed that there was one passenger who seemed, by virtue of his smart blue worsted suit and the hard brown Samsonite-type case on his knees, to be more prosperous than the rest. He was reading a newspaper—with some difficulty, as the crush meant he could only open it a fraction.

There were also several serious-looking young men in ill-fitting Western clothes. One was seated directly behind me. I suspected these were civil servants returning to the country; Swanepoel had said they'd been laid off by the new regime. The one behind me, though, turned out to be a student of Food Science at Makerere University in Kampala.

"You are a doctor then, sir?" he said, having enquired after my name and the purpose of my visit to Mbarara.

I nodded.

"You will be at the clinic with Doctor Merrit?" he asked.

"That's right."

"I am glad that you are coming there. We have a great need of doctors, so long as they do not cost too much money. Doctor Merrit is very costly. Even the African doctor there is too expensive for many of our people."

"I'm sure they try not to be," I said, "any doctor does—but it's the same problem everywhere, I'm afraid. In my country there are terrible arguments going on about who should pay for medical care. And in America, you have to have insurance to get anywhere at all."

I watched his expression as he absorbed this information. A furrow went across his high brow. I wondered—twisted awkwardly backwards to look at him, with his black plastic spectacles perched on his nose and his limp-collared white shirt—whether I had said something out of place.

"Sir, I do not think you have been in Uganda very long," he

said. "Even wealthy families here suffer from many deaths in a single year. When I listen to the BBC World Service or go to read the newspaper in the British Council in Kampala, I am amazed, sir. They make so much fuss in Britain when just one person is killed. In Uganda we are the world champions of death by comparison, but I never hear a single mention of this. I never see or hear a single report in all my life."

I made a kind of sympathetic gesture with my mouth, unsure of what was expected of me at this point. "I'm sorry," I said eventually. "I'm sure I'll be confronted with the worst of it all pretty soon."

"My family are from Mbarara," he informed me then. "So I know that place. I am shifting there to see them. My name is Boniface Malumba. You must call me Bonney. Because I know some white people who never use first names, if they ever speak to us one bit."

He sank back into his seat—as uncomfortable as mine, so far as I could tell.

"That's very rude," I said, confused, "I won't do that." I wish you'd leave me alone, I thought to myself.

Then he grinned sheepishly. "Doctor Garrigan, I am sorry for my words. It is not your fault. You are good man, I can see. You are welcome at my father's house in Mbarara. I will send word for you."

"Thank you," I said. "That would be lovely."

I turned back round, glad to be relieved of the double burden of having to conduct a conversation like that while twisted round on those torturous springs. The old woman next to me, who had a turban on her head, appeared to be the proprietor of the goat beneath the seat. It was getting restive. She gave the poor creature a kick, then smiled at me with toothless gums.

My thighs were still hurting as we carried on into the countryside, in spite of the folded jacket. We passed clumps of banana plantations by the side of the road and open lorries going in the opposite direction, most of them piled high with the waxy fruit—it's eaten green, in a savory dish, not yellow like at home—and belching out clouds of black exhaust. There were boys with bananas, too, the large bunches of forty or fifty balanced precariously on the back of their old-fashioned bicycles.

The towns along the way had intriguing names—Mpigi,

Buwama, Lukaya, Masaka, Mbirizi, Lyantonde—but were all run-down and rather dull, most of them simply a string of single-story shops and houses along the road. Only Masaka was of any substance. We stopped there for a break and I grabbed some beef and rice at the Tropic-o'-Paradise Restaurant, where—on a crude poster of a dusky pirate clutching a struggling girl—"mouthwatering food" was advertised. It wasn't.

Near Sanga, the next village along from Lyantonde, the main incident of interest on my trip took place. There was a blast on the horn and we came to a juddering, wheezing halt—you could actually hear the driver pumping on the brakes. The goat-kicking woman tugged at my sleeve and pointed, saying something I did not understand.

Looking ahead, over the other passengers, I saw a pile of branches in the road and farther along a lorry slewed across it. The branches, I realized, were the Ugandan equivalent of traffic cones, or a danger triangle.

I leant over to get a better view. It was not a banana but a tea lorry, with the name of one of the main trading companies, James Finlay, emblazoned across the door of the cab, which had swung open. All across the tarmac in front were sacks of tea, some of them split open so that the black powder spilled out. Only it didn't look as if the powder had spilled out, but as if the tarmac had crumbled and was climbing into the bags.

Next to the road a man, who must have been the driver, was sitting on the ground with his head in his hands. I could also see a number of soldiers, a couple of them perched on the sacks of tea, drinking beer out of bottles, and more next to a canvas bivouac under a mango tree.

The chatter in the bus fell silent. One of the soldiers had climbed in. He was wearing a shabby green uniform and a crumpled forage cap, and he carried an automatic rifle. It looked heavy, with at least three curving magazines of ammunition, one stuck in, the others taped on, side by side, ready to be flipped up. I was also intrigued to see, as he walked down the aisle, that on his feet he wore a pair of pink fluffy slippers.

The soldier said something loudly and people began to reach into their bags and the folds of their clothing, bringing out tattered identity papers. I dug around for my passport. When it came to my turn, I handed it to him meekly, keeping an eye on the end of the gun which, hung over his shoulder with the ungainly bundle of magazines banging into his hip, swung dangerously near my nose.

The soldier flicked through the pages of my passport, looked at me, closed it, and then opened it again, flicking through once more. I glanced up at him expectantly, but he obviously didn't speak English. Then he beckoned to me to come with him, waving the passport like a reproach.

I turned round and looked anxiously at Boniface. He said something to the soldier but the soldier just snapped at him and began to pull at my clothes.

I stood up. "What does he want?" I asked Boniface.

Boniface made the money sign with his thumb and forefinger. "He wants shillings," he whispered. "You will have to give him some. If you don't, he will be troublesome."

I turned to face the soldier, raising my palms in a gesture of surrender, as if he was pointing the gun at me—which he was, more or less—and nodding stupidly. Don't be frightened, I told myself. I reached down and fumbled in the inside pocket of the folded jacket on the seat, trying to extract a 200-shilling note without showing my wallet. When I managed to get something, it turned out to be 500 shillings.

The soldier tucked it into one of the pouches on his belt, without a word, and moved along up the bus as if the encounter had not taken place. Everyone else had got their money ready by now, from the civil-servant types to the poorest-looking old women. They were all so calm (even the babies seemed to have gone quiet) and apparently inured to the procedure that he might as well have been making the collection at church.

Except for one. When the soldier came alongside the prosperous-looking man with the blue suit, he leant over him and slammed his hand down on the brown case, barking an order in Swahili—meaning, I supposed, that the man should open it.

I was surprised to hear the man reply in English. "I am a Kenyan diplomat doing government business in Uganda," he said, as if he were making a statement in court. "You have no right to make me open this case. I can show you my passport, I can show you my papers."

The soldier's face turned ugly—he let off a barrage of abuse at the Kenyan and then went to the front of the bus, shouting.

"It is not good," whispered Boniface.

Two more soldiers climbed aboard. They approached the Kenyan and started to pull the case off his knee. The man bent over, hugging the case as if it were a child.

"You have no right to do this," he protested. "What you are doing is wrong. My visas and my permits are in order."

The soldiers kept saying something, kept repeating a word over and over again.

"They are saying," Boniface explained, "that he is a spy."

One of the new soldiers (this one was wearing no shoes at all, and a pair of trousers so ragged they were indecent) swung his gun round. Hard. The ugly sight sticking up at the end tore into the Kenyan's cheek. The original soldier wrenched the case away, as the others started slapping the man about his bloodied face.

The man moaned. The long noise of it came down the bus as the soldiers clattered off with the case. I watched them walk towards their fellows under the mango tree, one of them hefting the case up onto his head.

People began to talk again, and the driver started up the engine. As we skirted the sacks of tea and the lorry, which hadn't moved—the driver was still sitting there with his head in his hands—Boniface tapped me on the shoulder.

"You see how we have to suffer in Africa," he said, "you see how we have a life that is very hard."

"Yes," I said, nonplussed, "yes."

Feeling guilty, I reached under the seat, where my bag was (the goat, having stopped thrashing about, had sunk into a near catatonic state), and rummaged around. I stood up and pushed through with my plastic first-aid box to where the Kenyan was sitting. He was just looking straight ahead. Blood was running down his cheek, falling onto his shirt in thick globules.

The wound was nastier than I had imagined. A flap of skin hung down, raw, where the sight had caught him. I could see at once that it would need stitching. "Excuse me," I said. "I am a doctor. I can treat your wound."

I leaned over him. Several of the other passengers had got up and were crowding behind me, intrigued at what the muzungu was doing. The Kenyan, as if snapping out of a trance, lifted one of his hands. He turned round to face me, the blood streaming down.

"How dare you come to me like this?" he said, quietly. "What good are you to me now? You said nothing when you should have come forward. The soldiers, they would not have harmed me, or taken money from these people if you had stepped forward. They are afraid to hurt white people."

"But they took money from me as well," I said, rather too defensively. "Look, let me just see to your wound. You're losing blood."

I pulled some lint out of the kit and moved to press it on the gash. But the Kenyan, to my surprise, hit my hand away. The watching group gave out a little gasp. Several of them started shouting at the Kenyan.

He stood next to me, great gouts of blood coming out from where the flap of skin hung.

"I do not need help from you," he said. "You did not step forward when you had the power. You say you are a doctor but in fact I think you come to Africa to take from us, like all muzungu."

He gave a dignified nod on finishing his speech and then sat down, oblivious to his wound. I didn't know what to say. The heat in the bus made me feel slightly faint—the heat from the sun, from the press of the bodies behind me, and the hot uproar of the engine coming through the soles of my shoes. I stood for a moment, looking at him there, the flap of skin hanging on his bleeding face, embarrassment and confusion rising in mine.

And then I thought—I'm almost too ashamed to put it down—I thought of reaching over and pulling the damn thing off, pulling it off his face in one swift, uncompromising movement. As if I were removing a plaster.

I don't know what came over me, I really don't, and I don't remember getting back to my seat, only the consoling and dirty looks for him and me from the other passengers, who had launched into a discussion. Some, I think, may have been sniggering, whether at me or the Kenyan I didn't know.

Boniface was kind, though; he appreciated my predicament. "Do not be sad, sir," he said, rubbing my arm. "It is not his fault. Since the soldiers came, it has been like this everywhere."

6

The matatu arrived in Mbarara at about four o'clock in the afternoon. It was a dusty sort of a town. Bonney, having made me promise again to come and visit his family as soon as possible, showed me to a hotel. The Agip Motel, it was called; the Speke seemed quite luxurious by comparison. After checking in and taking a shower, I tried to ring Merrit from the front desk. But the phones were down.

So I set off to find his house, asking people in the street for directions. Everyone seemed to know who he was and where he lived, but it still took me quite a long time and a number of enquiries. On the way I passed an army barracks and a group of government offices with tatty signs: "Central Bureau of Forestry," "Ministry of Agriculture and Fisheries (South-West Rehabilitation Project)," "Centre for Continuing Education (Makerere Outreach Unit)." A little more imposing—"Local Government Court, Southern Province Kikagati / Ibanda Sub-Districts."

As I walked, I collected a wondrous group of small boys about me, running alongside and calling out.

"Muzungu, muzungu!"

They capered around.

"Where are you from?"

Several of them were pushing along little toy cars, about the size of shoeboxes, twisted out of steel wire. They bowled these along showily in front of me. The toys had an ingenious steering device, involving a bicycle spoke attached to the front axle of the toy and a steering wheel at waist height. You would never, I thought, see kids making that kind of thing at home.

"Muzungu, are you married?"

"No, I'm not," I said. "Are you?"

They giggled, spurring on their vehicles to ever more deft maneuvers in the dust. The more sophisticated models had mannequin drivers made of stuffed cloth; one even with a soldier's camouflage uniform, perfect down to the peaked cap perched on top and the deathly grinning face marked on with charcoal.

"My name is Gugu," the driver of that one said. He was a snubnosed little fellow in a grubby T-shirt, with an infectious smile. I glanced down at him, at his big eyes and perfectly rounded head, his dusty knees and surprisingly aged-looking feet. The price of going barefoot, I supposed.

"Why do you want doctor?" continued the boy. "Are you sick?"

"No. I am a doctor. I am going to work here."

"I am going to be a mechanic," he said, proudly. "This is my car. It is a VW Beetle."

"It's very good," I said, "but shouldn't he be driving a tank or a jeep, if he's a soldier?"

"What is tank?"

"One with a long gun at the front."

The boy nodded sagely, and then pointed at a gated fence surrounding a group of buildings.

"Doctor there."

I had reached the compound. It was by now about six, and quickly getting dark. Next to the gate stood a building, a sort of military pillbox, except that it was made of mud and straw. A list of names and numbers was painted on a board, nailed into the dried mud of the hut. A hurricane lamp was hung on another nail. Its breathy roar seemed too quick, too bold, for the faintness of its light.

1. Waziri
2. —
3. Canova
4. Chiric
5. Ssegu

6. —
7. Seabrook
8. Merrit
9. Zach

The boys, who had stopped in a ring behind me, suddenly scampered off as I was reading.

"Bye-bye, muzungu! Bye-bye!"

There was tinkling laughter as they tumbled down the hill. I thought of elves. Then, smelling tobacco smoke, the word "Woodbine" wound into my head. I realized then that there was someone in the pillbox. Wisps of smoke a-coming out of it that I could smell.

I peered inside. A boot, a fold of cloth, the glow of a pipe. There was a presence there, for certain—the sweeter smell of long occupation overlying the harsh tobacco—but nothing was said to my intrusion. So I carried on blithely into the compound and knocked at number eight.

The man who opened the door had a moustache the color of rust. He looked at me for a moment, startled.

"I'm sorry . . ." I began, conscious of it being too late just to turn up on someone's doorstep.

"Goodness!" he said. "You must be Doctor Garrigan."

I shook his hand. He was about fifty, and slightly overweight, with a bizarre white streak down the middle of his brown hair.

"We've been expecting you for ages," he said.

"Oh—I thought I was here on schedule."

"Spiny, don't make him feel it's his fault," said another voice.

A woman in a blue dress was standing behind him. "The ministry said you were coming last month," she explained as he stood aside for her. "We sent them a telegram but they didn't reply. So we didn't know when you were coming."

"Anyway, I'm Alan Merrit. Come in. Pleased to have you on board. This is my wife, Joyce. I'm really embarrassed you've had to hunt us out like this. Let me get you a drink, then we can sit down and talk. Sorry about the mix-up. This place is completely bloody, you know."

The living room was dimly lit, except for where it opened onto the veranda, through a pair of louvered doors. Insects flitted under a row of spots beyond the doors.

"We're out here," Mrs. Merrit said. "Come through." She was wearing a pair of heavy lapis lazuli earrings that caught the light as they swung.

"What would you like?" said Merrit, calling from the kitchen.

"A beer, please, if you've got it," I said.

There was the rattle and heavy clunk of a fridge door being opened and closed. Mrs. Merrit motioned me to a cane chair and then sat down herself, crossing her legs. A curl of green pressed powder was burning on the table, attached to a wire stand. Next to it, a packet: DOOM Mosquito Coils, Van der Zyl pvt, Bloemfontein, RSA. The trickle of smoke rose directly up into the rafters. It smelt perfumed, oriental.

"Now, I want to hear all about your trip," she said. "Where have you left your things?"

I told her about the man on the matatu, about Boniface and the Agip Motel.

"Oh, but it's horrible there," she said. "There's no question. You must stay here. We'll send the watchman down to collect your bags."

She walked to the edge of the veranda and shouted into the night. "Nestor!"

Merrit came in and put a beer down in front of me, the glass foaming, with the half-full bottle alongside it, and opened another for himself. The legend on the bottle said SIMBA, across a painted picture of a lion with its mouth open.

"Nestor!"

"What are you shouting about, darling?"

"Nicholas is booked into the Agip, he can't stay there, can he? I'm going to send Nestor down to collect his bags."

"Look," I protested feebly, "there's no need. I'll go back later."

"Don't be silly," Merrit said. "It's dark. You'll fall into the ditch. Stay. We've got plenty of room since the kids left."

"That's very good of you. Are you sure?"

"Of course," he said, nodding his head. With the white streak down the middle, he looked a little like a badger.

Mrs. Merrit stood up, rubbing her palms together briskly.

"Now, have you eaten? We already have, I'm afraid, and the house-boy has gone home, but I could rustle something up for you. How about a toasted ham sandwich?"

"That would be great," I said, realizing that I was quite hungry.

"I'll just go through and make it," she said. "Shout for him again will you, Spiny, it annoys me he takes so long."

"Probably asleep."

Merrit—why, I'd been wondering, did she call him Spiny?—got up and walked down the steps into the garden, going a little way round the corner of the building.

"Nestor! Nestor!"

"Will you have mustard?" his wife called from the kitchen. "I can make some up. We get Colman's powder from the duty-free shop in Kampala."

"Oh, don't bother, I'll be fine."

"Nestor!" His voice grew fainter as he ventured deeper into the garden.

She came back out holding a bowl of peanuts. "Here's something to keep you going."

"Thank you," I said, as she put the bowl on the table.

"And do have some mustard with your ham. I think the powdered version's nicer than the bought stuff back in UK, actually. More oomph to it. It's the kind of treat you'll miss when you face the shops in town. Even the Indian dukas only have the very basics."

"All right, then," I said, grasping a handful of peanuts.

"If we'd known when you were coming, I'd have got you a proper meal," she said. "The ministry are hopeless like that. I've made sure they've cleaned the bungalow up for you, though. It's one of those across the way."

She pointed over the flowerbeds, where I could see the outline of another three houses. "The middle one. It's fully furnished, but you'll need to get bedding and so on from the market. I can lend you things for the time being. And you must eat here till you're organized."

"That's very kind of you," I said. My voice sounded distant—all I could hear, inside the bones of my head, was the noise of the peanuts as I crunched them.

"Oh, don't worry, I know how hard it is when you're setting up somewhere. I've done it enough times. Now, I'm going to toast your bread."

She went back to the kitchen. I drank some of my beer, enjoying the sensation of bubbles on my tongue after the stickiness of the peanuts.

A few seconds later, Merrit came up the steps, puffing. "I don't know where the old bugger is," he said. "Perhaps it's time to get someone younger."

He sat down, and we talked. I noticed that he had that peculiar waxiness of skin which certain men get as they pass out of middle age. When I told him about the incident which had taken place on my journey, he just laughed; and then—the froth of the Simba gathering on his moustache—took a sip from his glass, as if to wash the laugh away.

"It's just Africa nonsense, Nicholas. You'll get used to it, or you'll get used to not being used to it. You have to see the funny side, or you'd go mad."

"I suppose I will," I said, wondering how what had happened could be thought funny at all. "I think I've got a lot to learn. You feel like you can cope with it all and then something like that happens and everything seems impossible again."

"Not really, it's very simple. This place—chaos, you just have to expect the worst. You think it's a matter of it getting worse for it to get better, but actually it just gets worse and worse. Take this new business with Amin. I hear they're all happy as sandboys right now up in Kampala, but it'll end in tears, I promise you. Our own stupid fault, of course."

I reached for the peanuts and he sipped at his beer again. Simba.

"Lion," Merrit explained, when I asked. "It's a Swahili word, simba's king of the beasts; there's even a Simba battalion in the army. Their barracks are in town. Sometimes they come into the hospital for treatment."

"Bullet wounds?"

"Well, more often syphilis."

I picked up the bottle. *The beer of strength and quality*, that's what the label announced, underneath the lion picture.

"They don't really speak Swahili round here, though," he

continued. "Not as such. It's from the Arabic . . . *sawahil*—people of the coasts."

Merrit said *sawahil* in an affected voice, twisting his mouth down so it came out as "sour heel." He frowned as he did it, his moustache looking funny-fierce.

"Mombasa, Zanzibar, down there. Where the slavers came in. I went there once. It's all narrow alleys and overhangs. They have some very beautiful carved doors on the houses. Arab, hundreds of years old. Here they're mountain people. Totally different, with a totally different language. Some do speak Swahili, though, as a lingua franca, and if you're going to learn any language in East Africa it might as well be that."

He took another mosquito coil from the packet next to the peanuts, fixed it into the springy steel holder and lit it. It flared and then settled down into a comfortable glow.

"Syphilis, too, actually. That came up from the coast as well. Trade routes."

"Do you think I should learn?"

"You'll pick things up. In Kinyankole, too, that's the local one. But to be honest, you're fine with English."

He looked up at the doorway. "Here's Joyce with your toasties."

"Any sign of Nestor?" she asked, from over a tray piled high with golden-brown triangles.

"Not yet."

She put the tray down in front of me. "I did some cheese ones too."

As she stood looking into the garden, with her hands on her hips, I bit into one of the crisp parcels—and immediately took a sharp intake of breath as hot cheese burned my tongue.

"Nestor! Where is he, Spiny?" she exclaimed. And then, to me: "We have terrible problems with servants here. Stealing and so on. Let me know when you're ready to get one and I'll put out the word. Otherwise you'll just get someone one of the other expats has sacked."

"I don't know if I'll really want one," I said, finishing my molten mouthful. "I think I'd rather look after myself."

Merrit snorted. Spiny. I wondered whether the nickname was from the streak in his hair.

"Everyone thinks that when they first arrive," he said. "You'll change your mind soon enough, when you have to wash your own clothes by hand."

"And in a way," she added, sniffily, "you're doing them a favor. They're very keen for the money, you know. They earn a lot more from us than they would on the plantations or going down to the tobacco estates in Rhodesia. Nestor!"

Just as the word left her lips, Nestor—I guessed—materialized out of the night, carrying a hurricane lamp. He was a bent and wrinkled old man, with a khaki greatcoat hanging loose about his bony shoulders; a former soldier, I thought to myself, realizing, as a tobacco smell came to me, that he must have been the ghost-like inhabitant of the hut at the gate. He saluted smartly as he approached us.

As Mrs. Merrit gave Nestor instructions, her husband questioned me at length about what I'd seen of the coup.

"Were you scared?" he asked. "I'd have been scared if it had happened when I first arrived. That was over twenty years ago, mind, when it wouldn't have happened."

"More bewildered than scared," I said. "It was scarier with the soldiers on the bus, really."

"Spiny," Mrs. Merrit said, having sent Nestor off, "it's terrible that Nicholas has had to find his way here in such a haphazard way. I think you should send a memo to the ministry."

"There's no point, darling, they don't listen to me. Don't worry, we'll soon get you fixed up. You'll find it as comfortable as England once you've settled in."

"Scotland," I said.

They laughed—together, in that harmonic way of long-standing couples.

"That's exaggerating," she said. "It's quite a hard life here. I often wish we could go back."

"Why couldn't you?" I said.

"There'd be no point. We're African now."

"No, we're not," her husband said. "And we will go back. When the time is right."

"There's nothing for us there, Spiny. You know how depressed you got on our last leave."

"Hmm."

He looked cross, and then she turned to me, her lapis earrings gleaming. "England has changed so much since we left. You'll find, if you stay here a few years, that half your mind is back in the UK. You're living in two places at the same time. And then you do go back there and you realize it's a different place altogether from the one you had in your head."

"It is the same," he said grumpily, getting up to fetch more drinks, "and, as far as I know, you can't be in two places at one time . . ."

"Don't mind him," she said. "He gets bad-tempered when he thinks about the future. We haven't got a pension, you see. It's a bit of a worry. I think he should go into private practice in South Africa, but he won't agree. Anyway, why am I bothering you with all this?"

Merrit came back in and poured another half-bottle of beer into my glass. I watched the Simba picture turn on its head as he tipped the bottle. The lion's design put me in mind of those black-and-white films (with titles like *Safari!* or *Return of the Hunter*) I had watched as a child—but it was stylized, too, like a heraldic sign from long ago.

Rex rampant, I thought later in their guest room. Mrs. Merrit's crisp sheets were wrapped around me and the thin white gauze of the mosquito net obscured my sleepy view of the blue suitcase, across the other side of the room. It was dusty on the bottom, from where Nestor must have put it down on the way. Rex rampant, I said to myself again as my eyelids closed, rex rampant and leopard couchant . . .

7

The following morning, we had a delicious breakfast of coffee, homemade bread and oranges. The malaria pills sat in a little saucer in the middle of the table, and Merrit made me take one. I'd checked it out before leaving Scotland and knew I wasn't headed for a high-risk malarial district, so I hadn't planned to take daily doses. But he demurred.

"We're not exactly plagued by mosquitoes here, like in the areas we spray, but you can't be too careful."

Halfway through the meal, Merrit got up to fiddle with the dials on a big Eddystone shortwave, pointing out to me the aerial wire draped on the avocado tree outside. It was then I heard for the first time the BBC's "Lillibullero," a tune with which I would become familiar when I sent off for my own Grundig Music-Boy through a coupon in the *Uganda Argus*.

"This is the BBC World Service . . ." Always an upper-class English voice, except for those football Saturdays with Paddy Feeney. It was he who kept me sane later, when things got bad with Amin: amazing how you can get everything in perspective, even a dictator, when you hear just a single mention of Raith Rovers.

After the pips, the news came on. Gathered like one of those families you see in pictures from the war, the Merrits and I listened to the broadcast. Another British Ambassador kidnapped by guerrillas, this time in Uruguay. The post strike still on at home, and telephone lines between East and West Berlin reconnected for the first time in nineteen years.

Afterwards, Merrit took me over to my own bungalow. I noticed a wasp's nest attached to one of the wooden fascia boards under the eaves. Its greyish material made me think of papier-mâché, of the rough dolls I had made at primary school. Cows and pigs. Humans.

"We'll have to get rid of that for you," Merrit said, seeing me look. "Smoke them out."

We went inside. I dumped my suitcase in the center of the empty lounge. Our feet were loud on the bare floorboards as we walked around. The bungalow was light and airy in a desolate sort of a way, with its bubbly, whitewashed walls, crude wooden furniture and—strangest of all—a concrete bath. One item bore witness to Merrit's suspicions about malarial incidence: a mosquito net, its coarse muslin ruched up into an iron hoop hung from the ceiling. Yet I felt, on that first day, that I might be happy there. Clean lines, that's the phrase—bungalow number six certainly had those.

"Why the bars on the window?" I asked, going over to look out, through the ornate, curled-iron bars and the insect grille, at the green valley and mountains beyond.

"Kondos," he said, "what they call armed bandits here, and the usual petty theft. I had my toothbrush stolen the other day. Someone actually put his hand through the bars on the bathroom window and filched it out of the mug."

"It's a beautiful view," I said.

"They call it the Bacwezi valley. It's just swamps really."

We went back outside into the early sun and began the climb up towards the clinic. On the way, Merrit stopped to lace his shoe, and I looked down at the shrinking compound below me. It had been hastily thrown up, obviously, but was quite pleasant nonetheless: three sets of three uniform dwellings, tin-roofed and settled neatly among the high-banked flowerbeds, with paths weaving in between and a high steel water tower glinting above. The blades of its rotor moved slowly in the wind.

Each bungalow had a white picket fence around it, which added a villa-like note to the communal—that is, fenced, with a curlicue of barbed wire on top—feel of the place. I wondered what the Africans (there were some passing by below, on the track between the fence and the banana plantation) must have thought of this strange encampment in their midst. It was a little like those dinky almshouse squares you sometimes see from a bus and wish you could live in.

The clinic was basic: nothing but another fenced circle of one-storied buildings on wooden stilts, partly shabby Western brick, partly built of clay, with drooping banana-leaf roofs in the local fashion. I'd hardly have credited it as a medical establishment if it hadn't been for the line of patients (women with squealing babies, old men, the occasional soldier) waiting in the queue that stretched from the main door down to the outside gate we came through.

"Ah," said Merrit, as we walked in, "the hordes are upon us. Well, Nicholas, welcome to my parlor."

I noticed that the patients had plywood boards with numbers painted in white hanging round their necks, or were putting them on; this process an energetic young man in a lab coat was organizing, handing out the splintery tags from a box hung over his shoulder and remonstrating with those who wanted to go before their number came up.

"Morning, Billy," called out Merrit, ignoring the cries of the patients when they saw him and pulling away from a woman who tugged at his sleeve.

"Bwana," he replied, solemnly, nodding his head as we passed.

Merrit waved at a couple of whites—both with dark curly hair and wearing red shorts—getting out of a dusty Peugeot. "Those are our two Cubans, Chiric and Canova. They're alike as peas in a pod."

We walked towards the path that went round the perimeter, past an outhouse where a generator was yammering away, shaking the leafy roof and staining the air with the smell of diesel.

"They're both brilliant surgeons. Canova especially. I must tell you the story of Canova's heart one day. He actually performed a minor cardiac operation—here! Astonishing. I couldn't have done it."

We had stopped underneath a tall steel structure with fans—like the one in the bungalow compound, only bigger.

"This is our borehole," said Merrit, patting one of the struts affectionately. "The water's pumped up into the tank and filtered through silver catalysts on the way down. Cleanest H$_2$O around. Though that's not saying much."

"Why are the buildings on stilts?"

"We had terrible problems trying to find the right site. The land round here is relatively boggy and in the end we had to sink in wooden piles to shore up the foundations . . . Look, there's the hospital Land Rover."

He waved, calling loudly. "Waziri, come and meet our new recruit from Scotland."

The vehicle, its white paint covered with bright red dust, slowed down as it came towards us, turning around the central flowerbed in the little car park. It pulled up close to us. An African with grey sideburns and a safari shirt held his hand down to me out of the open window.

"Hello," said the man, smiling broadly. "So, another Scotsman. I think Scottish doctors must be taking over Uganda. You know of Mackay, presumably, who set up Mulago, the big hospital in Kampala, way back when? I was trained there by Scottish doctors myself, before I went to the US."

"We get about," I said, squinting against the sun above the Land Rover roof.

"Nicholas Garrigan, William Waziri," Merrit announced grandly. "William's mainly in charge of our field trips—we do vaccination and spraying programs all around the villages here—in fact I was thinking it would be good, William, if you took Nicholas out on one soon. Familiarization."

"Certainly. I'm going out again next month." He smiled at me again. "Come along, by all means. See how the wananchi live."

He drove off, the spare wheel case like a badge on the back: Cooper Motors, Kampala.

"What are the wananchi?" I asked Merrit.

"The common people. The citizens. It's like a term of respect."

We continued our tour of the perimeter. "That's the X-ray darkroom. We made a mistake putting it on the eastern side. When the sun is at its highest, it beats on the wall. Makes it like an oven, spoiling the negatives. We haven't got the money for much radiology anyway. You'll find you have to be quite sparing here, equipment-wise. And with drugs."

"How do you get supplies?"

"Billy Ssegu, he's our business manager, the one who was doing the queues. He goes up to Kampala in the Land Rover once a month to beg from the ministry. He does his best but sometimes we can't even get antibiotics or simple analgesics."

We were right at the far edge of the fence now. I noticed that there was a funny smell where the ground dipped unnaturally— in the way a grave does after a year or so, when the earth has settled down.

"But all my other problems pale in comparison to this," said Merrit, pointing at the subsiding ground, which was covered with grass except for an uneven brown crust at the edges. I moved forward, wondering what he was going on about.

He grabbed my arm. "For God's sake, be careful. It's not solid. Well, it is solids." He chuckled. "This is our cesspit, Nicholas. It may not smell like it now but, believe me, it does when the water table's up. The problem's the marshy ground. The stuff doesn't drain away and in the rainy season water comes into the pit from the surrounding area and makes it overflow. Tidal wave of shit. Very unhygienic. On the worst days we have to close the clinic down until an engineer comes from Kampala to siphon it into a tanker. We really need a proper septic tank but I can't see it happening in my lifetime."

"It's funny," I said, "with the grass on top, you wouldn't know it was there."

"You would've done if you'd stepped in. Look." He pushed at the grass with his foot and the whole thing moved, swaying gently on itself as the crust touched and parted from the neighboring turf.

We turned around to go back.

"Oh, yes. There's that, too."

He pointed to a tarpaulin-covered mound some way over the other side of the fence; nearby, the wire was broken by a small gate made of flattened, pale blue Stork margarine tins nailed on to a bit of wood. We went through the gate and down a well-trodden clay path through the scrub.

"Cleanliness next to godliness, litter next to the latrines," Merrit said.

I could see a circle of ash under the edge of the tarpaulin.

"This is the rubbish pile for burnables: everything from old dressings to lousy blankets. There's a rule that everyone on site brings a bag a week—you have to rush at it or the flies get you—and on Guy Fawkes Night we have a bloody great fire."

"Isn't that waiting a bit long?"

He gave me quick look from under his wiry eyebrows as we walked back towards the buildings—as if to say, don't tell me how to run my hospital. But all he said, and mildly, was: "It's too dangerous to have a lot of fires, we have to watch for the bushes going up. Anyway, the locals like it big."

Near to the entrance to one of the buildings, hard by the pathway, was a tentative effort at a little garden. It was mainly full of weeds, in between which a few cabbages and tomatoes were losing the battle with nature.

"We encourage the families of the longer-term patients to grow vegetables," said Merrit, "but they haven't quite got the hang of it. Everyone has to provide their own food, you see."

We came in through the laundry door. Piles of sheets and towels and faded green theater gowns were stacked on either side. We passed through an archway into a long ward full of cast-iron truckle-beds, each with their neatly written reports and fever curves pinned to the end. Auxiliaries moved around the patients, patroling wooden equipment trolleys down the aisles. Merrit clapped his hands.

"Hello everybody," he said loudly. "This is Doctor Garrigan, who'll be joining us."

Then he took me round, meeting the staff. One, in particular, I noticed immediately. Leaning over what looked like a severe smallpox victim (his legs covered in eruptions), she had luxuriant auburn curls tied in a slightly severe bun and was wearing a pair of canvas trousers and an open-neck white shirt with buttoned, military-style breast pockets.

"This is Sara Zach," said Merrit. "She's here with us from the medical faculty of the University of Tel Aviv."

"Hello," said Sara Zach, as she turned round to look at me.

Her skin was a deep coppery color, almost as dark as her hair. I could see a faint glistening of moisture standing out from the pores in it.

"Welcome to our clinic."

Her accent came out strong on the word "clinic" and I toyed with its ups and downs in my head—*klinik, kalinik, klienik?*—as she put her lint and tweezers aside. I noticed how strong her hands looked as she did so, the outlines of the tendons in them clearly visible.

"Is that smallpox?" I said to her, as the man in the bed groaned.

She laughed powerfully, the muscles in her throat moving the collars of her shirt.

"We would have him in isolation if it was. No, it is just a bad case of putse fly. It lays its eggs in your clothes while they are drying on the line and then they burrow into the skin. You have to draw the larvae out with Vaseline—it suffocates them—and then pick them with tweezers when they come out to breathe. There is no way to do it but mechanically."

"Of course," I said, blushing.

"I made similar mistakes myself on arrival," she said, smiling. "Tropical medicine here is very different from in Israel."

A ray of sunlight, shooting suddenly through one of the windows in the ward, alighted on her forehead. The bones in her face were brutal in the way they stood out, almost ugly; or at least, not attractive as usually considered. In fact, her whole way of carrying herself was like this.

"I am afraid I must get back to work now," she said to Merrit curtly.

She reached into the trolley for the tweezers and bent back down over the old man's gleaming, Vaseline-covered leg.

Later, I met the Ugandan auxilaries, who lined up to shake my hand as if at a wedding. Later still, Ivor Seabrook, an old Englishman wearing a broad yellow tie that clung to his white shirt as if it had been thrown there. Above that flopped the desiccated grey hair and smiling, destroyed features of the long-term tropical alcoholic.

"Tsetse fly. Tryp, y'know," he said, pointing a finger down at the sweating, shaking boy he was attending. "Not much of it up here at all, but it's a kind of speciality of mine from Bulawayo days."

"One of the old school," Merrit whispered as we toured the beds. "Bet you a hundred shillings he tells you his soldier-ant story before the end of the week."

We peeped into the mortuary and then through the windows of the isolation ward and the operating theater. In the latter, the glass was steamed up from the sterilizer but I could make out the two Cubans. They looked comical in full surgical fig—green masks over their faces, and bare legs poking from under their gowns as they moved around the table. One of them looked up from under the steel lamp and waved a pair of forceps at us.

Then we went up a long corridor to have a look at the pharmacy, where a big white fridge was burbling away among the racks of labeled bottles. On the floor next to it was a small green plastic bucket with a dozen or so paper spills in it, their ends blackened from where they had been lit and extinguished.

"It works on paraffin," said Merrit, opening the door. "A bit old-fashioned, I admit, but—you can't trust the generator."

I spent the rest of the day acquainting myself further with the clinic and its procedures. Then, before supper, I went out on my own for a walk above the compound. I stepped warily up the grassy tracks, yet was still a little breathless by the time I reached the top of the biggest hill.

I stood there—in that evening air, in that coming primal light of ancient stars—and listened to the crickets and the bullfrogs as they sang in their peculiar counterpoint. Looking over the valley, which seemed as if it might go on for ever, I spied out the land, taking possession in my head of the darkening papyrus swamps, the slopes dotted with banana and coffee, and the brown smudge of the Rwizi River—and I felt wonderful.

I don't know how long I was there—it could have been half an hour, it could have been an hour. I went down on my knees at one point and on the grass in front of me I saw a cricket, struggling about in foamy stuff—like cuckoo spit—its perfect serrated legs moving pathetically to and fro in the close, white bubbles. I wondered whether the muck might be shot out by the bullfrogs, some kind of anesthetic projectile to dull the senses of their prey. I poked around in the undergrowth but couldn't find one, though the croaking, incessant during all my search, seemed ever so near. It was only when I heard a crack of thunder that I realized I ought to be getting back to the Merrits', as night was falling swiftly. My eyes had dimmed along with the light, which I had not noticed going.

It rained heavily on the way down, vast theatrical swaths of the stuff whipping up the banana plantations and pulling at the coffee bushes. The track made a natural watercourse down to the bridge over the Rwizi, and I had to watch my footing as the dust turned to mud. As I passed a village above the clinic, I could hear the sound of children's laughter, and splashing too, as figures cavorted in the lamplight.

I felt refreshed and calm as I got into bed. Even the machine-gun noise of the rain on the tin roof didn't disturb me; in fact, it made me feel oddly impregnable, in a castle-keep sort of a way. The storm got much worse, and from where I lay, as I dozed off, I could see flashes of blue lightning through the mosquito grille in the window, making the whole room flicker. I thought of the old cinema in Fossiemuir, and I dreamed that night of a horrible, Godzilla-like encounter between cricket and bullfrog—the saw-bones legs of the one, the glaucous eye and long tongue of the other. Where I was in it, spectator or actor, I didn't know, I couldn't tell.

8

The days came and went. I put some plants into old paint pots and hung them from the joists in the veranda roof. It was there that I came to write up my case notes in the evenings, and the journal I started keeping. Not every night. You couldn't rely on the electricity. In fact, everything there was uncertain. There was morning mist and oppressive heat, and the time passed in an unholy mixture of languor and franticness. Like bursts and blips against the static of the radio. Or the way the million sound of the massed cricket band seemed to punctuate the fabric of the land itself. Sharp against flat.

Someone died of an amoebic liver abcess one week at the start, and I was soon treating more intestinal parasites than I had ever dreamed existed. And other nasties: feet mangled from gangrenous tick typhus; yaws with their look of a burn or a brand; the florid measles rash on a malnourished child.

Another time, an infected dog bite on a young girl's nose. The pus pulsing beneath like an underground spring. Me holding my breath as I lanced and packed it, with Sara keeping the screaming child down on the plastic couch. Her hand was strong and bronzed, her nails as hard and bright as diamonds. We left the wound open overnight to dry.

Sometimes, with the parasitic cases, elephantiasis had set in, and the swollen legs were particularly horrible. I remember one poor woman who presented. It was as if someone had knelt down in front of her and blown air into her big toe.

"Like a cartoon," I said to Sara as we scrubbed up.

She looked at me sternly over the basin. "Nicholas, you are not clinical enough about things. You ought to learn to be."

We locked up and walked down the hill to the compound. We could see the moon over the papyrus swamps. She asked me about Scotland.

"I never met a Scot before," she said, parting from me slightly to skirt a puddle. "I don't know what they are like."

"I'm a reasonably typical example," I said. "I suppose. But is any nation *like* something nowadays?"

"Of course! So how do you think you are typical?"

"Well, I like football. And rugby. And I like a drink."

"Rugby? What is that?" Her voice, with its strange accent, rose high and curious in the falling darkness.

"You don't know what rugby is? Seriously?"

"No, I don't, what is it?" She gave me a sideways look, the waves of her hair brushing in the opposite direction over her shoulders as she turned her head.

"It's a game. With an egg-shaped ball."

"An egg-shaped ball? Are you joking?"

"No, not at all. It's like football, soccer, only you use your hands."

We'd reached the compound, and were standing facing each other between the flowerbeds. Light flooded down on us from an arc lamp on the water tower, her with her canvas bag, me with a sheaf of papers under my arm.

"So that is what it is to be Scottish?" she said. "To like these games?"

"Obviously not just that. But it's very important."

She smiled. Her eyes seemed enormous in the half-light. "You are a very funny man, Nicholas," she said. "An Israeli man would never define himself in terms of a sport."

I looked down at her feet. "Well . . . good night, then."

"Good night," she said—and then, mockingly—"and you must tell me more about your rugby sometime."

I watched her walk over towards her bungalow, her canvas bag on her shoulder.

As I lay in bed that night, after finishing my journal entry, I realized I was a bit cross about her saying I wasn't clinical enough.

It was difficult constantly to take that approach, the diseases being so disgusting. The worms were the worst. I nearly threw up the first time Merrit flipped a patient over and all this, this stuff, like pale brown vegetation, dried ferns or something, spilled out of him and started moving around on the sheet.

TB and gastroenteritis were other common complaints—and then there were the special tropical fevers that Ivor liked to get his hands on, like blackwater and dengue. The latter puffs up the face with bruiselike hemorrhages. I would have sworn, if I hadn't known better, that it was from being beaten up.

And yellow fever. I remember Ivor coming over excitedly with a dish full of dark, heavy liquid. "Look," he said, thrusting it in front of me, "coffee-ground vomit. Sure sign."

Ulcers and suppurating panga (machete) gashes were quite frequent too; one of the problems was that after we'd dressed them they put native medicines—cobwebs, ground bark—on later, and infection would set in again. There were some we could simply do nothing for, like the young man who came in with a flail arm, long and thin as a willow branch, expecting us somehow to unravel the mature development of infantile polio.

Most of my time was spent doing simple things like percussing patients' chests, listening for tubercular spots on their lungs, or administering injections. Hour after hour, I found myself wearily changing needles, routine as a factory worker, the orderly rubbing with alcohol the buttock of the next one in line.

Or analyzing stools (each one brought in neatly wrapped in a lush banana leaf) in the evenings in the laboratory, gagging at the smell and swearing as the light of the lamp dipped up and down with the unreliable current. Naturally, we looked at blood too: samples usually went bad on the journey to Kampala so we had to do the best we could with old-fashioned brass microscopes.

I was fascinated by all that side of it, the shapes as much as what they meant: the smear on the slide of *Trypanosoma brucei*—"Tryp the light fantastic," Ivor trilled every time it was mentioned, fluttering his fingers—like a raindrop on inky paper; the squashed mulberry look of gonorrheal cells in urethral discharge. Diplococci.

The snakebite cases were a fright. The patients sat there with their swollen feet and calves—usually the bites were from when they'd been tending the matooke plantations—and, in a clay pot or old maize-oil can on their knees, the snake itself. We'd check it against the description in the Fitzsimons snakebite pamphlet and select the right antivenom.

One time a snakebite case came in, the snake wasn't dead. It escaped from its pot. Everyone ran out of outpatients screaming. But Waziri knocked it senseless with the tire iron from the Land Rover. He brought it out hooked over the curl of the iron and tossed the black-and-yellow thing at me for a joke. It landed at my feet.

"That's not very funny," I said. "It might not have been dead."

"Don't worry," he said, grinning broadly, "I knew it was."

Then we all crowded round, looking at it where it lay in the dust like a withered piece of rubber hose.

There was less midwifery than you'd expect; most of them gave birth in the villages, having worked in the fields up until the last minute. This resulted in a considerable number of cases of vaginal fistula, where the fetus had rubbed a hole in the tissues. Even the Cubans threw up their hands then, and we had to send those cases up to Kampala. The journey did for a lot of them, making the hole bigger.

"A snowball's chance in hell," Merrit said as we watched one of the worst ones—she could only have been fourteen—set off down the track.

On my way out of the compound one morning, I bumped into Sara. Oh, all right, I engineered the bumping—why is it I seem to fall in love with women the moment I clap eyes on them? It is an inadequacy (another!), not a gift.

Climbing the hill together, we stopped for a moment to look at the army barracks on the edge of town. Squatting in the parade ground, in the shadow of the redbrick building, one little group of men looked as if they were checking their guns or something (we could just make out blankets spread on the ground, with dark bits on them). Another group was loading kit into a phalanx of jeeps. We could hear their voices, rising up faintly like shreds of ash from a bonfire.

"There'll be a big troop movement this afternoon," Sara said firmly. "Come on. We'll be late for work."

During the week that followed, an increasing number of patients with bullet wounds and blade lacerations presented at the clinic. Mostly farmers, but some soldiers too.

"They're getting restless," Ivor said gleefully one evening, slinging an empty blood bag into the over-full bin.

Wrinkled, sucked out like a dried tomato, the bag landed on top of a scrump of white paper: obsolete fever curves torn off the clipboards, and old drug requisition forms. As Ivor went off to lock up, I stared at it like a dumb animal—lethargic, disengaged—and wondered what I was doing there. All the staff had gone home except for us and the night sister.

I heard Ivor's rich, Christmas-pudding voice behind me. "We're running out of blood again, you know. You'd think there were vampires here. Come and see this old girl."

I walked down the dim ward, eyes following me from the stark metal beds, and joined him where he was leaning over the latest case of wounds. The woman groaned as he pulled back the sheet to point out the passage of the bullet: through her breast, from the side, and then down into her hand, shattering a knuckle.

"The breast is fine but the hand is done for. She says the soldiers accused her of feeding the Obote guerrillas from over the border."

We said good-night to the sister and went out into the car park. Bats were swooping around under the trees. It was so quiet you could hear their wings.

On the way down the hill, Ivor placed his hand softly in the small of my back. I edged away and carried on talking, pretending it hadn't happened, and then it was just as if nothing had. I liked old Ivor, he brightened the place up, but I didn't much fancy being one of his laddies.

"He's got *another* new cook boy," as Mrs. Merrit said from time to time in shock-horror tones. "It can't be right. Somebody'll complain to the police one day and then we'll have trouble on our hands."

. . .

I became quite friendly with Waziri. We went out on our first vaccination safari together after a month or two. East Ankole: Ruhama, Rwampara, Isingiro, Kashari, Nyabusozi, Mitoma, Kiruhura. On rough roads, with the Ruwenzoris stretched high above us, it was quite a trip—we even crossed a river—and the Land Rover bumped about so much that I had to hold onto my seat. Waziri's sunglass case skittered about on the dashboard as we negotiated rocks and potholes, tree stumps and the odd stray goat.

"The steering needs correcting," he said, when we stopped for petrol: from a jerrycan on the roof. I walked to the edge of the road for a pee while he filled up.

The sound of me going, together with the glug-glug of the petrol behind, made it feel like we were by a brook. As my bladder relaxed, I stared out into the various landscape: dust, marsh, mountain, forest, farmland—smooth green carpets of tea, cotton bushes, grazing for cows—and a clutch of different diseases for each locale.

On my way back to the Land Rover, one of the largest butterflies I had ever seen alighted on my shirt. It was easily as big as my hand. I watched its blue and red wings slowly opening and closing on my chest. It was very beautiful indeed, but seen close up, with its antennae searching the air just below my breast pocket, it was also slightly threatening.

"Ekwihuguhugu," said Waziri, softly.

"What?" I whispered. It sounded like "Chattanooga Choo-Choo."

"The butterfly. In Kinyankole-Luchiga, the mountain dialect, we call them Ekwihuguhugu. It means: this one is very fragile. They are the biggest butterflies in the world."

I looked down at the insect and said the word. It flew off then, as if I had uttered an occult command, flapping over the eroded red earth at the side of the road and disappearing into the bush.

"It was probably attracted by the smell of your urine," Waziri said, as we got into the Land Rover. "Or the petrol. We don't usually see them this far down off the mountains."

We drove from village to village, spraying the huts with their wobbly roofs: you had to spray the cone at the top especially or else the insects could still breed up there, thus becoming immune. Mosquitoes and mbwa—the small black fly *Simulium damnosum*—were what we were after. The dog fly, it used to be called. Its bite produces a worm which swells up the blood vessels, causing ulcers and, in the worst cases, blindness. The larvae live in river weed.

And then we inoculated: TB, polio, cholera, smallpox, the empty vials chinking as I threw each one into an old biscuit tin.

Though I knew that they were not, to my stranger's eye each village seemed the same. The chickens would scatter as we drove in and the women look up from their mats of drying millet, or the matooke they were steaming on charcoal grates. Everyone would gather round. A hubbub. We'd set up our white trestle table and lay out the syringes. They'd all queue up—excited, mistrustful or just plain scared. I'd rub the arms. Sometimes people would wince more from the coldness of the alcohol on the cotton wool than they would from the needle.

Afterwards, Waziri would read the riot act in Kinyankole, the smoke from the matooke grates swirling behind him. This was how it went:

1. All persons to vary their matooke with other fruits and vegetables and to have meat when possible.
2. All persons to wash at least once per diem.
3. Each sick person to have a well-ventilated hut.
4. All dead persons to be buried not thrown in the swamps.

On the penultimate day of the tour, night fell before we could get to Butogota, a village in the Bwindi district. It started to rain, bringing the smell of tropical vegetation into the cab. On the way we passed a track on the right and a wooden sign with "Bwindi Impenetrable Forest" written on it, flashing up wet in the headlights. I couldn't believe it, but it was for real.

"Your explorers called it that, not us," Waziri said. "Bwindi just means dark. Bwindi dark, omushana light. The pygmies live inside, what's left of them. It's not a nice place. You must never go there, Nicholas. It is full of army as well now, anyway."

So was everywhere. The following night, as we got back to Mbarara, we nearly ran into a roadblock that had just a single hurricane lamp as illumination. And I do mean nearly ran into it: stopping just short of the spiky mat laid out to burst the tires.

"Simama hapa!" a voice shouted. A figure emerged, rising up from the bushes on the side of the road as if from the wings of a theater.

"What's that mean?" I whispered to Waziri.

"Stop there."

As he replied, the tip of a rifle appeared on the windowsill. I could smell beer on the soldier's breath when he leaned in, his camouflage hat pulled down tight. He said something. Waziri replied, quite short with him, I thought, and then there was silence for a few seconds, with the soldier just leaning there over his gun and looking at us. Eventually Waziri flung a 200-shilling note at him and we drove off, skirting the mat.

"Goatfuckers," Waziri said, shaking his head.

To calm our nerves, we went for a drink in the Changalulu, one of the bars in town. We got quite drunk, or I did at least. I was upbeat, in spite of the roadblock incident.

"I really feel like things are coming good for me here," I confided to him. "It's like I'm in the real Africa."

He laughed. "You muzungu are always saying things like that, as if there's some kind of secret to be discovered. We had one man here looking for the site of King Solomon's Mines. The idiot thought it was up in the Ruwenzoris. I told him he'd find it in a maize patch if he looked hard enough."

"The alien corn," I said. "You know the Bible story."

"Of course. I went to the mission school. We all did. Well, those who went to school."

He drained his glass and stood up, his tall ascetic frame a shadow against the wall. "Want another?"

I looked round the bar as he went to get them. A woman in a red bandanna was wiping tables. It was getting late and there was just one other customer, a soldier, quite high-ranking, I could see from his peaked cap and brass pips. He was staring moodily into his glass. I noticed that he had fierce-looking ritual scars on each cheek.

"So, you want to see the real Africa, my friend?" Waziri plonked the beer down in front of me. There was a slight mocking tone in his voice. "You should go down to the hotel some time. Every third Tuesday they do the devil dance or the witch sniffing or whatever you want to call it there. For the tourists."

He scratched his head. "Though God knows, there's not many of those nowadays. It's fun, though. The usual thing: the dancers moving their knees up and dropping shells and powders in the dirt."

"Do they really believe it all?"

"Who, the tourists or the dancers?" He raised his eyebrow.

The officer got up to leave, giving us a hard look as he passed.

"That's Major Mabuse," Waziri said, turning to watch him go. "He was just a taxi driver before the coup. A nasty piece of work."

"They all seem to be."

"Not all," he said, after a pause. "Well," he continued. "Amin is the nastiest, I'll grant you that. You know he's coming here next month? There's going to be a reception at the football stadium."

"Will you go?"

"Of course not. I wouldn't be associated with that monster in any way whatsoever."

We sat in silence for another moment and then I asked him more about the dancing. "Is it just like a custom or something to believe in properly?"

He nodded, or half-nodded. "Properly."

"Really? In this day and age, even here?"

"Here is my country, Nicholas. Well, they do in a way and not in others. When it suits, like any belief. Sometimes it's useful, though: for explaining the inexplicable. And the frightening aspect of it is like a form of psychotherapy. Shock treatment. In that way, it's the show of the thing that's interesting. It all depends, I've come to this conclusion, on the rustling of the dried leaf skirts. It's like a form of vagueness that lets you imagine things, only you hear it. And obviously the masks as well. They have a big lion one that is very wonderful."

"And tom-toms?"

"Naturally. And beans in gourds and a big blue cockerel whose blood you throw down in the dust, whatever you want. They whip the bad spirits out of the place and the tourists all stand there clicking it with the cameras and then the man in the lion mask comes round for the collection. You know it is Nestor, the night watchman from our place?"

"No! I wouldn't have thought he has the energy to leap around."

"He does when he gets the fever in him and there's some young girl bouncing about. Then his legs spring like a young goat. But he helps people, too. They go to him and he rubs the stuff— the magic substance, the muti—on their bodies. And sometimes it works, too. Not often, but now and then."

9

The boy I had talked to when I first arrived, the one with the T-shirt and the wire toy car, was waiting for me outside the clinic one evening. He handed me a folded note: "Dear Doctor Garrigan, this is my brother Gugu. I believe you have met him. I am writing to ask if you can come for lunch on Sunday. Yours sincerely, Bonney Malumba."

So at the weekend off I went to the Malumbas'. Boniface, smart in a pair of bell-bottom trousers, greeted me in the hall.

"My long-lost friend Doctor Nicholas."

Gugu scampered about between us. Mrs. Malumba, a portly matron in a long gown with tufted sleeves, offered to wash my feet, but I declined, of course. It was quite a swish house, by local standards. They even had a television, a small black-and-white one with a V-shaped aerial on top.

The father was stout and distinguished-looking. He retired relatively wealthy, Boniface told me later, having been Chief Headman for the Directorate of Overseas Surveys. Also wearing a long gown, he was sitting on a straw stool when I came in, with a glass of beer in his hand. Boniface introduced us with great formality and I sat down on another stool to talk to his father. We started with politics and I soon learned that he was no fan of Amin.

"That fellow is no better than Obote, let me tell you. It is because of Obote that we had to move away and I believe many will be moving on account of Amin also."

I learned that the family was Baganda, from near Kampala, and had emigrated down here to Ankole country when Mr. Malumba retired. I asked him about the different Ganda words, which had been puzzling me.

This was how it went:

Mu-ganda (a single Ganda person)
Ba-ganda ('the people')
Lu-ganda (the Ganda tongue)
Bu-ganda (the land of Ganda).

Before long, he was telling me the story of his life with the Directorate, from its early days as part of the Colonial Office to after Independence, when he had helped run the East African triangulation project for ODA, the same people from whom I was seconded.

"What exactly is triangulation?" I asked.

He leaned forward on his stool, making gestures with his hands over the straw mats on the floor. "It is dividing an area into triangles for mapping. Distance and height, so you can put hills on a map that is flat. We had to make chains of triangles which would be connected to chains in other countries. The chain had come up from Tanzania and Zambia through to the border of Burundi. Just over there. In my time, we extended it through Uganda and Sudan to connect with Egypt. This was done a long time ago. It was called the Thirtieth Arc."

"That's a lot of ground to cover." I thought of the map in my guidebook and tried to imagine the vast distances he was describing.

"We went from one mountain to another, making stations. I was a helioboy to begin with. I held the mirror and the surveyor caught my light in his theodolite, many miles away. Sometimes as far as sixty miles. Other times it would be dark and we would send lighting parties. Then the surveyor would send the closing-down signal with his light and we would move to the next hill. And the next, and the next, and the next. Until we met with the other party. The other triangle. That was how we made the chain."

"Hard work," I said. Mrs. Malumba smiled at me over his shoulder. Then she went into the kitchen, leaving me with Bonney and Gugu, who were listening to their father as closely as I was. Though I suspected this story was one he had told many times before.

"Yes," he continued, "and much walking. And much heavy equipment to carry. We went in Land Rovers and lorries and camped each night. And other things, too, were hard. I began in Karamoja. Up north. It was difficult there. Very rough place. The Karamojans kept taking the wire the beacons were tied with. So we tied them with bark cloth, but they took that too. And also herds of buffalo and elephant would knock them over."

"It must have been exciting to see them, though. The animals."

"I suppose so. The soldiers have killed them all now. For food, and I believe sometimes for pleasure also. It was different in those days. Now and then we went up in planes. With the RAF. I had to carry the heavy camera which took pictures of the shape of the ground. The Fairchild K17. Fifty thousand square miles we covered. Very far. Below we could see the white wooden crosses we had put on the ground."

"What were they for?"

"To mark the points. We paid the wananchi to repaint them once a month or they would become faded by the time we took the shots. And you know, in some parts they are still painting them now, so many years later. I believe they thought we were missionaries. So many of those crosses became holy sites."

"I don't believe it," I said, laughing.

"It is so. But in the work, the films would go to England, and there the cartographers would scale and plot maps from the shots—one-to-fifty-thousand, one-to-twenty-five-thousand—putting the films over. Then the maps came back, when we were already in a different place, and we studied them with joy. For they were very beautiful. Hill shades, roads, rivers, vegetation. All in color: pink, green, blue, yellow. I can show you."

He went to a shelf, selected a couple of maps and spread them out on the floor. One was an old one, the folds nearly developed into tears. On it were notations like "Rudolf Province" and "East African Protectorate." The other map was new.

"We put on the names, we would ask the people and they would tell us the name and why it was used. Like here. Kumam, it is 'went to the dance but did not get there.' Kololo, that is from a chief who went mad. He was put there in isolation. It means 'the only one.' Muhavara is from 'what shows the way' because we put a beacon there. Mbale is from King Omumbale. In the legends he would fly to that place from the Ssese Islands in Lake Victoria and land on a tree there . . ."

"Father you must leave Nicholas now," interrupted Boniface. "He cannot be wanting to know all this."

"Just a few more. It is very important that all people know our history. It has been hiding. So. See this one, Namagasali. When the Uganda Railway came there, the people were amazed at the train. They would go there and say, 'Namusa gali.' That is, 'I am greeting the train.' Semuliki: 'river without fish.' When the white men came, we thought you would steal the fish, so that is the name we told you!"

He traced some blue on the map. "Nakiripiripirit. There is a lake there. When the wind blows, the water moves and so from this the name, which means 'moving shining.' "

"Shimmering," said Bonney loudly.

His father increased his own volume and velocity as if to compensate for the loss of face. "Mubende, there was a palace on a hill there. Very very steep. So when the king's subjects came with heavy packs of gifts for him they would be on their knees. Thus, you see 'kubendabenda,' this bend-down-double climbing. So, you see, even your English language has added to our store."

"What about Mbarara?" I asked, smiling.

"Oh, that is very boring. It is from the name of a green grass round here. Better is Koboko, Amin's town. There is a hill there called kobuko, which the story says was blown by a mystery power from Maya, in Sudan. This strange force pushed it in space to Uganda and where it landed it killed all the people who were there before. For kobuko means in Kakwa the thing which smothers or covers you, stopping your breath. I tell you, Nicholas, all things I am telling you are real. Instance, maya means hill also in a Sudanese tongue . . ."

"OK, OK, but this is more real than your crazy talk," said Mrs. Malumba, bringing in a steaming bowl.

"That smells delicious," I said. "What is it?"

"It is matooke with goat-and-groundnut sauce," she replied.

We sat down and Mrs. Malumba said grace. "God the Father

bless this food which has been given to us by You, through Jesus Christ Our Lord."

Amen, we all said. I watched the others to see how to scoop up the gluey mush with my hand. As we ate, we soon got to talking about tribes again: the bad-penny topic, black and white.

"Why am I called a muzungu?" My mouth was full, and the word came out scrambled, as if I didn't properly know the name for what I was.

"It is the same as before," said Mr. Malumba. "Mu-zungu, except you say Wa-zungu for many people."

"But what does zungu mean?"

"It's just you European people, like the Asians are just the wahindi. Except that there is also kizunguzungu, which means dizzy. Only I don't know which came first, muzungu or kizun-guzungu. Or if they are connected. In any case, muzungu is what we christened you when you turned up. Only the tribes here have more complex names."

"And the big men in the Mercedes-Benz," shrilled Gugu, "at school we call them wa-benzi!"

We all laughed and then Mrs. Malumba said, seriously, "Be careful what you say, boy. It could be bad for you in these times."

Bonney, meanwhile, was looking despondent over his plate. I sensed that he wanted to show me off but also show off to me, and was irritated that others were taking center stage.

Or maybe I was just imagining it. He put his oar in, anyway: "It's not always tribes, though. Sometimes ba just means from, or a small collective unit, like the Abanabugerere means people who live in Bugerere. We don't like to think about tribes now anyhow."

"When someone's attacking you, you need to have a tribe. You need to stick together when the knives are out," said his father sternly.

"You are not modern, Father. These old things, we do not need them now."

"You will see. When I went back to Kampala I saw all those Anyanya and Kakwa thugs Amin has brought down from the north to put into the police and the army. It is not good. Those people are not like us. Even their bodies are different. They are bony and look angry all the time. No wonder they cut so many people. Even they have brought some here, to the barracks."

"They are still people, Father, whatever tribe they belong to."

They broke into Luganda to argue. I sat in silence, trying to deduce something from the ebb and flow of their words. Mrs. Malumba smiled at me as she cleared up the plates, and then took them through. Gugu ran outside, the mesh door swinging behind him on its spring.

Irritated, Boniface changed the subject, I supposed, and the language, asking me if I could get him into a university in Britain. "I want to do postgraduate food science at Reading University," he said, "It is the best place. But I will need a scholarship. Then I can come back here and work for the World Bank."

As I tortuously went into why there was not much I could do, Gugu saved me by coming back in. He was holding—by the tail—a chameleon. Mr. Malumba got up and started shouting. It was apparently bad luck to injure or interfere with them. There was a brittle rustle as the reptile fell from the boy's hand on to a straw mat. Ignoring his father, the kid got down on his knees and started poking at it.

Mr. Malumba shook his head, and went off for his post-lunch nap. "Ah, Doctor Garrigan, never have children. I must go for my sleep now. It is very kind of you to have eaten with us."

"No, no," I said, embarrassed. "It's been a pleasure. It's been fascinating."

When he had gone, Gugu said something to Bonney in Luganda, and flicked at the poor animal again.

Bonney replied in a cutting voice. The boy shrugged.

"What did he say?" I asked Bonney.

"He wanted to know what is going to happen. The colors of the chameleon, people think they are all the spirits of your ancestors passing by. It's crazy—the idea is that you must not disturb them. The bagagga, the magic specialists in the villages, pretend that you can tell your own fate from the changes. Well, they tell it and you pay them."

We looked at the piebald creature on the floor, motionless except for one moment when it lifted a front leg, like a dog holding up its paw to beg. But its lidded eye seemed oblivious to us, and it didn't change color for me, not once, whatever Gugu held next to it. Eventually, Bonney told Gugu to take it back outside.

I stayed quite late into the afternoon. We watched a kung-fu film on the television. It was fuzzy enough already—bad reception—and when the electricity current dipped, everything faded to grey. Walking back, I rehearsed Bruce Lee's intermittent acrobatic maneuvers in my head: lots of leaping about and crunching of bones, all in the cause of some complicated and improbable revenge. Hong Kong Phooey. Yet it was fun and, having seen it, I suddenly missed British television. Or perhaps I was really just missing Britain. Or Scotland, anyway. Home.

10

Another Sunday, the week before Amin's visit. A page or two from my journal, which is in front of me as I scratch away, under these iron skies. My God, do not look so fiercely down upon me! I am too tired to redo it (so tired I nearly wrote, *I am too tired to read it*), but perhaps copying it verbatim will give a richer flavor of the place. It's an argument. Anyway, here it is:

> Church bells, and the sound of the women in the village pounding millet in a pestle and mortar. Thump thump thump. I have felt lonely all weekend and done nothing. There hasn't been much to record, except that I saw a snake in the garden. No one ever said how boring Africa can be: just the slow sweat of time.
>
> The veranda, the valley, me. The Bacwezi valley. Waziri says that the Bacwezi were a tribe who lived here long ago—around 1350, migrants from Ethiopia or Sudan. They lost all their cattle in a plague and were then wiped out themselves in an invasion by the Luo. The latter seem to be gone from here now, leaving the Ankole with some of the Bacwezi traditions: a drum of national unity—now lost, apparently—and a belief in cattle as the center of life. They certainly do have hundreds of cattle, the long-horn type. There is even a concrete statue of one in the middle of the roundabout in town. So strong is the identification, in fact, that at four days old every boy child,

dressed in the soft, suedelike skin of a premature calf, is placed on the back of a cow and given a miniature bow and arrow with which to defend it.

As well as cows, the Bacwezi used to worship fig trees, and there is a sacred grove of them somewhere near here. Waziri says that the local people think it is full of ghosts, and that he'll take me there sometime. Then he tells me that the Bacwezi themselves had actually ousted the Batembuzi, who had ruled since 1100. Isuza was their last king, but he fell in love with a princess from the underworld. He followed her there and couldn't find his way back. And yet it was his grandson, Ndahura—"the uprooter"—who founded the Bacwezi. And now the Ankole claim that dynasty as their heritage; and there are still Bacwezi cultists around today, who scatter coins and cowrie shells in the soil beneath the holy trees.

I couldn't get to grips with it. "So really, it's all the same tribe?" I asked him.

"Oh, no," he said. "You'd be totally wrong if you thought that. And in fact, there are two sections of the Ankole, the Bairu and the Bahima, the one aristocrats, the one slaves . . ."

Or was it the other way round? So much for tribes.

My tin breakfast plate is on the table beside me, a spoon and the empty half-scoop of a pawpaw lying side by side upon it. A canoe and its paddle. I love the fruit here, but I crave a decent joint of meat. I'm still holding out against a cook boy, which means I have to wander round the market in town once a week, haggling for produce. A trip to the butcher involves watching a fellow with a panga hack at a carcass hanging from a tree. Longhorn beef doesn't taste like beef and the pork is too liable to tapeworms—which leaves scrawny arse of chicken or goat so tough it really needs to be chewed by Eskimos for a few months first. That's how they soften their hides. The Nile perch is quite coarse, too, and quite far gone by the time it gets here from Lake Victoria. It's best to curry it, Mrs. M. says, but I don't like curry.

Every now and then they kill a cow in the marketplace,

roping in a soldier with a rifle to do the dirty deed. I saw this last week. He shot it through the neck. The poor dun creature standing there looking into the middle distance with mild interest. When the shot rang out it crumpled to the ground, looking amazingly human (all knees and elbows) as it did so. Like someone who has to sit down because they've been told some really bad news. Then they cut it up, with everyone crowding round, ready with banana leaves in which to wrap their piece.

So. Things go on. There is the view. The sun that shines. Banana plantations creeping up the hill. Their ranks of gleaming leaves going off into the distance. When I look at them, I think of the roofs of the housing schemes in Edinburgh. Here in front of me, there is the odd hut scattered about, but most people live in Mbarara and come out to tend their plots. These irregular squiggles and torn-off corners of produce—millet, cassava, maize, groundnuts—are shored up against erosion by plucky little terraces of red earth. Otherwise, when the big rains come, everything would slip down the hill: down to the marsh at the bottom of the valley, and that ditchy little spot of brown water where the Rwizi River wills itself into being from a confluence of tiny streams.

They're not so tiny, actually, when the rains do come and throw into the gullies all of their thunderous, psychopompic, kitchen-sink performance. Like on my first night. The skies rattle and for anything between a few minutes and whole weeks, the land turns dark as death, barely visible. When it is over, it is as if something that needs to have been said, has been said—but you're not sure if you believe it because the performance has been so over the top. Then the sun shines again and eagles and kites come down off the Ruwenzoris to hover for mice and bushrats.

Recently, a bird of prey dropped something from its beak onto the lawn: I'm not sure if it was an eagle or a kite—or for that matter whether the creature I picked up by its tail was a mouse or a bushrat. I swung it over the fence. Every now and then a troop of vervet monkeys shows up too (I heard some on the roof the other night, which frightened the life out of me) and there is a family of banded mongooses that dash around looking for snakes. They look like ferrets, except plumper, and rather beautifully striped with grey and brown. I hope they get that snake I saw.

Things are getting a bit out of hand on the garden front, but it'll be a few years yet before it returns to the wild. The previous occupant of the bungalow—like Merrit, a Medical Officer from the colonial administration who had decided to "stay on"—was a keen gardener. Steps from the veranda lead down into the overspilling flowerbeds: frangipani, bird of paradise, elephant grass, roses, African marigolds—they grow like weeds here— succulent cacti, too, pagoda flower, prickly pear, poinsettia and shrimp plant.

Mrs. M. has taken me round, showing me what they are, but they're soon enough only words to me. Some of them are not indigenous, she told me proudly. "Old Saunders—he died in his sleep, you know—actually introduced species to the country, sending to Kew for packets of seeds."

So that was how my ordinary life went. And then something happened: Amin came. They put up bunting—banana leaves— round the stadium that day. A Saturday. I went down there with Sara. We couldn't see very much because of the crowds, except for his big helicopter coming down in the middle of the pitch.

There was a tremendous roar when he stepped up to the podium, the bulk of his large body hidden beneath traditional robes. This was the first time I actually saw him, and it was an impressive sight. He had this aura that is difficult to describe, and it had much more to do with the rhythms of his voice than the furs, hides and feathers of his headdress.

"It is astonishing he is so popular," Sara said. She was holding me by the arm, the swell of the crowd was pushing us so much.

"I have come," Amin said into the microphone, "to talk to you about the god. Because it is he who has been helping you people in Mbarara to make yourselves the best citizens of Uganda. Yes, I am very proud of you."

The crowd wailed with happiness.

"But," Amin continued, "better worlds than this are possible. To make them happen, you must believe in the god very strongly. Even if you are Christian, Moslem, or whatever you are. Because his rule is a rule beyond what has happened, beyond all that you can think of. Just because you cannot think of him, or what it would be like to shake his hand, it does not mean that he is not there."

"Quite a philosopher," I said to Sara.

"You think so?" she said, seriously. "Don't be fooled."

"You always take things literally," I teased her.

"Who do you think made this world?" shouted Amin. "Who do you think made me? It must be the god. That is why you must work very hard. If you do not, and the god wishes it, the sun will not rise tomorrow."

"They should try this back home," I said. "It would work wonders with the unemployment figures."

"Don't be silly," Sara said. I noticed that she was writing things down in a notebook.

"So," Amin continued, "you must do your duty in the fields and the factories. You must be with the god for that reason. Now, let me say this. I have been receiving some complaints about the state of affairs in Uganda. Wananchi have been complaining about searches and seizures. Well, let me tell you, anything that is done in my name, it is the right thing. Any bad thing done, it is by those who are disobeying me. I cannot be everywhere at one time, I cannot make myself invisible."

"Why are you writing it down?" I said to Sara.

"Just out of interest," she said, looking up at me quickly. How could I have been so thick-headed, I wonder now, so impervious?

Amin's voice echoed round the stadium. "I have all power in Uganda, it is true, because the people support me. But I am not the highest power. I lift my hand, I let it fall—in government, I do this. But it is your own self you should be guarding. At the same time, as an ordinary Ugandan, I myself know all that you are. I live inside each one of you, knowing your hopes and your dreams."

I stared at him up there on the podium, just as the hundreds of others around me did. Without question, there was something fascinating about him; a quality of naked, visceral attraction that commanded the attention, mustering assent, overcoming resistance—fostering the loss of oneself, or so it felt, in the very modulations of his voice.

"That is why we must work together, and stop corruption," he said. "Constant dipping empties the gourd of honey, and if we want Uganda to continue as a paradise, we must build hives— hives and factories and farms. We must act. For he who desires but does not act breeds pestilence. And we do not want that in Uganda. Do we?"

The crowd roared.

"Otherwise," he continued, "we will be under the power of the white man again. Or his African servants. Two wrongs do not make a right. That is why we must know the causes of civil strife in Uganda and pull them out straight. Like doctors, we must proceed from a knowledge of the causes of illness. Myself, I know that events are going to happen. They have to happen. But I don't know how. I am only a human being, like all of you. That is why I must ask you to be the doctors of Uganda in your everyday lives. It is necessary. We must continue to heal our country from the illness of Obote and imperialism."

Sara looked about us. "We better go," she whispered, "we could be attacked."

"Do you really think so?" I thought she was being a touch overdramatic.

"Come *on*," Sara said, forcefully.

We pushed through the crowd, whose eyes were fixed on Amin, his every word, so it seemed, corresponding to some need in themselves. As we walked up to the compound, with the loudspeaker noise of Amin's speech and the cheers of the crowd fading away, Sara was silent, replying to me in monosyllables when I spoke to her. I myself was excited by it all, but she declined when I asked her in for coffee.

"I have work to do," she said.

"But it's Saturday."

"My own things."

On the Monday morning following Amin's visit, I saw Merrit next to the big pile beyond the clinic boundary. I went over to see what he was up to. He was standing in front of a small but particularly foul-smelling bonfire, with a little bag at his feet.

"What are you doing?" I asked, looking more closely. There were bottles and vials popping in the heat, their shiny metal caps twisting with a slow, agonized turn. "I thought you only burned once a year."

"It's the charity groups. They send us out-of-date medicaments. Absolutely useless. If I don't burn them thoroughly, the patients steal them from the rubbish pit and sell them in the market. See this"—he reached into the bag and pulled out a handful of capsules, half-red half-yellow—"tetracycline: useless if you don't have a proper course. Do more harm than good."

Waziri and I went into town for lunch later in the week. Barbecued chicken at the Riheka Guest House ("All-in-one 24-hr Pub for Comfort and Leisure"), with chips and a salad roughly chopped.

"You shouldn't have gone," he said, when I told him about Amin's speech.

"Why not?"

"You're just giving him credence. If whites turn up, they will all think he is even better than they already think him."

For all that, he still wanted to know what Amin had said. And when I told him the bit about the wananchi being the "doctors of Uganda," he told me an interesting story. His grandfather had told it to him, he said. An anti-doctor religion apparently took hold here in the 1920s. Because the European doctors couldn't cure all the diseases they were presented with, and because the Bible didn't mention modern treatments, a militant Christian cult evolved around the refusal of Western medicine.

"They used to smash the bottles—it's understandable, really. They'd been offered all these things, all these explanations, and yet there were still some other things—plague, the sleeping sickness, leprosy—that weren't being explained. Not then, anyway. You have to remember that this wasn't long after a time when every muzungu was perceived as a musawo, a doctor, whether they were a soldier, a merchant, a civil servant. Whatever. You fellows were all miracle workers in those days, Nicholas."

"So they went back to the Bible?"

"Correct, and often it was only the Old Testament. Some even became Jews. I'm not joking. They trusted the white word but not the white man. They trusted that the Supreme Being, he who dispensed justice and punishment through illness and healing, would take up their case. Katonda omu ainza byonna. God omnipotent, in other words. The strange thing was, this was a European god, really. Before, I mean the African deity, he had just created—and then slipped away quietly. Now he was a kind of consultant, on call."

I laughed.

"I'm serious," he continued. "That sense, of them being protected by one God, it had really come from the muzungu in the first place . . . All those missionaries, thinking it was their chosen mission to educate us. Spreading the light. Omushana, except only in English."

He shook his head. "That's what happened to me, that's why I became a doctor. A true son of the White Fathers."

I said, "I promise not to spread any light."

11

To the Merrits for supper, as I put it, rather Jennifer's Diary-ishly. Ivor and Sara were there, the latter in a dark blue silk shirt. I couldn't keep my eyes off where her hair touched the collar. Auburn and dark blue, honey and blood mixed together: the color of a bruise.

Ivor got drunk during the meal, which was slightly tense at one point. Merrit had launched into some interminable tale about an Oxford friend of his who had made a fortune in the clothing industry, in the course of which he described the friend as being "very Jewish."

He broke off and looked at Sara, who was sawing away at a tough piece of chicken. "Oh, Christ, I'm sorry," he said, clapping his hand to his forehead.

"Why be sorry?" she said, continuing to cut at the chicken. "If he was very Jewish, then he was very Jewish."

There was silence for a moment.

"You really should get yourself a gardener, Nicholas," Mrs. Merrit said, eventually. "It's just not fair on the garden."

"No, but the garden wasn't fair on Adam and Eve," slurred Ivor, his chin sliding into the grubby knot of his yellow tie.

Mrs. Merrit eyed him coldly, and then her husband continued with his story.

"Anyway . . ."

On the way back, after we'd poured Ivor into his bungalow, Sara invited me in for whisky. Her place was even more sparsely furnished than mine: not much more than a desk, a chair and a sofa. And a bed, I supposed, though I didn't get to see that.

She also had a big short-wave radio. Like Merrit's, only it was a send-and-receive, with the aerial whip up on the roof and a black microphone with a coiled wire. The latter looked odd on the wood.

"All doctors get them in Israel," she said, when I asked her about it, "it comes with my grant."

"But who do you talk to? Martians?" I was already quite tipsy.

"Don't be silly."

She got up and walked across the room towards the radio. I watched the light play on her shirt.

"I could even call Tel Aviv if I wanted; the idea is that you can have medical advice on rare diseases. Or whatever."

She turned a knob and a wave of white noise came out. On top of it or behind it, or wherever things happen in radio world, was an eerie electronic neighing, going up and down jaggedly, and a deep squelchy voice choppily declaiming in a foreign language some repetitive sounding set of orders or other permutation of words and numbers. Altogether, it was as if the football results were being read by one of the prophets. In a snowstorm. On a runaway horse.

She turned it off and came to sit at the other end of the sofa. I edged closer as we talked. Centimeter by centimeter. And I would happily have stayed on drinking for longer, and edging closer still, but eventually she threw me out, patting me on the shoulder.

"Nicholas, it is time you went home. You will turn into a drunk like Ivor."

I pecked her on the cheek at the door. About this her eyes were completely neutral, not revealing whether it was a welcome move.

God, I was awkward.

Walking in the bush a few days later I saw—to my great surprise—a leopard on the hill above the clinic. It glanced at me, and then just lay down mellow in the grass, washing its paws like a cat. I was terrified at the time, but quite pleased with myself when I told Sara about it.

"You just have to keep calm when wild animals are around," I said. "You mustn't let them smell your fear."

"You obviously know a lot about it," she replied, coolly.

The following Friday I saw a pair of cranes in the garden. The national bird of Uganda: magnificent yellow crest, black-and-white face and long beak sticking out like a comic surprise. All the better for killing snakes with. Tall, manic creatures, with big personalities, they strutted about on the lawn and came over to tap on the living-room window with their beaks. They thought it was an enemy but it was only their own reflection.

Once a year, Waziri informed me, others will come and together they do a special mating dance in a circle on the lawn. But I never saw it.

In April I went on tour with Waziri again. We stayed in government rest houses, hotels, and once in the room above a bar. West Ankole: Buhweju, Bunyaruguru, Kajara, Shema, Igara. Tuesday to Friday. We traveled along the volcanic ridge, at one point passing a border post for Zaïre, which is Francophone, after a fashion. There was a sign there which made me chuckle: "Bienvenue à Zaïre, prodigieuses visions d'enfer"—and a picture of mountains spewing forth lava and ash.

As well as conducting the vaccination safari, we stopped in Kabale, a hill town on the Uganda side, and visited a banana wine factory there. The sickly "Banapo" vintage was made by a Belgian called Grillat, who wore a crumpled white suit and had a gold tooth. We sampled some from little glass tumblers. Grillat said that bananas were not just the staple here in Uganda.

I see that I made a note about it. (I suppose I am quite an orderly person, though the way my life has gone it doesn't feel that way.) As well as food and wine, bananas were used for:

Roofs
Cattle feed
Clothing (Adam and Eve)

Medicine (poultices)
Dye
Vinegar
Packing material (guns, bodies).

On the Thursday, Waziri left me at the White Horse Hotel (up in the hills) and went off for the afternoon. "My folks are from round here," he said. "I have to go and give them money."

He didn't come back till morning, which annoyed me, as I had waited up to eat with him. I noticed that his clothes (usually spotless) were all dusty when he came in.

"Old flame?" I asked him.

"You could say that," he said, looking irritated.

We drove through one of the most intensive areas of banana cultivation on the way back. Waziri said that he liked to watch the tree go through its calendar. When the time comes to flower, the plant—by this stage five or six feet high—forces a reddish bud from its center, which then curves downwards, slowly opening up to uncover three rows of small flowers.

According to Waziri:

1. The top row becomes bananas
2. The bottom row makes pollen
3. The middle row drops off
4. The tree dies.

"It is a fascinating spectacle," he said. "The cycle takes about eighteen months to complete and I watch it every year. I missed it when I was doing my post-med in America."

When we got back, I went round the other side of the fence at the bottom of the compound, to look for myself. The fruit is green while on the tree, grouped twenty or thirty close, pointing upward in serried ranks, with the red bud hanging below. The latter looks like a placenta and has the same consistency, too. Living tissue.

Only one bunch of bananas comes from each bud. The tree does die, but a new plant springs up each season at the foot of each dead tree. God is great, as the Moslem patients used to say when they recovered. Most of them went to Doctor Ghose in town, though.

In May a young woman—a girl, really, overweight but with an astonishingly pretty face—came in with her mother, complaining of backache.

"I have been hoeing too much," she said to me, groaning.

So I put her on the couch and, not seeing anything immediately obvious, was about to send her in for X ray. Suddenly she sat up and started thrashing around. She went into labor right there and then.

The poor girl appeared to have had no idea. Feeling foolish, I had to deliver myself, as none of the other doctors was available. It was my first since arriving in Uganda, and basically Nyala, the African sister, did it. As I watched the delivery, I remembered the chilling, yet slightly comical words of one of my father's more stringent colleagues, delivered in a broad Fife accent on hearing that the birthrate in Fossiemuir had gone up sharply: "Why do they do this? By being born we already—the most of us, anyway—exist in sin. The best the others can hope for is a little to be pardoned. That drop of forgiveness is sparely poured."

I initially supposed that what had brought the girl to such a dramatic change in her vision of herself was a form of denial. I thought to myself, this "hoeing too much" stuff is obviously a doubling up of her own conscience: she is "guilty" about backache rather than pregnancy. I later realized I was wrong: there was no stigma attached to pregnancy in Uganda. The girl's mother was happy to find out what was wrong.

It struck me that if something as basic as pregnancy could be overlooked, then how much else? No diagnosis is infallible. It took me (medical training encouraging the opposite) a long time to understand this. To understand that there is no comprehensive system of understanding, at least not in the way that the organs of the body are part of a common structure.

I didn't always use to think so. One of my favorite books as a child, alongside the adventure stories, atlases and stamp albums, was a leather-bound, encyclopedic, calendar-anniversary affair of my father's called *Odhams' Book of Knowledge*. Published in the 1920s, it listed the important events that happened on a particular day and noted where you could find information about them elsewhere in the book: everything was connected, each element ratified by another. As a matter of fact, the hospital library was full of similar stuff: *Harmsworth's Household Encyclopedia, Squire's Companion to the British Pharmacopoeia* and so on. They must have been brought by my predecessors, and found their way across the continent, from mission-station to mission-station, hospital to hospital. A light seeking a light. A guide.

Talking of which, I must relate what Waziri told me about the honey badger. The honey badger and the honey guide. The guide is a small bird that hops about, thereby leading the badger to a hive too solid for the guide to break into. The badger breaks it open with his long front claws, eats his fill, and what's left is plenty for the honey guide. I had heard something like this before—what surprised me was how the badger escapes bee stings: apparently, he first claws a small hole in the hive, then turns around, holds on tight, and stuns them with a blast of noxious gas from his behind.

12

My God, how the time passed. I went inside and came back out with a hurricane lamp. The veranda again, my second year in Uganda. Getting too dark, too quick, as I recall. Writing in a failing light, a light you actually notice failing—as there on the equator—is like staying in the bath with the water running out. That is a curious feeling. How it might be if your soul was leaving you. Just displacement, really, your body realizing its own true mass. But odd nonetheless.

A lot of noise at the barracks one night, shooting and then a loud explosion. I could see the flames below. The next morning we heard from Waziri that a detachment from the north had killed all the Langi and Acholi soldiers.

He looked drawn as he told us about it, sitting staring at the table in the office and speaking in a monotone. His green surgical mask hung at his throat.

"Scores of them. I saw the lorries taking the bodies myself, even an arm sticking out from under the tailgate. It was disgusting. They say they have dumped them in the forest and that they had put them all in one room, with dynamite. Stacked up round the walls. They cut the throats of those who survived."

It was in June that the two Americans disappeared. They had apparently come up here in a blue Volkswagen asking questions about the soldiers. I didn't see them but Sara told me she had actually spoken to one of them.

"He said he was a journalist. He wanted to know about the killings."

We were lying next to each other, naked and looking up at the ceiling. It was the first time. More or less the whole weekend in bed. Like a sexual training course for the rest of my life, as I rather foolishly thought back then. Her hair spread on the pillow and the flame tree in bloom in the garden outside.

I wanted her to stop talking about those other, darker things. I could only think of us. "Tough but tender Sara from Israel," I said, turning over onto my side and stroking her stomach.

She smiled, in spite of herself. "Don't be a—what is it you say in English?—don't be a . . . twit!"

I moved up my hand and tried to tickle her but she held my wrist hard, and then climbed on top of me, pushing my hands into the pillow.

"You're my prisoner," she whispered in my ear. "You must do as you are told."

"The Americans argued with Major Mabuse," Waziri said at the clinic on the Monday. "The rumor is that they were bayoneted and buried just off the road."

The very next day I saw Major Mabuse in town. He was driving a blue Volkswagen, his peaked cap on the dashboard and the scarification on his cheeks so noticeable, in broad daylight, as to make me touch my own to check their smoothness.

"That's a bit daft," Ivor remarked, when I told everyone in the clinic canteen. "You'd think he'd be a bit more secretive than that."

June was also the month I saw the corpse in the Rwizi, below the Ngaromwenda bridge. It was blown up with putrefaction, like a sheep's carcass I'd seen once back home, and the head was wedged between two rocks. The balloon of the man's torso rose and fell with the current, a ghoulish instrument of measurement.

And that month, too, the flimsy blue airmail letter came from my sister, Moira. It was about Father's death. And then the one about Mum. The two events brought closer by bad post. Consequences, consequences: the whole thing is that. Me wondering whether I should go back each time, and then feeling guilty about not doing so. Now I cannot understand how I was so callous. But perhaps even then, as early as that, something in me had begun to close down.

As if to top it all, we had a small fire at the clinic. A bottle of ethanol was knocked over in the dispensary without anyone noticing. It trickled down the corridor to the paraffin fridge. No one was killed, luckily, but part of one wing was destroyed, including the library. Merrit raged—and obviously I couldn't tell him I thought it might have been my fault. I wasn't sure, though. I just remember, the day it happened, hearing a clink as I shut the dispensary door. Having put the fire out (which involved all of us running with buckets of water—and any container we could lay our hands on), the smell of burned building hung around, even after we had got the builders in to demolish the damaged parts.

Against the grain of all this, things were going very well with Sara. Borrowing the clinic Land Rover one Sunday, we went for a picnic by one of the lakes up in the mountains near Kabale. I spread out the rug on the meadow grass like a magician. I never saw a lovelier or more romantic spot: the hills a deep green, covered with cacti, ferns and giant lobelia, and farther below the terraces where the coffee bushes were in blossom. Higher up, the Ruwenzoris proper were doing their volcanic thing, compressing and twisting their moss-covered rocks and misty, tree-covered plateaus. I remembered the words in *Uganda for Travellers*: "confusing for petrographers"—students of stones, describers of rocks. Not photographers, as I'd misread it at first.

Sara's head was on my chest, her chin digging into it. I could see our shoes, which we had taken off, piled on each other by the edge of the rug, then the platinum brooch of the lake, pinned on the mountainside. Far below us—where the ground fell away into the valley—an eagle was circling, looking for monkeys on which to feed. All around us were the sounds of pigeons calling, or whirring down forest slopes, and those of a hundred other birds I could not begin to name.

"They say it moves one millimeter a year," I said, into her hair.

"What?" Her voice was muffled too, I could feel the vibrations of it against me.

"The mountains . . . the range."

"I thought you meant this."

She moved down, pulling up my shirt, and into my head there

came images of ridges and fissures, the Mountains of the Moon bending and stretching, heating up to impossible fahrenheits as, deep beneath us, they piled fold upon fold, layer upon layer, sediment upon sediment—all leading, a million years hence, to what end? For a moment, less than a moment, a malachite sunbird hovered near to where we were lying. And then its plumage exploded like a thunderflash between my eyes, and it was gone.

Afterwards we got up and walked around, going over to inspect the meadow's edge. Some rock hyraxes were chattering on a shaggy outcrop. They dashed into a crevice as we approached. Below the rock was a large yellow flower.

"Look," said Sara. "It is somebody's house."

I peered inside. The cup of the flower was full of rainwater. Floating in the liquid was a very small, very green frog, motionless except for where its eyes rolled back and forth.

"At least he doesn't need a bathroom," I said.

As we walked back to the rug, hand in hand, I was as full of joy and love as I have ever been. The damp grass moved between my toes and from a moss-covered branch a hornbill gave a loud squawk out of its curved double beak.

We had just sat back down when there was another strange noise. There, in the foothills of the Ruwenzoris, we heard, of all the sounds in the world, bagpipes. As if from nowhere a detachment of soldiers in full Scottish paraphernalia—kilts, sporrans, white-and-red-checkered gaiters, drums and pipes—appeared over a hill, marching along the dirt track just as if it were the most natural thing in the world, the sound of their wonderful lungs of leather skirling out over the bush. They must have been a border patrol. But what a border patrol. Around their tunics of khaki drill were navy blue cummerbunds, and on each head sat a tall red fez with a black tassel.

The strangest thing of all was that they ignored us totally, as if we ourselves were part of the whole bizarre parade. Not observers but participants. We sat there, stunned, as they tramped off, and we might well have thought they were nothing but ghosts coming down out of the mist on the Ruwenzoris. Except that the music kept on for miles later. Dumbstruck, we watched them march down the track to town, their outlandish figures getting smaller and smaller.

13

Things went along smoothly in the second half of the year, although I was dogged by an ear infection. Well, I thought it was an infection and had been dosing myself with antibiotics accordingly. But in fact it was nothing but a blockage. I was all plugged up. Sara scoped and syringed me and afterwards it was wonderful, my ears as fresh and glowing as petunias in a window box after rain.

"It's like someone's turned the volume up," I told her.

She emptied the fluid into the sink. "You've got the longest ear canals I've ever seen," she said. "Like seashells turned inside out."

We made love tenderly that night. In the morning when I awoke, with my bright new ears I heard her talking urgent Hebrew into the radio. I read the *Uganda Argus* as I waited, and then a fortnight-old *Observer*. Amin was in Rome, visiting Pope Paul. Back in the UK, a Labor MP was warning of "another Ulster" in Yorkshire following the death of a picketing miner. There was a committee of enquiry into the coal dispute, and another into Bloody Sunday. Better to be here, I thought.

"Who were you talking to?" I asked, when Sara had finished.

"Just Tel Aviv. I want a pay-raise."

"Get one for me too, will you?"

She moved her head to one side, looking troubled.

"What's the matter?"

"Nothing," she said.

That morning I had to give a class for the two interns we'd taken from Mulago Medical School. To get things going, I read out to them sections from Bailey and Love's *Short Practice* on the happy topic of the day:

> Syphilis derives its name from a poem by a Physician, Girolamo Frascatoro, published in Venice in 1530. The poem tells of the shepherd, Syphilus, who was struck down by the disease as a punishment for insulting Apollo. On his return from Haiti in 1493, Christopher Columbus brought back syphilis, parrots and rare plants. The King and Queen received him with the highest honors . . .
>
> When a patient presents a fissured tongue, it used to be assumed that he or she is suffering from hereditary or acquired syphilis. Fissures, even deep fissures, are usually due to congenital furrowing. John Thomson, after a study of a large number of cases, showed that the furrowing of the tongue was not present at birth, but was acquired in early childhood . . .

And so it went on, until we did the rounds and I showed them the disease in the flesh. I think they were quite shocked.

In the evening I got home to hear on the World Service that they had declared a State of Emergency in Britain.

"It is not quite the same as with us," Sara said, spikily, when I told her. "Israel is a permanent state of emergency."

In September, I went on tour on my own for the first time. Waziri was on holiday. It was OK, at least until I got back. I came home that evening, tired and dusty, to find a child standing in my doorway—stiff, his eyes glazed, Adam's apple stark and pulsing.

It was Gugu, messenger and chameleon trainer.

"What's up?" I said, patting him on the head.

He didn't reply, just raised his hand and pointed down at the town. I could see a plume of black smoke, and suddenly realized that something terrible had happened.

"What's the matter?"

Again he said nothing, just stared at me. So I let him into the bungalow, turned on the World Service and sat him down in front of it with a bottle of Coke. I then went over to the Merrits' to see if they knew what was going on. No one there. Sara, too, was out.

Leaving Gugu, still silent, in front of the radio as it chuntered away, I ran down into town to the Malumbas'. When I arrived, there were lots of people milling around and shouting.

I couldn't make out the words at first, and then I realized it was "Amin daima!"

Amin for ever.

I was confused. A whole section of the street was burning and some twenty or thirty bodies lay outside the houses, surrounded by a large crowd. I spotted Sara, Ivor and the Merrits, a little circle among the black faces, like fans in the wrong place at a football match.

"Amin daima! Amin daima!" the crowd were shouting again, punching their fists in the air.

The other three standing over him, Ivor was winding a bandage round the head of a young woman with a wounded temple. Her eyes were rolling and she was making a kind of mewing sound.

"Nicholas! There you are," cried Sara, reaching over through the crush and gripping my arm. "We thought you might have been caught in it."

"In what?"

"You mean you haven't heard?" said Merrit. "The Obote guerrillas came over today. They drove in with lorries. About a thousand. They attacked the barracks with a mortar but it landed here. We've been at it all day."

"Field hospital," Ivor said. "It reminds me of the war. Anyway, it's no go for her." He nodded at the young woman who was being helped up by two men from the crowd. "We'll have to take her in. I think the lung is punctured."

"Nicholas," said Sara gently, "you should know. Your friend is dead."

I said, "What friend?"

She led me over to where the bodies were laid out on the street, their limbs sticking out. Crazy paving, I thought, wildly.

The face was a mask of blood.

"Amin daima!"

I hardly recognized him. His parents were laid out next to him. There was a rip in Mr. Malumba's torso where the coils of his intestines showed blue-grey, falling to one side outside his torn gown.

The map, Mr. Malumba's map—it flashed into my head and then great holes started to appear in it, like plastic melting. I started to be sick on the ground. Sara held my shoulders tight. A crowd started to gather round, the sight of a muzungu throwing up apparently as much of a spectacle as a row of bodies. A little way away from me, four men lifted a corpse into a truck, holding it by the arms and legs. Limbs seeking limbs.

Bonney.

As I retched, I dimly heard the voices of two women wrapped in bright, colorful cloth, one with a baby strapped to her back, the other with a bundle of wood under her arm.

They spoke slowly and carefully, as if taking part in a ritual.

"Is the lake calm?"

"No, the lake is not calm."

"Is this how we live in Uganda today?"

"It is not us, it is because a great calamity has fallen on the town."

"Is God driving?"

"No, God is not driving."

Gugu remained with us for a short while afterwards. By then, Sara was spending many of her nights at my place. We didn't know what to do with the child. He never spoke again. We tried all the recognized methods, but it was no good: that kind of trauma needed the sort of treatment the clinic simply wasn't able to provide. However, I felt a duty of care (did I really, I wonder now?) and in the end the boy stayed for nearly a month. In some ways, it was a happy time—Sara frying up some delicious Israeli dish with peppers on the stove and us coaxing Gugu into a game of tag round the living room before tucking him up in bed.

But he never spoke, not once, and one day Nestor came with some other men and said he had to come away to his relatives. There was almost a feeling that we had done wrong by keeping him with us. Sara and I stood at the door, watching them go, the old watchman in his khaki coat resting his hand on the boy's shoulder.

"There's nothing more we can do," she said. Then she turned and looked at me, her brown eyes full of pain. "You should leave Uganda soon, Nicholas. Things will go badly here."

"What do you mean?" I said, following her back into the house. "How do you know?"

Her feet were loud on the wooden floor of the living room. She stopped in the middle, with her back to me.

"I just do. It's like in Israel. You do know, you know it in your head, when there will be trouble. I remember once, when I was in the army, we were going through an Arab village and it was all quiet and the only thing you could hear was a dog barking in the distance and the noise of the wind. But we were all afraid nonetheless and sure enough there was a sniper that night. It killed my friend."

I went over to put my arm round her, but she shrugged it off. I presumed she was upset over the departure of Gugu.

She began sleeping back in her own bed more often after that, and in general behaving differently towards me. Often, when I said I wanted to see her, she would say she was too busy. Then I'd back off, and we'd be awkward with each other at work—until suddenly one night I'd hear a tap on my door and she'd be there again, sliding on top of me in the heat.

The trick of making love in the tropics, by the way, is to sweat a lot, and keep on sweating, else you stick against each other.

There was another thing. Every so often, the team of Israeli engineers working on the Fort Portal road would come down here for a break, and she would go into town to visit them. I was terribly jealous when she did this, sure that one of her own countrymen would have more appeal than I did.

One night, I went after her into town, more out of curiosity than jealousy. I found her in a bar. A map on the table. The tough-looking engineers were with her, all talking rapidly in Hebrew. She saw me but pretended not to notice, so I had just one beer and left.

Around midnight she came over and tore a strip off me, saying that they were her people and it was her business what she did with them anyway. We still fucked, though, after the shouting, but it was a disaster. She cried a bit when it was over, and said she might have to leave one day. She wouldn't tell me why when I asked.

You can't ignore it when things go badly in bed. You can't put your head in the sand. But thinking about it, still less talking about it, seems to make it worse. The fact is, her dark little breasts started to taste sour to me every time, and the wet slick I'd grown used to reaching down for—it was no longer there. She became irritable and began spending more and more time back at her own bungalow.

I realize now that she, like me, had been using Gugu to live out some kind of fantasy family life—both of us, aware how things were going downhill at the clinic, must have been craving a kind of normality.

And things at the clinic were going downhill. Waziri had just taken off, we discovered. He never came back from that holiday. I never got the chance to see the Bacwezi grove. Merrit was furious—about Waziri and just about everything. We were finding it more and more difficult to keep the place running. Money came through from Kampala less and less frequently.

Meanwhile, strange items of news were reaching us about Amin. The World Service reported, in its usual po-faced way, that he had sent a message to the Queen, with copies to the UN Secretary-General Doctor Kurt Waldheim, Soviet Premier Brezhnev and Mao Tse-Tung: "Unless the Scots achieve their independence peacefully," it read, "they will take up arms and fight the English until they regain their freedom. Many of the Scottish people already consider me last King of the Scots. I am the first man to ask the British government to end their oppression of Scotland. If the Scots want me to be their King, I will."

This kind of thing simply made the place seem more unreal. For me, then and in that place, little reminders of home began to take on enormous importance—like finding a bottle of Bell's or a packet of cornflakes in one of the Asian shops in town. Though that soon became impossible.

There was worse in store for me, and much worse for the Asians. One day in town, I was shocked to see a group of them surrounded by soldiers. They were scratching their faces with broken bottles.

Amin had said in a speech that the idea of the Economic War had come to him in a dream. "Asians came to Uganda to build the railway. The railway is finished. They must leave now."

A sign was erected outside one of the government offices in town: "Bureau for the Redistribution of Asian Property." And during that time, a new song was being played on the radio: "Farewell Asians, farewell Asians, you have milked the cow but you did not feed it."

There was some confusion, initially, about only Asians who weren't Ugandan citizens having to go, but nearly all went, in the end; 50,000 from the whole country, the BBC said, many to Britain. Amin himself called it Operation Mafuta Mingi, which translates as "too much cooking oil"—a valuable commodity that in this case symbolized Asian dominance in East African commerce.

Everything was to be given over: the Sikh mechanics' garages where they'd grind a new set of valves for you; the grocers where you'd get English tinned meat; the fabric shops with their bolts of colored cloth stacked up to the ceiling. Mr. Vassanji, the solicitor. The thin-faced GP in town, Doctor Ghose, whose qualifications Merrit used to say were dubious (but who did quite a good job, so far as I could tell). It was all to be "allocated," as the euphemism had it.

When the deadline came, the Asians piled up their belongings in boxes near the bus park ready to go. But the soldiers took most of it, especially watches and cameras, and the Asians left for the airport penniless, a lot of them. The worst thing was seeing the Sikhs have their turbans knocked off, and their beards cut with bayonets. I stood by, I know that now—there was nothing I could do, I thought. Not all of the Asians made the deadline, which only increased the brutality, and it was some time before all of those in Mbarara had actually left.

It was during this period that Popitlal, Dr. Ghose's assistant, turned up at the clinic. He had cropped his hair and put boot polish on his face. He wanted us to take him in as an orderly, and go along with the pretence that he was an African. And he was, in so far as these things mean anything: his family had been in Africa for nearly a century. We gave him a cup of tea—he was trembling with fear—while we discussed what to do. He was now a stateless person.

"If he stays, we'll get into hot water ourselves," Merrit said.

"We can't just turn him in," I said.

Billy Ssegu was the only one of the Ugandans who wasn't laughing at the boot polish. The Asians weren't too popular, because of the money. They were close enough to be envied by the poor in a way that the muzungu weren't. Or so I thought back then.

"I know," Billy said, "we'll put him into Rwanda. My brother is an immigration official at the border. He'll let him through. We can take him up in the Land Rover."

"Be quick, then," Merrit said crossly. "I don't want soldiers turning up here."

So he took him. I often wonder what happened to Popitlal, what sort of life he made for himself.

As for the others, Major Mabuse simply gave a lot of their businesses to his fellow officers. One restaurant was renamed "The Exodus." With khaki behind the counter, the prices went haywire. A lot of the shops closed, because the import lines of credit from Bombay and elsewhere dried up overnight. Salt, matches, sugar, soap: even the most basic things became hard to get. The army slaughtered a whole herd of milking cows for beef, which meant we had no milk either. And we soon had to abandon our vaccination safaris, being unable to get spare parts for the Land Rover.

Sara wouldn't say much about it all, simply, "It's Amin, what do you expect?" and a shrug. At that stage, we weren't sleeping together at all. You're a failure, I told myself.

And then, one day, she didn't turn up at the clinic. When I went down to her bungalow at lunchtime, the door was unlocked. I went inside. Many of her things were gone. Open cupboards and drawers showed signs of hurried packing. I walked slowly back up the hill, feeling wretched and dismal and wondering what I was going to say to Merrit.

It was the beginning of October, and I remember sitting that night listening to the radio while I fretted about her. At their conference in Blackpool, the Conservatives had just defeated Enoch Powell's motion condemning the government for allowing the expelled Ugandan Asians into the country.

Given the Asian scenario, I should have known, following

Amin's announcement about Zionist imperialists and their "secret army, six-hundred-strong," that Sara would go too. But I wasn't prepared for it. He seemed to me to be mainly attacking a sect of black Ugandan Jews called the Malakites, perhaps the ones Waziri had mentioned, as much as Israel herself. Once I had pieced it all together, I felt foolish, deficient in an almost physical way—it had all been there before my very eyes. *I should have known*, that is the phrase of my life, its summing up, its consummate acknowledgment.

She still could have said goodbye, though. I suppose she was afraid I would try to stop her. Nestor, it transpired, had actually seen her go. "The men from the road gang, bwana. They came to take her in a jeep at sunrise. The people say all the tractors, they went over the mountain to Rwanda. Amin says all Israeli personnel to leave within three days."

So I could only imagine her going. Perhaps it was less painful that way. Standing watching the yellow graders go into the sun. The graders and the jeeps and the wide-mouthed bulldozers.

14

Oddly, once Sara had gone, the problem with my ears came back. It must have been an infection after all, and I began a course of antibiotics again. It was also about this time that the stories about Amin began to fascinate me. And when, with my gummy ears, I heard him calling himself the last rightful King of Scotland again on the radio, I thought, in a wild moment, that it had some special relevance for me. As if I were his subject.

Meeting him in person for the first time, when the soldiers came to call for me at the bungalow, and I had to go and bind his sprained wrist—that was a bizarre experience. The cow he had hit lay bleeding on one side of the road, its gasps loud amid the murmurs of the soldiers and the birdsong of the bush. Nearby, nose-deep in vegetation, was the red Maserati. On the other side, no less impressive a spectacle, sprawled Idi Amin Dada. Even on his back he was physically dominating. I felt as if I were encountering a being out of Greek myth—except, I must confess, for his smell, which was a rancid mixture of beer and sweat.

He held his hand in the air, muttering Swahili curses as I wound the fabric round. Then I began checking him for concussion, fractures, signs of internal bleeding. I was in professional mode, but I couldn't help feeling awed by the sheer size of him and the way, even in those unelevated circumstances, he radiated a barely restrained energy. As my hands moved over his body, undoing the buttons of his camouflage battledress, and touching his chest and abdomen, I felt—far from being the healer—that some kind of elemental force was seeping into me.

Suddenly, he shouted something, his voice loud in my ear. But it wasn't directed at me, being simply an instruction to the soldiers. They began pushing the Maserati back onto the road. The bonnet was deeply dented, but the engine started when one of the soldiers tried it.

I returned to my checks, trying to concentrate. I was gentle with him, worried that his incomprehensible grumbles—occasionally punctured by the English word "stupid"—might explode into anger.

Once I had finished attending to him, however, he was charm itself. And Anglo-fluent once again; it was as if, in treating him, I had given him back the words.

"My dear Doctor Garrigan," he said, grabbing hold of my shoulder with his good hand as he clambered up. "Thank you very much indeed. This calls for a celebration."

He barked in Swahili at one of the soldiers. The man went over to the car. Idi—Amin, I should say—followed him slowly, and I followed Amin. Leaning into the boot, the soldier emerged with a bottle of Napoleon and a stack of steel tumblers. We watched as the man balanced two of the tumblers on the dented bonnet and filled them to the top with brandy. I noticed his hand was trembling as he poured—he was terrified.

"You know," Amin said, taking one of the tumblers and handing it to me, "every president has a bar in his car. Cheers!"

He took a deep gulp. I sipped nervously, reduced to a state of hopeless perplexity. I was drinking with Idi Amin, on a dirt road on a burning hot day, standing next to a pranged sports car, with a dying cow a few feet away. I noticed that one of the beast's horns had snapped off and was lying in the middle of the road, like a projectile fallen from the sky.

I realized that Amin was studying me closely. "This is excellent brandy," I blurted.

"Well, you know what they say in Swahili," he boomed. "Mteuzi haishi tamaa. A connoisseur never comes to the end of desire."

"Oh, don't worry," I said. "I won't drink too much."

The sound of a shot made me jump. I looked round quickly. A soldier was climbing off the cow, a revolver in his hand.

Amin chuckled. "Do not be afraid, he is just putting it out of its misery."

"Poor thing," I said.

"It is only meat . . . they can take it back to the barracks."

He paused, and then assumed a pose of some formality. "Now, I would like to thank you for coming at such short notice. Public opinion maintains that a gentleman is judged by his actions—and on that front you are most definitely a gentleman."

"It was the least I could do," I said.

"I would like you to have something as a token of my gratitude," he said. Reaching into his pocket, he pulled out a bundle of shilling notes and thrust them towards me. "Here."

"I couldn't possibly," I said, taking a step back.

"Ability is wealth, Doctor Garrigan. You should take advantage of your skills."

"I only bound your wrist," I said.

He frowned and turned away, staring into a tall clump of elephant grass by the side of the track. I wondered whether I had said something out of turn.

And then he spoke again. "Maybe you should come and work for me on a more permanent basis. Because, you know, he who tastes honey makes a hive—yes, he who dips his finger into honey does not want to dip it once only."

"I'm sorry, I don't understand," I said. The brandy was making me feel dizzy.

"I'd make it worth your while," he said. "You've obviously got a very good brain. Well, I have, too—but brains are like shoes. Everyone has his own kind. Yours is the one of the medical, mine of the military. It is like . . . a barber does not shave himself. If he does so, he will cut himself."

"That's true enough," I said, "but I'm happy in my job here."

"As you wish," he said. "I will speak to my Minister of Health, in any case. Now I have to go and speak to the chiefs of this area. They are very backward, so I have to tell them everything twice. Some of them even wear wellingtons when presiding at trials."

He straightened suddenly, almost coming to attention. "Well, goodbye, doctor—and my best thanks again."

"Goodbye," I said, going to shake his hand and then realizing it was the bandaged one.

He smiled and got into the vehicle, bending under the low rim of the door. "This car has a good engine. It can survive crashes."

I saw the white of his bandaged hand resting on the steering wheel, and wondered whether he would be able to drive OK.

"I will see you again," he said. "Of this I am sure."

He looked up at me from the car, something unfathomable—half-fascinating, half-frightening—in his eyes as he spoke.

"Doctor Garrigan, when you make your decision, remember this: water flows down into a valley, it does not climb a hill."

"I will," I mumbled, finding it hard to focus because of the brandy and the sunlight reflecting off the shiny red car. My pericranium glowed like a stove-hob.

Amin wound up the window and started the engine. After a couple of throaty revs, the Maserati pulled off and went some way down the track. Then it came to a sudden halt and reversed back towards me with a high-pitched whine.

Down came the glass. "And if water is spilt, it cannot be gathered up."

Without a word of further explanation, he sped off again. Confused and slightly drunk, I stood there as the soldiers heaved the body of the cow into one of their jeeps and prepared to follow him. I watched them go off. Only as the last vehicle was obscured by a baobab did I realize that I had no way of getting back myself. It was quite a long walk home.

15

By the time Wasswa's letter came, inviting me to become the President's personal physician, everything in Mbarara simply reminded me of Sara. It couldn't be borne. So I was happy to leave, although it was quite tricky with Merrit, who made out that I was letting him down.

A few days after I had replied to the letter, Wasswa phoned me up, saying he would send a driver the following week, and on the appointed day a car duly turned up. I said my goodbyes, such as they were, stowed my luggage in the boot, and began the journey into a new part of my life. Going in the opposite direction, we followed the same string of towns I had watched from the matatu: Sanga, where the Kenyan man had snubbed me, Lyantonde, Mbirizi . . .

A strange incident took place on the way, in a spot not far beyond Masaka (I had given the Tropic-o'-Paradise a miss this time). Barclay—the driver whom Wasswa had sent for me—suddenly pulled over, saying there was a tourist attraction that I ought to see. And so there was. Surrounded by bush, we got out and stood under the concrete rings painted with the words UGANDA EQUATOR in big letters.

Leaning there, with my arms up on one of the rings, I turned to look east and west and tried to work it all out—the thing about water going round one way down the plughole on one side of the line, the other way on the other. I looked towards Kampala, and wondered what my life there was going to be like.

"It is possible to get a cold drink here," Barclay said, interrupting my reverie and pointing at a homestead on the left, some way away from the road.

"OK," I said.

"But we must be careful because a madman lives there."

"Oh."

Intrigued, I followed him through a field of millet—thistles and African daisies, yellow and pale orange, poking up among the brown bushels—to the gate. The homestead was half-hidden in an encirclement of trees. Within stood an irregular palisade of thin sharpened logs, and through that I could make out the house, the mud-hut norm except that everything was thicker, with the same sense of fortification suggested by the fencing.

The gate was made out of three or four sheets of corrugated iron fastened onto a wooden trellis. Next to it a bell—very old—hung on a post. Barclay rang it.

"People, people, I see you. Come inside my place," shouted a voice.

We opened the gate and went in. To the left, under the shade of a tree, sat a man with dreadlocks, wearing a suit jacket and shorts. The plaits poked out from under a deer-stalker hat. Next to him was a battered-looking cool-box.

"Welcome, welcome," he said, leaping up. "This is Uganda equator refreshment center. We can please you any way here."

Barclay said something in Swahili and the man reached into the box and brought out two dusty bottles of Coke.

"You will have to give him 100 shillings," Barclay said, turning to me.

"It is very cold," said the Coke man, opening the bottles with his teeth and handing them to us. "But sometimes the machine is breaking."

I swigged the sweet liquid a bit queasily. The man had bad teeth.

"My name," he said, "is Angol-Steve."

Barclay tutted, shaking his head with embarrassment.

"I am the chief in these parts. No person comes from outside to tell me my business."

He tugged at my sleeve.

"No, of course not," I said, "we were just thirsty and—"

"I am the top person," he interrupted, sitting down again and glaring at us. "Even when there is trouble in Kampala they do not touch me."

"He is a crazy fellow, sir," said Barclay. "Do not take any notice."

"I am perfectly sane and very clever also," said Angol-Steve. "For I see things from many angles. That is why I am called Angol-Steve."

I burst out laughing in spite of myself. I'd thought it was some kind of tribal name.

"Ahh, this man, sir," Barclay said. "He is called that for one reason only. Because he is a fool who cannot see straight or talk straight about anything."

"Do not laugh at me. I have crossed to many places between here and Mombasa. Even Paris and Amsterdam I have been inside there."

"You are a fool," said Barclay. "That is why you live here alone."

"I tell you. I have been many places, I am not just manager of this refreshment center. I have been a magnet for many professions of the earth, and I change all things. Even I have been a policeman. You see. Wait here."

He rushed into the house, the vents of his suit jacket flapping behind him.

"I am sorry, bwana, it is the only place to get a soft drink here," Barclay said.

"It's fine," I said, shrugging.

Angol-Steve came out with a dented brass bugle.

"Listen," he said, and blew.

The sound went out over the bush, the two tones of it making me think of the cavalry in Westerns.

"So you see. I did parade call for Uganda Police. It is truth."

"When was that?" I said.

"It was before. I have done it many times a distance ago. So, you are from London?"

"No, I'm from Scotland, in fact."

"Scot-land. I know that place. Come, come with me just nearby here. There is a Scottish man lying near here."

"Eh, Angol, do not bother us with your lies," said the driver.

"It's all right," I said, fascinated.

We followed him out of the gate and through the trees, towards a patch of untilled ground among the millet stalks. A pied crow started up, disturbed by our passage. I watched it rise up and then bank away to the right.

"No, no, that is only bird. Look here," said Angol. He squatted down and pulled away some vegetation. Underneath was a rock with a brass plaque riveted to it.

Astonished, I got down and read the faint letters:

HEREABOUTS
lies Alexander Colquhoun Boothby born 5 December 1842
and left Scotland his native country in 1871
and died 5 July 1893
Altogether he lived highly respected and beloved for his
integrity and his humanity and
died most sincerely regreted
His Death was occasioned by the great fatigue
he endured during the course
of the campaign against the Waganda Mohammedans
in which he bore a distinguished part

"That man, I believe," said Angol-Steve as we walked back towards the car, "was a very great fighter. There again, the acceleration of history is the job of ruthless men."

"What do you know about anything of this," said Barclay. "Were you alive in that time? Are you a ghost? Eh?"

"I was not there but my spirit was there. For all sides are this side to me. It is truth. I have seen dog whips and batons and I have held diamonds in my hand in Johannesburg. And I know also the cure for serpents."

Barclay shook his head despairingly and turned the ignition. Angol-Steve stood waving at us as we moved off—and then suddenly started running after us.

"Wait, wait," he cried, "you must pay me for soft drinks."

We slowed down. Barclay turned to me. I fumbled in my back pocket and handed him the crumpled note. Taking it through the open window, Angol-Steve said something in Swahili.

"What did he say?" I asked as we drove off, the road stretching out straight as a die in front of us.

"It is nonsense. Everything he says is nonsense."

"No, but tell me."

"He said this: look behind you, the child might get burned."

"What does it mean?"

"Bwana, I do not know. Even in our country, we have some crazy people."

Bewildered in Uganda, and not for the last time, I looked into the rear-view mirror and watched the rolling ground recede. Still waving, the figure of Angol-Steve diminished into a speck, and then nothing.

Part Two

16

I have been able to find out little of the history by which Idi is come to us. After all, who knows where any of us is come from, who could go to the cause? Our current Prime Minister, indeed, might be distantly descended from the conjunction of a stone breaker and a lady's maid caught short on the highway. But this is the story of H.E., as I have had it recounted to me—by himself and by others. He wasn't always to be trusted.

I wouldn't be surprised if they say, in the region of the Kakwa tribe on the scrag-treed borders of Sudan, where Idi was born, that he was eleven months in the womb. Or some such monstrous thing. It is, so far as one can ascertain, New Year's Day, 1928 (though it could be as early as 1925), that he comes into the world, in a village not far from the dusty little village of Koboko. Who knows what curses beat down on the straw roof of the hut that night, what blessings rose from the hard earth floor?

Such questions are germane to the Kakwa territory. I recently found an excellent book in the Fort William library, by a Mr. George Ivan Smith. He says:

> It is a barren region where stones are set on the hills to attract the rain. The wise men of the tribe, faced with questions of life and death, human hope or fear, sought answers by tying a long string to a chicken, attaching the string to a stake, then beheading the chicken. Its reflexes and death throes would cause it to fly. The string confined

flight to the limits of a circle, like a satellite voyaging around the earth. Answers to deep human concerns lay in the direction to which the body of the dead bird pointed as it came to rest, like the last breathless click of the roulette wheel. Superstitions and visions drifted up through the tribes and peoples like evening mists along the Nile.

Power, in this landscape, was vested in rocks and trees, in streams and animals. And power, as everywhere, was one of the forces that determined human intercourse. Only here it was more naked. I've underlined in thick dark pencil where Smith writes:

The Kakwa question is not: "Who are you?" It is: "What are you?" "What kind of a man?" "Are you a big man?" "Are you a slave?"

The Kakwa people, numbering some 60,000, are identified as often as not by a series of tribal markings: three parallel cuts on the cheeks longways. Later, in Amin's regime, these would become known as "one-elevens." And the people who wore them were feared by those who did not.

But back to the mother: a Lugbara (another of the Nilotic tribes) impregnated by a Kakwa man, she is that rare thing, a slave with power. For even as she is heaving in her labor to expel her twelve-pound burden into the sweating night, she is by many accounts held to be a witch. Though I am not so sure.

But let us follow the other historians in their garish story. She offers amulets and fetishes at market: the backbones of birds and the skulls of small reptiles, powder ground from the bark of rare trees, berries, roots, coffee beans and seashells . . . A child with colic, or an uncle in debt, a thief in the village or rats raiding the wicker maize bins—these are her charges, this the genus of problem that her charms will solve.

Others, contrarily, have her as a camp follower. Nicknamed "Pepsi Cola," she makes herself available under canvas, in the tents of the army lines. Others still say that Pepsi was actually a mad old woman, possessed of a devil, whom Amin's real mother failed to cure, lowering the stock of her reputation. Who knows?

Sex or sorcery, these are the options. Otherwise starvation, no doubt about it: the land is fertile in places but Pepsi (if it is she) is landless, a traveler whose ambiguity the peasants can only countenance when—out of necessity, all else failing—they turn their face to magic. Looking up from where they are bent at their plots, hoes in hand, to the strange figure passing on the roadway—the baby wrapped in a colorful calico bundle on her back—they recognize what Pepsi is. They call her to them, bid her service, and feed her for it. Then, the next morning, send her on: Lugazi, Buikwe, finally Jinja.

The father, he is unknown, most people believe he was a soldier—a trooper, with trooper's ways. Perhaps, beer on his breath, rifle leaning against the chair, he pierces Pepsi against her will, brushing aside a whimpered plea for payment. Or perhaps they make love with mutual joy and care, each softening like tallow the pain of the other's hard life. Or perhaps the noble fellow means to spill his sons on the bed but sloppily forgets. That being so, did 300,000 deaths ensue from a single accident of birth, or would another tyrant have come, certain as the steam engine or automatic flail?

Ah well, I have said it before: the cause—that is the place where we cannot go.

So the father disappears, as fathers do, and the mother plies her wares in Jinja—King's African Rifles town, town of factories and godowns, town of foul vapors and gunny sacks, town of the source of the Nile and the great railway lumbering up from the coast. Idi, he thrives here, beefy enough from an early age to make his mark in the dusty scraps that kids get into.

Then a gap. Some say Idi is briefly a bellboy at the Imperial Hotel in Kampala, bright buttons shining. Some say—he has said, in fact—that he sold sweet biscuits in boxes by the roadside.

In any case, by 1946 he has enlisted in the 4th King's African Rifles. The KAR, E Company. A thumbprint is the accepted signature for enlistment. Rations and equipment are issued. Idi works his way up for seven years, perhaps for some time as a cook. But his military merits soon become apparent, and he is made company sergeant-major.

What a passage that must have been. In idle moments, I have often pictured Idi in the training camps, climbing netted gantries.

Or, on the barked command, running full-tilt, bayonet at the ready, at the wooden rick where men filled with straw are hung by the neck. Then retiring, his gear trim at the foot of the green truckle bed, to sleep soundly on a belly full of rice and beer. Already a six-footer, he is noted for keeping his uniform neat and clean, and for excellence in sports. Boxing and rugby are his forte. He would later become boxing champion of Uganda; later still, I understand, he would challenge Muhammad Ali to a bout.

As for real work: 1953–1954, operations in Kenya against that country's notorious Mau Mau freedom fighters. I recall the occasion he explained, those great paws describing the motions from the podium, his special garrotte technique to the horrified Organization of African Unity conference, Kenyan delegates included. Later on, there is hunting-down of cattle poachers among the nomadic tribes, the Turkana and the Karamojong, who inhabit the far north of East Africa. The pursuit of shifta—bandits with ancient First World War rifles or home-made "daneguns," bound with wire and muzzle-loaded—is said to take his patrol across the borders of Somalia and Sudan, trudging through the desert landscape, razing villages or, still under the British aegis, looting them for food.

An eccentric Scottish officer, meanwhile, has put some of the KAR into khaki kilts. This, and subsequent involvement with Scottish soldiery, has a significant effect on Idi. Later in his career, asked by a Canadian reporter why he has demanded Scottish bodyguards from the Queen, he will reply: "The officers who promoted me to major were all Scottish. One, I think, is now commander-in-chief in Scotland and I would be happy if anybody came from there to be an escort to me or a bodyguard . . . and I will be talking to them about their traditions, because I have been with them for a very long time and they are a very brave people in the battlefield. I remember very well that when they are going to war at night they played their pipes and they were very brave. I am very happy to remember what we had with them during the Second World War, in North Africa."

Like Cecil Rhodes's Cape-to-Cairo Railway, Idi's penetration into northern Africa in those days is the matter of myth, extending itself in the telling: there is one tale of a beating in a brothel in Mogadishu, Somalia's Italianate capital. Which seems unlikely.

North, as an idea, is important to Idi, though; it is this country that suckled him, these borderlands of Arab and Bantu Africa where things are unsure. Here the Nubians live, the Moslem Nubi, the colonies of black mercenaries imported years ago by Captain Lugard, the crafty British soldier, to do his dirty work. It is this translated people that Idi will draw on, too, bringing them down in lorries for enlistment into the army or to fill the cohorts of the Public Safety Unit and the State Research Bureau—latterly as part of his Moslemization program. Alarmed at the prospect of an independent Uganda in which, as colonial bloodhounds, they have no place, they are only too happy to comply.

By 1959, after taking a course in Nakuru, Kenya (where he learns English), Idi has been promoted to "Effendi," a junior officer. On the eve of Independence, as Obote takes up the reins of power, the small matter of the murder of some Turkana tribesmen nearly comes to court. But it is all swept under the carpet by the British administration. These are new times, after all. The big day is only six months away.

Uganda's kingdoms are all to come together, in the blueprint, under a federal government. And so it is, on 9 October 1962, that the flag of free Uganda is raised. Idi, promoted to captain, his misdemeanors forgiven, is put in command of a battalion in the new Uganda Army. He is sent to Britain on an officer-training course, at the School of Infantry in Wiltshire and also up to Stirling, where, as he later said, "The warmth and kindness of the Scottish people increased my love for them."

Most intriguing of all, Idi makes a trip, in these early years, to Israel—for a parachute course. He is, so the story goes, awarded his wings without making a single jump.

Oh Israel, who could have been Uganda. I've often wondered what would have happened, actually, if it had been so, if the Zionist homeland had been there, as was mooted—if there had been synagogues on the savannah, kibbutzes in the bundu. If it had been Africans, not Arabs, who had fought for their territory. If it had been in Kampala that Eichmann was arraigned.

It was not so. Instead, Israel takes an interest in the land it could have been, in the shape of military and economic aid.

Another tribe, the Baganda, represented by the Kabaka Yekka ("the King, he only") party in the Cabinet, is meanwhile trying to shore up its own position. This follows the reinstatement of the Kabaka himself, Mutesa II, King Freddie, whom the British have deported following a political spat. Now he has returned, Edward William Frederick David Walugembe Luwangula Mutesa II— Professor of Almighty Power and Knowledge, Lord of the Clans and the Land, the Father of All Twins, the Blacksmith's Hammer, the Smelter of Iron, the Power of the Sun, First Officer of the Order of the Shield and Spears, the Cook with All the Firewood— is "back on seat."

And Obote doesn't like it. Just as the King didn't like Obote. "My first twinge of foreboding," he wrote, "came as I watched Milton Obote raise the flag of independence. My anxiety had no precise form or cause. It was more the sensing of an unfamiliar shift of emphasis, a gap between what was fitting and what was not."

Grandest of all the old Uganda kingdoms, a mighty dynasty in its time, Buganda had given its name to the country. It was King Freddie's great-grandfather, Mutesa I, who had received the explorer John Hanning Speke, opening his tall gates of reed to greet the ragged traveler with ceremonious majesty.

"I cut a poor figure in comparison," wrote Speke. "They wore neat bark cloths resembling the best yellow corduroy cloth, crimp and well set, as if stiffened with starch, and over that as upper cloaks, a patchwork of small antelope skins, which I observed were sewn together as well as any English glover could have pierced them."

Speke gave a rifle as a present to Mutesa, who forthwith had a servant try it out on the first passerby outside the palace gates. It worked. So did the presents that others brought: a bicycle, its best Brummagem spokes spinning in the red dust, and a music box. This last—bequest of another Scot, Alexander Mackay—tinkled out Haydn's *Creation* under the shade of a mango tree.

But now the machinery is not turning over quite so well. With Obote making inroads into its power, Buganda attempts to secede. Loyalists are rumored to be arming themselves, with a view to throwing the federal government out of the kingdom. In May 1966, Obote responds by ordering Amin, by now Army Chief of Staff, to shell the Kabaka's palace. King Freddie flees to England, where he dies of alcoholic poisoning, according to the coroner. The Baganda believe Obote's agents have slipped something into his wine.

1969, a key year. An assassination attempt against Obote. The bullet goes through his cheek, but he survives. Amin hears the shooting, thinks it's he that is the target, and runs for his life. Climbing, barefoot, the barbed-wire fence of the garden, he tears his pink soles. Obote, recovered, as if out of piety institutes a "Move to the Left," a "Common Man's Charter."

In Washington and London, Tel Aviv and Johannesburg, officials ponder at their desks. Now, only true-blue Kenya stands between South Africa, where Communist demons lurk, and the Arab north, where Saudi and Libyan oil money fuels the flames of anti-Israeli sentiment. Otherwise, a red band of Soviet client-states tightens across the middle of Africa. Something has to be done, the men at the desks say to themselves.

Amin, meanwhile, pursues his own agenda, building up an individual network of support, staffed with Nubi and South Sudanese personnel loyal only to him, funded by his profits from selling ivory and diamonds and gold. Brought in by the lorryload across the border, the loot is supplied by Congolese rebels, who willingly exchange it for arms. Amin feels secure enough to go on pilgrimage to Mecca. Obote, suspecting him, orders his arrest, and then flies off to Singapore. But it is too late. Amin's plans are already in place.

H.E. himself told me later, in one of our taped sessions, how they found an armory at Obote's house on the night of the coup, in crates bearing the legend: A Gift of the Red Cross of the Soviet Union. "It proved Obote was a Communist," he said. "That is why he went to Tanzania."

Obote, at the time, tells the newspapers that Amin himself has gone through his belongings: "He blew down the door and then went in and took everything—including my underpants and my books—some seven thousand volumes. I don't know whether he is going to read them."

With his mechanized battalions in control (some in tanks given to the Ugandan military by Israel), Amin calls a meeting on the veranda at the Command Post, as he has renamed his house on Prince Charles Drive in Kampala. His supporters sit around him, waiting to see what he will do. Waiters serve tea and coffee.

A policeman, a good man, loyal to his service, is introduced among the party. The waiters pour him a cup.

Amin leans back in his chair: "I had this Obote man brought to me. I could have had him killed. But I didn't. I gave him coffee."

The policeman looks anxiously from side to side. He begins to hyperventilate, and collapses to the floor, dropping his cup and saucer, which smash on the hard parquet. The waiters are too afraid to rush forward.

Ignoring it all, Amin continues: "You see, I am not ambitious. Nor am I a tribalist. I have three wives—all from different tribes—living with me here in this house."

The assembled company, soldiers mostly, and a few civil servants, find themselves looking towards the entrance from the veranda into the house itself, as if they expect the wives to appear and parade in front of them. But they do not.

"I," says Amin, "have ordered the soldiers to help the people. If all the wananchi die, who is left to rebuild Uganda?"

Outside, the sound of gunfire shatters the night.

"That," Amin says, as if on cue, "is my men firing into the air. They are very joyful."

He looks around, nodding, as if daring anyone to gainsay him. The policeman is sitting on the floor in a pool of coffee, holding his knees into his heaving chest.

And then Amin takes up where he left off. "Indeed, the instantaneous public jubilation that everywhere has greeted my takeover has left everybody in no doubt whatsoever that my takeover is a very popular move. Otherwise what could be the cause of all this public joy and excitement?"

He pauses again. Everyone else pauses, too, or freezes: it's as if they are playing a schoolyard game . . . until Amin answers his own question.

"I will tell you. The public has reacted in this way because they felt a great relief at the overthrow of an oppressive and unpopular regime. A great heavy weight has been lifted off the shoulders of the general public, so they have gone almost wild with joy."

He puts his hands on top of his head and moves his scalp to and fro, as if thinking hard about what to say next. He looks up at the ceiling, which a gecko is slowly traversing. And then he continues.

"Obote's regime was one of great hypocrites. He was anything but a socialist. Obote had two palaces in Entebbe, three in Kampala, one in Jinja, one in Tororo and one in Mbale. All these palaces had to be furnished and maintained at great public expense, and yet all but one remained idle and unused almost all of the time. It is no wonder the people of Jinja in their great joy attacked and damaged the so-called President's Palace at Jinja, total destruction of the palace being prevented by the army. Obote's mode of living was also anything but socialist. He heavily indulged in drink, smoking and women, and carried a big retinue wherever he went. Furthermore, Obote's Move to the Left, the Common Man's Charter, is a lot of hot air."

Two waiters help up the gasping policeman, and carry him off, one taking each arm. Amin smiles . . .

"You see, my Government firmly believes in peace and the international brotherhood of man. The masses who are now rejoicing at the overthrow are remembering Obote's misdeeds, also his inaction, his ineptitude and political impotence at times of great need. Time will no doubt reveal more of his weaknesses galore. For my part, I can only wish great luck and good sailing to the Uganda Second Republic. If anyone troubles us from outside, they will get booted. Our air force is good, our army is mechanized. We are preparing a warm reception for invaders. We will fight them and we will fight them effectively: we will meet them on the ground."

Later that week, as a sign of his clemency, Amin releases some pro-Obote detainees. They present him with two gifts, a Bible and a Koran, and make a curious statement: "General Amin has delivered this country from tyranny, oppression and political enslavement, just as Moses delivered the Jews from Pharaoh's bondage."

Writes King Freddie, from his dingy London bedsit: "In the end I shall return to the land of my fathers and my people."

And he does come back, but in a coffin, his plane flanked by four Uganda Air Force MiGs—from the same squadron I had myself seen on arrival at Entebbe Airport.

But that's by the by. Amin responds to the restoration crisis (will Prince Ronnie take up his father's empty throne, as the

Baganda elders wish, or return to his studies in England?) by making the following announcement: "I want to take this opportunity to state clearly and categorically that the kingdoms will not be introduced and Uganda will not go back to the 1962 constitutional setup. It is my wish and, after all, the wish of the vast majority of Ugandans that Uganda should remain a strong and united country. We are inaugurating a year which will be characterized by the promotion of human understanding. This demands, among other things, that every Ugandan must free himself from the clutches of factionalism and tribalism."

As I worked at the clinic in my second year in Mbarara, during the summer of 1972, Amin's itinerary was (as I have pieced it together) as follows:

(1) To Israel, to firm up joint policy on the Sudan and military cooperation. Talks with Moshe Dayan and Golda Meir. Selective arms deal established. (Flight made on Israeli jet, Israeli pilot "Colonel Sapristi" at the controls.)

(2) From Israel to Gatwick. The government wasn't expecting him, but a black-tie dinner with Edward Heath, Alec Douglas-Home and Reginald Maudling takes place nonetheless.

"I want the Harrier jump jet," announces Amin.

"What for?" says Douglas Home.

"To bomb Tanzania," Amin replies.

That request is turned down, but an arms deal is discussed with Lord Carrington the next morning; finally, a new £10 million aid program for Uganda is thrashed out.

Visit by H.E. to Sandhurst. An impromptu lunch with Queen Elizabeth and Prince Philip at Buckingham Palace. "Mr. Philip," as Amin calls him.

"Tell me, Mr. President," the Queen asks, "to what do we owe the unexpected honor of your visit?"

"In Uganda, your majesty," he replies, "it is very difficult to find a pair of size thirteen shoes."

Later that day, Idi purchases shoes and clothes at London's "Large Man" shop.

(3) The highlight of the trip: Scotland. Visit to Holyrood, seat of the old kings. The Ugandan flag hoisted over Edinburgh Castle. Does it flutter in the wind, with a flesh-slapping flag noise, or does it hang limp? Who knows? Amin takes the salute. Shopping on Princes Street: scarlet plastic bags, boxes with ribbons. H.E.'s nine-year-old son, Campbell, wears a kilt for a Beating the Retreat by the King's Own Scottish Borderers. The end of an old song.

17

Following the diplomatic reception at State House on my first day in my new job, I didn't see Amin for some time. Whenever I approached Wasswa, the Minister, about being presented to him, I was fobbed off. As his physician, I thought that I should (at the very least) make a preliminary examination. It would only be right and proper. Otherwise, what was the point of me? But Amin was too busy, apparently. Not doing anything important, if the manner in which I was finally to see him was anything to go by.

It was about a month after the reception. I had gone up to the pool at one of the city's big hotels. As a nonresident, you could use it by paying a daily fee. I changed in the little concrete room. One side of it was full of chugging machinery—for cleaning or pumping out the pool, I supposed—with dials and a couple of green-handled levers sticking out of it. On the other was a steel door with a rubber seal, padlocked and marked PRIVATE in red letters.

I put my stuff in a locker and went out. There were lots of people out there, mostly whites, lying on sun loungers like Romans at a feast, sipping their Cokes and Fantas and reading paperback books as the waiters moved stealthily among them.

One of them, I realized, was Marina Perkins, the Ambassador's wife. She was wearing sunglasses. I toyed with the idea of going up to her but was embarrassed to do so in my swimming trunks. So I dropped my towel by the side and dived right in. I did some lengths, enjoying the feeling of it after so much time in the heat, and then hauled myself out next to where I'd left my towel.

With the water on me, and the towel in my hands, I felt bold enough to go up to Marina Perkins.

"Hello," I said. My eyes were stinging from the chlorine.

Hers were obscured by the dark glasses. She pushed them up. "Doctor Garrigan. I didn't count you as a swimmer."

"I do try to keep in shape." I was conscious, however, of a certain nervousness about the disposition of my body as I said this. I moved gawkily, fiddling with a corner of the towel.

"Come and talk to me," she said. "I'm tired of sitting around in the sun doing nothing."

I laid the towel out.

"It won't be comfy on the ground. Why don't you get one of those?" She pointed at one of the loungers.

I dragged one over as she suggested, its plastic feet scraping the concrete, and then lay down beside her. Well, a few feet away. I still felt a bit embarrassed. Talking to an attractive woman on a neighboring sun lounger is more difficult a matter than one might think—especially if she is someone else's wife. I found it hard not to let my gaze wander over the sideways-falling cup of her blue bikini. And so on, awkward cur that I was.

"So why did you leave Mbarara, really?" she asked. "It must have been quite exciting out there. An old-fashioned adventure."

Feeling the heat from the plastic lounger, an inauspicious augury coming up through the cushions and my damp towel, I decided not to tell her about Sara.

"Not really," I said. "Everything just becomes a job after a while. The problem was, I got tired of treating people with shoddy equipment and time-expired medicines. It became hardly worth it."

"It must always have been worth it, surely, to help people?"

"Up to a point. But a lot of the time, they were cases we just couldn't cope with. And anyway, it wasn't the most exciting life after work. I'm not cut out for endless dinner parties with the same people."

"Well, don't think it will be any different in Kampala. You'll find it gets the same here too. The list of things to do comes round again sooner than you think. There's hardly anything I haven't done: game park, Rwanda gorillas, Murchison Falls. The only one I haven't done is taking a boat out on Lake Vic. They say you can catch really big fish. I keep asking Robert, but he never has the time nowadays, after all that Asian stuff. He doesn't like water much anyway."

"I do," I said, and then suddenly felt gauche that I had shown interest where her husband had failed.

"I . . . used to go fishing a lot when I was a kid," I explained quickly. "With my father."

"Oh," she said.

I tried to change the subject. "You can't be that bored, though?"

"I am. It's all right for you. You've got an interesting job. You've got a use in the world. I'm just expected to hang around. I always feel as if I'm waiting for something."

I nodded, and looked down at my toes on the end of the sun-lounger.

"When you're a diplomat's wife, you've got to be like a diplomat. It's like you're under contract. I mean, I shouldn't really be talking to you like this. Not done—you know."

She pulled her dark glasses back down, like a spy in a comic. A Mata Hari.

"Don't worry," I said, jovially, "I won't tell anyone."

We chatted a bit about the political situation. She said that the same British journalists who had applauded Amin's coup were now writing critical articles, and that this was causing trouble for her husband. As she spoke, I noticed that one of the pool attendants was taking a keen interest in our conversation. I gave him a hard look. It was fruitless, and he continued to hang around while we were talking.

"I don't think it'll come to much," Marina said, when I asked her about the Economic War that Amin had announced. "There won't be a purge. Robert says it's just the aftermath of the Asian thing. It won't affect you or me."

Looking back, it seems crazy. All the time, in spite of myself, I was searching like a rubbish-picker among her words as they came out, poking about for an intimation that she found me attractive. None came. I must have been mad—what on earth did I expect?

"I suppose I ought to get back," she said, eventually. "We've got dinner with the East German Ambassador."

She gathered up her bag and towel and I watched her walk, little feet on the concrete, up towards the changing rooms.

I lay in the sun a bit more and then went for another swim. Pushing the water: forty lengths, changing my stroke every ten. Breast, back, side and a final burn of crawl. I can't do butterfly, it doesn't seem natural.

It was when I got out, as I was drying myself, that it happened. I had noticed several Ugandans, including a couple of soldiers, come into the pool area while I was swimming, and now they were sitting on the loungers, some fully dressed, some in trunks. One soldier was on mine but I didn't have the courage to challenge him.

On another lounger, over the other side, sat Wasswa. He beckoned to me, shouting across the water.

"Come and sit next to me, Doctor Garrigan. I have something to show you."

I went over and sat down on the cushioned plastic next to him.

"What is it?"

"You will see. It is very special."

He was wearing a pair of very skimpy trunks, I noticed— and then there was a kind of roaring sound from the center of the pool. A column of water, five or six feet high, rose up like a fountain. I spotted something dark underneath it. The roaring gave way to a mechanical grinding, and the Ugandans began to clap and cheer. A head came out as the plume cascaded down—oversized, like a bust of some great hero of the past— then broad shoulders, a stout belly in shorts, thighs, two doughty knees (one scarred) and finally a pair of surprisingly delicate ankles.

Amin waved at the jubilant bunch of flunkies and soldiers and dived off the platform. I could see the black X of him swimming underwater towards where Wasswa and I were sitting.

"It is a special machine His Excellency had put in," Wasswa said, pointing at the pillar in the centre of the pool. "It brings him up from underneath."

And then Amin's smiling face was breaking the surface in front of us, his eyes red and blinking. He pulled himself up, water falling off him on to the curblike edge. As if he had forgotten himself, Wasswa hurriedly got up and draped a towel around the President's shoulders. I stood up too.

Amin, at his full height, looked down at me closely. He wasn't smiling anymore.

"So . . . my personal physician. Why are you wasting your time around the swimming pool? You should be out healing the people of Uganda!"

"Uh-m," I said, bewildered, "I have been very busy, Your Excellency. I have been catching up on research. Anyway, in case you drowned . . ."

He stared like a bullfrog for a second, and then burst out laughing, pounding me on the back with his wet hand.

"Ah, Doctor Nicholas, you are a funny man. I was only joking. How is it going with you in Uganda? Do you like your new job?"

"Yes, but I really need to get the chance to check you over."

"Of course, of course. If I am sick. Now I am healthy."

He patted his stomach. "Very very healthy. Come, enjoy yourself at our pool."

He turned away but paused then, and spun back round. Involuntarily, I took a step back.

"No!" he said. "I want show you my secret weapon. Follow me."

He led me over towards the changing room, the retinue following too, whispering like naughty schoolchildren behind us. We went inside the room, past the bank of machinery. On the door marked PRIVATE, the padlock was hanging off its clasp. Amin pulled one of the levers and a noise came from inside. The pillar coming down, I guessed, from the wet suck of hydraulic air.

"This is very significant advance, this very important in our technology in Uganda," said Amin. "The Israeli people made it for me."

He turned to me, jabbing the air with his finger.

"Good engineers, bad politicians in Tel Aviv. Now, you look inside." He opened the door.

I did as he said. There was a dark little cubicle there, with a metal floor and walls, all dripping with water.

Suddenly I felt a hand in the small of my back pushing me in, and a deep laugh as the door closed behind. Complete darkness. The mechanical noise again. And then a wall of water coming down on me. The force of it almost knocked me over. The roof had opened and I thought was going to drown—except that, at the same time, the floor of the cubicle was rising and there were powerful jets of air coming up all around. I could see light above me through the falling water.

I emerged spluttering, crouched on the platform as it rose above the surface of the pool. The Ugandans, who had presumably rushed back outside, and the few Europeans who hadn't slunk off when Amin appeared, were gathered there—cheering *me* now.

Trying not to look cross, I slid into the water. Amin himself pulled me out at the edge. He hurt my arm, and he was laughing like a drain.

"Oh doctor, doctor. I am sorry. But it is good that you learn to swim in a proper manner. I myself have been swimming in more rough water. You should be better. One day you may be in a war situation, doctoring for the Uganda Army."

He gave me his towel, which was large, and decorated with the crested-crane symbol.

"You frightened me," I said, drying myself slightly queasily.

"Do not be frightened. It is foolish to be frightened. Come, sit down. Eh, you!"

He beckoned at one of his retinue. "Order sandwiches. And fried chicken. And Coca-Cola also."

The man rushed off: his immediate, mute response was something I'd get used to seeing around Amin. I sat down on one of the loungers, rather shaken.

"No, doctor, you must not be frightened. To be afraid is a coward, and I do not think my own doctor can be a coward. Not possible. All of you, listen to me!"

Amin dived into the pool. With powerful strokes, he swam across to the pillar, which was still elevated from my own adventure. He clambered on to the platform and clapped his hands.

"All of you people. Listen to me. I want to talk to about afraidness and cowardice in Uganda."

He smoothed the front of his wet trunks. "The truth is, afraidness is bad. I was not afraid to take the presidency from Obote or to send the Kabaka to England. It was the best thing for my country. I think God will not punish me for it."

There were murmurs of assent from the retinue. Beside me, Wasswa was nodding his head eagerly.

"It is true, I like to be head man. I do not like to be told, 'Amin, carry this gun,' or, 'Amin, dig latrine here.' " He pretended to dig on the platform, and then continued: "I like this not at all, it is not right for my people for the white man to come and tell him this thing, that thing. But I do like it after, when the officer in the army before say, 'Well done, Amin.' Just like when the Queen of England go and tell Scottish people, make planting here, build wall there. To keep antelope. The Scots eat antelope daily. Look how strong they are."

He pointed at me. Everyone looked, nodding at me, smiling at me.

"And myself, you know. You know in my heart, as I have said before, I am the king. That is why I like these machines. Machines are the things for kings."

He stamped on the metal, the funereal sound ringing out across the pool. I thought of my father and his Bell's, and then of that old Jacobite toast: "To the king over the water . . ."

"For it is true, also, out of my nature, I love to rule! No claim is first but mine. But the peoples of Uganda are good and therefore they deserve to have a good leader like me. If they were bad, they would deserve a bad leader. It is an obvious thing. It is logical. God would send this bad man to plague them. It would be horrible for them indeed."

Amin paused then and coughed, as if the water had got into his lungs.

"This man, yes, he would chase people and not be good, and he would take women from, ah, all over the place—black women and white women also. He could not make friends with any man who was a good man and he could not see a woman he did not want to make pregnant. He would say, this thing happen and then . . . this thing happen! Just because of his cleverness. And so he would slip here and run down there, thinking he is being very clever following his own plan. Eh, you, bring me some foods!"

A waiter from the hotel had brought the ordered refreshments out on a tray. He looked around nervously when Amin addressed him.

"Go, go," said Wasswa urgently. "Take it inside."

The waiter looked aghast.

"Take the tray into the pool."

The waiter walked round to the steps and gingerly went down into the water. Holding the tray above him he walked as far as he could up the shallow end, the water steadily soaking his white coat—until, forced to swim, he struggled to reach the platform. At one point the bottles of Coke and the plates nearly slid off the tray, and there was a palpable gasp around the pool. Eventually he got there. Amin squatted down and took the tray off him.

"Well, I am very glad you are not a diver in my navy, Mr. Waiter. You should get some training in swimming and sub-aqua."

He laughed at himself, and the whole gathering laughed, as the waiter swam back sheepishly in his heavy clothes. His white coat had ballooned up: I couldn't help thinking of the inflated corpse in the Rwizi, the sickening way it had moved up and down in the current.

"Anyway," said Amin, with his mouth full of chicken. "This bad chief, my friends. He thinks, what he is doing, that it is his plan not the plan of God. But it is in fact God's will what he is doing all the time. So he appears a very great man because of this. He believes in taking every chance and there is nothing he does not dare do. He never says—simama, finish, he is even like a brave man going on until the last minute when he is taken down. Then, too, he cannot realize his true situation. He just will not see it."

He waved the chicken leg in the air. You could see the joint move as he gesticulated. The loose, greasy skin was red from piri-piri. He took another bite, then dropped it on the platform by his side.

"So, things would be bad in that country until then. Every morning, when the sun shine, there is a new widow crying in her hut and a baby there chewing on her breast like a dry maize cob. And every day this bad chief is spitting at God in the sky. He puts a finger up at the moon, he does not know when is an equal measure of mealies flour in any thing. For he always goes too much in every area . . .

"Yes, for with his evil ways, he is like Shaitan and his country the whole of it will be his tomb. For him and many people otherwise. Even he, the top man, he asks himself, 'Is this Uganda? Or is Uganda hell?' For no kind of life is as wretched as this fellow's—

he is afraid from leopard dreams, false spirits which do come to him in the night—and when he dies he will die a cruel and an extraordinary death."

He swigged from a bottle of Coke, and then held his hand against his chest.

"For this is the truths. He goes steps up and it is too much good: his belly is fat and he empties his loins often. But there is a rope around his neck and when he reaches the highest step, God—He pulls this fellow into the fire by the end of the rope! Because he has now done His work for Him already, the will of God goes straight towards taking him, and when He does take him it is one for one, special parcel both ways."

With that he put down the bottle, clipped his palms together and dived into the pool smartly. We were still applauding when he came up.

"Well," said Amin, as one of the retinue dried his back with the crested-crane towel, "that is my story for you today, my friends. And now, now we will have a swimming competition—so we are fit on Lake Victoria in case of invasion."

And so they did, though I noticed that in all the races in which Amin took part the other participants allowed him to win. I crept off after watching it for a while. I felt, in one way and another, that I had done my bit. That no more would be expected of me for the time being.

I went to bed tired that night, and had a strange dream. Well, it was more like a memory returning to me, something I had once seen in a nook-and-corner antique shop in Edinburgh. It was a very small silver music box, not much larger than a packet of cigarettes but about twice as deep. The assistant wound it up for me, and this is what happened. The top of the box opened and a double bed rose up, all beautifully wrought in miniature, even down to the folds of the sheets. Lying on top of the latter, on their backs, were two naked ivory automata. The man was erect, his prepuce a tiny ruby set into the cream-colored shaft. As the music played—I can't recall the tune, except that it was seductive, very slow and Eastern—the male figure ascended and turned over. The woman opened her knees, and the man began to move between them rhythmically, his ruby-crested shaft disappearing into a cunning cavity. All this happened in time with the music, the process concluding with the end of the tune and the woman's head moving from side to side—except that, in my dream, it all kept going, as if there were no conclusion, no bounds.

Well . . . there were, in so far as I woke up with the familiar surroundings of my bungalow at State House around me. I lay in bed, running the story of the night over in my head, and then got up and showered. While I was eating my breakfast, I received a phone call (the first of many, as it happened).

"Hello, hello, doctor. President Amin here. Come now to my house. My son is very, very sick. Come immediately."

"I'll be five minutes," I said.

"How can you be five minutes? Are you a giant to make big steps or are you a fool?"

I didn't know what to say. "I don't know what you mean, sir."

"I am not in State House, doctor! On working days I am not in Entebbe. I am in the Command Post at Prince Charles Drive. You must motor here at once."

"But, I don't have a car," I mumbled. "It's quite a way."

"Ah. Then you must tell the soldiers at the gate to bring you. At once!"

He rang off, leaving me holding the receiver, bewildered. I looked down at the earpiece, and saw that it was glistening with sweat.

I gathered up my things and went outside to organize a driver. This took some time, but eventually I set off, in the passenger seat of an army jeep. Worried about being late, I tried to take my mind off it by looking at the brightly painted signs as we passed through Nateete and Ndeeba, the townships and light-industrial areas on the outskirts of Kampala: "Muggaga Auto Menders" (muggaga means witch doctor); "Cold Joint Meats"; "Volcano Dry Cleaners is the Answer"; "Desire Agencies—Unisex Barber and Dying Salon"; "Bell Lager—Great Night, Good Morning"; "Super Fast-Acting DOOM."

The most common advertisement was for Sportsman, a popular brand of cigarette. Red and yellow, the posters showed a picture of a slightly tawny English jockey, circa 1950, and carried the slogan, "Yee ssebo!"

"What's that mean?" I asked the driver as we passed a shop emblazoned with it.

His beret skew-whiff, he looked at me as if I were mad.

"Yes, sir!"

"No, but what does it *mean*?" I spoke slowly, thinking that he hadn't understood me.

"It means, yes, sir! Like, very good."

"Oh, I see," I replied, embarrassed.

We carried on into the city, past a coffin maker with his wares stacked up outside the shop, past the Hindu temple—deserted since the Asians had gone, it looked like a large, crumbling wedding cake, full of peaks and crenellations—Nakasero Soap Works and the market near Burton Street, finally going up Sturrock Road and into Prince Charles Drive.

It wasn't quite what I expected, the "Command Post": just a pleasant suburban house of the type many expatriate executives lived in, only a bit larger. You wouldn't have known it was any different except for a tall radio aerial on the tiled roof and the machine-gun emplacement at the gate. It was surrounded by spruce trees and bougainvillea, with a high bank leading up to the front door.

I was ushered in by the guards. One of Amin's wives—I supposed—greeted me at the door, wearing a blue cardigan, some kids pushing at her legs from behind.

"I am sorry, doctor. The President is now gone away on urgent government business. My name is Kay, it is my son who is ill."

I followed her in. The living room had a brown suite, a television and a drinks cabinet. Plastic toys were scattered over the carpet. There were dinosaurs painted in lurid green and red, and two big yellow Tonka trucks. And a couple of Action Man dolls in uniform, their limbs splayed at odd angles. A faint smell of cooking emerged from the kitchen. It was all quite normal.

"Through here," said Kay Amin. As I followed her, three or four children were shouting and running around us with the strange, pointless energy of the young. She gave one of them a slap.

I put my bag down. The boy—about ten years old, he reminded me very much of Gugu—was lying on the bed, curled up like a fetus, and wheezing. I turned him over. There was blood running from one nostril. I took his face in my hands and looked at him closely.

"Is it bad, doctor?" asked his mother, fiddling with the edge of her cardigan.

"Oh no," I said. I could see at once what the problem was. There was a slight swelling on the side of his nose. I pressed it gently, and the boy let out a yell. I crouched down to check with my penlight.

Definitely, I thought. "Don't worry, laddie," I said. "Now, you've put something up your nose, haven't you?"

The boy looked a little guilty as Kay Amin questioned him in Luganda, and then wailed when I took a pair of tweezers out of my instrument case. He leapt up off the bed. There was a little tussle before she could grab him and hold him down. I slowly inserted the tweezers—quite difficult since he was squirming around—and delved around. I hit a solid obstruction, and after a few attempts extracted a bloody something.

"What is it, in God's name?" cried Mrs. Amin.

I held the tweezers up to the light: between the pincers was a small piece of green Lego, dabbed with red.

"Tcha," she exclaimed. "Campbell, you are a very bad boy."

I swabbed the blood away from the boy's nose and aspersed the nostril with an antiseptic spray. As I pressed the plunger, I had a sudden vision of my father spraying the weeds along the fence of the paddock in Fossiemuir. He'd borrowed a spray canister from one of the farmers nearby. You wore it like a rucksack, waving the piped wand in front of you. It had leaked when he did it, burning his back with insecticide. I remember my mother leaning over his bare back in the kitchen, pressing cold towels against the weals . . .

"He'll be fine," I said, patting the boy's head. "Just tell him to watch where he tries to build his castles. They're more fun outside your head than in, Campbell."

She walked me to the door. "Thank you very much, doctor. The President will be very pleased you have cured his son so successfully."

And so he was. One morning the following week, I went out to find a Toyota van parked outside the door of the bungalow. On the side was the legend "Khan Fashion Emporium" and below, in smaller letters, "Latest styles direct Milan London Bombay tel. Kampala 663." There was an envelope tucked underneath the wiper.

Inside, on official government paper with the crested-crane device, was a message. "Well done! The President has insisted you have this van as reward for expert treatment of his son. The keys are under the driver-side mat. I am sorry it is secondhand, but if you bring it to Cooper Motors they will remove the sign on the govt. account. Give my name. Wasswa, Minister of Health."

I was delighted, and my life in the city began to open up after that. For a start, I could go out at night. I had Cooper's respray the panel and valet the innards with hot steam.

18

I missed my Mbarara veranda, having to write up my journal on a table dragged into the garden at State House. But still, it was breathtakingly pretty. A grapefruit tree stood right outside the bungalow, fifteen to twenty of the fruit hanging from its branches, bright yellow and oozing with odoriferous juice. I didn't pick one. They looked so gorgeous there I could hardly have wanted to.

I used to get up early on Sundays, while the air was still fresh, and listen to the morning noises over a cup of coffee as I wrote: the cawing of pied crows and the long trill and peep of plovers and cuckoos. In the distance, I could just make out the buildings of Entebbe town and farther beyond, Kampala itself, red and brown blocks piled carelessly over the hills. Marabous walked thoughtfully over the lawns and then took flight, laboring like some great, lumbering Lancaster or B52 until they caught a thermal and soared high above.

Three days a week, I did the rounds at Mulago, the main hospital in Kampala. I was a sort of consultant there, in addition to my as yet negligible presidential duties. I ended up mostly working in casualty. The hospital buildings looked like some Deep South plantation mansion, with a big clock in the gable of the entrance. The condition of the outside walls—a dirty yellow, as if something of the slums down the hill, the other side of Kitante Road, had found its way across—gave the lie to the grandeur of the place.

Towering above us were the aerials of UTV, Uganda Television, and every now and then a light plane buzzed over, to land at Kololo airstrip nearby. "That's Amin," everyone always said. The Command Post on Prince Charles Drive was just round the corner, as was Amin's third residence, Nakasero Lodge, where he lived most of the time.

Most of the work at Mulago—unlike in Mbarara, where it was fever that had busied us—was concerned with the surgery of infection. Infected muscle, infected cartilage, infected bone. So a lot of cutting, then—which was an education for me, since I am a physician not a surgeon (not that I think I will ever practice medicine again in any capacity). But in Africa needs must. Excursions with the lancet, adventures with the helpful knife, that was the excitement in my life in those days. You had to learn not to press.

Surgery of trauma also: wounds, fractures, amputations. The predominance of the last was on account of nothing more outlandish than car crashes. Colin Paterson, the senior surgeon there (another Scot), told me that more people died in Africa from motor injuries than from malaria. It was a gross exaggeration, but there was a grain of truth in it. No tests, no insurance, madmen at the wheel.

Serious research was also undertaken at Mulago, and I toyed with the idea of joining one of the teams on a part-time basis. We had several nationalities there: Vietnamese, Russians, Algerians, Chinese, as well as the Ugandan doctors. There was a bit of racial tension. One team ran a Lymphoma Treatment Center. Another, an American one, tested cultured polio vaccines on a bunch of monkeys brought in from Kivu province in Zaïre. They used the kidney tissue. I once saw the monkeys chattering in the cage when a lorry came in. One ran to the bars, gripped them with its little hands and looked—so I fancied—right at me. Deep eyes, like pots of maple syrup. Then one of its companions bit it on the ear.

But to be honest, I didn't know if I could be bothered with getting involved in the research side of things. I was having quite a pleasant life exploring the city in the van. Following the swimming-pool incident, I still hadn't actually got to attend to Amin properly, so I had plenty of time on my hands.

There were lots of clubs and bars to go to. It amused me that these favored names with connotations of air or space travel: "Highlife," "Stratocruise," "The Satellite." In fact, they were absolute dives, where Zaïreans in sharp suits and winkle-pickers played skipping guitar music and the bar girls milled around like tsetse fly. I supposed the aviation theme was popular because most of the Ugandans in those places wanted to escape abroad, to build more prosperous lives.

I took the van back to Cooper's and had them put a red cross on the bonnet. Swanepoel, the pilot whom I had met when I first arrived in the country, tipped me off to that one. Every now and then I would run into him in one of the bars.

"Helps you get through roadblocks," he'd said on that occasion. "I picked it up in the Congo. The mercs used to use it for ambushes."

"Mercs?"

"Mercenaries. Katanga."

"Really?" I said.

I never knew whether to believe Swanepoel's stories. The next time I saw him, I was out on the town with Peter Mbalu-Mukasa. He was one of the African doctors at Mulago. It was very noisy in the Stratocruise that night, the usual Friday crowd.

As meaty and coarse as ever, Swanepoel was sitting on a barstool, with a girl on his knee. Her hair was all glossy—treated so it hung down and caught the light off the trashy spinning chandeliers—and her arms were draped around Swanepoel's thick neck. One of his hands, meanwhile, was exploring her back, inside her red shirt. Cocking his head to one side, he raised a bushy eyebrow at me over her shoulder, as I pushed through the sweaty throng in the narrow gap behind them.

"Hello," I shouted. "You're back in Kampala, then."

"Well, we all come back here," he said. "Cradle of the human race!"

"What?" I said.

Peter, pushed from behind by carousers, was shunting into me in the gangway. The stench of beer, perfume and body odor was overpowering.

"Let's get a table," Peter said in my ear. "Tell your friend to come."

"Come and join us," I said to Swanepoel.

"Sure," he said. And then, to the girl: "See you later, sweetheart."

Once we found somewhere to sit, Swanepoel started banging on about the Semuliki discovery. That's what he'd meant, I realized, about the cradle of the human race.

"Yep," he said, "it's official. This is where we all came from. Did you see the news? It was your part of the country."

I had seen it. On the Zaïre border, in the Ruwenzoris but farther north than Mbarara, they had recently found a cache of prehistoric human remains. There had been a display of bones on UTV—femurs and a jawbone and other bits and pieces lying on a bit of dirty cloth.

"Missing link?" Swanepoel said, "You'd have thought they'd have filled the whole puzzle in by now."

"It's very complex," Peter said. "It is all going to New York for carbon dating." Then he sighed and shook his head. "They are saying Amin made a museum there go up to $500,000 to be able to export it."

"That doesn't surprise me," Swanepoel said. "Did you hear him on the TV?" He stood up and, puffing out his chest, did a passable impression of Amin: "Ladies and gentlemen, it may be that my ancestors were the first people on earth. I may be all your fathers, all the world's fathers are inside of me."

"Careful," Peter said, frowning. "You will be reported."

"He wouldn't touch me," Swanepoel said. "I'm too bloody useful to him."

"Everyone is useful to him—for a while," said Peter. "But now even some of the coup officers have been killed. They will come for the whites soon, I am warning you."

"No, they won't," said Swanepoel. "No offense, but someone's got to run the place."

I was a bit worried that Peter might indeed have taken umbrage at this, but he just looked at Swanepoel for a second over his beer glass, and then said, "You'll be the first!"

We all burst out laughing, and then I said, "I was talking to the British Ambassador's wife the other day."

"Hey, big man!" Swanepoel said mockingly.

"No, seriously. She didn't seem to think there was a purge on the way."

"Marina Perkins?" said Swanepoel, scratching his beard. "What would she know? I met her once or twice. She's a nice enough woman but, come on, she hasn't exactly got her finger on the pulse."

"But that is it," said Peter, "nobody has their finger on the pulse. Not even Amin. I know this, I know people in his household."

"Who?" said Swanepoel.

"I can't say," Peter said, looking nervous suddenly.

"You guys," said Swanepoel, shaking his head. "If you tremble in front of people like Amin, they'll stamp on you. That's how it is. Like when you're walking past a big slavering dog and he scents your fear."

"You don't understand," said Peter. "He stamps on us anyway. The soldiers have been beating up the students at the university."

"Don't worry," said Swanepoel. "Someone will knock him off his pedestal soon. They always do."

It was raining as we left, and by the time I reached home a full-fledged electrical storm had developed. The beer had made my throat dry, so I made a cup of tea before going to bed. I stood on the porch to drink it. Leaning against the doorpost, I watched as the blue and purple sheets of charged light flashed above the lake, and the wind shook the golden lamps of the grapefruit tree. It was terrifically noisy, more noisy than I can explain, but the strangest thing was how the noise had a smell, almost a taste: you could smell the charge dispersing in the air. A harsh metal taste of tarnished cutlery, battery terminals, or zinc supplement without the sugar coating.

19

It rained all weekend, as a matter of fact, and on the Monday morning I got a shock. The outside of the front door was covered with flying ants. Not the brown type but bright green ones. It was surreal. The rain had obviously brought them out in some seasonal sexual frenzy. I tried not to stand on them as I walked to the van, but in the end gave up and just crunched straight on. On the way to Kampala, the road was covered with them, and I had to brake several times to avoid the bands of kids who were collecting them up in little bags. As I drove, I remembered the whitebait taste of them from the banquet.

The rain had also turned the city to mud, not the usual red mud but a curious purple shade. And lots of it. As I sped through the puddles, it was as if the whole settlement was sliding down off the seven hills on which it was built. It was like Rome in that way, and the morning after the storm it was like Rome had been spilt.

Each hilltop was shrugging off its significant landmark: the King's Palace (or the ruins of it, since Amin and Obote had bombed it), the big water tank, the mosque, the UTV aerials, the barracks, the Anglican and Catholic cathedrals, the Poor Clares' convent . . . they were all coming down, sliding down in the slick purple mud. The same mud which sucked at my shoe, battening on the heel like an animal. It pulled it right off in the hospital car park, and had me hopping around. After that, I thought, as I checked the blackboard roster, it's bound to be a bad day.

It was the usual stuff marked up there: GSW for STS (Gunshot Wound for Surgical Toilet and Sterilization). That was debridement, when we had to pick out dirt and foreign matter (soot, fragments of cloth) with the forceps. I'd learned already that you had just to leave bullet wounds open for a few days. A gamble with infection. The latter is always a complicated business, in any case. As Bailey and Love's *Short Practice* puts it, "Staphylococci do not always cause sepsis; they may merely colonize an already discharging wound. Wound discharges containing staphylococci are sources of cross-infection . . ." But basically, if you see the pink flesh come and it starts to heal, you know you're all right. Otherwise—well, you can tell from the smell.

As it was Monday, we also had the the usual cases of "Monday Drip," as Paterson dubbed the venereals—the soldiers coming in after their weekends in the brothels.

"All bad things come from France," he said, his face crumpling into a conspiratorial grin as he waved about one of the bougies over the patient between us. "Except in this case it applies to the cure as well as the disease."

"What do you mean?" I asked.

"Bougie's a French word. It means candle as well as these."

"Actually," interjected Hassan, one of the Algerian doctors, "it's Algerian. Bujiyah is an Algerian town centered on the wax trade."

"You've got me there," said Paterson.

The poor chap over whose bed we were having this abstruse discussion had a urethral stricture on account of gonorrheal infection. Medically speaking, the bougie was the flexible steel rod we had to introduce into his penis in order that he could pee. But in this case it was all too swollen and weeping so we had to make a supra-pubic puncture and drain off the bladder that way.

It was a messy, nasty business, and so was much else we did. Tropical medicine is essentially pyomyositic. It centers on the collection of pus in areas of muscle. Or in the gut: we got a lot of abcesses as a result of strangulated hernias. This was often a direct consequence of bad diet: too much matooke and nothing else. Later that morning, in fact, we had a poor woman come in with a stomach so distended with wind that when we introduced the tube to—how shall I put this?—allow her to let off steam, the noise went on for eight minutes. Her kneeling the whole time, clutching a rosary as she said her prayers. She felt better afterwards, but we would still have to cut out the redundant piece of gut, the dead bowel, later in the week.

At lunchtime I rang Marina Perkins. Having made some plans with Paterson about going out on the lake, I remembered what she'd said about it. It was just a thought, inviting her, but when it came, I realized I'd been thinking about her a bit. I guess I was really missing Sara.

"It's . . . Nicholas Garrigan here," I said, uncertainly, into the big black mouthpiece.

"What a nice surprise!" Marina said. "I haven't seen you at the swimming pool recently."

I told her about my encounter with Amin.

"Oh, he's always doing that," she said. "I should have warned you."

"I wanted to ask you," I said. "What you were saying about the lake, well, my colleague at the hospital here, Colin Paterson, he's organizing a fishing expedition. The two of us, maybe some others, are going to hire a boat with an outboard motor and perch rods. Next weekend. I was wondering if you fancied coming along for the ride. What do you say?"

There was a pause. "Well, I don't see why not. But it couldn't be next weekend. Nor the one after. We've got Embassy functions. The first one in February would be good, though. Bob's going down to the Kagera Salient. Amin's invited a deputation of diplomats down there to prove he's not planning to invade Tanzania."

"OK, then," I said, relieved but still nervous. "I'll speak to Colin and ring you the Friday before."

"I could get the cook to prepare a picnic," she said.

With that over, I went back to the seemingly less awesome task of stitching up a panga wound. Pangas were the big cutlasses they used for agriculture—and the violent settling of a quarrel. It was a very particular type of injury. People would put up their arm to protect themselves from the assault, naturally enough, and what you got was a series of linear cuts, severing tendons and, usually, producing a compound fracture underneath.

Well, those were the easy ones. Sometimes, and it was like that with this fellow, they get cut on the skull. This one was fractured. The blade had gone nearly right through the dura mater, the fibrous layer beneath the bone. It looked as if he would be OK, but a damaged dura mater gave infection a direct route to the brain.

And if the blade had gone in farther than that, the case was altered substantially. Even with all the research teams, not one of us there, not even Paterson, could debride the brain. We'd need a proper neurosurgeon. But it will happen one day. There will be brain surgery in Uganda. Hospitals are like people: they grow, they develop, they learn. And they decay too, and they die.

Towards the end of the month, as a matter of fact, Paterson and I went out to one of the first hospitals in the country. Built by the missionaries in the late 1800s, it was once the best hospital between Cairo and the Cape. When we visited it was a dump, with no dependable electricity supply and so short of beds and linen that some of the patients doubled up on single mattresses, or simply lay on the floor. Several just had logs for pillows. There was a sign in the toilets—"Please do not expectorate in the sink"—but it was pretty pointless, so far as the prevention of infection went, since there was feces all over the floor.

It turned out that we had a transfer from there later in the week. Not just any transfer, but a top-level patient, a VIP. It was one of Amin's daughters. She attended a Catholic boarding school somewhere in the bush and had managed to sit on a needle during an embroidery class. I reckon it must have been a practical joke: someone sticking it in her chair. The needle had apparently disappeared into her thigh, so the nuns had rushed her to the hospital. There, a pair of North Korean doctors hadn't been able to find it in a cursory examination, so they had decided to operate.

For two hours they dug about. Steel seeking steel. No joy. Eventually, everyone panicking now because she's Amin's daughter, they bundled her into an ambulance with her bleeding leg and brought her to Mulago. Paterson and I were on duty.

We looked at the girl, who was face down on the trolley in front of us. Moaning into her pillow, she was already togged up in green gear by the nurses, with the relevant area of her thigh exposed, where black knots of dried blood had gathered round the sutures the North Koreans had made.

"We better put her under a general," I said. "There'll be hell to pay if she says we butchered her."

Paterson looked at the girl, and then looked at me, and then clapped his hand to his forehead. "Nick, I've just realized, we don't need to go digging around. We just need to run the X ray over her. They'll stand out bright as the Queen of Sheba's earrings."

So that was what we did. No joy again. Well, nothing showed on the film.

Then we realized. "So there never was a needle?" I said, when my colleague explained.

"Of course there wasn't—Scotland one, North Korea nil." Paterson shouted this down the ward, making the auxiliaries look up in surprise.

He held her hand. "You just wanted some attention from your nasty old dad, didn't you, sweetie?"

I felt uncomfortable about him saying this. What if she reported it back to Amin? She started to sob once we'd rumbled her, and didn't stop until we put her in the ambulance to take her back to school.

I spent the next few days fretting about what Amin's reaction to it all might be. One morning, a week later, the call came, as I think both Paterson and I knew it would.

"You go," said Paterson. "I'll be bound to say the wrong thing."

I walked down the ward to take it. Wherever there was a window, the sun was sending sharp-edged, mote-filled beams of light into the dark spaces under the beds. I felt odd as I walked straight through them, as if I were a hurdler ignoring his fences. I picked up the phone.

"Hello, hello, it is Doctor Idi Amin here," said the disembodied voice. "I am very pleased with my fellow doctors at Mulago. I would like you and Doctor Paterson to join me here at Cape Town for lunch tomorrow. One o'clock sharp."

The line went dead before I had the chance to reply.

Everyone knew about "Cape Town." It was the name given to a new residence directly on the lakeshore that Amin had just acquired—bringing the total to four in Kampala-Entebbe alone: State House, Prince Charles Drive, Nakasero Lodge, and now Cape Town. There was an island nearby which he used for bombing displays. The target was supposed to represent the South

African city (thus the name) at the moment of its capitulation to the liberating forces of African nationalism, in the guise of Amin's bombers.

"I saw them do it once," Paterson said on the way. "They always miss. Look, I know what this'll be like. He'll try to get us to do down the English because we're both Scots. He did it at the Uganda Caledonian Society dinner last year. That chap from the Embassy, Weir, he was there, gladhanding Amin to everyone. Very strange. Anyway, it's important to get Amin on to something noncontroversial."

"Like what?" I said, as the emerald expanse of Lake Victoria swept by on our right-hand side.

"Seat belts is a good one," he said, "the importance of seat belts on Africa's roads."

So that was how Paterson and I came to be discussing car safety policy with Idi Amin one afternoon, in the garden at Cape Town. It was hot and still, with only the smell of the blossom from the bushes and trees stirring the air around us, as we sat beside a wrought-iron table laden with a large jug of iced tea and a plate of cucumber sandwiches. As the other two talked—Paterson explaining the needle episode, Amin the concerned, if occasionally guffawing father—I looked about.

It was an impressive place; at least, it made an impression, with its pink-flowered oleanders and creamy, sickly scented frangipanis, its shaved lawns where peacocks flashed their spotted trains and white-coated servants hovered. The house was only single-story, but expansive in the Moorish style, with serial white arches and terracotta tiles. I spotted the amazed face of a child up at one of the windows, looking out at us. One of his, I supposed, though I couldn't tell if it was a boy or a girl.

I also caught glimpses of three young women in diaphanous gowns, strolling airily down the many paths that weaved through the shrubbery. I didn't know who they were. Amin himself was wearing white trousers and a jade-colored shirt which, hanging over his belly like a tent, suited exactly the green seraglio he had created for himself there at Cape Town. Well, in fact he had appropriated the place from an expatriate businessman. I wondered idly who had lived here originally, before all this lakeshore area had been developed for villas . . .

A peacock howled—a horrible noise—and then Amin's booming voice brought me sharply round. He was now fulfilling Paterson's predictions to a tee.

"You see, it is very true. Scotland and Uganda, we have both suffered hundreds of years of English imperialism. That is why I am going to extend the Economic War to British interests in Uganda. What do you think?"

Paterson stuck to his plan. "Your Excellency, as a doctor I'd like to talk to you about motor accidents in Uganda. You could save many lives."

At that point, Amin put down the half-eaten cucumber sandwich he had in his hand, and drew himself up for the full public address. It was a mode with which I was becoming familiar.

"There will be no accidents in the new Uganda. It has all been planned before. In the new stage of the Economic War, as I dreamed it from the beginning, BAT, Brooke Bond, Securicor, British Metal Corporation and the Chillington Tool Company will all become the property of the Uganda Government. Every one hundred years God appoints one person to be very powerful in the world to follow what the Prophet directed. When I dream, these things are put into practice. I am determined to wage the Economic War to ultimate victory. Before, Ugandan companies were controlled by imperialists. Africa has tremendous natural resources which could be harnessed for the benefit of the people of Africa, making it a modern and industrialized continent. African countries must cooperate to achieve their common objectives."

He took a deep breath and smiled at us. "You see, we must provide African solutions to African problems. Africa has its own laws."

"But Mr. President," urged Paterson, "the most important law you can pass will be to make seat belts compulsory in Uganda. You will save many lives that way."

A furrow went across Amin's brow. "Why do you keep on seatbelts? Every time I am meeting you, Doctor Paterson, you are talking about seat belts. There are more pressing problems for Uganda than seat belts."

He got up from the table, knocking it with his knees as he

stood up, so that the iced tea shuddered in our glasses. "Now you must go. You have made me angry with this talk of seat belts."

He turned on his heel, for all the world like the sergeant-major he really was, stomped through his stolen paradise and climbed some steps. He gave us a scornful look from his vantage point, and then went through one of the white arches along the side of the house.

"Maybe," said Paterson, on the way back, "seat belts wasn't such a good idea after all."

Getting up the next morning, I heard Alec Douglas-Home on the World Service, condemning Amin's proposed nationalizations as "outrageous by any standard." I retied my dressing gown—it had fallen open, and I always feel exposed when that happens, even when there is no one else in the house—and poured boiling water over the coffee I was making. The grounds expanded, fattening in the wet sac of the filter. I watched as the water subsided, leaving a crumbling brown crater. Breathing in the vapours, I suddenly realized that my bare feet were cold on the kitchen floor: the sun was already out but the wood had retained the night's coolness. I had no slippers in Africa, only a pair of handmade leather sandals I'd bought in Mbarara and seldom wore. Now Sara, she had worn them once, when she stayed with me. A feeling of sadness came over me as I tipped in the milk. I stared down at the swirling cup. She hadn't written. She hadn't called.

20

Someone else did, though. One day the following week, Stone summoned me to a meeting at the British Embassy. He wouldn't say what it was about over the phone. I wondered whether they knew about my invitation to Marina. What did it matter, anyway? As I drove down Parliament Avenue, I remembered that I hadn't yet told her that Paterson couldn't make the weekend she'd specified.

Stone opened the door. He was wearing brown slacks and brown shoes, which merged into one another uncomfortably at the ankle, and a dark blue blazer. "Nicholas, we're very glad to see you. Now, you know Major Weir, and our Ambassador, Robert Perkins."

"Yes," I said, looking at them in turn as I walked into the center of the room, with Stone behind me. I'd forgotten how fat Perkins was, noticing as I greeted him how uncomfortably his suit jacket sat upon him, and how thick the lenses of his spectacles were.

Weir, his turkey neck flapping over the olive-green collar of his army uniform, was standing in a corner, next to the intersection of two windows. He was smoking a cigarette, cupping a cut-glass ashtray in his hand. He put it down and came over to shake my hand, gripping it harder than was necessary—and then returned to his station. Behind him, the windows were curtained with white cotton, receding on a brass bar into the corner. Light came in dimly through the fabric, turning his smoke into mysterious ribbons of gun-metal blue.

"Right," Stone said, going over to close the heavy teak door. It clicked shut with an expensive, slightly sinister sound.

I looked around as he walked back over. A small Union Jack was hanging from a pole. Next to it, on a little table, stood a lamp with a pink shade and also a small photograph of Amin shaking hands with the Queen.

"Please, sit down," Perkins said, taking a seat himself on the other side of the table.

I did so, and then looked at Amin in the photograph in front of me, his face as full of joy as I had ever seen it. His expression, as he looked at the Queen, was not unlike that of a child gazing into the eyes of its mother.

"It's him we'd like to talk to you about," Stone said, following my eyes.

"Oh," I said, my mind racing to comprehend it all as Stone sat down next to Perkins. Weir remained standing behind them.

There was a tense pause. Weir's smoke made me think of djinn, genies from the bottle. Or something more Scottish, but equally exotic. Pale Kenneth, maybe, the soothsayer they called the Brahan Seer.

"The thing is," Perkins began, "the President has got out of hand."

Weir caught my eye. I noticed that he had a large number of tiny scars about his doleful mouth and chin, and, remembering what Stone had told me, wondered whether they were from when he had been shot down.

"We're looking to you to help us on this one," said Stone. "You'll remember I asked you keep an eye on things for us in Mbarara."

In fact, I'd almost forgotten about our conversation that first time in Kampala, so much had happened since.

"Look, I'm sorry I didn't do anything," I said. "But I couldn't really see what help I could be. I'm just a doctor."

Perkins and Stone exchanged glances.

"Oh, that doesn't matter now," said the latter. "But there is something where your particular skills might be the right ingredient."

Stone's custard-colored hair had got longer since I'd last seen him, falling over his ears at the side and making him look slightly girlish. He was still balding on top, though, and retained that shininess of forehead. I'd thought it was sweat last time, but it was obviously just the way he was.

"We need your help, Doctor Garrigan," he murmured.

Perkins nodded his agreement so forcefully that the plump flesh on his face trembled. I thought about the swimming pool. His wife's sideways-falling cup of joy.

"The point is," Stone continued, "the killing has got to stop. You've seen the trucks, same as all of us."

And I had—I'd seen the canvas-covered lorries heading off into the bush, three or four soldiers sitting in the back, and the half-glimpsed, white-eyed faces of the prisoners in the darkness behind. All the expats had seen them, I believe, and up till now we'd swept it under the carpet, carried on as normal, refusing to speculate on things we thought beyond our ken. To be honest, it was the only way to live. You had to cultivate a certain detachment—and now they appeared to want me to break that.

Stone was waiting for a response. I didn't know what to say, what they expected me to say.

"You see," said Perkins, finally, leaning back in his chair, "with the arrival of those Asians in London, I'm getting a lot of pressure. Top-level pressure."

He took a handkerchief out of his pocket and, removing his glasses, blew his nose.

"What has this got to do with me?" I asked firmly, once Perkins had stopped trumpeting.

"Well," said Stone, "you are in, you find yourself in, a very sensitive position. A position, I may say, we were partly instrumental in achieving for you."

"What do you mean?" I asked, surprised.

"We'd been pushing your appointment with Amin and Wasswa for a few months now. And when the accident happened with the cow, it was, well, it was fortunate."

"In one way . . ." Perkins said, cryptically.

I looked above him at the white curtains, and then at Weir, and suddenly realized that the latter hadn't said anything during the whole encounter. His grey eyes stared back at me intensely, as if right through me.

Stone pushed the hair back from his buttery forehead. "I'll

come to the point. We'd like you to . . . treat him in a more forthright way."

I was shocked by the implications of what he had said. I lifted my gaze over their heads and stared at the brass bar above the window. And then at the flag.

Perkins said, "He's going to nationalize British firms and tea estates here, as you've probably heard. We were hoping you might be able to reason with him."

"And if not that," added Stone, "give him something that will *make* him reasonable. Calm him down. That he has to take every day."

Weir was frowning at me, I noticed, as if I had done something wrong. I felt like a pupil standing before a headmaster. Mr. Laidlaw, the one at Fossiemuir. He used to hit us on the palm of the hand with a heavy wooden ruler. I remembered the red stripe it left, like a piece of bacon across my palm.

"I'm not sure I can do that," I said, shaking my head. "Well, I suppose I could . . . but it's not exactly correct practice, is it?" I was momentarily flattered that they thought me capable of such intrigue.

"Practice isn't the point," Stone said, tapping his finger on the desk. "Your job as a doctor is to return him to normality."

"What," I said, coming to my senses, "do you mean by that? What does that mean here?"

As the smoke trickled down over his cravat of flesh, Weir smiled at me, his eyes glittering with some inner amusement.

Perkins said, "Make him like a president should be. Otherwise Britain is finished in Uganda. And that will go for you, too, probably."

I felt ill suddenly. The smell of Weir's cigarette was making me queasy and lightheaded. He still wasn't saying anything, but it was as if he was looming in front of me as the other two continued talking in pressing tones.

"How about tranquillizers?" Stone said brightly.

Weir's drooping face had dilated to twenty times its natural size, it somehow seemed. That was the image in my head as I listened to the cajoling voices of the other two—and when they asked me once more if I'd agree to dope Amin, I didn't know what to say. In the end I left it open.

21

Perkins was right about one thing. Amin really did crack down on the British in Uganda during the next few days. It was almost as if he knew exactly what was going on—as indeed he claimed to. "Be careful," as Popitlal had said to Merrit and me as he got into the Land Rover all those months ago. "It will be your turn soon. First wahindi, then muzungu."

Well, it was Merrit's turn and that of a host of other Brits throughout the country. But not mine. Amin was furious on account of the Douglas-Home speech, and he ordered a series of summary expulsions. Some of the British who stayed were forced to carry him in a litter through the streets as a sign of their devotion, others to kneel in front of him and take an oath of fealty. Perkins lodged a formal protest.

Amid all this, however, I somehow managed to escape attention. I wasn't expelled, I wasn't even called to carry the litter. Meanwhile, my duties as presidential physician remained agreeable. Every now and then I was called to treat another of Amin's children, but it was hardly the kind of work one could call stressful.

"You're obviously his lordship's favored son," Spiny Merrit said sourly, when he came to see me on his way to the airport.

He looked unwell, thin and drawn—Joyce had gone home a month earlier, I learned—and it was all he could do not to blame me for the fact that the clinic had been run into the ground. Since I left, he said, there had been army raids on the equipment and several of the auxiliaries had disappeared.

"I was the last white there in the end," he exclaimed. "Ivor went, the Cubans . . . If you had stayed, it would have helped."

I said nothing. I felt it was an unreasonable line for him to take, but also that nothing would have been gained from trying to defend myself at that stage.

When I talked to Marina about Merrit going—during our boat trip, several days later—she wasn't surprised.

"It's not just him, you know. Bob says we might have to go ourselves if it gets any worse."

I didn't mention the conversation at the Embassy. I presumed that she wouldn't have been told about it, and from the way she talked about her husband and other pieces of Embassy business it seemed I was right.

"Everything is rather strange at the moment," she said. "We've had a bit of a time with Archie Weir. They've called him back. Too cozy with Amin, Bob said. I always thought he was odd anyway. Too quiet. I don't trust people who are too quiet."

"He's gone back to London?"

"Scotland. He's been retired."

"Why?"

"They—" she paused for a second, as if wondering whether to take me into her confidence—"say he gave Amin an invasion plan for Tanzania, that he drew up the maps and munitions lists."

I thought of Weir's face, inflating above me, and the smell of cigarettes. "Why on earth would he do that?"

She shook her head. "I've no idea. None of us do. Look, I really ought not be talking about it. Bob would hit the roof . . ."

As for the trip itself, initially everything went well, once Marina got over her surprise about it being just me and her.

"I thought we were having a big party," she said. "I've brought far too much to eat."

I'd hired the boat, and a nine-foot rod, from a boy at one of the villages on the Entebbe peninsula. Marina had brought a cool-box, and a basket full of food. The driver from the Embassy helped her carry them down to the pier, which stretched out between two beds of reed.

While the boat boy fiddled with the engine, we watched the

villagers lowering large bundles of split wood into the water. These stained the surface with a milky, poisonous cloud. Fish began to flop up.

As the villagers were splashing about in the shallows, collecting up the dead fish, the boy managed to get the motor going. We pushed off with a flourish, leaving the boy and Marina's driver at the edge. The driver looked a bit of a thug, I remember thinking—watching us intently as he stood there, legs astride, arms folded.

We were soon chugging happily along. I moved us away from the reeds into deep water, the wake from the propeller rippling out behind. After the rains, the streams were in full spate and the lake was swollen. The current, usually imperceptible, was making its presence known with little shreds of foam on top of the small waves. Overhead, the sky was bright blue.

"Do you think it's poisonous to humans?" Marina asked, looking back at the bundles of branches.

"I suppose it might be if you drank some of the water there and then. We should have stayed and waited for the kill to end. Apparently they catch hundreds in one go."

She touched the big, triple-hooked spoon at the end of the rod, which was leant up on the bows.

"It seems a bit easier than doing it this way."

"But less sporting," I said.

I moved the handle of the motor a little to the right to take us out of the way of one of the many sandbanks and large, tangled expanses of water hyacinth on the surface of the lake. The boat moved to the left accordingly (it was only a single-cylinder motor but did the job perfectly), and we sped on.

"The hyacinths were introduced by Belgian colonists in Rwanda, Colin—at the hospital—said," I told her. "He was the one who was going to come with us."

"Why couldn't he?"

"Oh, I don't know. Something on. Anyway, the hyacinths . . . They stole up the Kagera River, and now they are colonizing like mad. A million plants a year from a single flower, according to Colin. The hydroelectric people are worried it will clog up the whole lake. It's the same with Nile perch, in fact. We—the British—brought them here in the fifties, and now they've eaten up all the smaller fish. So we'll be doing the world a favor if we catch one."

"Look," said Marina, pointing behind me. "Weaver birds."

I twisted around, making the boat sway slightly. Sure enough, on the far side of the sandbank—which was gliding away from us now, as if it had been shot out of the stern—were the little yellow baskets of woven straw in which they make their nests.

"They're beautiful," she said. "It's funny, when we went up to Murchison Falls, we saw fish traps, and they were just that shape. Made of cane. You'd think they'd seen the nests and got the shape from them."

Once we entered a clear patch of water, I cut the motor and reached over for the rod. "Let's give it a go here," I said.

Taking care not to snag her, I sent the spoon some twenty yards out over the water.

"That was a good one," she said.

"Not really," I said, reeling it in with little bursts. "I used to be able to do it better."

After a few more casts—and no bites—I suggested that she have a go. I stood behind her, holding her wrist as I showed her how. I felt the heat of our two bodies close together.

"Now reel it in," I said.

We stood there silently in the swaying boat, under those African clouds touched with pink and red, and the only sound was the clicking of the line coming in and the lapping of the water against the side.

"Maybe I'm doing it wrong," she said, as the glittering lure suddenly flipped up out of the water.

I caught hold of the dripping line. "You've got to be patient. If you want it too much, they won't take. It's the unwritten rule of fishing."

"I don't think it's me," she said, handing back the rod. "You do it."

I cast out again, really putting my back into it this time. The line shot out, half as much again. But this time, too, nothing bit.

"Let's move somewhere else," I said.

"There might be some near that island," she suggested.

She pointed over to the west, where the outline of some trees and rocks stood up against the horizontal plane of water. I fired up the motor again and set off in that direction. Marina was sat in the stern, the wind moving her hair as she looked out over the water. I wondered what she was thinking.

"What about crocodiles?" she said, turning round.

"I guess there must be some. But you're more likely to catch bilharzia."

"That's the snail thing, isn't it?" she said. "The one that lays its eggs in you."

"More or less," I said, grinning at her. "We could stop here."

"Castaways," she said, with an engaging giggle.

The island was partly swallowed up by reeds, but there were a few gaps. I nosed the boat through one, to discover a small sandy beach. I cut the engine and we slid towards it. Then, unsteady in the rocking boat, I took off my shoes and rolled up my trousers. Marina laughed at me as I hopped out to tie us up against a tree. As I did so, there was a clatter. We both jumped. A flight of ducks, just like British mallards, rose up out of the reed bed. We watched them fly up, six or seven, scattered at first and then falling into triangle formation. I splashed back towards the boat, my bare feet sinking into the sand.

"I thought the noise of them was a gunshot," she said. "What's that over there?"

Where she was pointing, the outline of a vessel was increasing in size as it came towards us. We suddenly heard music.

"Maybe it's Amin, maybe it's the Ugandan Navy," Marina ventured.

I laughed. It was certainly possible. I stood and watched with her, the water cool around my ankles. Eventually the vessel got near enough for us to see that it was a passenger steamer. Low in the water, it had the words MV *Lumumba* printed on the side. There were two decks, all filled with people, some of whom waved at us as they went by. On one of the decks you could just make out the black boxes of two loudspeakers. The music was strong at that point, you could feel the beat of it across the water. But I couldn't work out the tune, and neither could Marina.

"I can't place it," she said.

"Quick," I said. "You better get out."

I had noticed the wake of the steamer coming towards us. I

pulled the boat right up to the shore so that she could get out without getting wet. I held her hands as she trod carefully over the edge. We stood in the sand, waiting for the wake to hit. As it turned out, it was much smaller than I'd expected, just rocking the boat a little.

Then we got out the picnic stuff and laid it on a grassy patch. After we had eaten—the sandwiches made me think of Amin— we lay side by side on the grass, the hot sun licking the moisture off our brows. At one point an owl, its feathers brown and honey-colored, settled in the tree above, seemingly oblivious to us. It only stayed for a minute or two, turning its head from side to side like a lookout, before flying off again.

"It must have just been resting," she said. "On its way across the lake."

"The owl of Minerva rises after dusk."

"What?"

"Wisdom is hindsight. The Greeks thought owls were the servants of the goddess of wisdom."

"They thought everything was like that, didn't they?" she said, brushing some crumbs off her. "Everything full of magic, everything following a pattern."

I thought, Lord knows why, that it was a hint. That this was the moment to lean over her, sending a tremor, a wake through the two of us under that hot sun, to put my hand lightly on her stomach, delicate as where the lake's slatelike layers of green and silver met the sky. Instead, I kissed her tenderly on the arm, just below the sleeve of her summer dress.

She sat up with a start, her shoulder bashing into my nose, and scrambled to her feet.

"What are you up to?" she shouted. "What on earth do you think you're doing?"

She brushed frantically at where I had kissed her, as if there was an insect there.

"I . . ." I stuttered.

"Take me back now," she said. "Right now. I don't know what you thought, but it obviously wasn't what I was thinking. I'm married to the British Ambassador!"

She went towards the boat, getting her dress wet. Sheepishly,

I started putting the picnic things back in the basket, before joining her. She was looking out over the water again, her hands clutching her sopping dress, her face pinched like a pair of pliers.

The outboard played up when I tried it, and for a dreadful second I thought we were going to be stranded on the island. Castaways indeed. But on the fifth pull the cord snickered back into the housing at the right tension, and a burst of blue smoke came out.

"I'm sorry," I said quietly, after we'd gone a little way. "I got the wrong end of the stick."

"There is no stick," she said. "I don't know what you were thinking of. I don't know what idea you had of me, but I had a very different idea of you."

We passed the journey back to the mainland in silence, me looking ahead for the landmark of the village, her staring coldly at the fishing rod lying in the bottom of the boat. I felt vaguely guilty, but not as uncomfortable as perhaps I ought to have been.

Vagueness, a freedom and an evasion. Vagueness, it could be something to do with feathers, or waves. Trying to be exact as I write, the material resisting me, I think about what that word means on days like today—days when the wind moans in the loose pane of the bothy and the seagulls sound like children in the grey, leaping skies.

It is a winter wind, lost in April and venting its frustration on ships and trees. There's a myth—up here in the northwest—that the island was whipped up in a storm, that it disappeared and landed elsewhere, settling, as one of the tourist brochures rather poetically has it, "like a butterfly on the churning waters."

The poor rowan outside is back in leaf, but it is still bitterly cold. There is some honeysuckle growing round the porch which I am amazed has survived the storms. I myself have been keeping indoors, alternating coffee with whisky late into the nights, breaking off every now and then to watch television. They've just shown a program in which a princess is executed in Saudi Arabia. I imagine Amin, with a big scimitar.

There was a phrase in the program—"malignant destiny"—and I found myself thinking it applied to me, to my time in

Uganda and what happened to me there. Then I knew it was the old thing again, that special vision of myself that took me there in the first place. My problem is that because the world doesn't deliver what I seek, I don't admit facts. It's no way to be going on.

It is terrible the way you think time is going to change you. The way you think of some future time when things will be all right. And all that happens is that you drop back into the previous stream of time and it closes over your head.

The kettle whistles on the stove. Uncle Eamonn's old-fashioned kettle. I should get an electric one, but I've grown attached to it.

22

It was about a week after the boat trip that Wasswa called me at the hospital. Choosing a reverse, vaccinatory way of trying to cheer myself up after the Marina disaster, I'd taken a long lunch to visit the Kasubi tombs. These were the long, dark grass huts in which the Kabakas, the Baganda kings, were laid to rest. An official called "Keeper of the King's Umbilical Cord" kept watch there. According to legend, the cord was the living king's twin and any harm done to it would affect him physically. Like voodoo, or sympathetic medicine. But at that time, as I have explained, the king was dead, and his young son living in exile in England. The new king, I suppose, if you can be king without a land.

Wasswa was frantic when he got hold of me, having tried to reach me for the last two hours. "Come quick," he said, "the President is sick. He is at Nakasero."

It was stormy that day, too, and busy. Though it was about three o'clock, there were still patients huddled in little groups outside the hospital. Several of them tugged at my clothes as I ran to the van with my emergency bag in my hand.

As I drove, I passed four women walking along the tarmac, shawls pulled over their heads as a pointless protection from the heavy rain. Suddenly there was a screech as a VW Combi overtook me and skidded to a halt in front of the four women. I passed the Combi in turn, just in time to catch a glimpse of the sliding door opening at the side and one of the women being pulled in. It was like something from a Punch and Judy show, but very disturbing all the same. I didn't see it properly, as it was raining so hard, and in trying to look in the mirror I nearly hit something—there were rocks and mud in the ruined road.

So I was pretty shaken up by the time I reached Nakasero. One of the guards led me over to the door of the Lodge, and I rushed up the steps to where Wasswa was waiting.

"He is inside, he has a pain in his stomach," he said.

Wasswa led me upstairs, through a mazelike series of rooms. We finally came to the master bedroom, which contained a large four-poster bed. Through the pink gauze of the bed curtain, I could see a hunchback mound of sheets and quilts, suffused with a mildly genital light. I don't know why I wrote that—*did I just mean gentle?*—but it seems right somehow, because that was the color, and it was mild. And all around hung an animal smell: fox's earth, badger's sett—something, in any case, rank and bolt-holeish.

On one side of the bed was a vast wall of books: smart, red-hide bindings, and the letters in gold—*Proceedings of the Law Society of Uganda,* followed by a roman numeral. On the other side was an escritoire-type writing desk, and a white vanity unit with mirrored wardrobes to the left and right. Scattered on the floor were clothes, records (some out of their sleeves) and a couple of men's magazines. A television was flickering grey and useless in a corner. Resting against the television cabinet was a baseball bat, with a leather catching-mitt lying on the carpet next to it. I noticed some pills scattered on the bedside table, next to a vial with the screw cap off, and also several empty bottles of Simba.

"Your Excellency?" Wasswa said nervously.

The pile of sheets moved. Wasswa pulled back the gauze, and suddenly the linen flew off the bed, to reveal Amin lying on his front in a pair of khaki underpants, his torso twisted round and one hand emerging from under the pillow, holding a very big, very silver revolver.

"Oh, no, sir, sir, it is me, Wasswa," shouted the Minister, jumping back into me.

"Eh?" Amin grunted.

Still pointing the gun, he turned over on to his back and squinted at us over the mound of his heaving belly. From the slow, gravid way the mattress was swaying about, and Amin with it, I could see that it was a water bed.

"Go away," he shouted. "I do not want you!"

"I'm sorry," I said. "I understood . . ."

"Doctor—not you," Amin said. "I mean my Minister. This is private thing, Minister."

He put the gun into a cowboy-style holster hanging over the back of an antique chair next to the bed. Wasswa went off, with a crestfallen look, and I began my examination. Finally, after several months in the post, I got to do my job.

"I am very ill. I have a pain here," moaned Amin, touching his right side.

I leaned over him and gently palpated the area, just to the right of where the dark curls climbed to his high belly button. There was a slight swelling. He moaned again—it was a surprisingly high-pitched noise, not unlike that a cat gives when it looks up to a passing stranger and enquires about its supper.

"Tell me what you have been eating," I said, quietly relishing the moment.

"Do not be stern with me, doctor. I have had matooke, two pieces of goat and also ice cream one tub," he said. "That is all."

"What about those?" I said, pointing at the tablets on the bed-side table.

He didn't reply. I stared at the mass of flesh below me: ankles, shins, thighs—the hooded eye of his penis, which had fallen to one side like a weary fish, was peeping through the gap in his Y-fronts—abdomen, chest, shoulders, head. There was something hypnotic about the mauve, sausage-meat slices of Amin's nipples. Nestling in their bed of black hair, they were almost all teat, no aureola. These stubby pistils had come smartly to attention as my hands had moved over them during the examination. It roused an intrigued disgust in me: never let it be said that doctors have an entirely neutral attitude to the bodies of their patients.

"Well?" I said, after a moment had passed.

He twisted his head to look. "Ah. That is just my medicine. It is aspirin."

"Your Excellency," I said. "You mustn't take aspirin with beer. It is bad for the stomach."

"It is my stomach that pains me, not drunkenness."

I picked up a Simba bottle and waved it reprovingly in front of his face.

"This is why. Or maybe too much food."

He sat up, resting his great weight on one of his elbows.

"No! It was paining me before."

"That may be," I said, "but these won't have helped. Now you lie back down."

I reached over and palpated his abdomen again. There was a hard, but not totally resistant lump between the lower ribcage and the top of the pelvis. About the size of a hen's egg. I could tell at once what was wrong.

"I think I know what your problem is. Now, I'm going to press quite hard. Try to lie still."

I pressed on the lump, pushing it more downwards than inwards.

"It hurts, doctor," said Amin, swaying on the bed. "I think maybe I need tablets."

"That's exactly what you don't need," I said, feeling secure in my command of the situation.

I tried again, but nothing happened.

"It's no good, Your Excellency, I'm going to have to employ more drastic measures to alleviate you."

"Anything is good that works," he replied. "That I am feeling full of health is the thing. I do not worry how you will achieve this."

"I need something long and hard," I said. "It isn't exactly standard procedure, but I'm going to have to burp you."

"What is that?" Amin said. "What?"

"Like with babies," I said.

"Babies?"

"Never mind."

My eyes wandered greedily round the room. I was intending to attempt an unorthodox combination of the Heimlich, antichoking maneuver and the classic baby burp. But Amin's abdomen was just too vast for me to do it without some kind of mechanical aid.

I looked about. Among the clothes strewn on the floor was a safari jacket with great wads of shilling notes bulging in the pockets, and a pair of brown boots. On one wall was a tall, badly painted portrait of Patrice Lumumba, the Congo patriot. I vaguely recalled that Amin had named one of his sons after him. I noticed a clip of high-velocity ammunition, and then I settled on the thing that would suit my purpose. Of course—the baseball bat. I walked over and picked it up.

"What you do?" he cried, scrabbling for the gun hanging on the chair.

"It's all right," I said, holding the bat, cradling it. "Keep calm. It is the pain that is making you nervous."

He looked at me for a moment, and then put the gun down on the bed. It looked strange there, surrounded by the softness of the linen.

"Yes, it is true. You are right. You are right because you are a doctor."

"I am going to use this," I said, soothingly, "to expel the pain from you. It may hurt a little, but you will feel much better."

"I will?"

"You will."

He looked up at me, a trusting expression in his eyes.

"Now," I said, pulling over the antique chair with the holster on it, "if you could get yourself onto this."

I lifted off the heavy holster and helped him swing his bare legs over. The hair on them had been flattened by the sheets, making the tight curls into hieroglyphs on his skin. His feet were calloused by years of marching in hard army boots, but they looked monumental, too. As if they could be removed from those delicate ankles and marveled at on a museum pedestal.

"What you do?" he said, impatiently. "No doctor has done this before. Not the Cubans, not the Russians, and not the Koreans either. What is this trick known to Scottish doctors only?"

"If you could get yourself on to the chair," I said. "Then we can get it over."

He moved his great bulk awkwardly, like someone getting from a car into a wheelchair, finally plumping his body down on the leather seat. The flesh of his thighs, straining against the khaki underpants, spilled out over the sides. He put his face in his hands, his elbows resting on his knees.

"What you do?" The repeated question came out distorted this time, the sound of it twisted by his splayed thumbs over his mouth.

"Nothing. Just sit still."

I walked behind him with the baseball bat and passed it over his head.

"What strange rite is this that you perform?" Amin asked nervously, from below me.

"I am going to press now on your belly. It will be better soon."

"You speak truth?"

"I speak truth. Lean back."

Squatting behind him, with the lattice-work of the chairback tight against my face, I fumbled the wood of the bat under the overhang of his stomach, moving it about to get it into the right place. I stood up, hunched over him.

"Now, lean forward."

He did as he was told—and then I pulled on the bat at both ends, gently at first and then applying more pressure. I could feel the rubbery pad of his ear next to mine. What auricular secrets passed between us in that moment, I wonder now, what primeval tympanic drumbeats?

"Doctor Nicholas!" Amin cried. "You hurt me!"

I pulled again, and then one more time.

"Stand up!" I ordered.

He staggered to his feet, the moist skin of his thighs making a ripping sound, like sticky tape, as it peeled away from the leather seat.

"What was all that?" he said, staring at me as if I were a madman. "Why do you press me?" He rubbed his swollen stomach.

"It's not finished," I said. "Trust me. Now you must touch your toes."

He did it. President for Life Field Marshal Al Hadj Doctor Idi Amin Dada, VC, DSO, Lord of All the Beasts of the Earth and Fishes of the Sea, King of the Scots and Conqueror of the British Empire in Africa in General and Uganda in Particular touched his toes. And then let out a flatus of a resonance appropriate to his size.

It was not, I thought as I pranced away, as long as that released by the woman with the sigmoid problem in the hospital, but it had more attack. And the smell, the smell was much worse.

Amin looked at me, and picked up the baseball bat. He approached me and for a moment I thought he was going to clout me with it. After all, I had made him suffer an indignity. But then he burst out laughing, banging his leg with the bat. It was a deep laugh, deep and dark, the laugh of one who saw comedy in the dead light and stardust of the galaxies. A universal laugh.

"You!" he said, gripping my arm—I could feel his thumb where it pressed against the bone. "I thought you had gone crazy. With this."

He held up the bat, and then flung it on to the bed, where it clunked against the revolver.

"You are a very clever man. You saw my problem. Now we must celebrate my cure. We must go to a bar."

"I would like to give you a proper medical," I said, "and then I ought to get back to the hospital."

"Oh, that is not a problem. Tell them I have given you permission. And you can do the medical another time. We will go to the Satellite and drink waragi. But first I must wash, and put on my smartest clothes."

"But I must . . ."

"There is no but, there is no must. I am above those things in Uganda," he said, striding across towards the bathroom.

I sat on the edge of the bed, suddenly lowered by the whole experience. I stared at the flecks of grey snow on the dud TV screen and thought about winter in Fossiemuir. How one December morning, at the age of six or seven, I'd wanted my father to take me sledding and he wouldn't and I'd run in a tantrum out into the garden, and round and round the house like a whirling dervish—until suddenly the large figure of my mother was in front of me and I'd been gathered up into her voluminous arms. That afternoon, looking down from my bedroom window, I had watched the tracks I'd made disappear under fresh snow.

In the near silence of another bedroom, I became aware of the scrape of a razor from next door and, intermittently, the frying sound of running water. A moment later, Amin poked his head round the door, his face half-covered in shaving cream—a clown, a minstrel.

"Do not be sad, doctor. Are you tired? You must be tired as you have done good work."

"I'm fine," I said, "I'm fine."

"You will be rewarded for your professional behavior. But first, waragi!"

Waragi was Ugandan gin, and in the bar Amin called for five bottles of it. Everyone crowded round, fawning at him and readily taking up his offer of free drinks. I had only a few sips. The fiery stuff made me gag, and the music made my head spin. At one point Amin got up and played the accordion with the band. Then he danced, and made me dance too.

When I said it was time for me to go home, Amin frowned.

"It is not time. I say when time is. But since you have helped me, I will agree. But you must drive me as I have had too much of this spirit. I will sleep at State House tonight."

So that was how I came to be driving Idi Amin home. He had dismissed all his bodyguards and retainers when we had gone to the bar: it was like he wanted, that night, to make me his special friend.

He had the silver revolver in his lap as I drove us through the dark along the potholed road to Entebbe.

"I am sorry I was fearful when you cured me," he said. "You see, I thought that you, too, wanted to kill me. So many people want to kill me."

"I'm sure you have enough protection," I said, nervously.

"Yes, it is true. Because the god is on my side. I dreamed it, but it was impossible. They couldn't do it. Because I know, I dreamed that. I know that exactly: when, how and what time I am going to die. This I know. And which year and which date. All this I know already and it is a secret . . . I have said this clear . . . And I know exactly that, who will be making something against me. Very soon, I can notice him straight and he can get punishment from god straight. Because I work only according to the god's instructions."

Once we reached Entebbe (the guards peering into the van were shocked to see that it was Amin who was my passenger), he made me come over to his quarters and talk to him some more.

We drank more waragi, just the two of us sitting at the long mahogany table in the banqueting room at State House, with the loathsome masks and the paintings of the colonial governor-generals looking down on us. I looked up at them, at the white-polled one that parroted my father especially, and Idi Amin's voice echoed in the big, gloomy space.

"It is good of you to speak with me," he said. "I cannot tell you how tired I am getting, from all this work. Leading Uganda. It is very difficult."

"You should delegate more," I said. "Get other people to do things."

"You do not understand. I cannot trust. There are many who are my friends today, who would betray me tomorrow. The one that is famous in the sea is the shark, but there are many others."

"What do you mean?"

"I have to be on my guard always."

I sipped my waragi thoughtfully. "Have you ever thought of retiring?"

He gave me a strange, benevolent smile, his cheeks gleaming under the dim light of the lamps suspended over the table.

"I will be in charge here for the full distance. As a man of destiny, I cannot go to a shamba and raise chickens. Yes, I must run for the distance. And, as you know, Doctor Nicholas, there is no distance that has no end. That is my tragedy."

"It's not necessarily a tragedy," I said.

"No," he said, sharply. "I know full well that it is. I know that I know I must keep on for all miles, until the god says."

"Who . . . is this god?" Though slightly frightened, and very wary, I was enjoying this rare moment of intimacy.

"It is the Lord Jesus Christ, and it is Allah, and it is the colobus monkey whose flowing white fur makes him look like a priest. And it is the River Nile and the mopani bee who drinks the sweat from your neck. It is many things."

He pointed up at the colonial paintings. "Yes, even it is them."

"You know what you were saying," I said, probingly, "about knowing when you would die?"

"Yes," he said.

"Well, do you believe in an afterlife?"

Amin was thoughtful for a moment. I thought about Stone and his plans. At that moment, there was no way that I felt I could do anything like put this man on tranquilizers. Flushed with drink, I even felt a sneaking sense of affection towards him.

"I do not know," he said, in answer to my question. "I have my sons, of course. It is maybe like this: when the lips die, the saliva is scattered."

He looked down at the tiled floor. "My own father . . . I did not know him. All I know is that he was soldier in the King's African Rifles. He could have been the king himself, for all I know—yes, except that I am the wrong color. Or the governor, at the least."

I laughed. "Do you think it was better before, when the governors were in charge?"

"No," he said, shaking his head slowly. "An ivory tooth is not a cure for a gap. Although it is true that I learnt many things from the British. Your empire was a shameful conquest, but a good teacher."

He poured some more waragi into his tumbler. "And yet some days, I am afraid that the same things I learned from them will come to fetch me into a trap, and that is when I am afraid for my position as the savior of Africa. Because your countrymen, doctor—well, the English anyway—they are not good to me anymore. And this makes me sad. And angry."

"Things have changed," I said.

"Yes," he said. "But maybe it was always so. I see all this rottenness around me, all these people—here in Uganda and in all the world—pulling the skin to their own side when they stretch the skin for the drum, and I do not know what to do is best."

"You . . . could stop the corruption," I said, edgily, "and stop the army killing people."

He sighed. "Doctor Nicholas, in Swahili we say, la kuvunda halian ubani. There is no incense for something rotting. And that is the condition of the world. This I know."

23

A lot else happened during that time (in all I was in Kampala for six years, having been in Mbarara for two), and I don't blame myself for all of it. Life went on, of course, as it usually does. I went to work. I ate. I slept. I got older. Every now and then I thought of Stone's instructions—flirted with the idea, and then dismissed it.

Naturally, this happened most of all when I was called upon to treat Amin. He himself had nothing serious wrong with him during all my tenure: overweight, certainly, and a touch of gout, but otherwise reasonably healthy, physically speaking at least.

This I discovered when I was finally able to give him a proper medical. I'm recalling my notes of that episode from memory, and have expanded them, since doctor's shorthand would be incomprehensible to the lay reader.

On examination:

Man in late forties, early fifties [it depended on the uncertain birthdate, of course, and I don't think he knew the exact date himself], looks fit and well. Height: 6 ft 6. Weight: 20 stone.

No jaundice, no anemia, no cyanosis, no clubbing, no lymphadenopathy.

Blood pressure: 130/90. Temp: 37.4C. Pulse: 84 bpm, and normal. Jugular-venous pressure, not raised. Heart sounds normal, no murmurs.

Abdominal: soft, obese, tender in the right subcostal region [the bloat problem again]. Bowel sounds, normal. Cranial nerves, II–XII intact. Pupil reactions, normal. Power, tone, coordination, sensation normal. Reflexes right and left, present and normal. All +.

This achieved with the usual business of auscultation (listening to heart and lungs with the stethoscope), opthalmoscope, reflex hammer and torch. I remember the sound of his heart, its reassuring *lub-dub, lub-dub, lub-dub*. I remember saying to him—it seems unbelievable now—"Follow my finger with your eye, Your Excellency . . ." I do wonder, in fact, how many other people have actually looked into Idi Amin's eye: less, if I may gainsay the poets, a question of the window being open to his debatable soul than of the red cup of the retina, glazed with blood vessels, and the end of the optic nerve like a drop of milk in the center.

In any case, nothing critical was wrong. I did have to drain an abcess in his throat at one point. He was quite anxious about that, as it was affecting his voice, making it higher.

"Thank God you have done it, doctor," he said, as I dabbed at the incision. "I might have died."

"I don't think it was quite that serious," I said, chuckling.

"Mzaha, mzaha, hutumbuka usaha," he countered. "Joke, joke, discharges pus."

"What do you mean?" I asked.

"Even a little scratch can be dangerous."

All those rumors about brain-lobe epilepsy or tertiary syphilis, they simply weren't true. The mental problems were there, yes— a type of impulsive grandiose delusion that I now see might have been common to dictators—but nothing clearly organic. Once, I never quite understood why, I had to pretend he was in a coma at Mulago.

I carried on with my duties there and, even though Amin later offered me a house of my own on the lakeshore, I remained in the bungalow at State House. I had grown used to it and didn't fancy a change. It was nonetheless curious that I had been billeted there in the first place, since he was hardly ever in residence: he preferred the Lodge at Nakasero.

Every now and then I would be invited there for tea, or to

attend some function. Idi would invariably hold forth. I remember him doing so when Heath resigned as British Prime Minister in 1974. "I told you so!" he cried. "How sad it is that Heath is now so very poor, having been relegated from Prime Minister to the obscure rank of bandmaster. I understand he is one of the best bandmasters in the United Kingdom."

A month or so later, President Nixon released the transcripts of the Watergate tapes. Wanting my opinion, Idi sent me over a copy of the telegram he planned to send to his beleaguered counterpart, in the context of the US having recently withdrawn aid to Uganda:

> My dear brother, it is quite true that you have enough problems on your plate and it is surprising that you have the zeal to add fresh ones. At the moment as you are uncomfortably sandwiched in that unfortunate affair, I ask Almighty God to help you solve your problems. I wish you a speedy recovery from this business. I am sure that any weak leader would have resigned or even committed suicide after being subject to so much harassment because of this Watergate affair. I take this opportunity to once again wish you a quick recovery and join your well-wishers in praying for your future success. P.S. I know that you have been very sick and had to be taken to hospital and that people were very worried you were going to die and might not give the answers on the case of Watergate for the whole world to know. Allow me to extend an invitation to you to come and rest in Uganda, so that you will be able to answer all questions with a healthy body and a clear conscience. You are not damned. You needn't be doubtful about salvation.

"I think it might be taken in the wrong way," I said, when he called me on the phone to ask what I thought.

"But that fellow Nixon," he said. "Even prostitutes on the street are more respected than him. I don't care what you say, I will send it."

And he did. By such encounters, in those early years, I thought I got to know him. But it was not so. He was too full of contradictions, just as my head is too full of images of him, even now. Him sitting in an armchair in his bright blue air force uniform a few weeks later, legs crossed, a stick across his knee. Big braid on his shoulders, the customary array of medals across his chest. One was a Victoria Cross made up by Spink's, the London jewelers, at Amin's request—except that they would only emblazon it "Victorious Cross."

Him raising his glass at yet another banquet, or walking through the streets surrounded by his retinue.

Him reaching up to pat a big bronze statue of himself on the shoulder.

Him in an English three-piece suit, addressing the business community.

Him wearing an academic gown and mortar board during a speech in his capacity as head of the Department of Political Science at the university.

Him (again) by the poolside, lighting a cigarette for a female companion. Him inspecting a fleet of black Mercedes-Benz.

Him with Kenyatta, with Yasser Arafat, with Mobutu.

Him dancing a warrior dance, jabbing with a spear.

Him showing visiting dignitaries the squadron of MiG fighters at Entebbe.

Him with Castro, with Kurt Waldheim, with Tito.

Him with his family: the sons, little Maclaren, Mckenzie, Campbell, Mwanga or Moses dressed up in camouflage like their father; the wives as they came on the scene, fell out of favor.

Him (again) with Mwanga, pretending to shoot a toy gun at the boy. The boy holding a gun too, but pointing it at the floor, uncertain what to do.

Him frowning, laughing, holding his clenched fist up to his mouth.

Him with a baby.

Him driving a jeep through jubilant crowds.

Him alone.

Him with me.

The day they tried to kill him, I wasn't with him. I was at the hospital. He turned up there, roared up there, rather, in an open jeep, dumped a man in casualty—the driver—and shot off again. The man seemed normal at first but on examination we realized that there was an inch-long, needlelike shrapnel splinter in his temple. There was nothing we could do.

I heard later what happened from one of the Ugandan doctors, whose wife had been among the crowds.

Amin had been due for some time to attend a police review at Nsambya Police Recreation Ground, where there was a football pitch. He obviously knew someone was out to get him, as the word was that he had already changed the site of the review four times. Crowds thronged the worn-out grass of the pitch.

He sat in the covered stand. The parade included march-pasts and a martial-arts demonstration by a South Korean–trained unit. During the display, Amin took out a rifle with a bayonet. He ordered a constable to defend himself against his mock lunge.

The bayonet horseplay lightened the mood, and afterwards Amin and the various ministers and army officers went off to a reception nearby. After three-quarters of an hour of drinks and canapés, he set off for Kampala.

He took the wheel of the jeep himself, telling the driver to move over. The jeep swung towards the gates of the sports ground, where more crowds were in place to cheer him. The dignitaries, as usual, waited for him to go first.

As Amin turned out on to the main road, there were two explosions, in quick succession. Smoke billowed and there was a faint rain of debris. Then two shots rang out. The ministers, my informant told me, judiciously fled through the same gate as Amin, lest they be accused of being involved in the attempt. The crowd ran away less thoughtfully, screaming. Already the police were pulling imagined perpetrators from among them.

The first grenade, it emerged, had exploded where Amin would have been sitting, had he not taken the driver's seat. As my X ray later showed, it forced the splinter into the driver's brain. The moment after the blasts was pandemonium. Amin, opening his briefcase, pulled out a grenade himself, ready to throw it if there was another attack.

That night, I remember, troops flooded Kampala. Civilians were haphazardly killed and beaten as punishment for the attempt. No one knew who were the culprits, but the reprisals took place nonetheless.

"Three grenades hit me," Amin told me later. "They killed thirty-nine people. My driver was killed and so was my escort—it was only I that escaped. I was saved by God's wish. I will not die until the date God has ordained. I know it, but I don't tell you to stop your suspense."

24

Idi got married again. Wife number four. I attended the ceremony at the cathedral. It was packed, not to mention the thousands cheering themselves hoarse outside. It had been announced
that he was also having a Moslem ceremony—"I love all the religions in Uganda," he'd said on the radio—but I wasn't invited to
that. The Christian one was a strange affair, not least because the
ushers were high-ranking army officers, except for Wasswa, who
was best man. I took up my seat at the back on the right, along
with the other expatriates—among whom, I was embarrassed to
see, were Marina and her husband, and Stone as well. Nearer to
me, half-obscured by a pillar, was Swanepoel.

The cathedral was very big and grand, and I concentrated on
its high pink-and-blue-painted ceiling while the organ was playing
before the bride came in. I tried not to look at Marina. It was now
over a year since my gaffe, but I still smarted—though it wasn't
much, really. I hadn't done anything that offensive. My eyes fell
instead on Idi, his back taking up a sizable portion of the first pew.
His jacket was dark green. Sea green. He kept looking round, with
a puzzled expression one saw often on his face, manifesting itself
in frowns and darting glances. The soldier sizing up danger, I supposed. The strange thing was he smiled when he did this. As if two
parts of his brain were working totally independently.

The music stopped, and we stood up. My eye swiveled inevitably towards Marina. I couldn't help it. She was wearing a plain
white blouse buttoned up at the neck and, so far as I could see

below the pew, a green skirt with flounces. Not the same color as Idi's, more like parsley. She was also wearing a hat, under the brim of which—she didn't look at me.

The procession started and the ushers, two by two with the scarlet stripes on their military trousers crisscrossing like scissors, walked up the aisle. A few paces behind walked the bride on her father's arm, her long heavy train and the bridesmaids behind her. The father's suit didn't fit. He looked like a Scottish farmer on market day. At the top of the aisle, the bridesmaids and groomsmen peeled off to left and right respectively. The new wife's name was Medina. Almost as tall as Amin, she was a dancer with the Heartbeat of Africa troupe, which was used for entertaining visiting diplomats and at official state functions.

"Please sit down," said the Archbishop of Uganda, Rwanda, Burundi and Boga-Zaïre. A tiny man, in spite of his title, he was dwarfed by the altar. His head, with its greying temples and kind creases round the eyes, had the statesmanlike look that many senior churchmen seem to acquire.

"Dearly beloved," he intoned, "we are assembled here in the presence of God to join this man and this woman in holy matrimony. Marriage was instituted by God in the Garden of Eden when He saw that it was not good for man to be alone. It thus is an institution of God—ordained in the time of man's innocence, before he had sinned against the Maker, and been banished from the Garden. It was given in wisdom and kindness, to repress irregular affection, and to support social order. Older than laws of merely human origin, it lies at the basis of all human legislation and civil government, and the peace and well-being of the community and country."

A slight frisson went through the congregation. Idi's shoulders, I could see even from that distance, had tensed up.

"A relationship consecrated in this manner should not be formed lightly, but advisedly, in fear of God, and for the purposes for which He, its Divine Author, has ordained the blessed state of matrimony."

The muscles in my back were already beginning to ache from the hard pew. I wanted to stand up and stretch. The strange idea came into my head that my body and Idi's were connected. Like the King's umbilical cord.

"Let me thereby remind you, Idi and Medina, that your home will never be what God intends for it to be if you leave Him out of your relationship. As you are obedient to the Word of God, and allow God to control your relationship, your home will be the place of joy and testimony to the world that God intends. You must recognize that this covenant you are about to make is more than a legal contract . . ."

I looked over at Marina again. She was looking in my direction, I could see the lashes of her eyes. But she wasn't looking at me. She was staring at the pillar.

". . . it is a bond of union established in heaven . . ."

Those pillars. Scrollwork like a piece of sweet rock. All that Catholic stuff. I couldn't be doing with it, not with my background. The whole place smelt overripe: God in the plaster, God in the wood of the pews. The incarnation of mortar. Hopeless. Or too hope-full, rather. As if one drop, half a drop even, of that blood-red wine would redeem any number of sins.

". . . and not to be broken on earth."

The first lesson was taken from Romans. Wasswa read it, his voice reedy and shaking. I swear I could see a hard gleam in the Archbishop's eye as the words came out.

Everyone must submit himself to the governing authorities, for there is no authority except that which God has established. The authorities that exist have been established by God. Consequently, he who rebels against the authority is rebelling against what God has instituted, and those who do so will bring judgment upon themselves. For rulers hold no terror for those who do right, but for those who do wrong. Do you want to be free from fear of the one in authority? Then do what is right and he will commend you . . .

Who is he? I thought, madly, as Swanepoel's beard came into my field of vision, Swanepoel winking at me like a drunken sailor.

Then the psalm, and another lesson, and the Gospel.

When everyone said "Amen," it sounded like "Amin," and when the Archbishop proclaimed, "You stand before us as individuals redeemed by Christ," I thought of those drops of blood and of my dead father.

"We are free," he used to say, "and we are not free. That is the mystery. It is mystical but it is also scientific. Biology, society, God knows what else (and He does), are pushing us in this or that direction all the time. And yet we can choose, also. It's like that new motorway. You're on it, like it or not, but you can come off it at a junction—should God will there to be one where you want one—and take another road. But it's still His road. Do you understand, Nicholas? Do you understand that when people say there is no mystery in the Presbyterian church, they've totally misunderstood? There is a mystery and it's a scientific mystery an' all."

This was his standard line, God as civil engineer, and it provoked much mirth amongst the congregation of Fossiemuir.

As if in divine confirmation of my train of thought, when Idi stood up for the vows, he was wearing a kilt. The sea-green jacket was just part of the Highland getup, spats and sporran, skean-dhu and brogans . . . the full, romantic, nonsensical lot, the same as I had seen in the mountains.

And then the questions.

"Are you prepared to love Medina as Christ loved the Church, are you willing to love . . ."

I looked round the walls, at the tableaus of the Stations of the Cross, representing the successive stages of Christ's Passion. The folds of cloth and angular faces jutted out in plaster relief. They were painted in bold, relentless colors: one could not doubt (and yet one could) that this was blood, that this was wood, that this spear would pierce flesh, this sponge drip vinegar that really stung. To me, they did seem a little theatrical, but they were moving, for all that. My father wouldn't have agreed, however.

"In the full knowledge that this love is not to be diminished by difficult circumstances, and it is only to be dissolved by death, will you now speak your marriage vows?"

"I have prayed you as my wife," Amin said, "and the god has truly answered my prayers. I have talked to him straight—"

The Archbishop interrupted "—you praise and thank Him for His faithfulness for I have delighted in knowing you and loving you . . ."

"Yes, that is the correct, for I have delighted in knowing you and loving you . . ."

"If these vows be discharged, they will add to the happiness of life, lightening by dividing its inevitable sorrows and heightening by doubling all its blessedness. But if these obligations be neglected and violated, you cannot escape the keenest misery as well as the darkest guilt. What token do you give of the vows you have made?"

"This ring."

"The ring that symbolizes the never-ending love you have pledged: for that love—a perfect circle as far as the eye can see, and for that love also—gold, as the emblem of that which is least tarnished and most enduring. Through these rings, let the light of Christ shine upon you for all of your life together, delighting in the society of each other as you conduct yourselves by His law. For it is also true that rings have, in history, been the traditional sign of authority, used to seal documents and sign proclamations. Before you exchange rings, will you therefore accept the authority of Christ in your life?"

I will. I willed Amin to say "I will" but I didn't hear it. Just a muddled and hardly audible—

"I accept the authority of the god . . ."

Then the Prayers of the People and—crowning moment—the Blessing of the Union.

Idi rocked back and forth on the balls of his feet. No words came out.

"I do, I do." The Archbishop muttered insistently.

"I do." Finally it came.

I looked for Marina, but all I could see was the back of Swanepoel's head.

"Medina, your husband is going to look to you for encouragement, cheerfulness and confidence . . ."

"I do."

Quietly, like the brush of a hand.

". . . I charge you both before God, the Searcher of all hearts, and before the Lord Jesus Christ, who shed His precious blood to redeem you from sin, that if either of you know any impediment why you may not be lawfully joined together in marriage, you do now confess it. For be well assured that if any persons are joined together otherwise than as God's word allows, their union is not blessed by Him. Equally, if any person present here today . . ."

I smiled to myself. It wasn't likely.

"Ministering in the name of the Lord Jesus, I now pronounce you husband and wife. May Christ be the head of your home. May He be the unseen guest at every meal, the listener to every conversation. May Christ's love rule your hearts and lives. You may now kiss the bride . . ."

Idi craned over her, like a boy biting an apple.

Then the Archbishop blessed them. Once that was over, the rest of the Mass felt like an anticlimax. I stole the odd glance at Marina during the closing hymn. Our eyes met for one moment but she turned away, and as I followed the crowd out after the Recessional—Idi sweeping by with a look like thunder—I lost sight of her.

Her attitude having put me in a sour mood (which was, I know, more than a little unfair on her), I decided to miss the big reception that had been laid on at the Imperial Hotel. According to the *Argus*, they had killed 300 goats and made 70 vats of curry—of which, as I have said, I am not fond.

Driving back home, I thought about the new wife. She had light-colored skin and the gossip was that Amin's nickname for her was Kahawa: coffee in Swahili. As well as being in the dance troupe, she was the official "face of Uganda" on tourist material, though I had heard that she was to be deleted now they were married. Poor girl, I suspected she would not derive much pleasure from that relationship. Amin's sex life struck me as likely to be, if not monstrous, then rather tender and geriatric. With a body that size, one imagined that the only genuine pleasure he could get was to lie on his back and let the world spin about him.

Medina would take her place within his households, I supposed, much to the irritation of the other wives, who had enough problems competing for his attention as it was. Sometimes, looking out of the bungalow window, I saw them walking in the gardens, chattering and arguing like a bunch of schoolgirls. Only one of them actually lived at State House, but they all got together from time to time. They were of different ages, but the situation was so confused that I was still not quite sure which was which, having been introduced only at functions when they were all togged up in white robes and turbans and difficult to distinguish. So I made some enquiries of Wasswa on the matter, and this, it seemed, was about the sum of it:

Wife Number One: Malyamu, a schoolteacher's daughter. Six foot tall. First love of the then army sergeant, who fathered a number of children on her before paying the bride price (after the old fashion) in 1966, to formalize the engagement.

Wife Number Two: Kay, a student at Makerere University, and daughter of a clergyman. The ceremony (also in 1966) took place in a registry office, though Kay did wear a wedding dress. Amin, Wasswa said, was in army uniform.

Wife Number Three: Nora, a girl from Obote's Langi tribe. This (1967) was by all accounts a political marriage, its purpose to persuade Obote that Amin was not plotting against him.

Wife Number Four: Medina . . .

25

As the months went by, Idi began to take me into his confidence more and more. He would phone me up—he loved the telephone, that man—and as often as once a week I would find myself dragged away from Mulago to perform some task entirely nonmedical in character. Such as briefing the many journalists, mainly British but latterly Americans and Germans, too, who came to see the President during this time, or talked to him over the phone. From time to time they would turn up at a designated hotel or at one of Amin's residences, with their train of rubber leads, bulky black television cameras on their shoulders and spongy microphones on spearlike poles.

Inevitably, they'd prod him into saying some outrageous thing or other. I remember how they knelt down in front of him, some fiddling with their equipment, some scribbling in little notebooks with spiral wire bindings. They always wore light brown, or even khaki, as I recall, and sometimes it seemed as if one soldier was interviewing another.

Except for on one occasion I remember, when Idi—all his elephantine bulk—was stuffed into an orange jump-suit. We were in the banqueting room at State House. The dark wooden table had been pushed against the wall, like a longboat moored at a quayside, and Idi sat in the displaced carver chair, with a semicircle of journalists in front of him.

"This is my astronaut suit," he announced, as the press conference began. "I will wear it when Uganda goes to the moon. I have been having words with NASA, and they say it is possible for me to be the first black man to go there."

Everyone laughed.

"I am serious," Amin protested. The collectively dour, bewhiskered gaze of the governor-generals seemed to say otherwise, as they frowned down from their portraits on the unfolding scene.

"Mr. President, do you sleep with all of your wives at once?" began one of the journalists.

"You are a very cheeky man."

Everyone laughed again. I noticed that there were a bunch of thuggish aides—probably State Research Bureau men—standing at the back of the room, under the crested-crane dish. The latter needed a polish, having become tarnished and covered with verdigris.

A correspondent from one of the US networks put up his hand. "Why did you expel the Israelis from Uganda, after all they had done for you in terms of building roads and supplying aircraft to the Uganda Air Force?"

Amin looked surprised, as if it was inconceivable that anyone could ask such a question. I thought of Sara, her feet—their thonged skin the color of olive oil—in my sandals, the feeling of her long hair brushing across my chest.

"Because Arab victory in the war with Israel is inevitable and the Prime Minister Mrs. Golda Meir's only recourse was to tuck up her knickers and run away in the direction of New York and Washington. Also when the Israelis were in Uganda, yes, the Americans and the Israelis made Uganda the headquarters of the CIA in Africa. If you see Mrs. Meir, tell her I am not a person who fears anyone. I am over six foot tall and a former heavyweight boxing champion. When Muhammad Ali finished with George Foreman across the border in Zaïre, I told him, come and fight me now in Uganda. But he was too scared!"

They all scribbled furiously. For a moment the room was silent except for the sound of rustling paper and the faint hum of camera equipment.

The *Daily Mirror* reporter broke the silence. "How do you find it, being President of Uganda?" he asked.

"It is very hard, but I like it very much and enjoy it very much.

One must have a very good brain, work very hard and not be a coward. But I love Uganda and was given the insight to lead the country, so it is OK."

"Why did you ask Britain to supply you with Harrier jets?" asked the *Sunday Times* stringer, a tough-looking Rhodesian. His accent reminded me of Swanepoel's clipped South African tones, though I seemed to recall him telling me that a native of either country wouldn't think they were similar. Well, not a *real* one . . . So many traps and pratfalls in describing these things.

"I was sincere," Amin replied. "I asked the Defense Secretary in my meeting with him. I had to go and attack South Africa. I asked them even for a destroyer and an aircraft carrier so I could move on to South Africa with ultimate force. The common enemies of all Africa are South Africa and Rhodesia. Military might will eventually displace the racists from Southern Africa. Imperialists will face fire. A truly volunteer African army is already being raised to fight unless Pretoria and Rhodesia give majority rule to their black populations. A division of thousands of South African exiles has been trained and is ready to fight at a moment's notice. Some of these people are already there and are simply awaiting the green light from me."

"Will you therefore be joining the Communists in South Africa, to fight against the apartheid regime?"

"Oh no! I am very grateful for the free gifts such as tanks, mobile trucks, guns and fighter planes that the Soviet Union has given me, but I am not a puppet. No way. I don't dance for criminals who try to act like the Vice-President of Uganda. The Soviet attitude is equivalent to me going to Moscow to advise what policy to follow in Czechoslovakia."

He got up and started walking around in the space between the carver chair and the knees of the journalists—like a schoolmaster, or a football manager giving a pep talk.

"It is always the same. Everyone is always telling me what to do. Even the Israelis, when they were on my side in the great struggle with Obote, told me to liquidate all people in the army who were opposing me. They did tell me that, you know. In all truth. Their agents and the British ones, too, they helped me with the coup. Though I could have done it on my own, without him."

I wondered vaguely whether he was referring to Stone. Or

Weir. Probably both. Amin started to run on the spot and box the air in front of the journalists.

"Yes, though the British also have told me many bad things. When I thought they were a good people. BBC, you must say it. Though I know very well that you are the voice of the British Empire, a criminal organization which I have conquered and which was built by the sweat and labor of people in chains. Ugandans. Kenyans. Tanzanians. Burmese. Even Scots."

With mention of each of these nations came a forceful punch into the air until, with the last, Amin collapsed back into his seat, breathing heavy as a bull, his legs wide apart. There was silence as we stared at him, the orange fabric of the jumpsuit staggered here and there by the black plastic wires and other gadgets that were attached to it.

"How do you feel about being surrounded by so many pro-Communist states?" said the American, eventually. "Does it make you nervous?"

"Well, yes, you are right. It is quite tough. You see, we are not Communist here in Uganda. I very much want the wananchi to be free. In Communist countries like Tanzania, you do not feel free to talk: there is one spy for every three people. Not here. No one is afraid here. It's like Ugandan girls. I tell them to be proud, not shy. It's no good taking a girl to bed if she is shy . . . Do you get my point?"

He laughed, and a barrage of flashbulbs went off. It was a favorite trick to print pictures of him laughing maniacally. That Prince-of-Darkness, dead-of-night laugh he pulled off so well.

"What is your policy attitude to the United States, Field Marshal Amin?" the American asked.

"I love the American people very much and I love Ford very much also. But I wish to alert him to a situation fraught with dangers, namely the position of black people in his country. He is aware Africans were kidnapped from Africa by whites and forced against their will to leave their motherland and to go in chains to the United States. For the smooth running of his country, President Ford must not discriminate against them. Not only should he appoint them to high offices in his White House staff but he should also appoint them as secretaries of state. They are entitled to their rightful share in the running of the country."

The journalist glanced anxiously up at his cameraman to see if he had got this. And he had, hunched over the matt-plastic sucker of his eyepiece—like part of a sea creature, I'd thought, when they were setting up—recording for posterity Idi Amin in full flood: legs akimbo, arms a windmill.

"And the British?" asked the *Mirror* man.

"They are my friends, they just forget sometimes. Long live the Queen! Yes, I love them very much, until recently, when they have been attacking me. Nor do I want to see them kill the Irish Catholics, because, as a former colonial of Britain myself, I feel embarrassed. Regrettable developments in Ulster call for Britain's true friends to come to her assistance. The leaders of Ireland, Catholic and Protestant and English and Irish, should come to Uganda and negotiate peace—far away from the site of battle and antagonism."

He sighed and spread his enormous hands out wide, like a pair of oars before they hit the water.

"I don't know. What is to be done about Britain? I am the greatest politician in the world, I have shaken the British so much I deserve a degree in philosophy. But . . . when members of the same family quarrel, they are always ready to forgive and forget. I have many Irish, Scottish and Welsh friends, also. I like the Scots best, because they are the best fighters in Britain and do not practice discrimination. The English are the most hopeless. I really don't understand why Scotland does not decide to become independent and leave the English to suffer."

"When are you going to hand back power to a civilian government?" asked a woman with her hair in a bandanna.

"I am not quite able at this moment to hand back the reins of government to politicians because corruption is still rampant among civilians. Let me remind you that it is only through my efforts that we have undone the effects of many centuries of underdogism in Uganda. Uganda is a paradise in Africa. If you have a shirt and trousers, you can live in Uganda for years—even without working. I am the hero of Africa because of this."

"So why is everyone afraid of you?" she said, bravely I thought.

Amin beamed. "It is my brilliance that frightens them. And perhaps also I am not liked because I am not a puppet leader. The

Europeans carried me on their backs on a litter into my reception. Why did they do that? Because they considered me a brilliant, tough African leader who has done much to help create better understanding between Europeans and Africans."

"But what about atrocities committed by your soldiers?" The woman said this with emphasis, and an air of uneasiness fell over the room.

"There have been a few mistakes," Amin replied, quietly. "It is only true that a few badly trained soldiers have misbehaved. And some criminals pretending to act on my orders have been killing drivers and then stealing their cars. I have told them, if you are not happy with me, then kill me or make me resign—but don't disturb the people of Uganda at night by running about shooting. Uganda is going at supersonic speed and the people should not be made unnecessarily to panic."

"If it is just mistakes," she persisted, "why are there so many stories within Uganda about soldiers killing people?"

Amin replied with a question, and a curious look. "Are you married?"

There was laughter from one or two quarters.

"What's that got to do with it?"

"Because if you are, I am sure your husband finds you very difficult to deal with. He should divorce you."

More nervous laughter. And then silence.

"What about the killings?" she said, emphasizing her syllables again.

The atmosphere in the room was piercingly apprehensive.

"Let me repeat. We are a government of action. If we have evidence that an army officer is guilty of kidnapping and murder, then he will face justice. But there is no evidence to back up your allegations. You should not suggest these things about the Uganda Army. I have served with the British, Italian and Indian Armies, even with the US Army in Korea, and I can tell you, Uganda forces are up to international standard."

He stood up abruptly then and looked at his big gold watch—a present from King Faisal of Saudi Arabia, he had once told me. Then he approached the woman, wagging his fat finger in front of her face.

"My dear," he said, "don't forget that no one can run faster than a bullet. You people are very bad. You ask me so many questions. How much do you need to know? By Allah, do you want me to pull down my trousers so you can see my behind?"

He walked up and down in front of them in the orange suit, and then pointed at a reporter with a BBC badge on his lapel.

"Yes, instead of rectifying colonial wrongs of her own making, Britain has found fit to wage a dirty press war on Uganda. Certainly we cannot help thinking that racism is the motivating factor in this situation."

Then he turned to one of the thuggish aides, and said, angrily: "Get these people out of here, clear them all out the way."

"He's Mad—Official" was the headline in the *Mirror* the following day, citing the opinion of some famous psychiatrist, and that night five journalists, including the woman, were detained at Nakasero. When they were released and finally made their way back to Europe, the stories about their imprisonment incensed Amin still further.

"The Western press," he said to me one afternoon shortly afterwards, when I was seeing to his gut problems again, "has the habit of exaggerating everything. These magazines and newspapers select the worst photos, which show me like an overfed monkey. Whether or not they agree, my face is the most beautiful face in the world. That's what my wives and mother say, and they are surely right. Eh?"

"Yes, Your Excellency," I replied wearily, and turned him upside down on the steel trellis to which I had strapped him. I was in the process of administering a barium enema. The process involves pressing in the barium sulphate from a bag with a rubber nozzle—like a cake-maker's icing piper. It was a curious sight— the naked President of Uganda turned on his head so that the white radioactive paste would flow through his bowels while I took the X rays.

There was nothing much wrong, except mild colitis, though he complained about it mischievously for months afterwards.

"You made me do white in the toilet for many days," he said. "I think it may very well be an imperialist plot. You know, I have my suspicions, Doctor Nicholas, that you are trying to retard development and turn me into a child once again."

26

My sister, Moira, has asked me: how did you let yourself get so close to such a man? How could you not see? I couldn't really explain. It wasn't like that at first. As I said, life went on as normal with these little bizarre interventions butting up in between. Like those telegrams. There was one to Mrs. Thatcher, when she defeated Heath in the Conservative Party leadership contest.

"What do you think of this?" Idi said to me, and read it out:

> Dear Margaret, it was on Tuesday when I happened to look at your photograph which was published in one of the East African papers. You were depicted laughing at Mr. Edward Heath whom you have defeated at the party leadership elections. From the photograph you appeared very charming, happy, fresh, intelligent and confident. Long may you remain so. Yours faithfully, Idi Amin.

"I don't think you should send it," I said.

"Oh, I will," he said. "I most definitely will. It is very important."

Shortly afterwards, President Gaddafi of Libya came to open the new airport at Entebbe. I attended the ceremony. Amin greeted the Libyan leader warmly: "You are the only revolutionary leader who speaks what is on your mind and one who believes all the people in the world must lead equal lives. You are not in the pockets of any superpower and I want to assure you that we in

Uganda are not controlled by any superpower. That is why when I learned of your policies, I became your best friend."

It was following Gaddafi's visit that they opened the Libyan Arab Development bank in Kampala, and we began to see a lot of Libyan soldiers and PLO troopers in the city.

The week of the opening ceremony, Amin sent a telegram to President Julius Nyerere of Tanzania, with whom he was having one of his periodic tiffs about the Kagera Salient, a disputed border area of Tanzania which—a triangulation mistake on the colonial map, Mr. Malumba had told me—stuck into Uganda like a sore thumb.

"With these few words," went the missive, "I want to assure you that I love you and if you had been a woman, I would have considered marrying you, although your head is full of grey hairs, but, as you are a man, that possibility doesn't arise."

"Why do you send these telegrams?" I asked Amin.

"It is simple," he replied. "They are based on the truth. I mean to advise the leaders when I realize they are doing wrong. I am a messenger from the god."

Sometimes, though, these messages were nothing short of repellent. "Hitler was right about the Jews, because the Israelis are not working in the interests of the people of the world, and that is why they burned the Israelis alive with gas in the soil of Germany," he fulminated in one telex to the UN Secretary-General, Kurt Waldheim.

I heard Willy Brandt, the West German Chancellor, attack the statement on the World Service as "an expression of mental derangement." I agreed with him, obviously, and yet there I was in the middle of it. My life had already fallen into a pattern that concentrated on Amin. The closer I got to him, the fewer my illusions about him—and still I stayed, more fascinated than frightened.

Until one fateful month when everything seemed to happen at once. By then, Wife Number Five had come on the scene. Just nineteen, she was a soldier (a member of one of the Revolutionary Suicide Mechanized Units) and had been Idi's co-driver in the Organization of African Unity rally. I didn't attend that ceremony, though I heard from Wasswa that there had been a large cake—three tiers high—and that Yasser Arafat, the PLO leader, had been best man. The bride was called Sarah, which of course made me think of another one, without an "h," and what *she* would have thought of Mr. Arafat.

Anyway, between Medina's wedding (Number Four) and this one, I had seen various women coming in and out of Amin's quarters on the rare occasions when he stayed at State House. His bodyguards would usher these mistresses (some unwilling—it was not unusual to hear screams in the darkness on those nights) into his bedchamber. He also reportedly kept several concubines in towns around the country, for when he was on tour. The three wives up to Medina, I had gathered, were bored.

It was presumably this boredom which led to an episode that I wince to recall—medically, ethically, in just about every way possible, it was extremely disturbing. I still don't know if I did the right thing.

One night, during a severe storm, there was a knock at the door of the bungalow. I was just going to bed. It was Peter Mbalu-Mukasa, my colleague at Mulago—the one with whom I'd had the drink when we ran into Swanepoel. He looked awful, drenched to the bone and shivering; but also something else.

"Come in," I said, stepping aside. "What's up?"

"Close the door," he said, breathlessly. "I had difficulty persuading the guards to let me into the compound. I had to tell them it was Mulago business."

"Well, what is it?" I asked, perplexed.

He didn't answer, pushing past me into the living room.

I followed him through. "Calm down," I said. "Look, do you want a brandy or something?"

"No!"

He sat down abruptly on a chair in front of me. His head was in his hands, dripping water over the wooden floor.

"Nicholas," he said, his voice muffled, "I'm in trouble, real trouble."

"What is it?" The stains spread on the dry wood.

There was a pause before he lifted his head and began to speak. "For almost a year now, Kay Amin has been my lover. It is stupid, I know, but we love each other very much."

"My God . . . But you've got a wife," I said, stupidly.

"That's not the point. The fact is, Kay is pregnant, and she's going to have to have an abortion. I want you to help me perform the operation. Amin hasn't slept with her in years, and if he finds out she's going to have a baby, we will be killed."

"I can't do that," I said, appalled. "I think you are better off fleeing the country—you could get to the Kenya border by morning if you left now."

"I've thought of that. They would arrest us in any case; they'd be bound to recognize her. Please help me. I was going to do it on my own earlier this evening but . . . I became scared. She asked for you. We have to go now . . ."

Against my better judgment, I finally agreed to come and see her—but only that. I drove off with him into the night. We took my van. He hadn't got a vehicle, having come by taxi—an expensive journey, all the way from Kampala to Entebbe. You are being foolish, I told myself, as the lights of cars and houses skated by. Oily dollops of rain burst on the windscreen as I followed his directions to a flat in the suburbs of the city.

Kay Amin was lying on a sheet on the living-room floor, her cardigan tight on the globe of her belly. She wasn't aware of us coming in. I was aghast to see that Peter had spread the instruments for the operation on the dining table. They were gleaming in the lamplight, like the cutlery at some demonic supper party. He had obviously been just about to start. There was even a bowl of water.

It was a ghoulish and, I knew immediately, untenable situation. I had never conducted an abortion, and I wasn't going to start like this. Kay was in no state for such an operation—not to mention the Amin connection, the lack of hygiene of a domestic lounge, still less the question of abortion itself.

I looked down at the poor woman. Evidently terrified out of her wits, she had become delirious, mumbling incomprehensibly, her hands rubbing her stomach. She didn't recognize me. Sick with anxiety, I recalled the competent, reasonably happy-seeming housewife who had greeted me at Prince Charles Drive.

"This isn't possible," I said to Peter. "I'm not having anything to do with this whatsoever."

He grasped my arm. "Nicholas . . . please."

"It's not right. You must try to escape. It's your only option. Or take her to Mulago in the early hours and chance it."

"Don't be stupid. This is the only way." He started tugging my shirt. "You must, you must."

He pulled me close to him, as if I were a lover, and whispered hoarsely, "Plee-ease. I am not sure I can do it." His face was dark grey, the color of cement before it has set.

"I'm sorry," I said. A certain sort of grimness came into my voice, as if expediency had now to take over. I pushed him away gently.

He walked over to the kitchen door, resting his hands on the posts and rocking himself to and fro.

"For the last time," he said, "will you help me? If you do not, I will do it on my own."

The room fell silent, with the exception of Kay's anguished mumbling. I hesitated for a second. If the alternative was that Amin would kill them, and probably the baby, too, then surely it would be better to do the operation, however unsatisfactory the conditions. An abortion, after all, was by no means the worst thing a doctor could do, but then . . .

"It is better I leave now," I said, finally. "I can't be found here. Please . . . Peter, don't do this. Take my advice. Find some other way out. I will help you if I can. Ring me."

I turned sharply and left the room. I ran out of the block of flats and across to the van, my feet splashing through deep puddles. Driving back to Entebbe at high speed, sliding about on the wet road, I was in a state of panic: fearful of discovery and, at the same time, knowing that simply running away was not the right course of action. But what was I meant to have done? It would have been medically dangerous to operate; yet I couldn't have turned them over to the authorities—which to all intents and purposes meant Amin.

Perhaps I should have done. That night was the last time I saw either Peter Mbalu-Mukasa or Kay Amin. The rumors began to go round the hospital during the next week. He had botched the operation and Kay Amin had died of blood loss. Peter committed suicide the next day with an overdose of sleeping pills.

It was all true. Amin ordered an investigation, during the period of which I was in a constant terror. My secret consumed me—whatever I was doing, wherever I was, my mind returned to that awful scene.

My own part in it did not come to light, for which I thanked the Lord—though I remained haunted by that possibility for the rest of my time in Uganda. What about the taxi driver who had brought Peter to State House? The guards at the gate? What if someone in the block of flats had seen me—especially noticeable as I was white?

Nor was the affair over, so far as I was concerned. The following week, I got a call in my office at Mulago. "There is something you must see," said the mortuary assistant, who knew that Peter and I had been friendly. I joined her in the mortuary.

Opening one of the refrigerator doors, she slid out a body. It was the corpse of Kay Amin. All four limbs, neatly severed, were lying beside the torso. The head, still attached, was twisted to one side. I turned away, feeling sick, and ran out of the room.

To this day, I don't know what really happened to Kay Amin's body. Some say that Peter cut it up himself—the torso was found in a box in the boot of his car, the arms and legs in a sack on the back seat—others that Amin had done it. He was, I knew, an expert in disjointing animals, a skill he had learned while foraging as a soldier in the bush.

What happened afterwards was stranger still, and equally disgusting. Amin ordered that the body should be sewn back together. As his physician, I was ordered to be present at a peculiar ceremony once this had been done. Amin had also gathered his other remaining wives, some twenty children (including those by Kay) and various officials.

Amin waved his hand over the bruised and discolored body, its limbs spikily attached by means of rushed and amateurish sutures. The wives looked frightened—Medina especially—and the officials solemn, and several of the children were crying as he spoke.

"This one, she was a bad woman. See how she has used cream to change the colour of her face and her legs and her arms to look white while other parts of the body remain black. See how she looks as if she has been suffering from leprosy because of this cream. See how unnatural she looks, how like a half-caste. See the judgment of Allah on a Christian woman."

It is difficult for me to recall all this, not just because of the horrific nature of what I am describing. My journal is confused, almost cryptic on these matters. Even I myself find it hard to decipher.

27

Later that month, one Wednesday evening, I went to collect the van from a garage on the outskirts of the city, where I'd taken it to be serviced. It wasn't ready, of course (you couldn't really find a decent mechanic once the Asians had left, and most places had simply been boarded up), so I went for a walk while they finished it off.

The sky was gun-metal grey, and my spirits were low: on account of the Kay affair, obviously, but I was also feeding off a more general depression that sometimes settled over Kampala evenings. You had a sense of people not having gotten what they wanted during the day. The street vendors, for instance, with all their scraps of food, square tins of paraffin (Shell, Agip), pear-shaped plastic mirrors and crumpled boxes of cosmetics.

One vendor always sat directly under a poster advertising part of his stock, Envi body cream. As I walked past I found myself humming the tune to the words on the poster, realizing that it was a jingle I'd been hearing on the radio:

> *She's got the looks*
> *She's got the style*
> *She's got the kind of skin*
> *That drives 'em wild*
>
> *Hey what she got?*
> SHE GOT ENVI!

Then I remembered what Amin had said over Kay's body, and felt sick with myself. I walked on quickly.

Not many cars were about, just the odd army vehicle growling by, the scut of its bad diesel puffing out behind. I watched my feet and the small economy that thrived around them. So much of it, so much of life in that part of the city, was down by the curb. One vendor had a piece of plate glass over some tired-looking covers. The front page of an old London *Times*, yellowing. And *Drum: Africa's Leading Magazine*, with a picture of a woman in a leopard-skin coat.

Farther along I saw a kid standing in the gutter in a pool of brown water. He was clad only in shorts, and his belly button stuck out like a press-stud. He looked up at me.

"Muzungu," he whispered, staring: not a greeting, not an invocation or an appeal or a protest. Just a statement. He repeated it—"Muzungu"—and I walked on. Past a lone petrol pump with a padlocked handle, past a woman sitting on an up-turned plastic bowl, with another in front of her full of feathers and a dead rooster laid at her feet.

Night was falling. I reached Namirembe market just before the darkness became total. The traders were gathering up their wares under the tents and lean-tos, chatting to the remaining bunches of shoppers. At one place, a man in a Robin Hood hat was frying chicken over a brazier, tossing it with a spatula. The smell and the noise made me hungry.

Elsewhere in the market, with a little group swaying and murmuring around him, a man was scratching at a one-stringed Baganda fiddle. I walked on. Several of the traders had lit small oil lamps which they hung in front of their stalls. These glinted on stacks of hoes and pangas. When I had passed, and I looked back behind me, it was only the flickering lights that I could see, as if they were suspended in the darkness.

Now I was in the heart of the city, where street lamps gave out a different sort of light, as did the few shops that kept their displays illuminated. I stopped for a second outside a haberdasher's: razor blades, sewing needles, perfumes, and two pyramids of soap—Cusson's Imperial Leather, with its red and gold livery, and coarse green blocks of Palmolive. Next door was an electrical shop, its window totally bare except for a single television. Amin was on the screen, giving a speech. I watched his movements, the hands gesturing. Chopping. Lifted up on either side. The baton finger of some point or other, strenuously made.

Elsewhere a prostitute approached me, heavily made-up with purple lip gloss and wearing a brown leather jacket. I declined, but she insisted on following me for several hundred yards. Having thrown her off, I walked past a few more shops and into a park which skirted the gardens of the Imperial Hotel. The path I was taking ran close by the diamond-net fence and through its triangles I could dimly see a couple of the guests sitting at one of the lighted tables near the bar.

The table was done up in African-hut style, with a parasol made of straw. Hanging from the central pole was a hurricane lamp that suffused the man and woman with an orange glow. He was wearing short sleeves, khaki trousers, and a pair of up-to-the-knee field boots, she was in a summer dress. I strained my eyes to see their faces, my ears to catch their whispered voices. Then his hand moved to her knee.

I found myself running blindly back through the park, crashing into branches. I clattered down the street—my heels noisy as castanets on the curb—through to the market. The ENVI poster flashed by, the woman's face laughing at me. I ran on. Reaching the garage, I spoke to the mechanic hoarsely and thrust the bundle of shillings in his hand. He looked at me pop-eyed, surprised at the sight of this agitated muzungu.

I calmed down in the van. I calmed down as the road took me on its way, the potholes and all of it, bumping the sighs out of me, bumping the hurt out of me. There was a full moon. The good light of it came down through the curve of the windscreen, sweetening my bitterness. It was Freddy Swanepoel's hand that had reached for Marina's knee.

I was very down that night, and drank most of a bottle of whisky. What about her husband, whom she was meant to be with? What was wrong with me, if she was going to have an affair? What about "I'm married to the British Ambassador" and all that crap?

All this, I knew, was something of an overreaction to the event itself. It was the way one thing had piled on top of another that did it. Sara going, Stone and his machinations, that macabre business with Kay, the strangeness of Amin and, perhaps most of all, my fascination with him and my reluctance to get the hell out of there.

I spent the rest of the next week in a kind of foolish daze, so much not myself that even Amin noticed.

"What is the matter?" he asked. "You look as if you have seen ghost."

To my horror, I broke down in front of him and started hyperventilating, pulling acres of vacant air into my chest. Idi looked at me penetratingly and his voice when it came was soft and deep, soft and deep, like you think an angel's would be.

He patted me on the shoulder. "Doctor Nicholas, I can tell at once that you are in love. I have been this way myself, oh, many times."

I was opening and closing my mouth like a goldfish, and there were little amoebas of light exploding on my retina. Idi rubbed my shoulder harder.

"My dear, dear friend, you have to accept that the god's plan is not always what you thought."

"I'm sorry," I gasped, getting my breath back. "I'm not . . ."

"If it is love you want," he said, the dark pools of his eyes pulling me in, "you must not be eager. I am a very successful lover through this tactic. If you walk in Kampala, you will see at least twenty-three girls pregnant by me. That is why they call me Big Daddy. It is obvious."

I managed a laugh, though the taste of tears filled my mouth.

"I think you must go on holiday. You must go and see the animals at Mweya Lodge, or even Paraa. Go, Doctor Nicholas, you will see double-tooth barbet and whale-headed stork, colobus monkey and, of course, Mr. Crocodile and Mr. Elephant. Hippo yawning because they are very tired. Even there are some simba. Lion!"

He made a clawlike gesture with both of his hands, drawing back his lips over his teeth. In spite of myself, I had to smile.

"So," he said, "who is this lady who does not see your beauty?"

I shrugged.

He said, "Well, it is all right. You see, you do not need to tell me anything that happens in Uganda. Because I know it all

already. I have many agents. For example, I know that the wife of
the British Ambassador is a bad lady and you"—he poked me in
the ribs—"were going to be chasing after her, but in fact she was
with another fellow who she should not have been playing with
either."

I looked at him, more dumbfounded by this than any of the
other ludicrous things he had said, in all of my encounters with
him. I felt as if my life changed direction at that moment, as if
I were on a railway and someone—someone not myself—had
pulled the points over.

My mouth was open. There was a heavy clunk as the heel of
his big army boot hit the polished floorboard. "You see!" he said
triumphantly. "All this my agents tell me and they are correct. But
listen . . ."

He came closer and put a hand on each of my shoulders, looking into my eyes as if to say I had his deepest sympathy.

". . . it is foolish to be sad because she commits adultery with
another man and not with you. You are jealous because his lips
have been on hers. Don't try to cover the truth under ten blankets. Because it is natural for women to be in love with men—a
handsome finger gets a ring put around it, everyone knows that.
Yes, it is impossible to control feelings of love. Let your experience be a lesson to all of us men. The main thing is, anyway, that
neither of you has introduced a bastard into the family. Once you
put children into the equation, it is another thing altogether."

I wiped my face on my sleeve.

"That fellow, he is no good anyway," Idi continued. "He is the
best pilot in Africa except for President Amin, but he is no good
all the same. Don't you worry about him. It is bad to play around
with other people's wives and bad also to spy on President Amin.
He is a spy and he works for a very greedy aero company from
Kenya who also want to make me pay too much. I asked them for
things, special things I needed from Nairobi, and they wanted me
to pay not in Uganda shillings but in US dollars."

He pulled a bundle of blue notes from his pocket and held
them aloft, like someone grasping a fluttering bird.

"What is the point of having my face on this money if I cannot
use it? It is a very bad situation."

. . .

Not—I thought later, lying on the sofa in the bungalow, clutching a bottle of Scotch like a baby—as bad as mine. I resolved to pull myself together, to build a castle in myself. Running away from Uganda was not the answer. Running away was never the answer. I thought of one of Idi's Swahili proverbs: "If you have an itch in your behind, it will follow you round wherever you go."

Impregnable, that is what I told myself I would be. And healthy: I had let myself go a bit and taken on a touch of that jaundiced, tired-expat look of Ivor Seabrook's. From now on, I'd go swimming and sunbathing a lot, get a good ruddy hue in my yellowing countenance, eat fresh fruit daily—and let nothing bother me. Yes, I'd stick it out here, do good work at the hospital. Help people, like I was supposed to. *Be useful.*

I got up from the bed and wrote it down in my journal, an instruction in capitals, and two phrases, underlined.

> CULTIVATE
> The discipline of my native land
> The focus of my profession.

And I was doing quite well with my resolutions, until Stone from the Embassy rang me up again and asked to see me the following Saturday morning. He didn't expand, but I knew it would be the thing about treating Amin again—in which direction, needless to say, I had taken no steps. It was too dangerous, I'd reasoned. And yet, as I thought more about it after Stone's call, the notion of using drugs to bring Amin to order did make some sort of sense; perhaps it was in that way that I was meant to be useful. And I was still, I have to admit, vaguely attracted by the murky James Bondishness of it all.

Here on the island, it's all clear. Clear as the things and people I see around me in my new life: the window of my new soul. My relinquished, immedicable self far behind me. That's the stocky figure of Malachi Horan going down the hill now. Malachi is one of the local fishermen. He mostly supplies the Ossian Hotel (a sort of health farm–cum–millionaire's knocking shop on the west side—saunas, jacuzzis, that kind of thing), but whenever he's had a big catch he brings something up here for me. He's just dropped off three mackerel, a piece of twine through their gills. I've put them outside the door for now—it's certainly cold enough.

So there they are, a bunch of silver hanging from a nail, their blank eyes trained on the path of their burly death dealer. And here's me, my neck aching from sitting and writing all day. Maybe it's a premonition: they say the aristos in the French Revolution used to get neck ache before execution. A sentinel symptom. A little like when people get a headache prior to sexual activity, a projection of the muscle contraction at the top of the spinal cord that will occur during orgasm. Real but not real—not like these fish. I'll scale them later. One fillet tonight, the rest in the fridge.

28

There was a funny smell in the room. Stone, sitting at a big hardwood desk, was wearing a herringbone sports jacket. And those dreadful brown slacks again. As if he didn't want to look me in the eye, he kept turning his head back towards the window as he talked.

"I'm glad that I've got you on your own this time. It didn't help having those two around before."

"But why isn't the Ambassador here?" I demanded. "If you want to discuss the same matter as on my last visit, I want to see the boss."

"He's not . . . really my boss," Stone said, silkily. "Only in name. Let me help you with something. Let me tell you how the world works. There's a show within a show here, Nicholas. People like me have to turn over the wheels when they stick. And, sometimes, people like me have to count on people like you. Bob Perkins is just ceremonial."

He turned his head to the window again. Maybe he was worried someone might be listening. The window was slightly open. It was the tilting type, one big pane of glass with a wooden frame, and the refraction from the tilt threw up strange distortions of the garden outside, piling up trees and lawns at impossible angles. I couldn't resolve them into what they actually should have looked like.

"What happened to Weir?" I asked. "I heard he was recalled to London. Because he was too friendly with Amin."

Stone, for once, looked slightly taken aback. "Let's . . . just say he was too talkative."

I was pleased to have scored a point. "He didn't seem that way to me," I said, rather too smartly.

Stone frowned. "Getting back to what we were talking about last time, I suppose you've done nothing . . ."

"No," I said shortly. " I haven't. I was too afraid. Can't you try another approach?"

He sighed and leant back in his chair. The room smelled of his aftershave, I realized.

"My work is nothing but approaches, Nicholas. There's no constant, we just have to do what policy dictates, on a case-by-case basis. And in Uganda now, with things as they are, London thinks it is the right thing to do. We stopped a £12 million loan once he began that business with the Indians, but it wasn't enough. We need you."

"Why does it have to be me?" I said. "I'm a doctor, not a secret agent."

"That's the point. It's your duty in that way. As a doctor. And as a British citizen. You must have heard, you must have seen what has being going on. There's all the violence, lots of Brits booted out already. He's even put the Kampala Club under guard. The next stage of his Economic War will be all of us gone. Including you, I'm certain."

"I'm just doing a simple job," I said. "I'm not getting in any-one's way."

"Well, you should be getting in the way. You should be getting in the way of the killings. The PM says that he must be stopped. It's atrocious what's happening. Law and order have collapsed, people are disappearing every day. We keep getting reports of massacres of soldiers, they're dumping the bodies in the lake or in mass graves in the forests. It's like Hitler."

"You're exaggerating," I said, irritably. "Nothing is like Hitler."

I was annoyed by the way he kept trying to take the moral high ground. There was a pause as he rummaged in his desk drawer, finally pulling out a manila folder.

"Look at these." He pushed the folder across the desk. "I'll make some coffee. You'll need it. Then tell me what you think."

There were about fifteen grainy black-and-white photographs in the folder. The first showed three soldiers in the cockpit of an armored car, two with helmets, one with a black beret. In the middle of them a man in a vest was looking up at the sky, his mouth open, as if he were calling out in pain. The soldier nearest had his shoulders slightly hunched, as if he were doing something with his hands at the front of the man—but I couldn't see below the edge of the cockpit. It was a horrific image. I wondered who had taken the picture.

Another one showed a boy in shorts tied to a football goalpost. There was a black bag over his head and he was slumped forward. You could see his weight on the rope where it pulled against the post. At the other side a man in military police uniform was looking on, one arm raised as if he were about to intervene. Or had just given an order.

Looking at the photograph, stark there on the desk, part of me felt frightened, another part wanted to know the rest of the story. There were others that seemed to be in a sequence. A party of soldiers walking through the bush with a prisoner. Then the prisoner tied to a tree. A flour sack covering his face, the frayed corner of it tucked under his collar. In the next, I was shocked to see Amin, talking to the man with the bagged face, as if consoling him. His hand was resting on the man's shoulder.

I thought of his hand resting on mine, less than a fortnight ago. I felt a shiver of fear, then, at the possibilities of what Amin might do if he knew I was here. The next photograph broke the sequence, showing another man's clothed body sprawled on a curbside, covered with flies, even—which was odd, I remember thinking—on the parts that weren't bloody. He had been bludgeoned about the head, and the bones around the eyesocket had shattered, turning out the white ball like a boiled egg.

I heard Stone's voice behind me. "That's only a fraction of it. We're getting reports that are quite disgusting. Unbelievable. They're putting . . . things in people's mouths. They're actually *cutting their things off* and putting them in their mouths."

I turned round. Stone was carrying two steaming mugs on a round tin tray. He came off balance slightly as he pushed the door shut with his foot, and when he put the tray down there was a little pool of brown liquid in the well of it. I could hear the nylon crackle of his slacks as he walked over.

"It's strange, that mouth thing," he said, sitting down. "It's as if they don't want even those that die to talk. The State Research Bureau, you've surely heard of them, they have a speciality of shooting people there. An enormous amount of the skulls we have reported to us have broken jaws."

"I didn't know it was as bad as this," I said, pushing the folder back towards him.

Stone put his hands on the desk. "Let me come to the point. Hundreds of people are dying every day, and what are you doing? Just carrying on as normal, just bumping along the bottom. Because if you don't do anything, you are at the bottom: you're in a cesspit, Nicholas, the whole place is, and you are one of the few people able to lift it out."

"This is not fair," I said. "It's your fault, anyway. If you hadn't put him in, none of this would have happened."

He sipped his coffee. "It wasn't us, not exactly. The Israelis as well . . . At the time, anyway, it was the right decision. Everyone said it was right for Britain, even the newspapers."

"But that's what it is, isn't it? It's all just policy with you. Expediency: that's meat and drink to you people. When I came to see you, you suggested that—anyway, the point is, I cannot do what you ask. He is a human being, after all, whatever crimes his regime has perpetrated."

"He's a lunatic," Stone said reprovingly. "One with a lot of blood on his hands and the ability to get a lot more on. He simply shouldn't be running a country. Look, he's just sent a message to the Queen insisting that she send an aircraft to take him to the Commonwealth Conference, and a company of Scots Guards to escort him. His latest thing is to send the so-called Pioneers of the Uganda Navy to Guinea-Bissau to liberate it from the Portuguese. He hasn't got any ships, Nicholas, and Uganda is landlocked anyway. It would be quite funny if it weren't for the thousands of people who are dying. All these silly larks of his, it's like pornography. If you laugh at it, you're stepping over the corpses. And if you work with him, well, it's worse."

I felt extremely uncomfortable. "I don't . . . work with him. I occasionally have to treat him. Look, it's not like I'm going out killing people. There are hundreds of Ugandans in the same position as me."

"You could do something to help them, and the whole country. You'd be doing Uganda a favor. You have the medicines for it. You're the only person close enough. Let me be honest with you: we need you to do more than calm him down now—I have orders to ask you to kill him."

"That's out of the question," I said, laughing at the preposterousness of it, but also deeply shocked. "Doctors don't do that sort of thing. We take an oath, you know."

"I know," he replied, quietly, "but the purpose of that is to save lives, and think how many lives you'd save by this. You wouldn't get in trouble, I'd see to that. Whenever you get the chance to give him some jabs, just pump him full of adrenaline and make it seem like a heart attack."

"Impossible," I said, getting up. Something was still niggling at the back of my mind, though. It would be rather grand to rid the world of a dictator. And then I thought of Amin—that brief moment at State House when he had appeared to open up to me—and what it would mean to kill him, to kill anyone.

"Please sit down," Stone said. "I know what we are asking you to do is difficult. But it would be the right thing. What is it they say—it only takes one good man to do nothing for evil to triumph?"

Stone the preacher again. That was what annoyed me most, not what he was actually asking.

"You've got a very misplaced idea of the right thing," I said, loftily. "You can't talk to me like this anyway. You can't order me about, certainly not order me to murder somebody."

"Sit back down. Please—just listen to me. This is straight from London."

Why did I do as he said, and not walk out? All this could go away, things could go back to normal. I didn't need to go out and look for this kind of excitement.

Seated again, I folded my arms, waiting for him to speak. Stone stood up and walked slowly round the desk. I could smell the aftershave again.

"Sometimes," he said, "—and everything gets smoothed out in time—the moral path is the one that doesn't seem so. It's been like that throughout history. We'll look after you, Nicholas. I've already arranged for a sum of money to be paid into your account in Scotland."

"I do not want blood money in my bank account," I said.

"You will," he said from behind me, "mark my words. Fifty thousand pounds, and the same when it's done."

"You cannot make me do this," I said. Yet it flashed through my head once again that he was right. I could actually kill Amin and get away with it. Who would be better placed? But there was, I conceded it to myself again, something in me that actually *liked* the man, monster though he was.

Stone sat back down in front of me. The sun was flooding the room with a deep red light.

"Think about it seriously," he said. "We can get you whatever you want. Whatever you need. Women, money, a job somewhere else . . ."

I suddenly came to a decision. "I am not a killer," I said. "I may be lots of things, but I am not a killer. Maybe it would be different if he were ill, and you asked me simply not to treat him. To let him die. But he isn't ill, and I will not poison him."

And then I left the room. Stone didn't try to stop me. "The money will be in your account shortly," he said, as I reached for the door. "It'll stay there, but if you're going to do it, get on with it, for Christ's sake."

As I walked over to the van, between the well-tended, sculptural plots of the Embassy garden, I regretted having come, and resolved that this would be the last time I had anything to do with Stone and his schemes. I had to keep to my own agenda—though I didn't really know what that was. I drove home slowly, the sun on my hand on the steering wheel. When I got there, I made myself lunch. Delicious: avocado salad, some grilled perch, and a bottle of Pilsner.

29

As it turned out, I needn't have troubled myself over any other business with Stone. The following week Amin expelled him, Marina and her husband, and most of the remainder of the Embassy staff.

"I have broken the backbone of the British spy ring in Uganda," he announced on the radio. "Any other foreign embassies with spies in their midst will be dealt with accordingly. Especially if they offer bribes. Even me, the President of Uganda, they were offering bribes to."

In his usual contradictory spirit, he also said that he had sent yet another message to the Queen, professing his undying friendship for her and declaring his intention to pay her another visit.

"I said to the Queen of England, I hope that this time you will allow me to meet Scottish, Irish and Welsh liberation movements who are fighting against your imperial rule. I am sending this message early, so that you will have ample time to arrange for what is required for my comfortable stay in your country. For example, I hope that during my stay there will be a steady supply of essential commodities because I know that your economy is ailing in many fields. Yes, Mrs. Queen, you better believe it. I am coming to London and no one can stop me. Whether you like it or not, I am bringing two hundred and fifty Ugandan reserve forces as my bodyguards. I want to see how strong the British are and I want them to see the powerful man from the continent of Africa."

Two things happened after the expulsions, in rapid succession. The first was that my bungalow was broken into, and my journal stolen. Nothing else was touched. This frightened me. I thought about reporting it to the police, but decided against it. I suppose I knew, in my heart, that it had something to do with Amin. Ordinary burglars would never have dared enter the heavily guarded confines of State House.

The second thing, which happened early the next evening, was that Amin called me at Mulago. I was daydreaming when the phone rang, looking at an old woman sweeping the courtyard with deliberate rhythmic strokes. She did it every evening, clearing up where the outpatients queued, so I don't know why my gaze should have settled upon her. But it did, just as Amin's gaze had settled upon me.

"Come immediately," said his voice in my ear. It was harsher than usual, and my heart began to beat itself out of my chest.

"Doctor Nicholas? I have urgent medical business to discuss with you."

Sweep sweep sweep. My eyes focused on the woman in the courtyard. "Yes . . . Your Excellency."

"Very urgent. Nakasero." The line went dead.

I did as I was told. Driving to the Lodge, my stomach turned over and over. The sweat was streaming off me, even though the cool of evening had settled, and my throat felt as if a lump of wood had been shoved down it. What did he know about Stone? The fact that I had seen Kay the evening before she had died? The journal—what had I said in it?

Night fell on the way, and the moon was soon high and bright over the swamps next to the road. Moving in the breeze, the mass of papyrus plants looked threatening and weird, their nodding, dandelionlike heads—some over ten feet high—making them seem like helmeted space creatures.

Calm down, I told myself as I entered the city, he's asked to see you before, it doesn't mean anything. He wouldn't harm you. Not NG.

I drove on. When I got to Nakasero the guards showed me up to Amin's living quarters as before. I walked through the door, and was greeted with the same familiar mess. The baseball bat, the pornographic magazines on the floor, the portrait of Lumumba, the floor-to-ceiling shelves housing the *Proceedings of the Law Society of Uganda.*

Dressed in military uniform—just plain khaki, not the bedazzling field marshal's outfit—Amin was sitting in the antique chair. Next to it was the same gauzy four-poster water bed with its twisted squall of sheets and pillowcases, and the mirrored wardrobes, vanity unit and escritoire. On the desk, I noticed, the cowboy holster was resting, the embossed handle of the gun sticking out of it.

He looked up as I came in and smiled pleasantly at me. There was a copy of the *Sunday Times* lying open at his feet, showing a picture of him holding a baby and grinning broadly.

"Ah," he said, "my good friend Doctor Nicholas."

"You called, Your Excellency?" I was still sweating heavily.

He looked down at the newspaper headline: THE BUTCHER IN THE BUSH.

"Though the English hate me," he said, "I still love and respect the Queen. I was thinking of maybe writing to her once more."

"Is that what you called me about?" I said, relieved.

"Yes," he said, standing up. "And also no. I did call, but you did not hear. I gave you many things, but you betrayed me."

I stared at him, speechless.

"Doctor, you have done badly because you have started to fight against me. Like an English, not a Scots. Very bad."

My eyes flicked over to the escritoire, to the holster. But he was reaching into his pocket. He pulled out a tiny revolver of the type used by gamblers in Westerns. In his big fist, only the muzzle showed.

"This is your last day. You are to die. This is your end."

I flinched, and then sank to my knees and began to babble. "Your Excellency, please. I have done nothing!"

The mouth of the gun was right in front of me. I could see the wrinkles in Amin's hand.

His voice echoed above me. "So you want to leave me, do you?" Then he squatted down, his face close to mine. "What is wrong that you do not love me?" he whispered. "Why are you no longer my friend?"

"Please," I said, hoarsely. "Don't kill me. Please don't kill me."
I was trembling uncontrollably, and I felt that I might soon void myself.

Then suddenly Amin had stood up and his head was raised and he was laughing, laughing up to the ceiling. "Kill you? Why on earth should I want to kill a man like you?"

I looked up. There was something stunned and childlike in his face.

"No, I wouldn't want to kill you, Doctor Nicholas. I thought you wanted to kill me. But I know you wouldn't. I won't take vengeance on silliness."

I remained on the floor, panting like a dog, as Amin put the little gun back in his pocket. He walked over to the escritoire, and pulled open a drawer. I could see myself in the mirrors—crouched, panting, panting—and behind me the ranks of bookshelves.

"I am sorry to have frightened you," Amin said, coming back over. "The fact is, my good friend, that I have heard from my intelligence operatives in the State Research Bureau that you have been engaged in activities against the state. According to this report . . ."

He waved a pink piece of paper in the air above me.

". . . which was written by my good friend Major Weir, who has sadly had to go now—you have been told to give me bad drugs by the government of her Majesty the Queen."

"I . . ." I croaked, confused. *Weir?* I thought of his limp and his turkey-wattle neck, the insistent buzz of the radio-controlled helicopter.

"There is no need to deny it. I know everything, you see. Including this I know—that you are too good a doctor, and love Idi Amin Dada too much to do this thing."

"That's true," I said. "I wouldn't do it, you know that I wouldn't do it."

"So," he said, a cunning look coming into his eyes, "they did ask you, then?"

"I refused," I said. "It is not right."

"Good," he said, and walked over to the escritoire and sat down.

"Good," he repeated, reaching into the desk. "Because then I am able to forgive you this other matter."

He held up the black notebook in which I had been writing my journal. I looked up at him in horror. I had forgotten about it while he had been threatening me with the gun, and now a new wave of fear surged through me. There was silence for a moment in the room, as he turned the pages. I feverishly ran over in my mind what was in there.

"You are a very good writer," he said, after a while. "I can see that plain. But when I talked to you about my journey to become head of state of Uganda, I did not know you would be writing these things down in a book."

"It's just a journal," I said. "Like a diary."

"You are a very clever man," he said. "But I do not like what you write here about my mother. Her name was Fanta, not Pepsi Cola. And what you write about my fourth wife is insulting. You should know that I am a sexual lion and that I have fathered over fifty children in Uganda and all over the world. If you continue to write things like this, you will be dead. Straight. From now on we will have radio-cassette and press button. Whenever you write, you will take the words from my mouth. Exactly. Because the mouth is the home of words."

He turned over a few more pages. I prayed again that I had not noted in detail any connection with Kay. I didn't think I had, but I was not in a state to remember.

And then Amin said something that threw me totally. "Now, this is very important. This fellow, Waziri, noted here. You say he was your friend?"

"Well," I said, thinking rapidly where this was leading. "He worked at the clinic in Mbarara."

Amin fixed his eyes on me. "He was not a good doctor—and thus I do not think he could be your friend. Because he is not my friend, and if he is not my friend, he cannot be your friend. It is true?"

"I don't understand," I said.

Amin got to his feet, walked round the desk and pulled me up.

"Follow me," he commanded. "I have something very important to show you."

He walked over to the bookshelves and pushed against one of them. A dark space came where one stack of the leather volumes went in on itself. He pushed again. The stack swung in farther, revealing a long, damp passageway, dimly lit with strip lights. There were pools of water on the concrete floor, and all around a smell of dead and standing air.

Amin turned to me, his eyes gleaming avidly. "Come," he said.

There was no question of my refusing to do as he said. I followed his burly figure as it ducked through the entrance, and went down some steps. My pace fell in with his, splashing through the water. I felt an oppressive sense of dread.

We walked on, the braid on Amin's shoulders flashing as he passed under the lights. My heart beat painfully again (medically, I suspected I was tachycardic, running at over 100 bpm). The echoes of our footsteps sounded in the tunnel—and then another sound came.

Two sounds. The first was a thump thump thump, reminiscent of the women pounding millet back in Mbarara. With its slow relentlessness, it mocked my sore-speeding heart. The other sound was more disturbing still—a faint yet piercing scream, or howl. I'd only once heard anything like it before, when I'd come across a weasel caught in a snare in the pine woods above Fossiemuir. I felt my bowels loosen.

We entered a chamber. It had several partitioned walls and alcoves. In one of the latter was a cubicle with glass sides, and filled with electronic equipment. Shifting in the glass, the dials and LED levels flickered in the dim light.

Amin crossed to the other side of the chamber and looked through a spyhole in the wall. Then he pressed a button and a big metal door slid open.

"Kila mlango kwa ufunguo wake," he said, grinning back at me. "Every door has its own key."

A fetid smell heaved into me. On the other side was the entrance to another corridor, where two bright red fire extinguishers hung like sentinels. They brushed Amin's thighs as he passed through in front of me. The noises were suddenly very loud: whimpers, moans, outright yells from the very throat of pain. A row of barred doors stretched down one side of the corridor, the walls of which were smudged and crumbling. The stench, the heat, the sounds—alone they would have been horrific, together they were almost unbearable.

I blenched, and I blench from the page as I write—those sights I glimpsed as Amin led me past those cells—it takes . . . an almost physical effort to realize them, so deeply have I hidden them in my mind. So deeply have I hidden—

In the first cell, a man was threshing about in a barrel of water, his wrists tied clumsily to the sides with rope. In the second, a man was curled up on the concrete floor. Two soldiers were striking him with thick leather straps. In the corner of the third lay the corpse of a boy, his leg shattered, a sledgehammer leaning against the wall beside him. There was blood everywhere and fragments of bone, scattered about like chips of chalk in the puddles.

In the fourth cell were three women. They stood there naked and shivering, huddled together as a soldier walked round them, prodding them with a baton. It was a desperate sight, filling me with feelings of outrage and revulsion—but I was too scared to do anything.

I was transfixed for a moment, and then flung myself against the wall opposite the windows. I crouched on the floor. Amin reached down and gripped me hard by the upper arm.

"Come on," he said, "don't linger here, it is not natural. I want you to see the medical wing. There is a doctor there I'd like you to meet. He is a friend of yours."

He led me beyond the cells, into a room full of beds. They were fully made up, and spotlessly clean. If it hadn't been for the overpowering smell of rotten flesh that pervaded the whole building, you would have thought you were in a new, or recently overhauled hospital.

All the beds were empty except one, which was surrounded by a group of soldiers—maybe about ten, perhaps more.

"Is this your friend?" Amin said to me. "Is this man your colleague?"

The man on the bed was Waziri.

His head was bent down where a rope, also tied to his ankles, pulled at it. He looked up at me, as best he could with the fiber rope pressing into the flesh of his neck, his eyes full of terror. For a second, it was as if he was trying to speak: but his mouth was stuffed with a piece of rough plastic. The hard tough plastic of a fertilizer bag had been bent over several times and forced between his teeth.

Waziri moaned through the gag, spittle and blood running from the side of his mouth. I began to feel unsteady on my feet.

"This man," Amin said, clapping me on the shoulder, "has done bad. He has associated himself with counterstate guerrillas from Tanzania and Rwanda under the leadership of Obote. He has been fighting me in the Ruwenzoris, operating out of Kabale. You have done bad also to be his friend."

"I have done nothing," I whispered, backing away from the hellish scene.

But I couldn't. The soldiers were crowding behind me, pressing into me.

"You should know this, doctor," Amin said. "When two men fight, one wins. You must not be disobeying me."

Then he pointed at Waziri on the bed and said just one word. The word was "kalasi."

One of the soldiers produced a knife with a white bone handle. It looked like an ordinary kitchen bread knife. I glanced at Amin; his face was as fixed and solid as that of a statue, his eyes locked on the man on the bed.

Waziri, seeing the knife, started blinking feverishly. With his neck and ankles still trussed, he tried to roll back into himself like a hedgehog. But by then the soldiers were already on him, pushing past me, pushing past Amin even and crowding round the bed. They dragged him onto the floor. One put a boot on his head. Our eyes met at that exact moment, and Waziri's blinked again, and then all was obscured by the mass of camouflage swooping over him. I heard a gurgling sound and then I caught a glimpse of his bare torso—that, and the long, hideous blade shuttling back and forth.

When I came to, I was in one of the cells, lying on a truckle-bed. I looked at the concrete floor and breeze block walls. There were smears of brown everywhere: blood or feces, it was impossible to tell.

I didn't know how long I had been in there. They had taken my watch from me. There was no natural light, just a bare bulb.

The mattress was solid as a board and smelt strongly of urine, so I took it off and lay directly on the springs.

Shortly after I had done this, the door clanged open and a soldier came in. He had those ritual, one-eleven scars on his face—similar to Major Mabuse's, but longer—and was carrying a tin plate of matooke. He shouted at me angrily in Swahili when he saw the mattress on the floor, and then switched into English.

"You filthy British," he said. "You come here to take our sisters and then you throw our beds on the floor. Pick or you die!"

I struggled up from the bed and made a halfhearted attempt to lift the mattress onto it. The soldier let out a burst of Swahili, then squatted down and slid the plate of matooke across the floor. As he closed the heavy door behind him, I took one look at the steaming grey mash and started to retch.

I don't remember much else . . . I've blocked it out. They only kept me there for a single night, I worked out later. I was delirious with fear for most of it. At one point, however, I remember hearing muffled rifle fire from outside; at another, whispered voices from the cell next door, to which two men had just been consigned. I listened to them talking:

"You have heard what happened to Felix Aswa?"

"No. How did it go with him? I was for running to my house when I heard the shooting in our quarter . . . Then they got me and took me into a car secretly."

"They did not act secretly with him. They just grabbed him and shot him. And then they cut off his head with a panga. In broad daylight."

"His head?"

"Yes, and then they took the head and made it drink from a cup. And they called the wife of Felix and said, Look, here is the head of your husband taking tea."

"That is how it is in our country now."

"And then they took the head to places unknown."

I was about to call out to them when I heard the key sound in the lock of my own cell. The door opened and the soldier who had brought me the food entered.

"You, muzungu. Come with me. We are going to give you these." He touched his cheek.

I looked up at him, not understanding. Then he patted the

one-eleven scars on his cheek again, and smiled. The breath went out of my lungs. He came over and pulled me up by the arm. I struggled and shouted as he dragged me out into the corridor.

He stopped and smiled again, and then started laughing, pushing me in the ribs.

"Yee ssebo! It's OK, it's OK. I am joking. Eh, you, muzungu. Now, take off your clothes!"

I did as he said, trembling, and then he thrust me into a shower room. Still not sure whether he was joking about the scarification, I slumped against the wall under the cold water for something like twenty minutes.

When I came out, Wasswa was standing there, with a towel and some new clothes over his arm. I was so relieved to see his familiar face that at first I couldn't speak.

"Are you OK, doctor?" he said, handing me the towel. "You have been a very foolish man to write about President Amin in that way and to plan subversive activities with Britain against Uganda."

"Why have I been kept like this?" I mumbled. "I have done nothing."

"You are very lucky that President Amin has given you clemency. He wants to see you right away."

Once I had dressed, we went back into the corridor. I caught a glimpse through the bars of the two men I had heard speaking, one old, wearing traditional clothes, the other middle-aged, in a suit and tie. They looked up at me, surprised, as we passed.

"Please," the younger one shouted, "help us. My name is Edward Epunau. I am an honest businessman."

I stopped in my tracks, wanting to go back.

"Come on," said Wasswa. "There is nothing you can do."

"Help us!"

Wasswa took my arm. We walked up the corridor, past the other cells. I tried to ignore the now more muted sounds of their inmates, keeping my eyes firmly on the floor. I couldn't bear to see those things again. We went between the two fire extinguishers.

The Minister pressed a concealed button. Part of the wall slid away, to reveal the chamber through which I had passed the previous night. In a corner I could see the glass cubicle, where the steaming electronics hissed and warbled like something living. I also noticed, stupefied as I was, that the door was plaster on the cell side—you wouldn't have known it was there—and metal on the chamber side.

We walked up the second passageway. At the end, Wasswa pressed another button. I heard motion on the other side. The door swung open.

Amin was wearing an electric-blue safari suit with matching sombrero. He hugged me. In the mirrors I could see his wide shoulders in front of me, and the red-hide *Proceedings of the Law Society of Uganda* swinging shut behind. Their gold lettering glittered in the light.

"Ah, my good friend Doctor Nicholas. It is very nice to see you again, yes?"

"Yes, Your Excellency," I said, in a careful monotone, trying to reacquaint myself with the nurserylike atmosphere of his bedroom. The toys and board games on the floor. The portrait of Lumumba. The television showing a boxing match.

"Now, first you must have some breakfast," Amin said, grinning. "Then you can go home and you will be strong to do work tomorrow. I myself will be busy also. For there are many things happening in Uganda at this time."

We went down to the dining room and I ate surprisingly heartily, speaking carefully when Amin asked me questions. I was, I realized, lucky to have escaped with my life and I was determined now to get out of this situation and take the next plane home. As I left, I felt faint from having eaten too much and too quickly.

"One more thing," Amin said, as I was at the door. "As proof of your loyalty I want you to renounce your British citizenship and take up Ugandan citizenship immediately. Then I will know you are truly my friend. Wasswa has drawn up the papers and contacted London."

I looked back at him, the beast, and wished that I had done as Stone had asked. Walking down the steps outside the Lodge to the van, I felt physically wrecked. My bones were aching, and the sunlight made me blink. I got into the van and drove home like a zombie.

Back in the bungalow later that day, I pulled myself together. I packed quickly. I just knew I had to get out. I took only a few changes of clothes, my passport, some traveler's checks I'd taped to the bottom of a drawer for safekeeping—and my journal. The latter Amin had returned to me during the meal, enjoining me once again to write in future exactly what he told me.

"Come back soon and I will tell you all of my life story," he had said. "It is very exciting. Because, as you know, I am the hero of all Africa."

30

Early the following morning, I got into the van and drove to the airport. I drove fast: I longed to be in Scotland, cleansed of this place and its horrors. And I drove fast because I was scared. I knew that it was likely Amin would be having me watched now—but there was nothing untoward in the wing mirror when I looked.

When I got to the airport, there was a crowd of would-be passengers standing outside the complex. The entrance was barred by a contingent of troops. I got out of the van and walked over. I struggled through the crowds to where you could see onto the runway through the fence. One of the planes there, Air France 139, was surrounded by more troops. Next to the walkway were two dark-haired Arabs, and a blonde woman chatting to a Ugandan army officer. The woman was wearing a black skirt and had a machine-pistol slung over her shoulder.

"What's happened?" I asked one of others who was looking.

"The PLO have hijacked this plane from Tel Aviv and brought it here. They've stopped all the flights."

I walked back to the van and sat there for a while, agitated and angry, cursing Amin, cursing the PLO, most of all cursing myself. I'd have to plan things more carefully. I decided the best thing to do was to go to Mulago, just as if it were a normal day.

I didn't tell Paterson or any of the others about my incarceration and the horrors I'd witnessed, just excusing myself as having been sick. Everyone was talking about the hijack anyway, and my odd disappearance was soon forgotten.

Later that day, the phone rang in my office at the hospital. It was Wasswa. "How are you feeling?" he said. "I didn't expect you to be back at work so soon. You've been very thoughtless, you know. You are lucky he didn't have you killed."

I said nothing.

"Nicholas . . . you have probably heard about the Palestinians hijacking this plane from Israel and bringing it to Entebbe. Well, the President wants you to come to the airport. He says it is very important that the hostages are given the best medical treatment Uganda can offer."

"Haven't I been through enough?" I replied, coldly.

"You are not in a position to argue. And neither am I. He says you must go quick."

So I drove to the airport again. They had taken the hostages off the plane into the terminal building. Two hundred fifty of them were huddled in little groups, the terrorists standing among them with machine-pistols and megaphones. The blond woman, I discovered, was Gabriele Krieger, a German member of the Popular Front for the Liberation of Palestine (not the PLO, as I had thought earlier). The Israelis on the passenger list, and all those with Jewish-sounding names, were soon hived off into a separate room. It was a depressing sight. We were able to give them malaria tablets and distribute blankets—and to take one woman, Dora Bloch, to Mulago for treatment after she choked on some food.

But otherwise Krieger, who said she and her companions had wired the building with explosives, wouldn't allow us near them. All looked to be in shock, naturally enough—as much from discovering that arrival at Entebbe was not the end of their ordeal as from anything else. They had apparently imagined that they would be released when they got to Uganda. I learned that the terrorists had given a deadline of two days for their demands about the release of fifty-three Palestinian prisoners around the world to be met—otherwise all the hostages, Jews and Gentiles alike, would be killed.

I was about to leave when Amin arrived in a large Sikorsky helicopter—together with Medina, a contingent of guards in white shorts and red berets, and some photographers from the Ministry of Information.

"Everyone stay where you are," shouted one of the guards as they clattered into the hall. "Sit down! Sit down! Don't move!"

Amin walked in. He was wearing full field marshal's uniform, with a resplendent complement of medals. As well as Medina, one of his young sons was there—Campbell, I think—also dressed in uniform.

At first Amin just strolled among the non-Israeli hostages, smiling as they looked up at him in bewilderment. He admired the blonde terrorist's machine-pistol, and patted a small French boy on the head. I saw the boy exchange glances with Campbell. Then Amin clapped his hands together. The room fell silent. It was like being in a theater the moment before the production begins.

"Hello, my good friends. Well, I have some good news to tell you. The bad dream is over. I have been negotiating with the Palestinians and I have been on the phone to Tel Aviv. As a result of my efforts, they have agreed to release all forty-seven hostages without Israeli passports or Jewish blood. I am releasing these people immediately as a gesture of my good faith. Right now there is a plane waiting outside to take you. OK, OK, goodbye."

Clapping and cheering, the Gentile hostages began to gather up their hand luggage. The photographers rushed about getting shots of them, and of a smiling, beneficent Amin.

Then he went through to the other room. In the confusion, I was able to follow him in. The Israelis stirred from their makeshift beds on the floor and looked at him expectantly. He clapped his hands again.

"For those of you that do not know me, I am Field Marshal Amin, President of Uganda. I want to welcome you to my country. I promise to do everything within my power to make your stay here as pleasant a one as possible. I have already arranged for food and water and medical care to be made available. It was I that per-suaded the Palestinians to allow you off the airplane and to release some of your fellow passengers.

"You must understand, I want to conclude this episode as soon as possible. The Palestinians are fair and just people. I myself am visiting Damascus and saw how well they treated the Jews there. So make yourself comfortable here also, please. I have already got the Palestinians to extend the deadline, but you must understand that negotiations for your release have failed up till now because of Israeli stubbornness. But I continue to try . . . because I am appointed by God Almighty to be your savior."

He paused for a moment, and smiled at his astonished audience.

"One more thing. And this is very important. This is very very important. Please, do not try to escape. As the Palestinians have wired the building with explosives. This is very important. In the meantime, look on me as your host. I shall arrange for your release as soon as the Israeli government stops its stupidity and agrees to the reasonable demands of the Palestinian people. I am sorry for your inconvenience. I do hope the Palestinian demands are met before the Israeli government forces them to use explosives on you."

He beamed at them—for such a man, he really did have a beautiful smile—and nodded his head, as if trying to convince them that he was doing them a kindness; as, no doubt, he genuinely thought he was.

"I have an idea: I think you Israelis should compose a letter to your government to persuade them to agree with the Palestinian demands. Then we can all have a party and you can go home. Isn't that better than the Palestinians blowing you all up? You see, the Israeli government is gambling with your lives. Anyway, I go now to negotiate your release and safety . . . Yes, it is true, I go to shape your destiny and save your lives . . . Shalom! Shalom! OK . . . Shalom."

He waved goodbye and walked out into the other room. Most of the non-Israelis had already made their way to the new plane— except for the Air France captain, who approached Amin as he was leaving.

"Excuse me, monsieur, I am the captain of the Airbus. Thank you for releasing some of the passengers. But those people in there are also my responsibility. They are just ordinary people, they have nothing to do with the war in Israel."

"Ah, Captain," Amin said, "it's so good to meet you. When you get to Paris, give a message to your government. Tell them the Palestinians only want a little piece of land of their own. Tell them the Palestinians only want one thing: peace!"

"Monsieur, I am not going to Paris. I feel it is my duty to remain here and look after my passengers. I beg you, allow them to leave now."

"As I said, Captain, it is very good to meet you. I'm afraid I must go now. I have urgent government business to attend to. I have to fly to the Organization of African Unity conference in Mauritius for a few days. It is my final meeting as Chairman and therefore very important."

He walked out of the hall abruptly, followed by his retinue. I watched him get into the helicopter. The sweeping wind from its rotors made the windows of the terminal rattle. As it lifted off, I wondered whether I myself would ever be able to leave.

Back at home that night, the phone rang while I was lying in bed. I got up to answer it, sure that it would be Wasswa once again. The line was crackly.

"Hello," I said.

"Doctor Nicholas Garrigan?" said the distant voice of the operator.

"Yes?"

"I have Colonel Sara Zach on the line for you from Tel Aviv."

I thought it was a joke.

"Nicholas?" said a voice I recognized, although its curt tones were curiously modulated by the wah-wah of the satellite.

"Is that really you? Sara?" I said. "Colonel? What is this?"

"It is me," she said. "I need to talk to you."

"You left me," I said. "Why did you leave without saying goodbye?"

"I had to," she said. "I should have thought that was obvious. But we can't talk about that now. There are more important things. Have you been to the airport since the hijack?"

"Yes. But how did you know I was here? How did you know I was in Kampala?"

"Nicholas, there is not time to explain. I need you to do two things. First, you must tell me everything that you saw at the airport. The layout of the hall in which they are holding them, how many soldiers are there. I also need descriptions of the Palestinians and what weapons they are carrying."

"Why?"

"Just tell me. You can save lives by telling me. Please, for the sake of us if not anything else."

So I told Sara what I had seen that day. She made me repeat it and asked me about some things in detail.

"There is one more thing I need you to do for me," she said.

"What?"

"You must go and speak to Amin when he gets back from Mauritius, you must tell him how he will be regarded as a great statesman and a holy man internationally if he releases the hostages. Tell him he will be admired all over the world. Can you do that for me?"

"I can't get involved in all that," I said. "I'm in enough trouble as it is. You know he put me in prison?"

"I did not know that, Nicholas. I am sorry."

"I'm not made for this kind of thing, Sara," I said. "I just want to go home now. I just want to get out of here."

"It's your duty," she said. "Please. Time is running out."

Time, time, time. It circles round me, overtakes me, stops me in my tracks with an outstretched palm. Simama hapa! Who goes there? I do. I will.

On the island now, in this bone-chilling winter, the journal—as I rewrite it in a colder, saner light—has become even more of a moldy pamphlet than it ever was. For it was touched by blisters of jungle green even before I sent it back. I have continued to make entries—obsessively putting in everything I discover, everything I glean. I'm as bad as a marabou stork collecting rubbish.

For instance, I read in the newspapers recently that the man who faked the Hitler diaries has put up a pair of trophy underpants for public auction in Germany. They are drab grey, and he claims that they belonged to Amin.

Equally, I hear that artist John MacNaught has recently represented Idi as Bonnie Prince Charlie in a show at Inverness Printmakers' Gallery. Crossing to Skye in a tiny boat named *Uganda*, dressed in tartan and wearing the Jacobite White Cockade in his beret, Idi is apparently shown against the backcloth of the saltire, the blue-and-white St. Andrew's–cross flag. Below the image are various inscriptions: Idi is My Darling; Rise and Follow

Idi; The Big Chevalier; Amin Righ Non Gael (Amin, King of the Gaels) . . .

This is the world, essentially mad, essentially true, that I have been inhabiting for most of the past decade. So forgive me, please, if what I put down reads strangely, stops and starts like an uncertain pulse.

31

Duty, that was the word Sara had used. I didn't know what my duty was, not then and not in the months that followed. I didn't ring Amin: I was too frightened, and was in any case too consumed by the idea of escape to think about anything else. But I had no clear idea how to proceed with my plans, now that the airport was closed. I would have to go overland, and that was a very different matter.

My nerves went to pieces after her phone call. The idea that she had been some kind of intelligence operative the whole time I knew her was ridiculous—but it seemed an unavoidable conclusion. It put a whole different color on her relationship with me. Was I really nothing more than a cover? That, and the memory of what I had seen in prison, which came back to me each night, left me in a state of constant agitation.

Going about in a daze, I carried on working during the next week. Things were deteriorating at Mulago, just as they had at the clinic in Mbarara. One day we ran out of water. Well, the whole city ran out of water. Suddenly toilets wouldn't flush and we were unable to sterilize instruments, mop the floors or bathe patients. We rang up the water company but they said they couldn't do anything, and in the end we had to rely on the good offices of one of the oil companies, which flushed out a tanker and started bringing us daily deliveries from Lake Victoria.

It was not just water: we were running low on many basic drugs, in addition to bandages and needles. There had also been a lot of thieving: the compressor we used for the anesthetic pumps, chairs and tables, even the lightbulbs for the operating lamps (which wouldn't fit an ordinary lamp)—all had disappeared into the night.

It was a chaotic time, during the hostage situation itself and afterwards. Shortages developed all over the country: I didn't see pyramids of soap in the shops anymore, nor of much else. Even the price of bananas had shot up, which was ridiculous, considering how many were grown. The story was that the farmers were not growing them for sale anymore. Because of inflation, they were growing just enough to feed their own families. The same applied to the cash crops, like coffee and sugarcane. The sugar problem was exacerbated by the workers on the estates having gone on strike (their own sugar allowance having been cut), and the small crop which had been harvested having been exported to Libya. They said it was being bartered for arms.

There were also stories about muzungus being killed. These had finally provoked several Western governments to complain to Amin, or—in the more extreme cases—to sever diplomatic links. Most of them, however, seemed happy to continue trading, even when the hostages were still captive.

Then came the raid. Most people probably know about that, so I won't rehearse it here in detail. A contingent of Israeli paratroopers landed at Entebbe in a Hercules cargo plane one night, having flown from Israel and refueled at Nairobi on the way. They killed all the terrorists and rescued most of the hostages.

Their inspired ploy was to drive a Mercedes-Benz down the cargo chute with a man in the front seat blacked up and wearing a Ugandan general's uniform. It was supposed to be Amin—Israeli intelligence had fed a false message to the airport authorities about his early return from the conference in Mauritius. This was enough to put the real Ugandan soldiers at the airport off their guard as the Mercedes rolled up to them. Most of the Ugandans simply ran off when they realized what was happening. As a parting shot, the Israelis blew up Amin's prize squadron of MiG jets.

At Mulago, we received about fifty injured Ugandan soldiers after the raid. Anti-Israeli feeling was running high in the city, but it was still a shock when other military men came to the hospital for Dora Bloch, the hostage we'd been allowed to take away for treatment. We stood by and watched, all too afraid to interfere, as they pulled her out of the bed.

"You shouldn't have told the soldiers she was there," was Amin's response to Paterson, when he made an official complaint. We later heard that Mrs. Bloch had been shot and buried in an unmarked grave.

The airport remained closed after the raid, and there was too much going on for me to make detailed plans for an overland escape yet. The next time I saw Amin—at his instigation, a month or so later—all he would talk about was his planes.

"They did not get the good MiGs," he said. "The planes they destroyed were waiting for repairs. It is very bad, but at least people all over the world will now agree with me that the Israelis are criminals."

I noticed, as he spoke to me, that he was still wearing the same Israeli paratrooper wings they had given him when he did his training there, all those years ago. He had very probably met some of the generals who organized the raid.

"Yes, it was a very bad thing to have happened," Amin continued. "But as a professional soldier, I have to admit that the operation was a good one."

He conceded this during one of the taped conversations that he made me come and have with him in the time after the raid. After having threatened me about it, he was now very keen that I should write down and record things about him; or, more properly, the things he wanted me to write down.*

Anyway, it was during that session—though at this point he asked me to turn off the recorder—that something happened which continues to fill me with anxiety.

"Doctor Nicholas," Amin said, clumsily taking the cassette out of the machine. "I have something to show you."

He pressed a buzzer. The door opened, and a servant came in carrying a cardboard box. He brought it over. Amin stood up and started to open it, pushing back the flaps.

"I have a gift here for my very good friends of Rafiki Aviation."

*Not wishing to get burned twice, I made my own notes in code in the margin, with a view to him being a possible reader again. It has just struck me that that could still be the case, if this book is ever published.

Out of the box he lifted something large, yellow and hairy. At first I didn't realize what it was—a stuffed lion's head, with glass eyes and a ragged mane, mounted on a plinth.

"Now," said Amin, "there is a favor I would like you to do for me."

As ever, when he said things like that, my heart dropped.

"I would like you drive to the airport and deliver this to the chairman of Rafiki Aviation, who is a Kenyan man, only a muzungu. You are on terms with the muzungu pilot Swanepoel also, I believe."

"Well, I know him," I said.

"Do not mind about that," Amin said. "If you do this well, we will forget about that as well as about all your crimes against the state. Take this."

He put the musty-smelling trophy back into the box and handed it to me. It was surprisingly heavy.

"But what is it for?" I asked him.

It ran through my mind that it could be stuffed with drugs. The marijuana grown in the Ugandan highlands was some of the strongest in the world. Perhaps that's what Swanepoel had meant when he said he ran "this and that" about for the Ugandan government, the first time I met him in the bar.

"Just go to the airport," Amin said. "You will find an aircraft waiting for you there."

"But it's closed," I said. "You closed the airport, Your Excellency."

"Not to small planes and to cargo planes. Listen to me. I have given orders that this plane should wait. It is a Piper Aztec. When you have done this, you can go home and resume your normal duties at Mulago."

"Why are you sending them this?"

"Mtumi wa kunga haambiwi maana," he said. "The carrier of a secret message is not told its meaning. No, the thing is that I give all the people who work for me presents from time to time. You'll get one too, once you have redeemed yourself. Now go!"

I didn't see that I had any option. Not willing to run the risk of another night in the cells, I carried the box over to the door.

"Wait," Amin said, following me over. "Your tape." He put it on top of the box and gave me a broad grin.

So once again, totally bewildered, I did as I was told. When I got to the airport, I saw that although the runway had been repaired following the raid, the terminal building remained in ruins. I made what enquiries I could of the staff, who were now forced to do their business from a clutch of canvas tents. They were quite suspicious of me, now associating all Europeans with the Israelis, until I showed them my government pass.

The Rafiki plane having been pointed out to me, I strode across to it, carrying the box. I hurried. I just wanted to be rid of it. The propellers were already spinning round. I could see a white face looking out of the back window at me and another at the front. The latter was wearing headphones, but Swanepoel's chunky cheekbones and beard were easily recognizable. In the middle window was his Alsatian dog, with its tongue hanging out. Its breath had steamed up the plastic.

The pilot door opened and a little set of folding steps descended automatically, like a magic trick. Swanepoel came out, and trod down the steps.

"What the hell are you doing here?" he said, shouting above the propeller noise. "Have we had to wait because of you?"

I thought of his broad hand on Marina Perkins's knee, and felt a spasm of jealousy. "I had to come," I shouted back. "Amin said I had to bring you this."

I put the box down in front of him.

"What is it?" he said, looking down. "Why have you had to bring it? Are you his errand-boy now?"

"He put me in gaol. It's a lion's head."

"What?" His beard ruffled in the wind.

"A lion's head. Mounted on a plinth. He says it is a gift."

"Mad bastard," he said, bending down to pick up the box. "He's done this before. Keeping us sweet. Last time it was one of those elephant-foot umbrella stands."

I was relieved that this was obviously a regular thing, and that I hadn't been drawn into some nefarious smuggling ring, with Amin as its sinister Mr. Big. I watched the plane take off, trembling as it left the ground and hauled itself into the sunset. Its small wings dipping slightly to one side, it gave a little lurch—and then sunk behind a hill and was gone. It was then I realized, with a crushing sense of my own stupidity, that I could have gotten on it and escaped.

They say the weather at the moment is the worst it's been in Scotland for twenty years. A tree fell on the electricity wires yesterday, and the power went out for an hour or two in the afternoon. I had to put up candles, as it got dark while I was waiting for it to come back on. A light seeking a light. It made me think of Africa before the bad times—me wrestling with the generator in Mbarara one night, the starting handle spraining my wrist. Sara wrapping it up in swaddling bands.

She would hardly recognize me now, I have been drinking so much and eating so unhealthily. Corrupted by the memory of acts I cannot abjure (unable as I am to grasp the extent of my own complicity), I have abandoned my flesh. My life has fallen into a terrible cycle. With each morning cool repentance comes, and by night I am in hell again. It is true, what the mirror shows: I am no longer the thin dark paleface who arrived in Uganda—qualified in healing arts but not so very different from that boy who was mad for maps and stamps. All that is gone, or ripened into something else: I am transformed into a suppurating beast, someone with a smell of evil about his person. Yes, I have become him. Oh my Christ—

32

The following morning—it was the same day my new Ugandan passport arrived in the post—I looked out of the window
of the bungalow to see that most of the grapefruit had fallen
off the tree overnight. I did not recall that the wind had been
very high, so I went outside in my dressing gown to investigate. Scattered on the lawn, the yellow globes looked as if they
were part of some Gulliverian game of pool. I reached down
for one. It had gone mushy and smelt rotten; they must fall off
the tree at a specific moment, I thought. Or perhaps it had
been one of the storms after all. Regretting that I had not picked
them in time, I went inside and had some stale cornflakes for
breakfast.

As I was finishing my coffee, I tuned into the BBC Africa Service. It was the only source of reliable information about Uganda,
the national media being totally under Amin's control. I listened
to a report on the growing tension between Amin and President
Nyerere of Tanzania, and on the killing of some Karamojong by
Ugandan troops.

The next item threw me into confusion:

A small plane crashed yesterday afternoon over Kenya's
Ngong Hills. The plane, owned by Rafiki Aviation of
Nairobi, burst into flames, farmers in the area said. On
board the plane, which was en route to Nairobi from
Entebbe in Uganda, was Mr. Michael Roberts, chairman

of Rafiki, a cargo firm, and the pilot Mr. Frederik Swanepoel. The cause of the crash is unknown.

I was shaking as I drove to work that day. Swanepoel dead.
The newsreader hadn't mentioned the delivery I'd made, but I
immediately suspected that it must have been explosives, not
drugs that it had been stuffed with. I realized, in my slow way, that
I had been the unwitting instrument of murder. Why would Amin
want Swanepoel killed, or his boss? Was I supposed to have got on
the plane too?

That event, and the mystery surrounding it, only made me
keener to leave. But I felt trapped. There was also something
more. Apart from my abortive effort immediately after the cells,
I hadn't been able to summon up in myself the will to leave.
Indeed, far from making practical moves towards an overland
exit, I began to invent reasons in my mind about why I couldn't do
so. The truth is, there were still things I wanted to know about
Amin. Now I wonder if it is that deadly, addictive curiosity, rather
than anything tangible, that makes me continue to feel uncomfortable about myself.

So I continued with my ghastly ringside seat. It was six
months before I plucked up the courage to ask Amin about the
lion's head. By this time, the ritual of my writing his "life story"
and recording his remarks on tape had become well established:
as I said, he insisted on it, almost as if he knew that, one day, his
tale would have to be told. I took the precaution, however, of
regularly mailing the tapes back to Moira in Scotland—she had
married and moved to Edinburgh—having already sent my original notebook.

"You know that that plane exploded, the Rafiki one?" I said to
Amin.

"Is that what happened?" he replied, ingenuously. "Well, you
know that whites are exploding all the time nowadays."

"What do you mean, exploding?" I said. "Exploding where?"

"Everywhere. They're just exploding and nobody knows why.
You've never seen anything like it. You ought to be careful,
Nicholas."

On other occasions, the conversations we had—the big Philips
tape recorder whirring all the while—were equally strange.

One time, feeling reckless, I simply said, "You know a lot of people think you are mad?"

"Mr. James Callaghan came here. That shows I am not mad. I released Mr. Denis Hills from captivity, after all, even though he was a bad man."

Hills was an English lecturer at Makerere University. He had made some disparaging remarks about Amin in a book, and escaped the death sentence only when Callaghan came out to plead for his life. I was on holiday at the time, doing one of the game parks, as Amin had suggested, so I missed all that.

"But what do you think?" Amin said, giving me a hard look. "Do you think I'm mad?"

"I think there's a sliding scale," I said quickly. "Everyone is a bit crazy in their own way."

He said, "Yes, you are absolutely right, and President Nyerere especially. He has got a chronic disease of bringing crazy mis-understandings between countries. He might well infect the people of Uganda with this disease. He is like a prostitute who has gonorrhea and every man who sleeps with her is infected with gonorrhea."

As a matter of fact, I noticed that Amin was obsessed with sexually transmitted diseases. Perhaps this was what gave cre-dence to the rumor about an STD being the root of his lunatic actions and remarks.

"I find that VD is very high," he told doctors at Mulago one day. "If a sick man, sick woman comes to the hospital, make them clean, or you will find that they will infect the whole population. I like Ugandan women very much and I don't want them spoiled by gonorrhea."

On another occasion, he said something quite odd, in view of the catastrophic incidence of AIDS that has taken place in the country since I left. "Doctor Nicholas," he said, "I have been talk-ing among the soldiers. I have been walking among their camp-fires. They say there is a new disease about and that it is fatal. I want you to investigate."

I did. Though I could find nothing out of the ordinary (that being a somewhat relative term in Uganda at that time), Amin made me publish my report. It was printed by the Uganda Sta-tionery Office in red covers and, I dare say, still exists. But I do wonder now, from time to time, whether some of the people I treated in Uganda in the 1970s might have been early cases of AIDS. Who knows? In the end it is just another death, and God knows there were a lot of those.

But it wasn't all doom and gloom with Amin. Sometimes he would talk to me about his children, and when he did so I honestly believed what he said. "I love my children, Doctor Nicholas. They make me very happy, and very proud. The child of a lion is a lion—that is how it is."

And then he would spoil it by doing something like coming to the hospital and insisting on being left alone with a corpse. I spied him once through the mortuary curtain. It was the body of a high-ranking military official who had been brought in by some other soldiers. They said he had died in a car accident, but his injuries were plainly the consequence of a severe beating.

Anyway, Amin turns up at Mulago and demands to be left alone. I see his shadow through the curtain. First he gives a military salute. Then I hear the stamp of his boot on the floor. Then he bends over the body, the shadow going out of my field of vision. There is a faint, liquid noise, like someone sucking a boiled sweet.

When I go in afterwards, there is an incision in the abdomen— surprisingly neat—and I see that the spleen has been removed. I don't know whether he ate it, or put it in his pocket, or what. Truly, in this case it was, as Galen put it, the *organum plenum mysterium*, the organ full of mystery.

That was about it so far as the cannibalism was concerned. All those stories about heads in the fridge . . . well, I didn't see any of them. Not in the fridge, anyway. But I wouldn't have done. I was close to Amin, yes, but it wasn't like he opened the fridge door every time I visited him.

I did confront him on this issue once, though. "There are many reports in the Western press about you eating human flesh. I remember you said that you had done so in that speech."

He just burst out laughing. "Ah well, Doctor Nicholas, you know the thing about cannibalism?"

"What?" I asked.

"You just can't prove it."

He slapped his thigh.

"Why?"

"Because the evidence—it has been eaten!"

As I say, faced with that sort of thing, what was I supposed to do? I just became quietly desperate. I hated the ambiguity of the whole situation. I knew that, by associating with him, I was being drawn deeper and deeper into a horrific morass—but I didn't know how to continue there without being associated with him. Killing him, after all, was not really an option. It would only mean endangering my own life. But there was one moment, just one, when I was tempted to carry out Stone's deadly instructions.

It was a Friday night. Amin was having a massage at the Imperial Hotel, and he wanted to see me—"immediately." Well, that was nothing new. He made me wait outside until it was finished. When the girl in the white coat pulled back the curtain, I went in. Amin was lying on his stomach on the cushioned leather of the massage table, so sated with pleasure that he was hardly conscious. His skin glistened in the light of an infra-red lamp. There was an electric massager, which looked a bit like a hair dryer, lying on a table nearby and also some mysterious tubes of cream. I noticed a screw of damp-looking tissue in a wicker basket at the foot of the table and then I saw, hanging on the back of the chair, the cowboy holster and in it the big silver revolver which I had seen in his bedroom.

I suddenly realized that I could reach for it then—that I could reach for the revolver and shoot him in the head as he lay there grossly. Part of me wanted to. I didn't do it, because I didn't want to do it for the reasons that Stone had outlined to me. What provoked me even to think about it was something much deeper and darker: I confess that I actually found myself thinking about how pleasurable it might be to kill him, to hold the heavy gun against his temple and feel the kick as it sent his hoggish brains over the wall.

And that was it, really. That was what finally provoked me to flee Uganda, that was when I crossed the line: the sudden and crushing realization that I had become enough like Amin to contemplate killing him for the sheer pleasure of it.

In the event, he simply turned over and started bellyaching about Tanzania. "They have been troubling my troops on the border," he said. "I am going to invade Tanzania with ultimate force. I would like you to provide advice on the healthiest rations for the soldiers involved in the operation. I want you to do this by tomorrow morning."

The murderous instinct having passed in me, I drove back to the bungalow and started to draw up the kind of nutritional schedule he seemed to want. I thought that if I gave it to him, any suspicions he had (though he hadn't voiced any) about me trying to leave would be allayed.

This is what I came up with:

Breakfast
1/2 lb maize/millet porridge
Coffee mixture or tea

Dinner
2 1/2 lb matooke (mashed, steamed banana)
6 oz boneless meat (goat or beef) or 12 oz Nile perch steak
1/2 oz fat (lard or ghee)
1 lb seasonal vegetables (tomatoes, okra, pumpkin)

Supper
1/2 lb bread (kisra pancake)
1/2 pt coffee
1 oz sugar
1 1/4 oz butter or margarine
9 oz meat or fish, as available
Also: beer and cigarette ration

Having done this, I went to sleep—not peacefully, however, as I had a hideous dream about Idi that night. He was sitting at a desk. I saw him from behind. He was holding something in his hand. It was frosty . . . calcified and jagged—like a splinter of rough slate dusted with chalk dust. Only, he was writing with it, scratching with it, and there was nothing on the paper. Just nothing. Then everything went to pieces and the silver revolver was there, lying in a corner on the floor of a cell. Something was on the metal. Grey viscous fluid lying on the shine of it. Then it all changed . . . How quickly do these things happen? A big rock came, and began to break into . . . into two parts. The sky red behind and a figure in the gap in the rock. The shape of a man, but huge and primeval and overbearing. Then I had that vision again, the one I kept having, of a vessel filling with dark liquid. It reaches the top . . .

I have been thinking about those times even when not writing. Peeling potatoes at the sink in the bothy and thinking about those times. Digging out the eyes with the triangular end of the scraper and thinking about those times. I was standing at the kitchen window and the sun, for once, was streaming brightly through. The wind has been quiet, too. Maybe summer's coming in at last.

It's been a funny week for more than the weather, though. A band of hippies, all dreadlocks and kaftans and grubby-faced children, arrived off the ferry in a convoy. They've parked their caravans in one of the fields next to the Ossian and the management are kicking up a stink. They think it will put off their guests. But the farmer who owns the field has given them clearance, so there's not much to be done. It's odd to see their campfires and hear their loud, strange music when you walk down the hill.

I suppose they have as much right as anyone to be here. The local people don't seem to mind, or they only mind as much as they mind anyone new arriving: we're all just "incomers" to them. That's what they call me, that's what they call the smart visitors to the Ossian, and that's what they are calling the hippies too. Malachi, my fisher friend, says they've come here because of Maelrubha's ruins. That's the old monastery that sits on the brow of the mountain. There's a stone circle nearby as well, and all the usual pagan nonsense is attached to it in the tourist brochures. Sacrifices, ancient rites . . . Saying that, a festival is still held here every year, and Malachi reckons that's why the hippies have come. He says if that's the case, they won't be welcome. One of the rules of the festival is that no stranger must take part in the work of it, or touch the tools used for the work.

Malachi has been the friendliest of all the people I've met since I arrived. He's been letting me use one of his boats: a lovely old, deep-keeled thing, clinker-built, its wide, overlapping planks calked with tar at the edges. Malachi says it's built on a model descended from the old Viking ships. Centuries ago, they raided these shores, and many of the locals think of themselves as Scandinavian rather than Scottish. Only I guess the Vikings didn't have a big lamp in the stern for night fishing like Malachi does. It's powered by a car battery. I don't take the boat out at night, of course, but I have seen him do so: the yellow fan of the lamp cutting into the dark fields of the Sound. I myself just potter around in the bay at the weekends. Only then do I feel cleansed and full of vitality: the voice of the sea, the amniotic rock of it, the burst of salt air in the lungs, they can do this to you. As if the old soul, the bad soul, had been changed into little water drops and fallen into the ocean, never to be found.

There has been another bomb, the television said. A police station in Lothian. You would think they'd sort the parcels more carefully at someplace like that. The same people, the Army of the Provisional Government, have claimed responsibility. No one was killed, but a police constable had her hand blown off.

Note to myself: Scotland and Uganda inextricably linked. Their Law Societies twinned, I read today. Another union. God knows why. Our Good Lord is in His heaven and He hath done what He hath pleased.

33

While I was planning the means of my escape, preparations went on apace for the invasion of Tanzania. Uganda Radio was carrying regular broadcasts about the situation. I remember hearing, at one point:

> Doctor Amin today briefed diplomats on the Tanzanian invasion into Uganda. He said that the force which invaded Uganda was a mixture of Ugandan exiles and Tanzanian soldiers.
>
> Doctor Amin said: "It was President Nyerere's army who set the ball rolling in aggressive military confrontation towards Uganda for reasons President Nyerere has not even bothered to explain to us, and to reveal the truth behind his motives of directing his army to courageously penetrate into Uganda with black ambitions. If Tanzania tries a second time to enter Uganda, they will suffer the consequence, because it is not difficult for Uganda to harm Tanzania more than what they have done to us."
>
> The Life President, however, stressed that he loves the innocent people of Tanzania very much and that is why Uganda did not react when the Tanzanian forces invaded us.

But they were reacting; I knew this myself. When I gave him the ration schedule, Amin said that he also wanted me to draw up guidelines for the army medics. I wrote a pamphlet for them, entitled *Treatment of Wounds in a War Zone*. I felt, before I left, that this would be one way in which I could do the right thing. At least it could save some lives.

I detailed various procedures that might be followed in the field. I described how the first duty of the surgeon was to prevent sepsis. I emphasized the difference between healing by first intention (closing the wound by joining its edges with stitches, as in a panga cut) and healing by second intention (allowing skin to grow over the wound of its own accord). I explained the importance of distinguishing between viable and nonviable tissue in a wound. How the latter could, if unexcised, lead to gangrene.

I also laid out the basic procedures for the management of shrapnel and bullet wounds. The theoretical mechanism was as follows: tissue necrosis occurs several centimeters to either side of the missile track. The missile releases energy which is absorbed by adjacent tissue particles, imparting to them an acceleration which flings them forward and outward. The kinetic energy can be calculated from the formula $KE = 1/2MV^2$, where M is the mass and V the velocity of the missile.

On delivery of the pamphlet, Amin was very pleased. I was very much back in favor. And still I hadn't gone. It was several months later before I was prompted, finally, to do so.

I was sitting in my office at Mulago when the post boy brought me a batch of letters. There was a bank statement from UK (which showed, to my surprise, that Stone's money was still in the account), a letter from Moira telling me that a great-uncle had left me a bothy on one of the Western Isles, and also a grubby envelope with a domestic crested-crane stamp.

This was the letter inside, jaggedly written on a scrap of lined exercise book in black ballpoint:

Bwana,
    i am having to write you because you were here before and hearing what happened in that time. The boy Gugu who you took in your house has been very bad. he is been done in great trouble. pliss move quick to Mbarara to help him from these bad tings.
    yours faithfully, Nestor
    (watchman).

The letter brought all the memories of Mbarara—now, as I see it, the happiest time I spent in Uganda—flooding back to me. I suddenly felt a rush of tenderness and responsibility towards the young boy I had left behind. The thought of Amin's brutal troops dealing out to him the like of what I had seen in Kampala in the last few years filled me with dread and guilt. I resolved that if I would do anything, I would take Gugu out of Uganda with me. It would, I thought, be my way of atoning for my association with Amin.

Once I had decided, I made my preparations rapidly. I took out as much money as I could from the bank in Kampala, filled some cardboard boxes with food and bought two jerrycans full of fuel. My plan was to drive down to Mbarara, pick Gugu up and make my way over the border into Rwanda, by bush roads if need be.

The situation was made more complicated by the increasing amount of military traffic on the road since Amin's offensive into Tanzania had hotted up. He was sending large numbers of tanks and troops down to the border. Only the previous night, the radio said, a Libyan Tupolev jet had dropped five bombs on northern Tanzania. Three thousand Ugandan soldiers had gone across the border into the Kagera Salient in northwestern Tanzania, led by the so-called Suicide Strike Force. The Tanzanian border guards had fallen back and hundreds of local people had been taken hostage. The Ugandans had raided a cattle ranch and driven thousands of cattle back across the border, and blown open the safes in banks and shops. Factories and homes were razed to the ground.

The US Secretary of State, Cyrus Vance, had cabled Amin, with the intention of persuading him to withdraw from Tanzanian territory. On the radio, Amin replied by accusing America of "interfering in an African dispute with the aim of creating a second Vietnam."

"The Uganda armed forces have made a record in world history," Amin continued. "In the supersonic speed of twenty-five minutes they have taken back this Kagera territory, which has been held by Tanzanian and Chinese imperialists for too many years. All Tanzanians in the area must know that they are under direct rule by the Conqueror of the British Empire."

President Nyerere of Tanzania broadcast a call for the Organization of African Unity to act against Amin, while defending his right to retaliate without negotiation: "Do you negotiate with a burglar when he is in your house? There has been naked, blatant and brazen aggression against Tanzania. I want to know what the OAU will do about this. I expect African countries to tell Amin to withdraw before people talk about restraint. I expect no dithering . . . Since Amin usurped power, he has murdered more people than Smith in Rhodesia, more than Vorster in South Africa. But there is a tendency in Africa that it does not matter if an African kills other Africans. Had Amin been white, free Africa would have passed many resolutions condemning him. Being black is now becoming a certificate to kill fellow Africans."

As I drove, though I didn't know it for a fact, Tanzanian infantry were marching towards the Ruwenzoris, the "Mountains of the Moon." I was worried that my escape route passed so near to a likely war zone. But I didn't have much choice. The crossing point to Kenya was closed. Sudan was too far. The Rwanda–Zaïre border would be the easiest to pass through, there being a large number of border crossings in the mountains. In any case, I reckoned that in the confusion of military operations I would be able to cross over unnoticed in that vast area. I toyed with the idea of getting special clearance from Amin to check medical facilities in the field—but in the end decided that this would only draw attention to me.

The first hundred miles or so were fine. I passed farms hedged with spiky green manyara plants, forests of blue-gum trees, fields of bright green maize stalks, the usual fleets of banana lorries—one with a bundle of pink tilapia fish tied to its wing mirror to keep them fresh—and the customary complement of people riding sidesaddle on the backs of bicycles, as the cyclists struggled in the heat. Children waved at my white face and cried, "Muzungu! Muzungu!" For a moment it seemed that all was well in Amin's Uganda.

There were also a lot of army trucks on the road, but I just overtook them in the van and carried on. Some of the soldiers even grinned at me from the back of their trucks. The van still had the red cross Swanepoel had suggested I have painted on it, so I suppose that helped.

I crossed over the equator—I could just see Angol-Steve's little encampment to the right—and began to recognize familiar landmarks as I got closer to Mbarara: Masaka, Lyantonde, Lake Mburo, a tree near Sanga where I noticed pelicans nesting, their great, scooping bills clearly visible from the road. I thought about the poor Kenyan—his bloody face and my gaucheness, the soldier with the bedroom slippers. That had been near here.

I had just passed through Biharwe trading center when I saw a sign for Nyamityobora Forest on the right: it brought to mind the sign I had seen with Waziri—the one for the Impenetrable Forest, farther west. It was at that point that I saw an army checkpoint on the brow of the hill. I came to a halt. The sun was going down by now and I could see the silhouettes of the soldiers, the apex of a tent, and the square shape of a Land Rover in the distance.

I didn't know what to do. I had my usual papers, but those might not be enough. They could send me back, even arrest me. I could try to brazen it out with my red cross, say I was Amin's doctor—but even that was risky in this kind of environment. I sat for a moment in the van, the engine idling, wondering what to do.

Then I saw that the Land Rover was coming down the hill. It was half a mile away but they had obviously, through binoculars, seen me waiting and come to investigate.

I panicked, hurriedly shifting the gear into reverse and turning round. In the mirror I could see that the Land Rover was speeding up. I looked about wildly—at the tarmac coming up at me and the bush on either side of the road. I put my foot down and the van's engine squealed. Then I saw the sign to the forest and I veered off left down the dirt track. I looked to see if they were still following me. They were, they had turned off as well. I pressed down harder on the pedal and it soon got very bumpy, and darker, too, since I had passed under the canopy of the forest.

The track twisted through the big curtains of green. My foot was on the floor, my eye flicking between the track and the mirror—but I couldn't see if they were still behind me because of the twists and turns. Why don't you just stop, I thought to myself, explain who you are? But fear drove me on.

I didn't know how far I was ahead of them when I saw another sign—"Nyamityobora Forest Game Lodge"—and suddenly I was in a clearing and the track had just stopped. There was a building made of logs there, like an American cabin, only it was deserted and broken down. I sat in the van, pulling at the steering wheel, not knowing what to do. I noticed a couple of paths leading into the forest but they were too narrow to take the van down.

I turned off the engine and listened. There it was: through the leafy baffles and side sweeps of liana I could hear the mechanical grind of another vehicle. I grabbed whatever I could—as it happened, only my wallet and passport—and jumped out. I looked about. It was all just bush: bush and the abandoned cabin.

I didn't know where to go. I looked about. Dark green everywhere, and then I could hear the other engine again. It was closer. I looked at the cabin: they were bound to go in there. The paths? Too obvious. I looked into the bush again. It was full of places to hide but that in itself put me off. It was as if there was too much to choose from and if I ran, I'd have to batter through the vegetation. My tracks would show and they'd easily be able to follow me.

Calm down, I told myself. Stay and wait for them, use Amin's name to bluff it out. It got darker quickly as I waited. I soon saw the lights of the Land Rover flashing against broad leaves and then they were chopped off again by an intersection of trees. This terrified me further.

The headlights once more, on and off. I looked about again, wildly. Then I spotted that there was a narrow space underneath the cabin. I rolled in just as the Land Rover pulled into the clearing.

The gap smelt musty and I could feel dried vegetation under my back. I heard the door of the Land Rover open. They had left the lights on and I saw a pair of army boots walk into the beam. Trousers with puttees. And then two more. A voice shouted out something in Swahili. By then I'd picked up enough to recognize the word "wapi"—where. Where are you? The voices continued for a little more.

Another light came: the beam of a torch, darting about. I heard them open the door of the van and then the dry hustle of their boots coming over towards the cabin. A creak on the step, the noise of them opening the door, and then their footsteps heavy on the boards above me.

More talking. An insect crawled over my face. I didn't dare

move to brush it off as I listened to the tread of the men above, the sound of them talking and opening cupboards. Looking for me. My heart thumped.

After a while they came outside and wandered about the clearing. The beam of the torch again. Then one of them came over towards the gap under the cabin. The boots—close by me, so close I could smell sweat and leather—and the beam was flashing about in the space. It flickered over me. I thought, this is it. They've seen me.

I stiffened. But then the light was gone again and they were walking back towards the van, opening up the boot and looking inside, rummaging in my boxes of food.

Suddenly there was a burst of automatic gunfire. I could see the man's legs juddering as they absorbed the energy of the recoil. He spun about like a top, sending rounds ripping into the broad-leaved grove around us. The bullets went into the cabin, splintering the wood and shattering was what left of the glass in the windows.

I was paralysed, except in my head, except where I was praying that he wouldn't lower his line of fire, wouldn't crouch and fire into the space underneath.

Just as quickly as it came, as if someone had switched off a light in a suburban room, the firing stopped. Quiet. Then one of the men laughed. I heard them get into the Land Rover and the diesel rattle of its engine. The arc of the headlights moved across the leaves as the vehicle turned. My breath came out of me in a long draught and I was about to roll back out from under the gap when I heard another sound, strangely familiar. Another vehicle starting up, its headlights coming on. I stiffened again and watched its wheels move off. They had taken the van. I'd left the keys in it, like a fool, and now they had taken it.

I lay there for half an hour, unsure of what to do. I couldn't stay here till morning. I couldn't walk into the forest. There was still some moonlight in the grove but if I was to go deeper into the forest, I would be bound to get lost, even if I followed one of the paths. I put up my hand and gripped the slimy edge of the wood to pull myself up. As I did so, I heard a rustle in the brush under the cabin, just to my right. It made me jump and I banged my head on the wood as I came out.

I stood in the grove, my back to the cabin, staring into vast obscurity of the forest. I was on my own now. I might as well have been naked. All I could see was a dark wall of leaves, broken every now and then by shafts of moonlight and intermittent pinpoints of gold: the living lamps of thousands of glowworms. What a fool you have been, their Morse code seemed to say to me, oh-what-a-fool-you-have-been.

I don't know what made me turn round. Maybe I heard another rustle from under the cabin. Maybe it was just a sixth sense. But there behind me, swaying vertically in the emphatic quietness of that moonlit clearing, was a snake. Four or five feet long, it was raised up on itself, with its small hood drawn high and each eye as clear and green as a good emerald. A mamba, I thought, stupefied.

I turned to run but it had already begun to strike. I felt—very precisely—the two points of its fangs go through the fabric of my trousers into the back of my calf. I didn't feel any pain at first, though, and carried on running, flailing blindly at the enormous heavy leaves that overhung the path. I ran until my breath burned in my chest. I ran and I ran, and all the while I could feel the dull throbbing rising up my leg. It began to hurt, and then it began to hurt a lot. Eventually, the swelling wave of pain flowed up past my thigh, over my pelvis, and I had to run slower. I slowed down, in fact, to a walk. And then I stopped.

I stopped in the darkness, amid the ceaseless soughing branches and the deep sappy smells of the forest, with its bird calls and strange animal squeaks. I started to cry, the tears running down my besmirched face. I wept and I lay down. I curled up on the forest floor and fingered the back of my calf, where I could feel the raised flesh around the puncture points. I suddenly felt terribly thirsty and I realized that it was because of the poison flooding through my body. As I frantically rehearsed my options, grasping at odd bits of snakebite pathology, I felt my nervous system start to revolt against itself, every bit of me seeming to go into spasm. My arms and legs began to jerk about and the last thing my rolling eyes saw was the face of Idi Amin, high up in the treetops and stretching from pole to pole.

. . .

I don't remember much about the next—as a matter of fact, I don't know how long the period of time was. My next memory was of something prodding me in the side and blue fragments of sky coming down to me through the forest canopy. Except that I couldn't see them properly, as my eyelids had swollen up. All of me, in fact, had swollen up. My head was pounding like a steam-hammer and my shaking limbs were pouring with sweat.

I felt an unseen hand hold something to my lips. The rough nozzle of a skin bottle. The hair of it—goat's hair? I thought, dumbly, *monkey* hair?—tickled, and then the cool water was coming down, splashing over my lips and chin and going up my nose. Then the hands were turning my body over, gently going over it. I winced as they touched the swollen calf. I heard a grunt and the sound of someone rooting around. I felt the fabric of my trouser leg being pulled up and then I heard the noise of a blade cutting through the material.

I yelped as the point of the knife searched the flesh where the snake had bit and then I felt a pair of lips close about the wound and suck. And then a spit, the gob of it tapping sharply as it hit a leaf. Another suck, another spit. And then, as my mind wandered off, my consciousness struggling like someone scrabbling to hold onto a cliff, I heard a series of piercing whistles.

The next thing I recall was being in the womb. At least, it felt how a womb might. I was moving—moving rhythmically—forwards and side to side. I realized I was going along a forest path. The dappled sky was still above and the broad-flanked leaves paddled my face as I passed by them in my cocoon. I was wrapped up, swathed in rank-smelling skins. I could hear, as I rocked from side to side, the sound of men talking and I could see the soles of their feet flashing up from the forest floor as they ran with me.

Every now and then I felt the weight of the ground on my back, and I saw the shapes of the tribesmen above me. And then they would lift up the poles again and we would continue our journey. When we got to the village, the hunters gave me more water and put me in a low hut. It was like an igloo, only it was made from branches and leaves that had been bent round and stuck into the ground. With the skins still about me, between me and the hard earth floor, I fell asleep once more.

On waking, I was able to gauge more about my rescuers through the oval gap in the hutment. They were a band of about nine—three women, three men (one old and bearded) and the rest children. They didn't seem to have much with them, if you didn't count hunting equipment, which included one high-powered–looking rifle, several bows and arrows (the heads of the latter bound tightly with string and coated in what looked like tar), and a couple of large nets. All were more or less naked, though two of the women wore skirts made from dried banana leaves and one of the men was wearing what looked very much like a Woolworths anorak: blue terylene, with a fur trim. Unfastened and almost in shreds, it hung about him like a greatcoat.

At one point a woman came into my hut with a lump of indistinguishable, half-cooked flesh, at which I gnawed hungrily. She squatted in front of me at the oval opening. With her long, dried-out breasts hanging down almost to her waist, she looked to me—in my hallucinatory, venomized state—like an athlete with a towel over his shouders.

Then she handed me a tin can full of a sour-smelling liquid, motioning me to drink it. I sipped the bitter, herby draught gratefully. I felt dozy then and hardly noticed as she turned me over and began massaging the swollen flesh around the punctures. I had a vague sensation of something sticky and warm being plastered over the place, and then I fell asleep again.

When I woke up, the taste of the herb potation was strongly present in my mouth—as if it had been reduced, like the mysterious caramelized sauces my mother used to make over the stove in Fossiemuir. I thought of her in her rose-print apron in that cold stone house, and then I thought of him, as impregnable as a strong-room door behind his newspaper in the lounge. I couldn't blame them for this situation, I knew that; nor, in truth, for the closed-in, oblivious temperament that had got me into it. I knew it was simply myself, this casket of emotional defects and diffident, inward-turning passions . . . Not once, I thought, as I lay there in that stinking hut, have you snatched anything glorious or courageous from the world as it passed you by.

I had an odd vision, then, of Amin in the driver's compartment of an old-fashioned steam train, dressed in uniform and cap, and grinning manically as he whipped past in a cloud of steam and dust. Strapped to the cowcatcher was Winston Churchill, my father, me . . . I didn't know, the faces kept changing.

As this surreal picture passed out of my feverish head, I felt—in that dark, stale space with its oval gap of light—something crawl over my ankle. I reached down and, pinching where it was, felt an ant crumble between my thumb and forefinger. I remembered another insect then, the moth—its dusty wings the color of dried blood—that had alighted near us in the beer garden when I had had my last talk with my father. Well, not quite a talk: we had just sat there over our pint glasses and squares of cheese, the day before I left, and we had hardly said a word. A smile had broken across his tight face when the moth settled on the wooden table, and he had taken off his spectacles—I can see them now, clenched in the papery skin of his hand—and spoken, something close to fierce emotion in his eyes. "The most important thing," he'd whispered, as if imparting heretical information, "is to minimize the harm you do to those around you."

As the thick tiredness crept over me again, I tried to retain the image of his face in my mind—the eyes with their grey mist of something half-said, the high forehead that turned into a bald patch between two clamps of white hair, the mouth that tended naturally downwards—but I couldn't hold it for long. I cursed myself for not having gone back for his funeral; perhaps she would have . . . *I did no harm*, I mumbled aloud, as if he was beside me in the furry semidarkness of the hut, *I did no harm*. O my father—

The irresistible force of sleep pushed down my eyelids, closing off him, closing off Amin in that runaway train, closing off my cloistered view of the hunters' camp, closing off light.

After another day, and more food and herb soup, I was strong enough to get up and wander round the encampment. The whole place smelt strongly of woodsmoke and roasted flesh. Busy mending their nets and skinning a baby antelope (its small, buttonlike horns covered in felt), they didn't take much notice of me once I ventured out. In spite of potbellies, and faces, even those of the children, that seemed creased like ancient parchment, they seemed in the rudest health—and totally contented. I felt like a strange animal that had been captured and was being allowed to domesticate itself. I wondered whether they were the pygmies Waziri had mentioned (but they seemed too tall), or even some long-lost strand of the Bacwezi.

That night, however, as I lay in the dome of leaves and branches, a furious argument took place. In the firelight I caught occasional glimpses of the faces of the participants. From time to time one of them—most often the old man with the beard—gestured towards me. I couldn't, of course, understand a word they were saying.

The following morning the man in the anorak shook me out of a deep sleep and gestured that I should follow him. We went for about two hours down one of the forest paths. He kept having to stop to let me catch up with him: I was still quite weak but wouldn't have been able to keep up in any case, such was the speed with which he moved through the vegetation. He picked out the path with ease, at moments when I thought it had simply vanished into a somber fence of green. More green than one can describe—except that everywhere there were clouds of white butterflies, so many it was almost unnerving. Not the big, mountain type, but small forest ones, floating around without purpose. Or so it appeared. There are no flowers, I thought dumbly, as I stumbled on.

On one of the rest stops, in a clearing much like the one where the soldiers had taken my van, the man suddenly looked at me and held his nose. I realized that there was a smell of decay about the place. The man pointed where the path in front of us bisected another: it was much wider, wide enough to take a vehicle and I noticed that there were indeed deep tire tracks there, pressing flattened leaves into the soil.

He began to walk down the wide path, much more slowly than he had been going before. As I followed him, the smell got stronger. We soon came upon a sight which made me quail with horror. In front of us was a large pile of bodies, nearly twenty feet high. They hadn't been laid neatly but they had the appearance of repose, nonetheless, as they lay breast upon breast of each other. Heads, some still in helmets, lolled on the shoulders of their neighbors; feet were put up, as if comfortably, on the stomachs of the same; arms and legs were intertwined like the lianas of the forest.

The whole thing was covered by a pullulating swarm of mottled blue insects, which rose and fell as if the mound itself were the gently breathing body of a sleeping giant. At the bottom, apart from shreds of camouflage, the gleaming bones of the oldest corpses were the only way of distinguishing where flesh met plant in the sweltering mush of organic material. At the top, the faces of the recently dead retained their dreadful expressions of fear or surprise or abject entreaty.

You could, in some cases, still see their wounds: here and there the simple dark hole of a bullet, elsewhere more disturbing signs of pain and torture—burns (one man's arm simply a charred stump), gougings and twisted limbs. The forehead of one had deep cuts in it like those on the top of a loaf of homemade bread, another's was simply caved in, as if some essential element had been removed. In front of the bodies—nearly all of which were male—were odd bits of clothing and military equipment: a forage cap, a brass buckle, a yellow plastic shoe. Beer bottles were scattered about the clearing too, and at my own feet I could see where cigarette butts had been stamped into the earth. My calf began to throb again and I felt unsteady: it was the sight of the butts and bottles, I think, that did it, more than the mound itself, or even the smell. The image of men standing here, smoking and drinking as they dispatched or disposed of their victims—that was what made me, finally, begin to vomit.

It was only when I had finished—by which stage I was on my hands and knees in front of that awful altar—that I realized that the man in the anorak had gone. I was suddenly struck by a fear of the trees again. I ran back up the wide path, crossed over the point where we had joined and carried on. I had only run for another hundred yards or so when I heard the loud blare of pop music, and rounding a corner I crossed the threshold of the forest.

As the unobstructed blue light poured down over me, my calf gave a valedictory throb. I crouched down and pulled aside the ragged flaps of my filthy trousers. The poultice the hunter woman had put on the snakebite was itching. Black, and crisscrossed with fibrous matter, it looked like a badge. I got under one of the edges with my fingernail and pulled at it slightly. It came away to reveal a medallion of white flesh, stark amid the grime. In the middle of the circle were the two eyes of the puncture, the skin around them dead: whiter than white.

34

The path out of the forest led into a meadowlike area. Beyond it, a road wound down into a town, nestling in a valley. With a surge of joy and astonishment, I recognized the valley as the Bacwezi, and the outline of the town as that of Mbarara. I walked on a bit farther through the tall, brown-and-yellow grass, weary and still faint from my venomous episode, but grateful to be back within the confines of civilized society. As I saw it—and that is how I saw it.

I stood in the grass, the stalks as high as my knees. In front of me, in a bare space under an acacia tree, two boys—one with a transistor radio under his arm, which explained the pop music—were driving a couple of longhorn zebu cattle to and fro over a pile of millet stalks. Threshing on the hoof. I watched as the thick, horny material, its tracks of brown and blue full of secret biological history, trampled the tiny seeds off the bulrush-like stalks. Out of calcium and gelatine shall come forth carbohydrate, saith the Lord. And out of the jungle, NG MD.

Flicked at with a little stick, the cows went round in a circle. One lad, smaller than the other, hung for dear life onto several skeins of leather in the middle. His job it was to keep the cows roughly in the area of the millet pile, while the other kept them moving. The pile itself was moving too, the seeds jumping up and down in apparent confusion. Like Brownian motion, I thought. Around me the pop music weaved amid the dappled grasses, and the meadow seemed to answer with its sweet breath, and I had this strange sensation of seeing deep into time. I thought of the

Bacwezi again, their rites of cow and fig, and of the Batembuzi's King Isuza, the one who couldn't find his way back from the underworld. As I did so, one of the beasts (its anus opening and closing quick as a camera shutter) was moved to defecate. The dollop of dung fell onto the millet pile, sending it scattering.

I walked past the cowherds—they looked at me amazed; I suppose I must have been quite a sight, a muzungu with his hair matted, his clothes the filthiest rags—and down the road into town. My old town.

A lorry passed me on the way, its dusty double wheels rolling their thick treads over the warm tarmac: so warm I could feel it softening beneath my shoes. Mounted on the lorry's flatbed, strangely, was its own trailer, so you had one set of double wheels right on top of another. A man stood on the mounted trailer. He had a white cloth wrapped round his head, half obscuring his face. I looked up at him as he went by (the flatbed-trailer arrangement meant that he was quite high up) and he moved his arm as if to cover his face further still. I thought of Waziri suddenly, his surgical mask at his throat, and feelings of guilt, but more of fear, sent a shiver through me. I hurried on, uncertain what to do.

As I got nearer to town, I passed four kids in uniform, sitting on a low wall under the shade of a bottlebrush tree. On their way home from school. They stared at me as I passed by—stared at this white man gone bush. Their uniform was bright blue, and I envied them its crispness.

I hurried on. I had no idea where I would find the boy, but even after my own troubles, Nestor's letter was still worrying me. You can imagine my surprise when, on reaching the army camp, I caught what I believed to be a glimpse of Gugu's face.

It was difficult, difficult to see and difficult to move. There were lots of people, a tight and shouting press concentrated on something in front of the camp gates . . . men and women, soldiers and civilians, young and old. Some of the soldiers seemed very young indeed.

I started to jostle through the crowd. As I got closer, through the thicket of limbs I could see someone tied to a chair. Then I saw Gugu's face again. An arm raised up, a hand gripping a rifle. The rifle came down. The figure in the chair rocked from side to side. Not him, too, I thought, not Gugu, please God.

I elbowed through. There was a booming noise. I heard one of the women wail and the crowd relaxed a little. And then tightened again. People started to move against me. They were running away. Given this opportunity I burst, mad and ragged creature that I was, into the central circle. One of the boy soldiers who was beating turned to me, and I could see his face and also the bloodied face of the figure in the chair. It wasn't Gugu.

Then I heard the booming sound again and the boy soldier, comic in his overlarge camouflage, swung his rifle at me. The brown stock of it connected with my ribs and the pain made me aware of something. That it was him after all; the face was Gugu's that I had seen. But not in the chair.

I was on the floor then and he—the little man, transformed, camouflaged innocent with viciousness on his brow—was above me, the barrel of the rifle trained on me. Then another booming sound came, only closer and with a whistle riding on the top of the boom. The noise came so close it filled my ears and nose, so close it was like a taste. There was a smell of metal and burning in the air, and the crowd was crying out, crying out at the flames above us.

The blast hit us. The one in the chair, he went backwards, his legs stuck up. And then Gugu above me, he too was going off the ground. Everything was going off the ground. The *ground* was going off the ground. The force of the explosion sent the breath out of my chest and my body rolling in the smoky air.

I tumbled—upwards! As I lost consciousness, what was in my head—slow, and reaching blindly at its own strangeness—was the thought of losing it. In front of me was Gugu, changed boy with camouflaged wings descending. His sternum was red and departing from itself, red and departing from its center like a half-opened flower.

35

At one time or another, I see a figure coming towards me, striding purposefully through the millet. The land stretches out steamy and blue behind the bulrushes. In front of me, behind him. Then the land falls. It is Amin.

In another place I see an elephant, one ear sticking out farther than the other; one tusk, also, longer than the other. He leans to one side in a camp pose. I can see the wrinkles in his rough grey-brown skin, the sheer thickness of each leg and the little plait of hair that hangs from the end of his scraggy tail. His other tail, his front tail, drops limply down between his tusks. Slaps himself then, flesh-slap with the sudden trunk. It is Amin.

Elsewhere I see a hippo standing in a grassy space, next to a tall cactus tree. It rolls. What surprises me is the lightness, the almost-pinkness of the underside of its body. But it is Amin, it is the soles of his feet, sticking up on the massage table as I enter the room.

By a river in the grassland I see three rhinos. Three rhinos standing on the savannah, solid in their armor by a long low river. They move their plates and—I need only say it straight in my sleep—the plates of the earth and the soft bones on the top of some baby's head would also move. A baby in Fort Portal, a baby in Fort William. But it is Amin, it is just three Amins by that long low river.

In a garden I see a peacock extending its fan, and howling like a banshee. It, too, is Amin, it is Amin's medals, his medals and his faraway eyes.

And then I see my father and I am free. He is reading the Scotsman. *But the headline on the back says: "The road dark, the destination obscure."*

Every time this comes round, it's like a rerun. A rerun of the first time as I'm traveling along, as I'm traveling along and eating up space. Yet it felt like a rerun then, too. And now, as then, I cannot sleep but see Amin . . .

What I did see, such as I could when I came to, was a concerned black face peering over me. A face topped by an American-style military helmet, a face with a cheroot sticking out of its lips.

"Ah, you have woken, bwana. We were worried if we had injured a muzungu. It would not be good for our international relations."

"Uhnn?" There was blood in my eyes.

I realized that once again I was moving along, except that now I was in a vehicle. I looked about. There were weapons and equipment hanging on the sides and up front I could see the heads of a driver and a passenger and a thick glass window.

"President Nyerere would be very unhappy with me if that was the case, so I am very happy to see you," said the cheroot man, who was bending over me, crouched under the low roof of what, I was becoming aware, was an armored personnel carrier.

"Where am I?" I struggled up on to my elbows, a ripple of pain coming up from my bruised ribs.

"You are in the custody of the Tanzanian Defense Forces. May I present myself? I am Colonel Armstrong Kuchasa, officer i/c the operation of our country against the Ugandan aggressor Idi Amin Dada."

He handed me a mug of tea and a lump of stale bread.

"Those boys," I said, "—just children."

"Kidogos," the Colonel said. "Kid soldiers. Amin has started to use them. They are the most vicious of the lot. They have been raping women in my country. Boys . . . raping grown women."

I sipped at the tea thoughtfully, soaking the hard bread with it in my mouth.

"Now," he said, watching me, "you must explain to me what you are doing here. Quickly. We have just completed a successful offensive against Mbarara. We are very busy."

In the distance, I could hear once again the boom of artillery fire and—much closer—the sound of men's voices.

"I was trying to leave," I said. "I had had enough. I thought I could get over into Rwanda."

"That would not be possible. Now you must stay with us. The problem is, our medics are very busy because of the fighting. You will have to come all the way to Kampala. You needn't worry, this is a war we will win."

I felt a jolt, searing my ribs, as the APC went over a bump.

"I've just come from there," I said. "But you don't have to look after me. I am a doctor myself. Maybe I can even help the medics. I am not badly injured. It's just my eardrums, they are very sore."

"You—a doctor? In truth? What is your name?"

"Garrigan," I said, sitting up. "I practiced near here first and then up in Kampala."

Colonel Kuchasa slapped his thigh and then sucked on his cheroot.

"This is very ripe. We have been giving Tanzanian medicine to a muzungu doctor."

The vehicle pulled to a halt, sending him lurching forward, his binoculars swinging round his neck.

"Well, Doctor Garrigan," he said, steadying himself. "I will have to go now. Stay in the APC: although they haven't yet stood and fought, there are still a lot of Ugandan forces around."

"Near here?" I said.

"Don't worry. You will be safe—unless they have RPGs."

"What are they?"

"Rocket-propelled grenades. For piercing armor."

He laughed. Then—picking up a stick, which, I slowly realized, was actually a short spear—he lifted the hatch of the turret and poked his head out. The noise of men talking was suddenly louder. I heard him shout in Swahili and then the reply coming back.

The Colonel called down to me. "The Simba garrison from Mbarara has retreated to Masaka. That is where we are heading now. Major Mabuse, the head of the garrison, has holed up in a church at the top of a hill. We must now make the assault on foot. You must stay here in the APC. It will follow as the action is completed."

He clambered out then, and I lay there for a few minutes, listening to the noises of the soldiers moving around me, their voices muffled by the steel walls of the armored car. I was still quite weak from the snakebite—though whatever gunk the hunters had daubed on it had been a triumphant success—and my head continued to ring from the blast. Yet I was curious to see what was happening, so after a few minutes I got up and cautiously looked out myself.

There were two or three other APCs next to the one I was in, also three fuel tankers, a couple of ambulances and ten or so lorries with howitzers and other artillery pieces pulled behind them. Otherwise the whole contingent, which was deploying across the road in front of me, was on foot. As I watched, a pair of scarlet-and-black shrikes flew up out of a bush, disturbed by the movement.

A little way away, the Colonel was waving his spear about, drawing lines in the dust in front of some other officers. (As I recall it, I can't help myself thinking of Michael Caine in *Zulu*— "Don't throw those bloody spears at me!" That old vision of Africa I'd had, the same that led me there and doomed me: it returns like a specter.)

A sergeant-major called out an order, and the body of men came to a halt. With the Colonel continuing to make his dispositions, the sergeant-major began to address the troops. They must have been up to a thousand strong—jaunty-looking in their grey ponchos, camouflage uniforms and jungle hats. Once he had finished, they began to move forward.

The road to Masaka cut on into the blank bush ahead: there was no target as such. I couldn't see where they were going to attack. Smelling petrol in the air, I turned round in the turret to see where it was coming from.

About a quarter of a mile away stood the remants of Mbarara. Even from that distance, and through billowing smoke, I could see that the Tanzanian shelling had been devastatingly effective. Through a gap in the opaque vapor—a space, in that odd perspective, no bigger than a man's hand—I suddenly caught a glimpse of something familiar: a steel water tower. I couldn't tell whether it was the one in the compound or the one at the clinic, but it made me sad all the same. The sun caught the steel again. Then I realized the tower was lying on its side.

Messages from the dead, I thought, as the steel glinted again. I watched the black smoke balloon up above the town. Then my mind returned to Gugu. How could he have become such a creature? From son of a distinguished cartographer to bloodthirsty kidogo in just a few years. Was this what Amin had done to Uganda? Or was it my fault—should I have looked after Gugu, should I have stayed there and been a father to him? Or killed Amin when I had the opportunity? By that stage, I reflected, it wouldn't have done any good.

The sharp rattle of machine-gun fire jerked me back to the present. As I turned round, I saw a Tanzanian soldier drop to the ground. The sergeant-major shouted. There was blood on the dead man's face.

The troops fanned out on either side of the road, running and then crouching behind the stumpy trees and tall sharp grass. They held their automatic rifles out in front of them, occasionally letting forth a jerking volley of fire.

Up ahead, flitting among the trees, were the indistinct shapes of Amin's fleeing soldiers. Beyond them, high up, a battery of artillery started a fusillade. I could see the yellow and red flashes illuminating the brow of a hill. The bullets whistled by, and shells began to fall round and about, many to the rear. When the high-pitched whine of a shell came in the air, the Tanzanians threw themselves down and curled up in tight balls. Once it had exploded, they got up again and continued their darting runs forward.

The APC—in which, probably foolishly, I felt quite safe—began to move forward slowly. We passed a detachment of gunners setting up mortar base plates down on my right in the soft earth. I watched them attach the three slanting tubes onto the plates, feed in the bulbous charges and turn away their heads in anticipation of the noise: thud! thud! thud! and then the awful wait before the explosion proper. I felt my eardrums press in, and the noise and brightness of it made me want to close my eyes.

When I opened them, clouds of blue smoke were drifting

over the battlefield. The Tanzanian infantry moved ahead, with the APC and other vehicles trundling after them. In front of me I could see the bodies of those I assumed to be Ugandan soldiers sprawled in the tall grass—both armies were wearing exactly the same camouflage fatigues—while behind the mortars continued to send their deadly charges in high loops over my head.

As well as the bodies, there were bits of equipment (rifles and ammunition pouches, knapsacks and canteens, crumpled items of clothing) sprinkled over the rough yellow vegetation. The road itself was also scattered with the debris of war—brass shell cases, the guide wires from rockets and other assorted bits of metal— all of which the caterpillar tracks of the APC crushed as it went over them.

The bombardment and mopping-up operation continued all afternoon. We passed through the deserted towns and villages that lined the road: Sanga, Lyantonde, Katovu, Kyazanga, Mbirizi. In every one, the shops were shut up, in every one there was not a soul to be seen—the inhabitants had all fled into the bush— not a soul to be seen, until the whip of a sniper's bullet was heard and we would stop and flush him out.

The Tanzanians slowly moved forward, with the Amin soldiers somewhere in front. The Tanzanians were much more disciplined, if the bunch nearest to the APC were anything to go by. Three of them manned a heavy machine gun, which they mounted on its tripod for each engagement. One man lay on the ground pulling the trigger, his legs apart, while another fed the belt of bullets into the breech. The third man lay next to them, his rifle at the ready, to provide cover for the others. I watched transfixed, heedless of any danger to myself. There was something hypnotic about the way the spent cases sprung out, each tumbling along the ground beneath the tripod in response to the orange flames that came out of the muzzle with every burst.

In between, while they changed belts, the man with the rifle would discharge a few rounds himself. He didn't seem to be shooting at anything in particular. His own spent cartridges flew over his shoulder and he, in turn, would snap in a new magazine as his two companions set themselves once more to their stammering, deadly work.

As they did so, patches of oily smoke emerged from the

breech. Perhaps because of the oil in them, these patches held their shape. Dark and mysterious phantoms they seemed like, as they drifted slowly across the tops of the tall grass on either side of the road or threaded themselves through the parched branches of the acacia trees. Then the APC moved on again. For a few minutes a pack of wild dogs appeared out of the trees and trotted along beside us, the females carrying their young in their mouths.

The closer we got to Masaka, the more vague and fleeting my impressions of the fighting became. This was as much a consequence of the increasing noise (which reached a crescendo as the APC crept up towards the vanguard) as it was of the fall of darkness.

Only it wasn't darkness, but a general, low-level blaze of munitions, light enough to illuminate the shapes of men and vehicles. The glow was of an uncertain color—yellow, red, purple, gold—and the whole of it was intermittently crossed by thick clouds of dark smoke. But all this, both the clouds and the dull glow, gave way to the screaming phosphoric trails of the rockets which the Tanzanians began to pour into the town as we came within range.

The tracers passed high over my head, their luminous track staying in the sky long after their passing—and staying in my head, too, when I shut my eyes: imprinted on the retina like a photographic negative. I thought of Amin's eye again, looking at it through the opthalmoscope, and wondered where he was, what he was looking at.

Every now and then there would be a still more blinding flash of light as one of the rockets hit an arms dump or the fuel tank of a vehicle: this would illuminate the outline of the town—an outline that changed with each illumination, as the bombardment took its toll. It wasn't just rockets. That evening the howitzers sent nearly three thousand shells into Masaka.

By the end of the barrage, the opposition had dribbled away to nothing. But they were weary Tanzanian soldiers who entered the destroyed town that night. Weary of marching, as much as anything. Only Major Mabuse had put up a fight, apparently, but that was all over by the time the APC reached the bombed-out church. I did see Mabuse's body, though, recognizing those peculiar raised scars on his cheeks. I might as easily have not recognized him: the bottom half of his body was nothing but an anonymous tangle of flesh, draped over the twisted wreck of a mounted machine gun. The Tanzanians said that he had fought to the last minute. I thought of him in that bar in Mbarara, his grim face staring into the bottom of his beer glass as if he were conjuring up demons from the flecks of foam.

The whole place smelt of burned flesh, and the whole place was smashed. Rubble and broken glass littered the pavements, and the tiled roofs of buildings—caved in and hanging at precarious angles—were curved into strangely beautiful, fragmented shapes. Below, among the piled bodies, dogs and chickens sniffed and scratched. I looked out for the Tropic-o'-Paradise, but could hardly distinguish one shelled building from another, still less spy out the pirate sign.

I slept in the APC that night, and so did Colonel Kuchasa, who climbed back in late and smelling of beer. I was lying on a blanket on the floor in the back, the driver was stretched out on the front seat. The Colonel took up a position at the far end. I could see his cheroot glowing in the dark.

"It has been a very good action," he said, to no one in particular. "Not only have we won, we have also collected much valuable equipment. Recoil-less rifles, six tanks, Pye 47 radios, plastic explosive, medicine, boots and tunics, even a bazooka—Idi Amin has been the best quartermaster we have ever had."

"Mmmh?" I said.

He rambled on. I fell asleep that night with the smell of cordite in my nostrils—it was like fireworks on Bonfire Night, but much stronger—and the sound of the Colonel's voice in my artillery-battered ears.

"I like this war," he was saying. "I was trained in classic infantry techniques by the British at Sandhurst and in guerrilla tactics by the Chinese. This war has both. It's wonderful."

Beyond his words persisted, real or in my head I no longer knew, the howl, hiss and chatter of exploding ordnance . . . And the sound of helicopters, too, came to me with the mind's night creatures, the glittering eyes of Major Weir chopping and changing with those of the Colonel in the vertiginous blur of the rotors.

36

I felt a little stronger the following morning and with Colonel Kuchasa's permission was able to help out in the ambulance wagons. The Tanzanian medics accepted me with brusque professionalism. This was war seen from a totally different point of view: not military capability, but the simple algebraic fact of KE = $1/2 MV^2$ and its attempted reversal. That is, once again, the laceration or crushing caused by the passage of a bullet or the more general tissue necrosis following the shock wave of an explosion (shrapnel, blast wounds). Cavitation ensues as the tissue is flung forward and outwards. Pathogens take hold at the entrance and exit wounds as they are sucked in by the negative pressure in the cavity.

So much for the theory. The man I was working on as I thought about all this had a small dark entrance hole next to his groin and (we discovered on turning him over) a bigger exit wound on the buttock, out of which trailed a skein of bloody tissue. His skin was covered with blood. I swabbed the wound and then went in, cutting away at the deep fascia. I trimmed the ends of two tendons and lightly tacked together the strands of a severed nerve.

The stretchers kept coming in, bearing men with various injuries: part of the shoulder taken off, or legs full of shrapnel, a bullet through the ear, a severed spine, or shell splinters in the abdomen. In each case: nitro under the tongue, a morphine plug in the hand, an IV needle and line into the forearm (the saline solution as a temporary replacement for lost blood). Then exploration of the wound.

It is first sluiced with an antiseptic solution. Then debridement (surgical toilet) takes place: the removal of bullets, indriven bits of clothing, loose bits of bone and obviously unviable tissue. The wound is incised generously and widely; the neurovascular bundles are identified; dead tissue is excised—tissue that does not bleed, tissue that does not contract freely when cut, tissue that looks green, yellow or blue in color, signaling sepsis and fulminating putrefaction—and the wound, after further antiseptic irrigation, is left open or covered with a gauze light enough to allow easy drainage. Suture may be attempted four to six days later if the wound is free from infection.

If there is a good blood supply and healthy tissue, no hematoma or tension in the tissue planes and, most important of all (and most difficult to achieve in a field hospital), freedom from pathogenic bacteria, healing can occur quite quickly. If, on the other hand, blood supply is poor or obstructed, tissue dead, damaged or infected, healing may take many weeks. It may be necessary to sprinkle antibiotic powder (ampicillin, cloxacillin) on the wound if the injury involves contaminated bone. The latter should in any case be cleaned with a curette, and on no account removed from the wound as this may result in limb shrinkage or nonunion.

And then the next case. In quieter moments came the simpler needs of an infantry regiment on the march: Vaseline for the callus that forms where boots rub the back of the calf, medicated talc for scrofula, ointment for septic toes—as well as more generalized cases of tick fever, hookworm, jiggers, tropical eating sores and the like.

By the end of the morning (the first influx of major casualties having been dealt with), I returned to the APC. I had to walk back down the line to get to it and, as my bad luck would have it, I chose to do so at the moment of a counterattack by Amin's forces.

I was walking along against the flow of troops—I could hear the swish of their knapsacks jogging against their backs as they walked, and smell the graphite oil from their guns—when there was a series of sharp cracks. A soldier near to me muttered an indecipherable exclamation and promptly fell on to his back. The column dived for cover and so did I. The bullets began to whip over us, lashing the air and tearing through the grass. For a few moments we were pinned down.

I realized that the man who had been shot was lying beside me. Blood was dribbling from his open mouth. I leant over him and gently lifted his hand away from where it was pressed against his chest. I saw that the bullet had passed through his ribcage and—the blood from the mouth suggested—pierced a lung. He would almost certainly die. I took off his hat and cradled his face in my hands. He was moaning slightly, and beneath his half-closed lids the whites of his eyes were fluttering up and down.

Using the hat, I tried to staunch the flow from his chest but it was useless. And then I realized that all of his lower body had also been sieved by bullets. I was lucky to have escaped unscathed. I blew the whistle that was hanging round his neck, and stayed with him until the stretcher bearers got to us, the pair of them looking like an insect with their low, crouching run and the poles between them. More daring than I, they took him off. One twitching leg hung from the stretcher as they ran, the boot full of blood.

The encounter raged for the next hour or so, the bullets piping directly above me and grenades exploding with dark red flashes to my right and left. Every now and then it would all die down and you would think it was over, and in these moments I would scuttle farther back towards the APC. And then the fusillade would begin again.

When I finally reached the APC, I had another close shave as I clambered in. A bullet passed so close that I felt the wind of it on my face. Once inside, the cabin resounded with loud metallic pings as bullets and pieces of shrapnel bounced off the armor.

Eventually the din ceased and we began to move forward. I looked out of the turret again. We soon came into a more fertile and—so it initially seemed—peaceful area of countryside. It appeared vaguely familiar. There was millet there, and a maize plot. I realized that we were about to cross the equator. I saw the concrete rings and looked out for Angol-Steve's odd little homestead, on the left-hand side. I was shocked to see that it was totally burned out.

There was also something else, a few hundred yards farther along. Hanging—by a rope, from a baobab at the side of the road—was Angol-Steve's body, swinging slightly in the wind.

There were blood and brains on his shirt. His shins, I noticed, were ragged. Wild animals had obviously gnawed at them. Hyenas, I thought, sickened. The APC speeded up. I felt an overwhelming sadness. I had liked him—he had certainly been harmless, and in his eccentric way he was a shaft of light.

Angol-Steve was not the only one. All along the way after that, at various points next to shell holes and tanks that had slewed off the road, were strewn the mutilated bodies of Ugandan peasants. It was senseless slaughter—the retreating army had no quarrel with these helpless people, except in so far as they might not have given them maize or matooke when they demanded it—slaughter born of fear and the knowledge that one period of brutal domination was coming to an end. Unable to look any longer, I climbed back down into the ringing steel shell of the APC.

About half an hour later Kuchasa's genial face popped over the circular hatch of the turret. "We got the devils who did all that," he said, seeing my downcast expression. "Come and have something to eat. We want to take Kampala on a full stomach."

I climbed out and joined the officers where they were standing around a fire. Two large black pots were hung above the flames and inside them, ugali (maize-meal porridge) and a stew of stringy meat. I dipped handfuls of the white goo into the gravy. It burned my hand and wasn't really very nice, I suppose, but I suddenly realized that I was very hungry. I listened to the officers talk in a mixture of Swahili and English as I ate. They planned, the Colonel said, to be in the capital by the following night. He sent a runner to tell the other troops. "Sika Kampala," the whisper went round the cooking pots. "Take Kampala."

And so we did. But it wasn't plain sailing. The next engagement was at a village called Lukaya, somewhere between Masaka and Kampala. There was a papyrus swamp there and when we reached it, water—two or three feet deep—covered the road. The APC sloshed through it like a prehistoric monster, sending columns of brown liquid shooting up on either side. As we went through, a couple of dark shapes leapt off through the papyrus: sitatunga, the aquatic antelopes whose splayed hooves enable them to walk through swamps and over floating carpets of vegetation.

More significantly, there were a thousand Libyan and Palestinian soldiers on the other side of the swamp. The Libyans had apparently been flown in from Tripoli by Colonel Gaddafi, who had issued a warning to Tanzania that he would come in on Amin's side.

It turned out that these Libyans were armed with Katyusha rocket launchers and soon the rockets, with their blood-red tails, were flying the other way. The Tanzanian ranks were thinned in this encounter—I saw three go down myself, falling together like ballet dancers—and the invading army had to pull back until air support could be brought up. Once the Tanzanian MiGs had strafed the Libyan position, streaking so low above us that they almost touched the trees, the infantry were able to move through the swamp towards the Libyan positions.

They did not take many prisoners from among the Libyans, and what few they did take seemed among the sorriest creatures I had ever seen. (Kuchasa said some didn't even know in which country they were fighting.) They trailed behind the APC during the final stages of the assault on Kampala.

The contingent of Tanzanians I was with was not the only one. Various other regiments had been securing strategic locations all through southwestern Uganda, from Mutukula to Murongo (where Tanzania, Uganda and Rwanda intersect), and then converging eastwards on the capital. The regular Tanzanian troops were aided by ragtag bands of anti-Amin guerrillas. All in all there were 45,000 Tanzanian soldiers and about 2,000 guerrillas.

Early that evening, as Kampala's seven hills came into view, it began to rain. By the time the first buildings came into sight, the road had turned to flowing mud and the verges were full of the noise of boots tramping in the sodden grass. The mud clogged the tracks of the APC, making it creak and rumble all the louder.

There was a little more resistance on the edge of the city, if the crackle of small-arms fire was anything to go by, but the Tanzanians advanced steadily, jumping into the concrete drainage ditches for cover whenever it was needed. As the light began to fail, I watched the vivid orange muzzle flashes as the soldiers moved forward firing. My eye was caught by the strange action of them shooting round the corners of buildings—holding the gun away from themselves as though it was something unpleasant.

Night closed around us, and the fighting continued in a half-light of street lamp and flame. Some of the defense was brave, not to say foolhardy. At one point, a Mercedes came careering round a corner filled with Ugandan soldiers brandishing weapons out of the windows. A Tanzanian trooper simply picked up one of the bazookas they had captured earlier and sent a vicious spout of fire in their direction. The explosion was loud, roaring in my ears. I once again felt my tympanic membranes flutter—to, I was sure of it, the very point of perforation.

The style of fighting changed as successive waves of troops got deeper and deeper into the city. The Tanzanians nipped from shop-front to shop-front, their rifle reports echoing among the masonry. There was also a lot of waiting, during which periods the troops would pull out sticks of sugarcane and chew them. The pavements were strewn with gobs of white fiber. If we had been a retreating army, it would have been forbidden, Colonel Kuchasa told me, as it makes it easier for trackers to follow your path.

During the periods of waiting, the Colonel would confer with his officers. Nobody seemed to know exactly where they were going, although I knew from the previous night's discussion that it was Kuchasa's intention to take up commanding positions on each of the seven hills, and to secure the UTV and radio stations, the clock tower at the center of the city, and Amin's Command Post at Prince Charles Drive.

Capturing the Command Post involved traversing a golf course, and also the moonlit gardens of Kampala's diplomatic quarter, where the flags of distinguished nations hung unmoving in the wet air. It was odd to hear the sound of machine-gun fire and the crump of mortars in that suburban environment. I had got out of the APC and was walking by this stage. At one point, while I was going past the gates of a house, a security light came on and a dog rushed out into the driveway and started to bark. A dalmatian, it stood there yapping in the pool of light. I looked at it and it looked at me, while behind me hundreds of booted feet tramped past wearily. And then I, too, walked on.

Most of the diplomats, like everyone else, stayed in their beds, except for the North Korean Ambassador, who came out as we went past and asked Kuchasa to join him for a noodle break-fast the following morning. Earlier, in a strange incident I heard about but did not see, Doctor Gottfried Lessing, the East German

Ambassador (and former husband of Doris Lessing, the novelist), made a break for it in two white Peugeots in the middle of the night, along with the First Consul and both of their wives. They went over the golf course just as the Tanzanians and Ugandan liberation forces were crossing it. The latter fired rocket-propelled grenades at the two cars, turning them both into balls of flame. There was speculation that they were trying to escape because of East German associations with the State Research Bureau, one of Amin's terror organizations.

As for Amin himself, rumor was rife concerning his whereabouts. The few Ugandans who were on the street that night said that he had been seen at Namirembe market the previous day, trying to drum up morale. At one point on the approach, during the day, one of the Tanzanian officers had seen his red Maserati through binoculars—but no one really knew where he was now. One road out of the city, that to Jinja, had been deliberately left open to allow diplomats and the remaining Libyan soldiers to escape: President Nyerere was keen not to bring Libya further into the war, which some outside commentators were representing as an Arab-versus-African conflict. Some said Amin had already fled down this road, others that he was still holed up somewhere in Kampala.

There was a peculiar moment in the early morning. Mist had come down along with the dawn, and the outskirts of the city were eerily swathed in the stuff. The troopers' teeth were chattering with the cold and they looked, as they tramped along there in their grey ponchos, like giant bats. And then out of the mist there suddenly loomed a tall, silver figure.

"It is him," whispered one of the troopers.

And the shape of the figure was indeed much like that of Amin—fifteen feet tall, mind, and dressed in swimming trunks, but the same muscular build and imperious air. It was, it transpired on closer inspection, a statue advertising a health spa on the edge of Kampala. The fact is, it would have been totally in character for Amin to have greeted the invading force dressed in his swimming trunks. The story went down the line, provoking much merriment.

As for myself, I didn't really know what to do once we were in the heart of the city, walking past the closed shutters and barricaded doors. There was still a little danger. Small groups of pro-Amin soldiers were moving through the streets in a confused manner, some on foot, but most in tanks, Land Rovers and armored cars. The odd bullet flicked off the walls of the buildings, and in the distance a burning oil-storage depot gave off the same sick yellow light I had seen during the advance. Salvos of artillery were still booming overhead.

The Tanzanian command, I learned, were planning to billet at State House. I realized then what a situation I was in. I couldn't simply go back to the bungalow there: my relationship with Amin might easily be misinterpreted. Already I had seen several pro-Amin citizens prodded by the bayonets of the Tanzanian soldiery, which by this time had got hold of crates of whisky and beer and (perhaps more worryingly) bundles of dagga: the strong Ugandan marijuana.

I decided instead to trudge up to Mulago. I went off in search of Colonel Kuchasa, to find him slightly harassed by the problem of keeping his overexcited troops in order. They were firing their pistols and automatic rifles into the air, and were I a woman, I should not have liked to have been in the vicinity. I said goodbye to their exemplary leader, who had been so kind to me, and began the long walk through the rain up to the hospital. On the way, I noticed that there were a lot more rats about.

When I got to the hospital, soaked through and covered in mud, Paterson was shocked—and at the same time almost too busy to see me. He was in surgical greens, and rushing about the ward. It was full of soldiers. They lay on the beds and they lay on the floor, moaning quietly and staring up at me as I walked past. I saw the dirty bandages, covered in brown and yellow muck, and I felt a rush of guilt. This was where I should have been, I thought, this was where I should have been all the time.

Paterson was exteriorizing a loop of damaged bowel, winding it around a spindle. The patient's stomach had obviously been opened by a bomb, and it was not a pretty sight. There were shreds of flesh and muscle all over his torso.

"Very nice of you to join us, Nick," Paterson said, his sarcasm making me feel even worse. "We thought you'd disappeared into the sunset with Amin."

"I tried for the border," I said.

"That was brave of you," he said. "Thanks for letting us know."

"I . . ."

"Look, we're run off our feet. I don't care where you've been or what you have been doing. Just scrub up and pitch in."

I did as he said, changing into surgical greens—at least they were clean and dry—and set to work. Stretcher upon stretcher was brought in, from both sides. A surprising number had broken thighs, from standing too close to their own artillery when the recoil came. As there were Africans with Arab features fighting on the Tanzanian side, and the Libyans and Palestinians on the Amin side, with the majority of both forces having Bantu characteristics—and, as I have said, the same camouflage fatigues, the same canvas packs and steel waterbottles—it was nigh on impossible to distinguish between them. Eventually we realized that only their undergarments provided a clue: the Ugandans wore olive green Y-fronts, the Tanzanians the same except in navy blue. And the Libyans, for some inexplicable reason, wore white woolen long johns.

The procession of those consumed by death and wounds seemed interminable—and so it was that I spent most of the day at the operating table. A single horrible image from that time sticks in my mind: a kidogo on the slab, not much older than Gugu would have been, Paterson leaning over him, opening his chest with the plastic spreader and then going in. A butterfly, I thought. Ekwihuguhugu. This one is very fragile.

37

Late in the afternoon I stumbled—crazed from overwork and lack of sleep—back down into town. I must have looked a strange sight. I had taken off the blood-spattered surgical gown and pantaloons I had worn for the operations and put on a clean set of the same from the store. My own clothes were simply too dirty and too torn to wear.

I didn't know what to do. Paterson had grudgingly offered me use of a room in his house, but I couldn't stay there for ever. I had no money to speak of and nowhere to go. Apparently a tank shell had landed in the grounds of State House. If my bungalow hadn't been destroyed, it was now no doubt home to Tanzanian soldiers. The rumor was that Amin had come running out on to the lawn as soon as the shell had landed and leaped into a helicopter.

Everyone was wondering where he was. We had heard him on the radio that day in the refectory at Mulago, more incoherent and deluded than ever.

> I President Idi Amin Dada of Republic of Uganda. I would like to denounce reports that Kampala is in the hands of foreign aggressors, that my government has been overthrown and that they have formed their rebellion government in Uganda. I myself am in a relaxed and jovial mood. I am in a very comfortable place. I dismiss as nonsense reports that I have run away . . . I assure that as

a conqueror of the British Empire I am prepared to die in defense of my motherland . . . which will survive completely. Though it is true that Tanzania and its Zionist friends—including Cuba, Israel, America and South Africa—have been attacking the country. They have killed very many innocent Ugandans, children, young and old, and women, killing doctors with long-range artillery. Destroying the whole Kampala including the Mulago Hospital, killing doctors, nurses . . .

—this last declaration brought a dry laugh from Paterson and the rest of the staff, since Mulago had come through the barrage more or less unscathed—

. . . making the mercenaries tyrannizing the wananchi of Uganda. Even changing completely the town of Uganda today. It is not a town, therefore I am surprised this so-called government wanted to form a government in Uganda after killing everyone . . . Yet Palestinian soldiers are fighting side by side with us on the front line. My good friend Gaddafi has sent us two thousand troops and large quantities of arms. This is, truly, the time when Arab countries should assist Uganda financially and materially . . .

. . . and Uganda armed forces must not surrender their arms to any rebellion completely. Coward officers and soldiers that . . . whoever will be found retreating from the firing line must be court-martialed and, if found guilty, must be killed by firing squad.

Yet we are in full control all over Uganda . . . Kampala we have too . . . We have got soldiers controlling the country, keeping the law and order . . . I am speaking as the President of the Republic of Uganda and the commander in chief of Uganda's armed forces. I want repeat this in Kiswahili. Mimi nataka kusema . . .

Where, people asked, was he broadcasting from? One of the mobile Land Rover transmitters he had fitted out? Or somewhere in the city? Certainly it was not the main radio station in

Kampala—from where, earlier, one of the officers of the Ugandan liberating forces had made a triumphant speech as soon as they had secured the complex.

"We ask all the masses of Uganda," the officer had said, "to rise up and join hands in eliminating the few remaining murderers. We appeal to all peace-loving peoples of the world to support the people's liberation cause and condemn the former Fascist regime."

On other stations, Western countries and various African ones were busily denouncing the Tanzanian invasion: "It was the first time," said one commentator, "that an African country had invaded with impunity the capital of its neighbor. If the borders are not respected, the invasions will never cease . . ."

I turned all these words over in my head as I walked through Kampala. Down Mulago Hill, along Kitante and Akii Bua, then round into Lugard Road. Overnight, it had changed beyond all recognition. Once residents had realized that the Tanzanians would not prevent them, indeed would join in—on the way down I had passed a soldier who was completely naked, except for the helmet on his head and the bottle of Simba in his hand—they had begun to loot their own city.

The process had obviously started early in the morning, and it was still going on, if the crowd that flooded the streets was anything to go by. In the main shopping precinct nearly every door and window I walked past had been broken down. I saw three youths pushing a brand-new Toyota along the road, and then farther up the enormous gaping hole they had made in the showroom window. Others contented themselves with bicycles, typewriters and televisions. Latecomers had to settle for pots and pans.

Elsewhere, crowds were gorging themselves on sugar. A warehouse had been found fully stocked and people were pushing their way through to get a sackful. Many weren't waiting to get the sacks home but were ripping them open on the spot, and simply filling their mouths with it.

At the same time as all this was taking place, there was also a kind of victory rally in progress. One portion of the crowd was cheering the detachments of Tanzanian soldiers who were combing the city for pro-Amin troops and officials. The people followed the soldiers in large groups, the body of them running slowly after with a heavy, unified tread. Some were beating drums, others calling out.

I stopped on the pavement and watched them go by—and then I saw something which made me fear for my own life. The crowd suddenly turned in on itself. Losing the rhythm of its slow jog, it started to contract and expand about a single point. I couldn't see anything but a whirl of clothing. The Tanzanian soldiers turned round and tried to break it up.

But they were too late. Suddenly an arm rose above the melee, flung up into the air. It spun round like a stick, and then fell back down into the threshing mass of bodies. Horrified, I realized that somebody was being torn limb from limb.

"It is an Amin fellow," said a young girl standing on the curb beside me. I could hardly hear her above the noise of the crowd. She was talking to a friend. Both were wearing maroon gymslips and cream blouses: the uniform of one of the big Kampala schools. As I watched the confusion in front of me, I strained to hear their voices.

"He would have been luckier if the Tanzanians had got him."

"It will be like this for a while now. Until the gogolimbo has passed."

"What is that?"

"It is the bad spirit that has come over this place. My grandmother says that it will only go away when you see a dog and a goat riding a bicycle together."

"That wouldn't surprise me. Nothing would surprise me now."

"It will be all right, though. Not now, perhaps, but at some point it will all be back to normal."

"We'll be able to get married."

"Are you kidding? All the good men are dead."

"Not all of them."

"Most."

"Did you hear about Cecilia?"

"What about her?"

"She was raped by a soldier. I saw her in the street. She looked very bad. Walking painfully."

"It is a horrible thing. A gun can make men very pleased with themselves."

"Look at that poor man! There is hardly anything left of him."

"Don't be sad. Like I said, this era will be over soon."

"You think so? I am not so sure. I have my doubts."

"About what?"

"About the new leaders. I am apprehensive."

"No, you're not. You're pessimistic. We must have hope if we are to be saved . . ."

Passing so close that one of its handlebars nearly hit me in the ribs, a droning, low-powered scooter snapped me out of my daze. Annoyed, I watched it weave through the crowd. Leaving the two girls talking, I found myself carried along by the mob. It was converging on Amin's city residence at Nakasero, which the Tanzanians were in the process of searching.

When the crowd got there, the guards tried to prevent them coming in, jamming the wooden doors against the wall of bodies. I saw Colonel Kuchasa among the people on the steps, shouting and waving a revolver around. He had discarded his spear and was wearing Amin's cowboy holster around his waist. I recognized the gun which he was holding: the silver revolver. And then the doors gave way and the crowd poured in. I followed, the tails of my surgical gown flapping behind me.

38

I am Idi Amin at Holyrood. I am walking the echoing corridor. My mind shuttles between past and present as the lights on the walls fizz and rustle. It is the sound of electricity, the sound of electricity meeting damp. My footsteps echo in front of me and behind me. I am like a ghost in my green gown.

The northwest tower. I am Idi Amin standing gleeful as Rizzio dies. I am Idi where Mary Stuart, Queen of Scots, gives birth to the one who will unite the realms. I am Idi walking on the gravel, watching it all recede, watching it where Jamie the Saxt watches it from his carriage as he departs for London. The window is chapped with frost . . . At Musselburgh we'll stop for the funeral of Lord Seton, at Berwick they'll sound the guns for us, in Buckinghamshire one Oliver Cromwell, landowner, will feast us royally . . .

I am Idi walking with Cromwell in the stables of the Palace. It is years later. The smell of blood, excrement and steel is everywhere. It is the smell of occupation. It is the smell of electricity.

Yes, I am Idi Amin at Holyrood Palace in Edinburgh. I am Idi as Prince Charlie, carousing smoothly under these high roofs. A few nights of pleasure. His round back massive as the Rock. I am Idi Amin as Cumberland the persecutor, sword flashing silver in his hand.

I am running. I am running away from the lights with their smell of blood. I am Idi running on the track at Meadowbank. You should know that I can run 100 yards in 9.8 seconds. I am Idi

*pressed hard against the metal starting gates at Musselburgh. I am
riding a horse called African Pard and I will make all the running.
Because I am running. I am Idi running with lion and elephant in
the Botanic Gardens. I stumble on melons as I pass. Agave and
araucaria, canna lilies and the heavy, sticky petals of angel trum-
pets catch at my face and hands. I put them up. I put them up
because I am Idi Amin boxing at the Sparta Club in McDonald
Road. I am Idi Amin sparring with Kenny Buchanan. You must
know that in boxing, when the referee is against you, the only
thing to do is to win by knockout.*

*Now I am running across Waverley Bridge. The light is in
front of me but goes away with every panting step. I am Idi stepping across the Union Canal. What are those rocks? Those rocks
are crocs. I am Idi at the Tron Kirk, and I am Idi spitting on the
cobbled Heart of Midlothian in front of St. Giles. No, I'm not: I am
Idi watching himself at the Filmhouse in Lothian Road—I am a
real bit part, a gun-happy mercenary in the film Zenga. Or I am
Idi at Murrayfield. You should know that pushing is very hard,
and that with my speed and way of getting the ball, when you
tackle me you should harm yourself.*

*I am Idi at Dalmeny, I am Idi at Comely Bank. I am Idi at
Dalkeith, I am Idi at Corstorphine. I'm Idi at Marchmont, Mer-
chiston and Muirhouse. I am Idi at Juniper Green. I am Idi down
in the schemes, walking among the poor, and I am Idi at Morning-
side. I wish I was somewhere else. I wish I was somewhere else
because I am somewhere else. I am walking along the corridor
between his bedroom and those other rooms . . .*

For that is how it was. Along with the rest of the crowd, slipping in
with the looters and the sightseers, I had tumbled from chamber
to chamber in the presidential residence at Nakasero. I'd had to
press myself against the wall as they'd brought the furniture down
the stairs: dressers, wardrobes, a rocking chair. I had seen the portrait of Lumumba go by at an angle, the martyr's face bisecting a
chandelier and a rack of guns in the space beyond the staircase. I
had seen cameras and sports equipment, including a whole multi-
gym, dismantled piece by piece, come down the stairs. I had seen
telex machines and telephones, night-vision binoculars and Racal

two-way radios. I had seen rhino and kudu horns and rugs made from the skins of ocelots and jackals. I had seen bottles of specially made whisky with Amin's face on them. I had seen trays of pellet-shooting pens. I had seen attaché cases with tape recorders inside. I had seen 240 suits and uniforms on wide-shouldered hangers, and I had seen a large boxful of exploding paperback books.

All these things, as the wananchi rushed out noisily with their new belongings, I had seen come down the stairs.

And then I had climbed them. I had gone into his bedroom. Evidently one of the first places they had lighted on, it looked as if there had been a fight in there. The water bed had been punctured, there was water everywhere. Nearly everything else had been lifted, fingered or ransacked, including the chests of drawers. The vanity unit was gone, the television was gone, the escritoire was gone. And now all was quiet, except for the shouts and whoops from other rooms.

While I was in there, the curtains blew out of the window suddenly, where the pane had been smashed. The fabric was whipped out by the wind as I watched. It made me think of Gottfried Lessing in his car when the RPG hit it: as they ignite, RPGs create a vacuum in their local atmosphere. The air would have been sucked out of his lungs.

One of the few things left untouched was the bookshelf with the long run of the *Proceedings of the Law Society of Uganda*. It gleamed gold and red, gold and red and irresistible. Suddenly alone, I looked around furtively. Two men passed by the doorway, struggling with a rolled-up carpet. I saw them behind me in the mirror. And then I was alone again, and I pressed the book door and it opened with a neat click. And so I crossed the threshold and was standing again in another part of my history.

39

I pushed the door closed behind me and walked down the steps.
Now I was in the damp passageway and the smell of electricity
was in my nostrils. The strip lights were flicking on and off. I stood
there for a moment, unsure whether to go back or forward.

I walked on. The tunnel smelt mustier than before. I could
hear, farther down it, the indistinct sound of a voice talking. I
walked in the direction of the voice, the slap of my feet loud on
the concrete.

Reaching the entrance to the chamber, I hesitated—and then
went in. The place was deserted, so far as I could see, and there
was now no noise except for the intermittent hiss of radio static
from the banks of communications equipment in the glass booth.
There were no operators inside, just a pair of headphones hanging
on the back of a chair. Then I saw, reflected back from one of the
alcoves in the glass wall, an appalling sight.

On a wooden table in the alcove stood a brown earthenware
plate. Next to it lay a bag of rough wool. On the plate stood, or sat,
a severed head. Its neurovascular bundles were clearly visible,
gleaming where they trailed over the edge of the plate. The hair
was frosty with ice.

In a chair behind the table sat Idi Amin. He was wearing
a large British admiral's hat. Its tricorn shape made a strange
shadow theater on the wall behind. His jowls were heavier than
normal and the skin under his eyes was grey and baggy. He was
holding a small staff—a swagger stick.

I stood there, unseen in my surgical gown behind the partition, and as I stood there the voice I had heard in the corridor came again. It was Idi's, and he was addressing the head.

"I am sorry," he said. "I know now I have spent much time worshipping false things. That I should have to make my confession here in this place. In your faith. Though I must stress again that I love all three religions in Uganda: Catholic, Moslem and Protestant. But that is the problem here in Africa today. Everything is broken up completely. Even in the ordinary brain in my head. There, it is true that the soldiers come at me again and again. They come at me, they come at me in my dreams and in my waking times, and they do bad deeds too much.

"That is why I had to hurt you. That is why I had to chop off your head. That is also why we had to kill Mr. Lion and Mr. Elephant for food in Mweya and Paraa. And expel Jesus from Uganda as a whole. Because the danger—the danger of hunger, and the danger of guns, and the danger of ill health—it is there all times. Danger . . . Even when you think it is a good gift put into your hands, it can be a danger poison. I say to the muzungus—bring me a banana, and they say, 'Yes, boss,' and they bring it and it is not good. It is rotten. So I am getting angry. That is why there are bodies. I say, 'Burn them thoroughly,' but still it is not good. Ah, I tell you: it was not always this way, but always it was hard. That is why I had to be in charge completely in Uganda . . ."

He looked into the distance with a large, numb smile on his face. He pushed up the tricorn hat and shifted in his chair. The movement allowed the silhouette of the head to fall on the plaster behind him.

"You see, I come from a very poor family. I want to tell you this. From where I came, my father had no money. I am to work digging and some people give me money for food. And then I studied hard. But then I was taken by force into the army and I was in Kenya during the Second World War and Mau Mau. After I fetched to Burma with the Scottish regiment and I had gone through difficulties, I got the rank of lance-corporal—and up till now when I became general and President. It has been a long struggle and it is because it has been a struggle that I am what I am."

I remembered Idi's impassive countenance at the moment I

had seen the knife go into Waziri. I remembered Angol-Steve, the rope grasping his neck to death, his ragged shins.

Idi continued, hitting his boot with the swagger stick as he spoke: "Yet I am not so bad. People keep saying I am Hitler. Why do they keep on Hitler? The Hitler problem is now past tense. The war from Hitler is a different war from today. I know things, though. I know that the Israelis tried to poison the waters of the Nile to be killing me. That is one reason why people are fighting towards me: because I know many things. In no book are these things written except in my head. When I hear the voice, it is the voice of the god speaking and I know that it speaks the truth and is meaningful and I must follow it. The same voice comes to all great leaders. If you were to follow General de Gaulle, who is a great leader, and Napoleon, who is a great leader, and Mao Tse-Tung, who is a great leader—you would hear this same voice.

"It is true that sometimes I mishear it—I know I have done bad—but I am still fighting for people all over the world and in Britain and her Empire especially. If it wasn't for the British press, my reputation would be different. They were inventing anything about me. They reported any rumor. Things were done in my name, without my knowledge, and I was blamed for them. Soldiers are soldiers, and I could not go to the ministries all of the time. I didn't know what to do. I was taught to fight. That is all. If I am a naughty boy, it is because I am a simple soldier. And because I have been abandoned, kicked at and trampled on."

I thought of Gugu, his chest opening up in front of me, and then of the other kidogo, the one at Mulago. At that instant Idi stood up suddenly, and started pacing round the chamber with the staff under his arm.

"Do you miss Kampala," he said then, turning back to the head, "up in that heaven of yours? I know that I shall miss it, when I have to go. Because Kampala is a city I love too much. And I know that it loves me: I feel greatly the warmth it feels for me. Believe me, I am greatly moved when the people cheer me. As for the aggressors, I don't care who is going to raise trouble: I am going to deal with him very squarely . . ."

He pulled the chair round and sat on it once again, putting the staff on the table next to the plate.

"Yes, and I know that very soon I will escape from here. Alive.

Because, as I have said, my dreams always come true. And I know that someone will foot it here swiftly to help me . . ."

I felt a deadly weight hanging around my neck.

And then he said: "Yes, I know many things. For example, I know that you are there, Doctor Nicholas, and that you have been listening to me for the duration of this time. You see, there is a mirror on this side of the room also. Why don't you come and join us?"

My voice stuck in my throat. I raised a hand before my eyes.

"Do not be foolish. You are my very special doctor. Come here."

I felt my foot go forward. There was, indeed, a mirror.

"You muzungu are never as clever as you think you are," said Idi.

I saw myself moving in the mirror. The one he had been watching me in. And now he was in front of me. The tricorn at a jaunty angle on his head. On the table, on the plate: the other head.

I stood there, face to face with him now, and shaking. Like a driver at the wheel, he spun round the plate. At once I recognized the grisly visage as that of the Archbishop of Uganda, Rwanda, Burundi and Boga-Zaïre, the very one who had married him.

"You didn't expect that, did you?" he said. "In truth I am sorry for it. It was done without my permission. It was one of those times. They brought me the head in this and I was very angry. It had been frozen."

He held up the wool bag. It was heavy with blood and melt water.

"Anyway," he said, "that was before."

He looked at himself in the mirror. "But tell me, why did you come back here?"

I opened my mouth to speak, but only a dry croak came out.

"I know, it is because you love me. Unlike many people, you do not think I am a foolish muntu and a savage man who eats babies. You are too intelligent to think that."

Again, I was speechless.

"Let me tell you the truth about that, Doctor Nicholas. While I was a sergeant in the English army and my mission was to infiltrate the Mau Mau organization in Kenya, Uganda and in the

Belgian Congo, I was captured by cannibals of a Mau Mau tribe and I was forced to eat flesh with other English soldiers. We risked death if we refused. We ate human meat only in order to accomplish our military mission, which I consider now as heroic. It was the English fault, you see. If they had not come to Africa, where we did not want them, and pushed us off our lands, there would have been no Mau Mau. If there had been no Mau Mau, I would not have been fighting Mau Mau. Therefore I would not have eaten human flesh. Do you follow?"

"Yes," I gasped, finally. "But . . . you know there are soldiers outside, and crowds of people. They will kill you."

"They love me really," he said. "They have forgotten. They will remember. Because I am like a father to them. There is a part of me in every one of those people. In Uganda and worldwide. Completely. Otherwise, how could they have supported me?"

"What do you mean?"

"They wanted to be me, to live in me, because they did not want to be themselves."

"Maybe . . . they were just afraid of you and the soldiers," I ventured.

"That is also true," he said, thoughtfully. "But they did want to be me also, or they wanted something from me. The foreigners more than any. The Americans and the Soviets, the French and the English, the Israelis and Saudi Arabians, the Pakistanis and the Indians and the Bangladeshis and the Koreans. And the East Germans. All were my friend. Only the West Germans did not help me. Yes, nearly all the world was my friend—militarily, diplomatically, economically. Like many were buying coffee from Uganda—especially the United States, where they like coffee very much and bought half of all our coffee. They were our top trading partner. Or they sold me guns and airplanes or other things. Britain, Israel, America—all of them helped me train the State Research Bureau, who, as you know, have their headquarters next door. By the way, I am sorry that you had to stay there. But I had to teach you a lesson. Please, sit down."

I did as he said. My mind was in turmoil.

He continued, "You can relax now. All that is over. A new era has begun. I do not mind leaving now. I have had all a man could ask for. It is only natural that things should change. You can't over-take time."

"Where will you go?"

"I have many friends worldwide. Colonel Gaddafi has offered me the hand of his daughter in marriage."

"How will you get out?"

He picked up the staff and gesticulated with it as he spoke. "I have two planes standing by at Nakasongola air base, a Lockheed Hercules C-130 cargo plane and my Gulfstream executive jet. They can take me anywhere I want in the world."

"But how will you get out of the city? It's swarming with Tan-zanians. How will you get out of the Lodge?"

"Doctor Nicholas, you know that I am the best commando in the world, and also a master of disguise."

"You won't get out. It's impossible. Why didn't you go earlier?"

"You heard me. I was thinking. Thinking and praying. Now I need you to help me!"

He snapped the staff in two, seemingly effortlessly.

I jumped at the sharp noise.

"Please." His voice was suddenly quieter, weaker in timbre. "I beg of you."

"What do you want me to do?"

"I have a plan. There is an exit out of here through the State Research Bureau, as you know. But that will be guarded. I have seen them through the spyhole in the wall. They are taking bodies from there even now. They are putting them into bags. You can look if you want."

"No," I said. "I don't want to look."

"Doctor Nicholas," he said. "You are a good man. Let me tell you a secret. There is also a tunnel that comes out by the road to Entebbe. I had it put in for just such an occasion as this. I would very much like for you to go there with a vehicle. The exit is by the ENVI poster. Do you know where I mean?"

"Yes," I said, "but why should I help you?"

"Because I ask it of you. Because you are good."

Idi was a man of enormous bulk, but his countenance could on occasion display a certain delicacy. It did so now. This wasn't

The Last King of Scotland

Idi the ranter, he of the knitted brow and grinding teeth, the hand hitting the desk with heavy dunts. This was something else.

He came round and leaned over me. "Please help me," he said again, leaning closer. I could feel his breath in my ear. His voice was slow this time, like dripping honey.

My head spun. The softness of his voice had awakened in me an emotion I could hardly begin to understand. I felt dizzy and yet my thoughts were as clear as fresh spring water. My imagination was feverishly vivid in that long moment, yet my powers of analysis and application remained intense. I knew that I had been in a reprobate condition for some time because of my closeness to him and now—having been mired in cowardice and indecision for so many months—I was presented with an opportunity to overturn that. Not by handing him over to the Tanzanians (though I noticed that there was a submachine gun leaning against the wall beside him), but another way.

The emotion I felt for him was pity, and I knew that the way out of the darkness into which I had allowed myself to fall was to help him. There it was. The path of my departure was free.

"All right," I said. "I will."

40

Well, I suppose I must confess it now. I failed even in that questionable resolution. You have heard the most important part of my tale, and I will not detain you long with the details of my escape from Uganda and subsequent events.

I did manage to obtain a vehicle. Colonel Kuchasa was still outside Nakasero when I emerged. I persuaded him we needed a Land Rover at the hospital for medical reasons—to transfer some wounded Tanzanian soldiers. I told him we didn't have enough beds. And then I drove to where Idi had said the exit was. It was dark by the time I arrived, but the moon was high and full and even without the headlights on I could read the ridiculous ditty on the poster.

> *She's got the looks*
> *She's got the style*
> *She's got the kind of skin*
> *That drives 'em wild*
>
> *Hey what she got?*
> SHE GOT ENVI!

It had taken over an hour to get the Land Rover, however, and I didn't know whether he had given up on me. I sat there at the wheel for a bit. Once again, I didn't know what to do. I didn't know whether to wait or to drive off. Either way, I didn't know whether I was being tempted by good or bad.

In the end, after another hour, it was simply irritation with waiting that made me turn the key in the ignition. I followed the road out of the city and then down to the lakeshore. I didn't know quite where I was heading, and even though no one could see me, I felt foolish sitting there with the folds of my surgical gown about my knees.

I drove on, past the marshes. Soon, I knew, I would come to State House, where there were more Tanzanians. And my bungalow. I couldn't go there. I couldn't go anywhere.

I stopped the Land Rover and looked about. I was in a village by the lakeshore, deserted and almost totally destroyed. I slowly realized that it was the one where Marina and I had hired the boat.

I got out and walked down to the pier. There were several dinghies moored there, a number with outboard motors. They were rocking gently, and the noise of the boats rubbing against the wood soothed me. Almost without thinking, I gathered some jerrycans of fuel from the boats and climbed down into the biggest one, untied the lanyard and pulled the starting cord.

I could see lights across the dark expanse of the lake. Kisumu, Kenya. I trained my eye on them. NG seeking a light. The motor rattled away, and I glided like a phantom across the lonely vastness of Lake Victoria. For the first time in years, I felt free. At the stern, the algae bloom thrown up by my passage glowed red in the darkness—not just one red but a coral-scarlet-salmon-ruby-crimson host of incarnadine, incandescent shades.

I don't know how long it took me. Six hours? Seven? At one point, a triangle of geese flew across the moon high above. Their throaty noise, summoning some half-buried memory from the past, made me long for Scotland.

In any case, it was almost dawn when I reached the port town. Climbing up the wall of the dock, I grazed my thighs and shins—badly, drawing blood—and also got myself covered in the brown slime that clung to the concrete.

There was no one about. I sat at the top for a few minutes, breathless, and then, pulling myself together, went in search of the police station. I must have cut a curious figure, walking in there in my gown. The sergeant at the desk wrote down my name and promised to follow up my request for a telephone with which to call the British Ambassador in Nairobi. It was time to go home.

At least, that is what I thought. In the event, I was taken to Nairobi in a police car. There, rather than delivering me to the Embassy, they brought me to an ancient fort and locked me in a cell. No one would answer my questions when I shouted through the bars. Shocked and exhausted, I collapsed on the bed and started to sob.

Eventually, I pulled myself together enough to look round the cell. There was no window there, only a ventilator high up in the walls. The latter were made of massive stone blocks, bigger and older than the ones at Nakasero. There was Kikuyu graffiti scratched on the blocks, which led me to believe this had been a place where the British had interviewed suspects during the Mau Mau emergency. But they could just as well have been written by more recent detainees . . .

As can well be imagined, I was extremely confused. I didn't understand why I was being detained until later that day. At around four o'clock, I was taken from the cell into an interrogation room, where a senior police officer was seated with a folder of papers in front of him on the desk.

"We are holding you on suspicion of murder," he informed me. "We are considering charging you with planting a bomb on a light aircraft bound from Kampala to Nairobi. Do you have anything to say?"

I explained about the lion's head and my total ignorance of what it contained.

"He was using me," I protested. "I had absolutely no knowledge of a bomb. I even knew Swanepoel, the pilot, personally. I nearly got on that plane myself. I wish I had."

"That is a very tall story," the police officer said. "How do you expect us to believe it? We know that you were closely involved with Amin."

"Amin put me in prison. You can check it."

He looked through the papers in the folder. I caught a glimpse of a photograph. My own face. I had no idea when the picture had been taken, or who had taken it.

"But you were his doctor. We have intelligence on this matter."

"It was just a job, and one I regret ever taking. I was never involved in any criminal activity."

"In our view you were as close to Idi Amin as anybody was."

"I want to speak to the British Ambassador," I said, horrified that I was once again in danger.

He kept asking me questions. "Were you a member of the State Research Bureau? How much were you paid to plant the bomb? Is it correct that you were present at scenes of torture at SRB headquarters?"

I replied, each time, that I was being held illegally, that I had nothing to say, and that I wanted to speak to the Ambassador. Eventually he stopped the barrage of questions and gathered up his papers.

"Well, what's going to happen?" I demanded, as he was leaving.

"I am sorry, Doctor Garrigan," he said. "The Kenyan government is of the opinion that you are part of the deposed dictator Amin's apparatus of repression, and therefore guilty of crimes against humanity. And that you knowingly planted the bomb, on his instructions, on that plane. We will either be charging you to that effect—and we would aim to get a confession—or we will be sending you back to Uganda to face trial under the new government there."

They returned me to the cell. I lay on the bed again—in great distress, as I would remain all night. I remember muttering to myself, and rocking my body to and fro. I also dimly recall a muzungu in a suit standing in front of the bars of the cell at one point, speaking English to me. But by then I was too delirious to reply.

The next morning a policeman came in and took hold of me roughly. For the second time in my life, I was dragged from a cell into a shower and afterwards given a set of clean clothes, in this case a safari suit made of thin black cotton.

Once I was dressed (the material stuck unpleasantly to the weeping grazes on my legs), the policeman delivered me into the company of three armed guards. They handcuffed and blindfolded me. I felt myself being taken to a vehicle. We drove for a long while. I was very frightened, in some ways more frightened than I had ever been in the company of Amin. From the arrangement of the seats, I could tell it was a Land Rover. As we drove, I rehearsed the options in my mind: I was being taken to court, I was being returned to Uganda . . .

They opened the back door of the Land Rover. One of the guards removed the blindfold, laughing cruelly as he did so. They pulled me out. The light hurt my eyes, and then I saw with relief that it was the airport. I knew, then, that they weren't sending me back to Uganda: they would have just taken me to the border in a truck in that case, cheap and easy. I began to think the British must have intervened on my behalf—the man in the suit must have been from the Embassy.

But before I had time to thank my luck, I found myself pulled along by the guards. They ran with me, the gang of helmets clustering around. They were almost lifting me bodily as we rushed through the departure lounge, my limbs all floppy in theirs and everyone turning—the officials in blue serge, a big Asian party with tin trunks and bunches of flowers, the Kenyan businessmen, the expat schoolkids with their blazers and comics—to see what was amiss.

It all blurred out then, just the faces and the suitcases and the white walls passing, and suddenly I was in a canvas-top jeep, the hot air off the tarmac hitting my face.

A jumbo was waiting there, its jets already roaring. More policemen were standing at the foot of the steps. I was pulled down, and they hustled me forward and on to the stairway. Climbing the steps, I got a chance to look behind me at the jeep reversing away. My guards sat shadowed under the flapping canopy, oddly formal and dignified as they gripped their guns between their knees. Above it all, the elephant ears of the radar spun round on the roof of the concourse. My last look at Africa.

The Kenyans made me wear handcuffs right up until I entered the plane. The stewardesses, on the other hand, were exemplary, bringing me my meal and my drinks, once we were airborne, just as if I were an ordinary passenger. As soon as I had eaten, I had a severe bout of diarrhea, spending over an hour in the toilet. I then returned to my seat and fell into a deep sleep—deep, yet poisoned by dreams of Amin and the things that I had seen.

We were within a few hours of London when I woke up. The scrapes on my legs had dried off, but were still throbbing painfully. And yet, as we circled over Gatwick, I slowly began to feel a bit brighter about things. Assuming I was able to get up to Scotland without too much fuss, things didn't seem that bad, I told myself. We landed, and they played a ridiculous sad song on the tannoy as we taxied and hung about—"What do I have to do to make you love me?" went the stupid chorus. I listened to it feeling sorry for myself, looking out at the flashing orange lights and painted yellow lines on the runway. Without any hand luggage to encumber me, I was quickly off the plane.

No fuss? There was. As soon as I stepped into the customs hall, my eyes blinking from the bright airport lights and the bustle, an immigration official came up to me. He had the kind of paunchy face one associates with steak houses and beer gardens.

"Nicholas Garrigan?" he said.

"Yes," I said wearily.

"Can you come with me, please?" he said, taking me by the arm. "There are some immigration queries concerning your arrival in Great Britain."

He led me to a small, windowless anteroom, furnished with plastic seats and a Formica table. There was an automatic drinks dispenser in the corner and, sitting at the table, a familiar figure. It was Stone, the Embassy man. He had put on weight since leaving Uganda, but his straw-colored fringe still flopped down in the same way.

"Hello, Garrigan," he said. "Long time no see."

"You," I said, dumbfounded.

"Yes, I arranged for your release." He seemed very pleased with himself, and I suppose I ought to have been more grateful.

"Well . . . thank you. But if it hadn't been for you, I might not have been in that situation in the first place."

"Let me get to the point," he said, coldly. "We are under no obligation to take you back into this country."

"What? You're joking. I'm British. I have rights."

He drummed his fingers on the table. "Not true. When you took up Ugandan citizenship, you renounced your British rights."

"This is preposterous," I said, standing up. "I refuse to be treated like—" The immigration official, who had stood behind me, pressed me down back into my seat, putting his hand on my shoulder.

"I don't think you understand," Stone said. "You can't just arrive in this country, without a passport, without citizenship, and expect things. There are formalities to be gone through. We will have to process a reapplication for citizenship. There is the question, in any case, of whether you are now a fit person to be admitted to Great Britain at all."

"Why?" I said. "I have no blood on my hands."

Stone waved his own hand. "You may like to know that out there, behind the arrivals barrier, is a whole bunch of reporters waiting to hear your story. They might say otherwise."

I said nothing. I heard someone walk past outside, their tread heavy and bouncing on the insubstantial airport floor.

"What I am concerned with," Stone continued, "is that your activities in Uganda be seen for what they are: the actions of one man acting on his own. You have to understand that your return in these circumstances could be embarrassing for us."

"That's not my problem."

He signaled for the official to leave the room.

"Look," he said quietly, as the door shut, "your relationship with me, so far as it went, doesn't exist in official terms. You were acting on your own. What we, as I say, are concerned about is that this information is not distorted by the press."

"I will just tell the truth," I said.

"Let me make it plain: your admittance to and residence in this country are conditional upon your silence on matters relating to the British Government's activities in Uganda. If you are not prepared to agree to these conditions, and to live quietly once the initial interest in your arrival has died down, we will be putting you straight back on a plane to Uganda. Do you understand?"

I was shocked. "Why . . . didn't you just leave me in Kenya?"

"The press was beginning to sniff around. And the Kenyans were preparing to have a public trial. We cut their aid last year and they planned to use you as a way of forcing our hand. Which is what has happened."

I said nothing. He pushed some papers across the Formica towards me and held out a fountain pen. "These forms repeat the gist of what I've been saying to you. I strongly advise you to sign.

Furthermore, that money . . . it is still in your bank account. It's within our power to freeze the account if you do not comply. It's as simple as that."

I became aware that I had no choice. I had set my mind on returning to Scotland, on some peace and quiet while I decided what to do with the rest of my life. If this was going to be the only way to achieve that, then so be it. I took the pen off him and signed, four times, at the bottom of each page, without reading a word of it.

Stone was all sweetness and light after that, bringing me a plastic cup of tea from the machine in the corner.

"I'm pleased you've seen sense, Nicholas," he said, as I held the hot, soft cup. "There's one other thing. We've arranged a publicity expert to help you deal with all the media interest. We wouldn't want you to be caught off guard."

I shrugged, and stared at the stippled plastic wall behind him.

"We've booked a room for you in a hotel. The publicity fellow—his name's Ed Howarth—will drive you there. We're going to take you out the back to his car to avoid the journalists. But they're bound to track you down, so he's going to organize some interviews to head them off."

"I don't want that," I said. "I haven't done anything to warrant that."

"You don't have any choice. Unless we're able to control the situation, the newspapers will hound you and exploit you, and you may find yourself being in breach of the agreement"—he held up the sheaf of papers I had signed—"without having meant to be. And we wouldn't want that, would we?"

I shrugged again, angry inside that he should be able to do this to me. He put his head round the door and called the official. They took me back into customs and down a long, carpeted corridor towards one of the areas where the airlines dealt with cargo. We came out into a yard where lorries were parked or moving off.

It was dark and raining. The lights of the lorries and the cargo hangars glistened, reflected in the wet tarmac. As I stepped outside, the night cold hit me; the British weather, those skies that I had forgotten, went deep into my bones. It was partly pleasant, though, the rainy air like something purgative in my lungs. I idly wondered, as we walked through the yard, how ironic it would be, once everything was said and done, if I died of a chill caught at Gatwick airport.

"Well, Garrigan," Stone said, interrupting my thoughts to point at a yellow Jaguar parked in front of the lorries. "Here we are."

He rapped on the car's window. The door opened and a large man in a double-breasted suit got out, a cigarette between his lips.

"Hi, Nick," said the man, throwing the cigarette like a dart into a puddle and shaking me by the hand. "You look like you could do with a bath, a drink, and a crash-out."

"Well, that's me done," said Stone, as I got into the car. He leaned in. "And don't forget what I said. We'll be keeping tabs."

We drove off. The car smelled of tobacco. Weir, I thought, where was he now? The wet black light of the road skidded by, and held no answer.

"Don't worry," said Howarth, "they leave you alone if you follow the rules. I've had cases like this from them before. It's just a matter of giving people what they want—the government, the media boys, everyone. He probably told you that I'm sorting out your press coverage. They'll be livid that they didn't get pictures of you on arrival, so we'll have to handle things quite carefully. I thought, if you don't mind"—he turned to look at me in the passenger seat—"we'd do the interviews tomorrow morning."

"I just want to be left alone."

"We'll have to deal with the allegations first, I'm afraid," he said. "Then you'll be left in peace, I promise."

"What allegations?" I said, "I have been locked in prison, and I worked in a country run by a dictator. That's it."

"They are saying that you helped him cut people up. That you helped with tortures in his gaols."

"That's rubbish," I said, horrified. "I was one of the ones who was locked up."

"Don't get me wrong," Howarth said. "I believe you. But you'll have to explain why you were so close to the old bastard. He's in Libya at the moment, by the way; no one quite knows how he got out. There's a rumor that a Tanzanian officer who had been in the King's African Rifles with him helped him escape."

"I don't care where he is."

Howarth looked across at me. "Tell me something. Why did you stay? Why didn't you just leave?"

I felt it was a question I could hardly answer. I didn't *know* the answer myself. I paused, and then, when I spoke, I spoke slowly, as if I were a robot. I stared at the walnut dashboard as I did so, its winking lights an uncomfortable reminder of that communications room in the bowels of Nakasero.

"I stayed because it was the right thing to do. I couldn't get out anyway, some of the time. And it would have been dangerous to refuse him things. You just do not do that sort of thing in Africa. Besides, I genuinely felt that by being there I could moderate his excesses."

"That's it!" Howarth said, excitably, when I'd finished. "That's the right tack. Exactly the direction we want you to take things in. Don't mention Stone, or the Embassy. You just have to plead that you were in a fix."

"But it's true!" I protested. "I would be justified in saying it."

"Again, I know that," Howarth said, turning to me once more over the steering wheel, "but they don't. When you talk to them, as I said, you have to find a form of words that will give them what they want and keep the government boys happy at the same time."

"But it's all just lies. Well, it's not lies, but the way you are thinking about it is lies. I haven't committed any crime."

He laughed. "Don't worry. It's my business. I know what I'm doing. You'll be right as rain when the time comes."

As right as what—that cold rain which fell, from high above the city, as I got out of the car? No. Its coolness had turned to bile, and it seemed to hurt as it touched my face.

41

I went to sleep that night with the dull hum of London in my ears, seeping in through the sealed windows of the hotel. The next morning, wearing some clean (if slightly ill-fitting) clothes Howarth had managed to get for me, I waited in the hotel for him to pick me up. The lobby was a swish one, filled with light from an enormous glass atrium and the tinkling noise of tea and coffee being drunk at the low tables.

From where I was standing, at a window next to the potted plants and racks of tourist brochures, I got a good view down the Marylebone Road. There was a lot of traffic—there'd been a security alert on the Underground and people were obviously taking their cars—and I realized how so many years in Africa had made all this strange to me. The day before, a bomb had gone off in a rubbish bin outside Baker Street tube, just nearby. The television in my room reported that two commuters and a flower seller had died. There was still red and white police tape sealing off the entrance to one of the streets I could see out of the window, and a general air of nervousness among the passersby.

I have to confess that I had thought, in the night, of doing a flit, and not bothering to attend the press interviews Howarth had set up for me at his office. But I still had to go to a Royal Bank of Scotland branch and take out some money, and I knew that the reporters would indeed, as Stone had said, not rest until they'd tracked me down. So I waited patiently for Howarth. Once he had picked me up, I listened complaisantly during the journey to further nostrums about how I should answer the journalists' questions without hesitation and without losing my temper.

Howarth's office was at the Angel Islington, up some narrow stairs next to a salt-beef bar on White Lion Street. Three workmen in plastic earmuffs were digging up the road outside. One had a pneumatic drill, his hands a blur where he held the rubber handles. The noise was unbearable outside, gradually lessening as we climbed the stairs.

"They should be here any moment," he said, opening a glass-fronted door with the words "Howarth Associates, Promotions and Management" etched into the pane.

He walked over to the window and opened the blinds, letting in golden bars of light, which came down at an angle to form a grid on the carpet. I could still hear the noise of the drill. I sat down on one of the plush velvet sofas and looked around while he made some coffee. There was a terra-cotta pot full of cyclamen on the table, and on the walls were various knickknacks—albums of pop stars he had promoted, and a photograph of a boxer.

"So," said Howarth, handing me a steaming mug. "All set, then?"

"I'll be glad when it's all over," I replied. "This isn't really me."

"Oh, everyone says that, it won't be so bad—you'll see."

He was right. Only three journalists turned up in the end, which was fewer than I had been expecting. I have to confess that I was just a tiny bit disappointed about this. They sat bunched up on another sofa, in front of me. There were two fine-featured young men in charcoal suits from *The Times* and the *Telegraph* and a tough-looking woman from the *Daily Mail*. I was surprised to see none of the correspondents who'd covered Amin when I was there, but I supposed they were off chasing other freaks, wars and wonders around the world. That's what these people do, that's what they're there for.

The journalists had notebooks on their knees, and photographers in tow. The latter took up various positions around the room as I spoke, fiddling with their lenses and, from time to time (though I didn't see quite how they worked it out between each other), letting off flashguns. These filled Howarth's office with a white glare that hurt my eyes, and as I was talking I realized that someone must have closed the blinds again, because the grid of golden light on the carpet had gone.

I'm listening to a tape of that interview as I write. Howarth made it, and I insisted he give me a copy. As I listen to the recording now, with my pen in my hand, the noise of the drill is clearly audible in the background. I've cleaned up the mumblings and hesitations, though. There's no point in trying to reproduce ums and ahs . . .

TELEGRAPH: How do you respond to the charges of assisting in torture that the new Ugandan government has been leveling at you?

NG: It's madness. It's all untrue. I was a doctor working at the main hospital in Kampala. I have been used as a scapegoat because I also treated Idi Amin.

TIMES: What was your relationship with Amin?

NG: I got my fingers burnt. Amin was a charismatic character. I got pulled in by him, during the time when things were all right in Uganda, and then things started to go wrong.

TIMES: But some people have described you as Amin's right-hand man, his lieutenant—how do you respond to such an accusation?

NG: I was not his lieutenant. I was doing my job like many others, as a doctor.

MAIL: And what did that involve?

NG: Just ordinary medical work. From time to time, I did get dragged into doing one or two other tasks for Amin, insignificant civil-servant–type activities: writing pamphlets for the Ministry of Health, and so on. You have to appreciate that there were very few capable people there, towards the end.

MAIL: But why did you stay there till the end? You must have known about the terrible things going on around you?

NG: I don't think you know what fear is. In a situation like that, your life goes on tramlines. You have tunnel vision and you sometimes don't see things for what they are.

TELEGRAPH: But what about the crimes and murders you have been accused of?

NG: At no time was I involved in any crime or murder. I am innocent. My only crime was that I got caught up in the machine and then stayed.

TIMES: What was he like?

NG: As I said, he had charisma. But the man was a ruthless tyrant. It is a great tragedy that someone who was commissioned by the British before Independence should have been allowed to get himself into such a situation, mentally and morally.

HOWARTH: Let's keep this to questions about Doctor Garrigan. He can't be held responsible for everything that happened in Uganda . . .

MAIL: Wasn't it your job, as Amin's doctor, to help put him right?

NG: I kept trying to get him to undergo treatment, but he wouldn't listen. He just used to take handfuls of aspirin and other drugs without asking me, with brandy and beer. He had this mania when violent moods came down on him. Even his wives were not safe.

TIMES: Do you think he's mad?

NG: Mad? How does one define madness? He certainly did things you or I would classify as insane. To tell the truth, I am not sure whether he knew when he was acting inhumanely and talking nonsense. He had a sort of wicked brilliance that took control on these occasions, of himself as well as of others.

TIMES: Did it control you?

NG: I tried to resist it. And I suppose I did so. But there was something mesmerizing about him. You felt he could read your thoughts.

TELEGRAPH: Are you angry that people are accusing you of things?

NG: Of course I'm angry. I merely did my job.

MAIL: But what about specific charges, about you being seen in the offices of the State Research Bureau, and assisting in their torture sessions?

NG: At no time was I involved in any torture.

MAIL: What about William Waziri? The Ugandan Government is now saying that you were actually there when he was tortured and killed.

NG: I was there, but as a prisoner. Held against my will. Waziri was my friend. Look, I don't know why you are doing this to me. I only worked in the interests of people's health, as a doctor should. I did nothing wrong, unless it was wrong to have seen some very terrible things.

TIMES: But how could you stay in the employ of the man who did the things you saw? Even be his friend. Would you describe yourself as a friend of Amin?

NG: Firstly, I was in the employ of the Ministry of Health, on secondment from a British government agency. Secondly, I was his enemy. I knew that by the end.

TIMES: But were you his friend to begin with?

NG: I got to know him. As many others did. It was inevitable. That's all I'm prepared to say.

MAIL: What was it like being close to him?

NG: Like walking on eggshells.

TELEGRAPH: How do you mean?

NG: Amin took sheer delight in playing cat and mouse with my life. Look, you have to understand that by the time I realized the extent of the man's Jekyll-and-Hyde character, it was too late. One day Amin would be good to me, and the next he would be calling for my blood. It wasn't just me. He thoroughly enjoyed humiliating all the whites in Uganda.

TIMES: What about the Kenyan charges? They were saying you put a bomb on a Kenyan plane.

NG: The fact that they released me is proof of my innocence. I did give the pilot of the plane a package. But I didn't know there was a bomb in it.

[I remember feeling faint at this point, my head pounding. All I knew was that I had to defend myself. Whatever I said to those people, they wouldn't believe I was telling the truth.]

NG: Can I have a glass of water, please?

[Howarth brings it to me. My hand, as I recall, trembles as I take it, the liquid slithering poisonously in the glass. A pause. Just drill noise and the rustling of paper on the tape. The squeal of a camera motor winding on. Then a cough.]

NG: It's all lies. Ridiculous lies. I'm being painted with the same brush as Amin because people are guilty about what happened there.

TELEGRAPH: What will you do now?

NG: I'll manage. Britain is a wonderful country—I'm very grateful to be back here. This democracy really does mean something when you have been through what I've been through.

TIMES: How will you spend your time?

NG: I'm planning to relax and enjoy life. I'm planning to go back to Scotland.

TIMES: After all those deaths?

[Silence]

MAIL: What is your financial situation? There have been stories that Amin gave you large sums from the Ugandan exchequer.

NG: My conscience is totally clear on that front.

HOWARTH: I think we'll leave it there. Nick has been through a hell of a lot, as you've heard. He's been under no obligation to answer your questions and I think he's given you plenty to be going on with. Now he needs to rest.

[Tape switched off]

After the journalists had gone, I believe I might have wept a bit. Howarth brought me a whisky. "It's all over now," he said gently, sitting down beside me.

He tapped his ash, and looked out of the window. "Things will get back to normal. Now, give me the address of this place in Scotland you're planning to hole up in."

The pneumatic drill noise again. Persistent.

"I don't know it," I said. "I've never been there before. It's a place an old uncle left me. A bothy."

"A what?"

"A small cottage."

"Well, let me know," he said, handing me his card.

I used his office phone to ring Moira then, and told her I was OK, and was coming up north. It was strange to hear her voice in my ear. *Why are you going to the bothy?* Imagining her anxious face as I spoke to her down the line. *Don't be silly, come to me.* I remember I could see Howarth smoking by the window as I talked to her, looking down at the workmen and pretending not to listen. *I want to be on my own. Can you post my stuff there? You know?*

Afterwards, I said goodbye to Howarth and went to draw out some money. By chance, there was a Royal Bank of Scotland branch right across the road. I felt half-pleased, half-angry that Stone's money was still there: it had a sinister taint to it, but I had no other means of support. And still don't, unless this writing venture is unexpectedly lucrative.

Aiming to catch the Fort William sleeper that night, I then took a bus back to the Marylebone Road hotel. There, trying to rest, I ended up watching television for most of the day. The flood of images was exhausting, after so many years in Africa with just the World Service and the studio-bound reports of UTV. And as I watched the news, I found myself unable to separate it in my head from Amin.

Almost hour by hour that day, it seemed, the Callaghan government was unraveling, spring coming in to its "winter of discontent": I thought of him in Kampala as Wilson's Foreign Secretary, shaking hands with Amin during his mercy mission to rescue Denis Hills. Strikes by grave diggers and dustmen were being lifted: the shots of British army lorries returning to barracks, no longer having to clear rubbish bins, brought to mind those comic, but deadly "Revolutionary Suicide Mechanized Units" which traveled in exactly the same vehicles. We must have exported them to Uganda. Moreover, as one of my countrymen grumbled about the outcome of the Scottish devolution referendum, I thought—ridiculously, I know—of Amin and a cassette of Black Watch pipe-and-drum music to which he had once made me listen. And there was, I dumbly realized, a general election campaign about to begin. There were lots of pictures on the screen of Mrs. Thatcher's birdlike face: she appeared to have lots of exciting plans in store for Britain, yet of what could I think but Amin's letter complimenting her on her looks—"charming, happy, fresh"?

That evening, my head buzzing, I caught a taxi to Euston station. The radio in the cab was playing a haunting reggae song as, with a lurch of my internal organs, we dipped down into an underpass. The blood-deep, bouncing beat—interrupted every now and then, when we stopped at traffic lights, by the Bushman tongue clicks of the door locks of the cab—stirred strange, uncertain feelings in me. I suddenly thought of another taxi journey, from Entebbe to Kampala, on that road I would get to know so well: a dark hole where the radio should have been, a Cyclopean aperture in the dashboard.

42

I should have expected it, but I was still shocked by a headline in one of the newspapers I bought on the platform at Euston: AMIN DOCTOR RETURNS TO BRITAIN, and below, in smaller, sharper type, *Is there blood on his hands?* So it was, during the first hours of the long journey, under the yellow spot of the lamp in my couchette, that I read various half-versions of myself and my words. As a matter of fact, I felt as if I were reading about somebody quite other, and that eased the pain of it. I've still got the cuttings, and reproduce one here to give a flavor:

A British doctor who fell under the spell of Idi Amin denied yesterday that he had tortured prisoners held by the Ugandan dictator. "It's all untrue. I have been used as a scapegoat," claimed Dr. Nicholas Garrigan, who returned to London after being released from a Kenyan prison.

But he admitted that he had watched as a Ugandan doctor was tortured and killed by Amin's thugs at the notorious State Research Bureau HQ in Kampala, the country's capital. "I was there but I was a prisoner. I did nothing wrong. I merely did my job," he said.

He also denied knowing that a lion's-head game trophy he delivered on Amin's instructions to an aircraft at Entebbe airport contained a bomb that killed a businessman and his pilot.

Dr. Garrigan, his hands shaking as he spoke, said, "Amin was a ruthless tyrant but he had charisma. I got pulled in by him, during the time when things were all right in Uganda, and then things started to go wrong. There was something mesmerizing about him. You felt he could read your thoughts. One day Amin would be good to me and the next he would be calling for my blood."

Dr. Garrigan did not know why he had stayed in Uganda through all of Amin's atrocities. "I don't think you know what fear is," he said. "You sometimes don't see things for what they are. At no time was I myself involved in crimes or murder."

The Kenyan Government, after intervention from the Foreign Office, has accepted that Dr. Garrigan was duped into delivering the bomb that killed Michael Roberts, a Nairobi-based company director, and his South African pilot, Frederik Swanepoel. Diplomatic sources suggest that Swanepoel may have supplied plans of the Entebbe airfield to the Israelis before their daring raid to rescue hostages held there by Palestinian guerrillas in 1976. Amin, now thought to have fled to Saudia Arabia, murdered Swanepoel as he did so many who dared to betray him.

The newly established Uganda Government continues to claim that Garrigan, who was personal physician to President Amin, attended at scenes of torture and killing. "He lived in the same compound as Amin," a spokesman said. "He knew very well what was going on. We want him to come back here and account for his actions . . ."

Account? I'll give them account. They all took pretty much the same line, and were written in a similar nudge-nudge fashion. I was, however, surprised by the part about Swanepoel helping the Israelis. It explained a lot. I wondered why the reporters hadn't asked me about it, and then I realized they must have got the information from correspondents in Kampala or Nairobi after they had spoken to me. Cursing the breed, and cursing myself, I turned off the light and fell asleep, lulled by the motion of the train.

I woke early and, as the morning light softened, watched the northern tip of Loch Lomond run alongside the track. I realized then, as we passed into the rusty wastes of Rannoch Moor—the ridges of grass and heather broken by impressive slabs of rock—how cluttered by trees and shrubs the Ugandan landscape had been, how oppressive its ripe, relentless swaths of green.

Once we had pulled into Fort William, I called Moira again from a pay phone, knowing that she would be worried. *I saw the papers. You didn't do any of those things?* she asked me nervously. *I did nothing I am ashamed of. What they are saying in Kampala is rubbish. It's typical of what happens when revenge is in the air.* She pleaded with me to come and see her again, and confirmed she'd sent the journal and tapes. I told her, *Right now I need peace and quiet, and Eamonn's old place can give me that.*

After I had spoken to her, I hired a car with the money I'd drawn out, and did a bit of shopping: clothes, mainly, as I hadn't anything at all beyond what was on me, plus two bottles of whisky and a boxful of basic foodstuffs. Then I began the long drive by loch and glen to the west. The roads were empty—but winding, and quite foggy, too, so I had to take care. In some places, the fog came wraithlike up the windscreen as I drove. I'd forgotten how eerie it was.

I was only fifteen miles from Mallaig when the car broke down. The power failed and I chugged to a halt on the verge. I'd gone through a puddle not long before. I supposed the water must have sprung up and got onto something. When the engine coughed itself into silence, it was like one had been turned off in my own head: all the bad Amin feelings came flooding back.

I stood by the side of the road, feeling sorry for myself. The fog had lifted and although it was still relatively cold, bright shafts of sunshine were coming down. I looked out over the moorland. Suddenly, in a bush right next to me, the ears of a hare popped up. The winter sunlight shone through them, turning tissue and cartilage to pink cellophane. I took a step closer—and in an instant it had leapt up and was shooting across the moor, jouking from side to side.

I watched it until it went out of sight and then I came back to the car. I opened the bonnet and poked about among the plugs. Then I got back in and tried the ignition. It nearly caught. I took a sheet from the sports pages of one of the accursed newspapers, wiped the sparking cables with it, and tried the key again. This time, thank God, it started. I got back in again, and soon the houses and shoreline of Mallaig swung into sight around a bend.

After a short wait I drove onto the ferry, bumping over the steel panels where it joined to the dock. Getting out, I breathed the sea air in deeply and found myself a pleasant situation in the bow, where I could watch the wake stream back to the mainland. The crossing took a while, gannets and gulls going past at eye level on the balcony. There were fishing boats and yachts in the bay: one came so close I could hear its sail rattling as it bellied out with wind.

I went up to the stern. The jagged, antlered peaks of the Cuillins were in view (the King's Chimney and the Inaccessible Pinnacle I would later climb), and soon the steel panels went down again. I got back in the car, queued, and rolled off. Then, with the smell of peat and heather coming in through the window, I drove up through Skye: Knock Bay, Isleornsay, Broadford, Dunan—and round to Sconser.

I'd arranged with the hire company to leave the car at its depot there. This I did, and then got onto a smaller boat for the last part of my journey: NG on his own with the boxful of food and the clothes in plastic bags. It was a less magnificent approach— the island smaller, the rock slabs and ridges less imposing—but I cannot describe the feeling of utter joy I experienced when Maelrubha's mountain came into sight through the mist, getting bigger every second, the vague outline of its ruins—the tall stone cross, the circle itself, the tops of the pine trees around it spearing the clouds behind them.

Once we docked, I noticed that there was a Morrison's right there on the quay, its sign oddly modern amongst the masts and heaps of nets and ropes. I need not have bought the food at all. A hotel, too, the Ossian, and an ironmonger's and ship's chandlers.

There are only about a hundred dwellings on the island, so the bothy wasn't difficult to find. A fisherman in yellow oilskins, who said he had known Eamonn quite well, gave me the simple directions. I followed the stony track through the pine trees as he told me. It was covered with sheep droppings: green-brown musket balls.

The trees eventually parted into a half-moon clearing full of hummocky grass, in the middle of which was a stone cottage with two chimneys and a slate roof. A lone rowan tree, its branches twisted by gales, stood outside the door.

There was a thick manila package on the step in the porch. I picked it up and recognized Moira's handwriting. It must be the journal, I thought. I hadn't expected it to be here by the time I arrived.

I opened the door. Inside, the place appeared almost exactly as Uncle Eamonn must have left it—a plate on the kitchen table, the kettle on the stove, doors open like someone had just passed through them, the bed unmade in the low-beamed bedroom— and six months' worth of dust over the lot of it.

I looked round. It isn't a bothy proper, I thought, it's got more than one room. He'd had it extended, and the power and phone put in: I was surprised that they hadn't cut them off, but I supposed things happened slowly up here. (They do.) It was still small, though, and it smelt stale—but it was a bolt-hole *par excellence*. As I explored it, I had the oddest sensation. I will be here for the rest of my life, I thought—and so far, that much is true.

My explorations of the place concluded, I fiddled with the blue Calor gas cylinder, finally managing to get the stove to light. I fried up some small, bitter sausages out of my cardboard box and ate them with bread and tomato sauce.

I then made a fire with some logs that were stacked inside the porch. Once it had got going, I settled into an armchair with Moira's package on my lap and one of the bottles of whisky at my side. Having poured myself some into a chipped china cup, I sat there in a daze for half an hour or so. The lamp in the rough-plastered ceiling flickered as the wind blew outside.

After a few sips of whisky, I found myself—in that dim light and half-conscious state—reading the label on the back of the bottle: *Eight years ago we began to make plans for today, laying down stocks of the finest malt and grain whiskies, to bring you a blend of unparalleled quality. The result? Bell's Extra Special is now even more special. In Bell's eight-year-old you'll find more character, more to excite, more to stimulate, more to discover.*

And then I tore open the package, and began to read what was inside. It was strange to see that old journal again, its bent black cover with the moldy red spine, my crabbed handwriting between the lines; and as I turned the pages, I remembered some of the times on the veranda in Mbarara or in the State House gardens when I had written things—and I remembered also Amin's thick fingers leafing through it at his escritoire, and then his face looking up at me.

43

Water laps the bow. The shore is at my back and the wide sea in front. There are gulls diving round my ears, and my hand is on the tiller of my life. Not really, but I am out in Malachi's boat again and the waves are choppier than usual, even for early morning. It is good to get some fresh air into my lungs after another night at my desk—the final one, I hope.

The gulls call. I keep my eye on the orange buoy I've taken as my marker.

It has been a struggle to remember everything, to put it all down just as it happened—to face myself squarely while avoiding the dubious benefit of hindsight. It is all over now, the loathsome mask has fallen, but I still find myself haunted by the image of Amin. Whenever I turn on the radio or television, he seems to be mentioned. The Ugandan government (such as it is—the fighting continues there, between different factions) has made an official complaint to the Saudi Arabians about their harboring of him, saying that he should be returned for trial.

Whenever I try to think about him now, a kind of mental speechlessness descends on me. He himself was so supple verbally, in some ways, and that is what I remember most about him: his gangster sophistry, his miraculous tongue. He had all the best tunes, yes, and we let him have them. Yet at the same time, he only half knew his spells. He got them wrong. As for my conscience, there is something about it all—at the point where I, Idi

The Last King of Scotland

Amin and the world came together—that I cannot fix. It all changes whenever I look at it. Mutability. Maybe realizing that is the answer.

I have been out long enough. It is at least an hour since I pulled off from the land into the cold grey brightness that is the Inner Sound. My face is starting to get chapped from the wind, and I'm ready to turn now. Ready to turn and happy in the knowledge that this world of Amin's, with all its blood and crazed illusions, is slipping away. Already it is all behind me. For the first time in a while I am happy, happy in the knowledge that, whatever happens, I can be myself now.

I push the rubber handle of the motor, feel the weight of the water against it, and then the world spins on its axis and I'm facing the island again. I can see the tall cross and ruins of Maelrubha, up on the mountain, and below that the slates and the two little gable-end chimneys on the roof of the bothy. If I draw a triangle with the bothy as the base, the cross as the apex, in the very middle of it would be the smudge of blackened earth where the bonfire for the festival was. The Burning of the Clavie.

This is how it is. An Archangel tar barrel is sawn in two. The bottom half is fixed to a salmon fisher's stake, by means of a specially forged nail, which has to be hammered in with a stone, not a hammer. All the equipment has to be borrowed, or given. None of it can be bought. Staves of a herring cask are attached to the barrel and the whole thing, filled with wood soaked in tar, is set alight and carried around the island by the Clavie King, followed by his retinue. It's bad luck if he falls or stumbles, for him and for the whole island. Later it is mounted up on the stone cross and the king and his men break it up. Everyone gathers up the broken glowing pieces and keeps them in the house for good luck.

Until the next year. This time—I saw it all—there was a fight between the hippies and the king's men, who didn't like them following. When I asked Malachi what the Clavie was, he said, It's the deil, can ye not see that? I wuld 'a thought ye could see that, doctor.

The motor throbs as land comes closer. I have a sensation of losing track of time. In front of me, the mountain floats up with the swell. Drifts away amid tendrils of mist. And then comes back into sight. Its gorse-pocked granite flanks—the surface rolling slightly where there are colonies of fulmar and puffin in the corrie—represent a scene of as wild a nature as I've ever seen. For though I have heard the weird moanings of Afro-montane forest giants, and the terrible yelps of leopard and hyena, this island of sheep and rocks fills me with awe. Maybe I will get used to it; maybe it is simply that one alien vision determines another.

One of Malachi's crab pots rolls around in the bottom of the boat. There are scales everywhere, from the fish he uses to bait the pots. They look like children's fingernails.

I know what I have become. I know what I have seen. I know about all those people who died—and yet also I do not know about them. And I know, also, that most of my life is now behind me, just as Amin's is. I wonder how long he will live, what shape that life will take. I myself could not settle back down into an ordinary existence. I saw all those people at the bus stops in London waiting to go to work. I'd rather take my chance in Uganda again than have to go to work every day by bus.

Yes, most of my life is behind me now, my powers—such as they were—dissipated, diluted, like the throb of this motor as it goes into the water, its sonar circles rolling out far from sky's light and land's edge, grazing the top of silver mackerel, greasy green fronds of seaweed and the lacelike skirts of anemone. The engine putters, fades, goes on . . . as, beyond it, both small fry and the bulky shapes of the deeper ocean lock their ears on its earlier motions, flail blindly away from or towards their threat, their promise.

I feel the cold salt wind at the back of my head. A buffet. A gust. The mock-Gothic battlements of the hotel are in front of me. I'm alongside the pier, tide wrack floating all around me.

I wrap the rope round one of the cast-iron mushrooms outside the Ossian and walk up through the pine trees to the bothy, past sloping rocks covered with lichen and a cluster of ruined cottages in a clearing, with cocoa-brown sheep grazing among the masonry. I suddenly think of the Bacwezi, their sacred grove of figs.

The honeysuckle round the door to my own dwelling, I'm irritated to see, has fallen away. I'll have to nail it back up. On the stone step, I see that the newspaper has arrived. I pick it up and go inside. I drop it on the kitchen table and put on the kettle to make myself a mug of coffee.

The Last King of Scotland

While it's boiling, I settle down to read. The headline on page three is: FRINGE TERROR, WITH A TARTAN TINGE. Below, this:

Late last night, Special Branch officers said that they believed they had tracked down the source of the series of letter bombs and radio-controlled devices that have been exploding throughout Scotland during the past two years.

Already being dubbed the most successful bomber in Scottish history, the nationalist extremist Major Archibald Drummond Weir was arrested at his home in Broughton two days ago, charged with terrorist activities. He is allegedly the perpetrator of a number of threatened or actual explosions, including a bomb detonated at the entrance to the Clyde Tunnel in June, and the letter bomb sent to Downing Street last week, which exploded just 75 feet from the Prime Minister. Other similar charges are being prepared in connection with bombs placed at or sent to targets as diverse as the House of Commons, offices of nationalized industries (British Steel headquarters) and Glasgow City Chambers.

Major Weir, a former British Army intelligence officer and an expert in radio technology, admits that he is leader of the Army of the Provisional Government, which has claimed responsibility for the majority of the explosions. But he denies that he was acting as an *agent provocateur* for the security services, as has been suggested.

"My client does not recognize the rule of Whitehall," the Major's solicitor told reporters outside Broughton police station yesterday. "He has asked me to read out the following statement: 'Since I was a young man, my cherished aim has been to restore the Stuarts. I believe in a fully independent Scotland with its own history, culture and industry—a country with its own natural genius, a country able to make choices according to its own spirit. Scotland did not choose the closure of coal mines, Scotland did not choose the closure of shipyards, Scotland did not choose nuclear power stations and the leukemia that they bring. That is why I have done what I have done.' "

Sources reveal that Weir has been active in nationalist circles since he was recalled from Idi Amin's Uganda, where he had been Military Attaché at the British Embassy in Kampala. A Special Branch insider said it was the Amin connection that had led them to Weir, who, while in Africa, had secretly secured the dictator's support for the nationalist cause.

"We knew that Amin had been in touch with nationalist groups before he was deposed. We became aware that some of the earlier devices were constructed from equipment originally earmarked for the Ugandan Army by the Ministry of Defense, in the period before Amin's reign of terror became well known. It was then a matter of tracking back to those the dictator had been involved with."

The kettle starts to whistle, but I don't get up.

Other nationalist elements, meanwhile, maintain that the Major is indeed an MI5 counterinsurgent posing as a clandestine extremist in order to flush out potential terrorists, and that his arrest is a bluff.

A statement put out by the Scottish National Liberation Army cites the notebooks of the poet and activist Hugh MacDiarmid, who died in 1978: "MacDiarmid was President of the 1320 Club. Their members, of which Weir was originally one, believed that the British imperial state would not yield power to Scotland without violence. The club was named after the year of the Declaration of Arbroath. MacDiarmid soon identified Weir as a police spy and denounced him. Then Weir disappeared. Now we know that he went to Uganda to engage in other British-sponsored activities against notionally independent states."

The Scottish Nationalist Party, which proscribes membership of both the APG and the 1320 Club, said that it did not condone violence of any sort. "Scotland urgently needs self-determination but violence is not the route to be taken. Bombs are not the answer."

The Last King of Scotland

To the right of the story, there is a picture of Weir being escorted to a police van from a rather squalid-looking cottage. He's wearing a tartan-trimmed beret and Arran stockings. The whistling has become insistent. I take the kettle off the stove and make the coffee in a daze, staring at the picture on the table as I do so.

The phone rings. I jump. For some reason, I wonder vaguely whether it might be Sara. I've been thinking about her a lot lately.

"Hello," I say.

"Hello, my good friend. Is it you, Doctor Nicholas?"

I say nothing, imagining Sara coming out of the sea like a mermaid.

"Hello, hello?"

Outside, I hear the deep moan of the ocean. I think of the island, my island, settling on the waves *like a butterfly* as that brochure had it, and of Mr. Malumba's hill, blown by a magic power through the skies of Africa, smothering all beneath it.

"I know you are hearing me. I know it. Yes, I am here in Saudi Arabia, studying democracy. I'm badly in need of your advice. The Saudi contact in London, he fetched your telephone for me. It is true. You were always a kind man to me, and I need your advice. The American government has asked me to intervene again with Ayatollah Khomeini, my old friend, about the hostages held there in Iran. Shall I do this thing? I think so, even though I will tell them that if I had commanded the foolish mission to rescue them, it would have been successful . . . like your SAS storming of the Iranian Embassy in London recently. They are good fighters, so good they must in truth be the Scottish Air Service. Anyway, the world is causing much trouble for Iranians, isn't it?"

I see the brown wings of a skua flap by the window, the great skua with the white patch, the robber gull, which feeds by forcing other birds to disgorge.

"On the subject of raids, I have been watching very closely the feature film of when the Israelis were visiting Entebbe. I say it is stupid and ridiculous to feed public opinion on bogus events and deceive people with falsehoods for the sake of money. You know that one of the actors died while the camera was running. It was a punishment by Allah and should be a lesson to those who want to imitate Field Marshal Amin . . ."

As he continues talking, my eye follows the steep fall of the island down to the sea. The whole is more fairylike and romantic than—I must confess my thoughts take this shape—anything I ever saw outside of a theater. It is exactly the sort of place, in fact, where, bridged across from one rocky sideslip to another, brigands or the supporters of some fanatical cause might assemble round their leader.

"... what do you think? Doctor Nicholas? Since you ask, I am very happy here in Jeddah. I have a Chevy Caprice, a nice house on the beach and one wife is easier, I have found. I am wearing white robes and reading the Koran most studiously. And I go swimming every day. In the Red Sea ..."

In the end, I just put the phone down on him, his voice getting fainter as my hand goes down. I stare at the receiver in the cradle. And then I say to myself, I must pin up that honeysuckle in the porch. I will dig out a hammer and nails from among Eamonn's tools and do it.

A NOTE ON THE TYPE

This book was set in Caledonia, a Linotype face designed by W. A. Dwiggins (1880–1956). It belongs to the family of printing types called "modern face" by printers—a term used to mark the change in style of the type letters that occurred around 1800. Caledonia borders on the general design of Scotch Roman but it is more freely drawn than that letter.

Composed by Creative Graphics,
Allentown, Pennsylvania
Printed and bound by Berryville Graphics, Berryville, Virginia
Designed by Soonyoung Kwon